Beyond the Badge: Fletch

Blue Avengers MC
Book 1

Jeanne St. James

Jeanne ST. JAMES

Credits:
Photographer/Cover Art: Golden Czermak at FuriousFotog
Cover Model: Paul Gutierrez
Editor: Proofreading by the Page
Beta Readers: Alex Swab, Author BJ Alpha and Sharon Abrams
Logo: Jennifer Edwards

---

www.jeannestjames.com

Sign up for my newsletter for insider information, author news, and new releases:
www.jeannestjames.com/newslettersignup

Warning: This book contains explicit scenes, some possible triggers and adult language which may be considered offensive to some readers. This book is for sale to adults ONLY, as defined by the laws of the country in which you made your purchase. Please store your files wisely, where they cannot be accessed by under-aged readers.

This is a work of fiction. Any similarity to actual persons, living or dead, or actual events, is purely coincidental.

Keep an eye on her website at http://www.jeannestjames.com/or sign up for her newsletter to learn about her upcoming releases: http://www.jeannestjames.com/newslettersignup

Author Links: Instagram * Facebook * Goodreads Author Page * Newsletter * Jeanne's Review & Book Crew * BookBub * TikTok * YouTube

BLUE AVENGERS
HONOR
LOYALTY
LE
MC
PENNSYLVANIA

Author's Note

I must thank my partner and the love of my life for his invaluable help on this series. His experience with being on a federal drug task force, working undercover, not to mention the rest of his accomplishments achieved while wearing a badge for over 28 years, helped make the series be as true to life as possible.

Any mistakes or discrepancies are mine and mine alone.

Also, a special thank you to Alex Swab! Your assistance is priceless!

Lastly, please remember that these stories are works of *fiction*. Certain rules had to be bent or broken to create them. But then, weren't rules made to be broken?

Terms Used

PLCB - Pennsylvania Liquor Control Board
LEO - Liquor Enforcement Officer and/or Law Enforcement Officer (used for both)
PSP - PA State Police
The Plant - a place away from stations/barracks/etc. for law enforcement/a task force to conduct clandestine criminal investigations.
Bid - prison sentence/jail term
MC Chapter - The National club with a National exec committee (President, VP, etc)
MC Charter - Each charter is run independently, does not answer to a mother charter or a national chapter
Sled - slang for motorcycle
A-Cert - Wire-tapping certification
TFO - Task Force Officer
UC/UCO - Undercover Agent/Officer
Printing - the outline of a concealed carry gun showing through either a shirt or garment that the person is wearing

AUSA - Assistant US Attorney
Goomah - Slang for mistress
RICO - Racketeer Influenced and Corrupt Organizations Act

Character List

BAMC (Southwest Regional Charter):

Axel Jamison - *President* - Sergeant, Shadow Valley PD
Shane Fletcher (Fletch) - *Vice President* - Trooper, PA State Police
Antonio Alvarez (Rez) - *Sergeant at Arms* - Officer, Southern Allegheny Regional PD
Aiden Cross - *Secretary* - Corporal, Southern Allegheny Regional PD, Nash's (DAMC) husband
Mike Miller - *Treasurer* - Officer, Pittsburgh PD
Daniel Finnegan (Finn) - *Road Captain* - Officer, Southern Allegheny Regional PD
Bradley Lennox (Nox) - Officer, Shadow Valley PD
Colin Crew - Senior Special Agent, DEA, Tri-State Task Force Leader
Owen Decker - Trooper, PA State Police
Danielle Montgomery (Monty) - Corrections Officer, SCI Greene

Timothy Frasier - Liquor Enforcement Officer, PA State Police
Roland North - Lieutenant, Pittsburgh PD

Other Tri-State Drug Task Force Members:

Luke Rodgers - DEA Special Agent
Luis Torres - DEA Special Agent
Ian Butler - Corporal, PA State Police
Ken Proctor - Officer, Uniontown PD
Carl Powers - Trooper, PA State Police
Sam Kruger - Corporal, Greensburg PD
Warren Reynolds - Corporal, PA State Police
Don Mullins - Narcotic Detective, Pittsburgh PD
Nova Wilder – FBI Special Agent, Organized Crime Division

Others:
Mitch Jamison - Former BAMC President, Axel & Zak's father, Retired from Shadow Valley PD
Bella - DAMC, Axel's wife
Valerie (Val) - Decker's niece
Liam & Laney Jamison - Axel & Bella's twins
Francisco (Frank) Russo, Sr. - Late boss of the Pittsburgh La Cosa Nostra
Francisco (Frankie) Russo, Jr. - Current boss of the Pittsburgh La Cosa Nostra
Gianna Russo - Frank Russo Sr.'s wife and Jr.'s mother

Dirty Angels MC® Members:

Zak Jamison - *President* - Axel's brother
Hawk Dougherty - *VP*
Diesel Dougherty - *Sgt at Arms*
Nash - Cross's husband, Dirty Deeds band member

Prologue

"This is all we can get after doing all those damn fundraisers?" Shane Fletcher, vice president of the Blue Avengers MC, squinted up at the three-story red brick building.

From the looks of it, the windows on every floor had been boarded up years ago. Graffiti decorated the rotting plywood, the brick, the front entrance, and even the sidewalk out front. Weeds sprouted out of every crack in the concrete walkway, too.

The place was a depressing dump. The industrial area surrounding the building didn't look much better.

"What the hell did you expect? A damn castle?" Axel Jamison asked sharply.

"Not this. It's a pile of fucking dog shit!" Fletch bitched, because what they stood in front of was worth complaining about. It looked like more of a headache than a potential new home for their law enforcement MC.

"Dog shit that will polish up into a shiny piece of dog shit," Rez grumbled.

"Look, assholes. What's important is it has good bones." Jamison opened up his hands, extended them out in front of him and swept them across the building's façade in an *imagine this* motion. "Think of it as a blank canvas. We can create whatever we want out of this. We can make it our own."

Fletch shook his head. "Jesus Christ. We could do the town a service and burn it to the fucking ground."

Beside him, Crew barked out a sharp laugh. "Agreed. Then when the firefighters show up we can play a prank on those fuckers. At least that would make this place worthwhile."

"Yeah, just like they like to screw with us," Nox grumbled. "Payback's a fucking bitch."

"When I arrived on scene at a brush fire the other day, they had a donut dangling from a hook on a fishing rod." Aiden Cross shook his head.

"Did you bite?" Fletch asked him.

The ongoing, good-natured "rivalry" between his brothers in blue and the hose jockeys had existed as long as he could remember. And he'd been a state trooper ever since turning twenty-one fourteen years ago.

The old joke was, men who couldn't become cops became firefighters.

Cross answered with a shrug, "Of course I did. It was a glazed cruller. Even better, it was fresh."

"Bet it wasn't as good as those filled cupcakes Jamison's ol' lady makes," said Mike Miller, the club treasurer and a sergeant with the Pittsburgh PD.

"Fuck yeah. Did you bring any of those, Jamison?"

Ignoring Finn's question, the current president of the BAMC sighed. "Can we get back to business and not talk about my wife's cupcakes?"

Owen Decker leaned into Fletch. "He likes to lick her filling."

With a twisted grin, Jamison said, "I won't argue that."

Decker clapped his hands together. "All right. Rule number one if we buy this shit-hole... We need a constant supply of baked goods from Sophie's Sweet Treats. Make it happen, Jamison."

"I'll try."

"There is no try, only do," Decker announced.

"If you're going to quote Yoda, at least get it right," Miller complained.

"He doesn't give a fuck about Yoda, only *filled* cupcakes," Antonio Alvarez, Rez for short, told Miller.

Decker shrugged with a grin.

"We might have to put that in the bylaws," Cross suggested. "Because I agree, their shit can't be beat."

"I'll bring it up at our next meeting for a vote," Decker said next.

"No, you won't. And we're not here to talk about stuffing your fucking faces. We're here to see if this place will work for our club's church." Jamison tried to get the group back on track.

Too bad he didn't bring his gavel along to slam it on the table. That usually got the executive committee's focus back on the subject at hand.

Miller pointed to the front door. "I'd say that's a sign right there."

The group got quiet—for once—and stared at the large anarchy symbol spray-painted in red.

"That's bad juju," Rez pointed out.

"No it isn't," Jamison assured him, "and we can paint over it."

Rez shook his head. "Hell no. Even if you paint over it,

it'll still be there, only hidden beneath a layer of paint. The door needs to be replaced."

"Some dumb punk spray-painted a symbol they don't even understand. It doesn't mean shit," Fletch said. "Don't be a superstitious pussy."

Rez cocked an eyebrow. "Says you, who does a whole routine before every Steelers game."

"Do you want them to lose?" Fletch wasn't going take the blame when his favorite football team lost because he was too lazy or embarrassed to do it. The whole ritual only took thirty seconds. If that.

He fucked himself the day the guys caught him doing it. Now they rode his ass about it every damn time they watched a game together. Being September, football season was finally in full swing.

If they finally got their own clubhouse, they'd be watching a hell of a lot more games together. He'd have to do his "good luck" routine before the game either outside in the parking lot or while hiding in the bathroom.

"Just think. If we get a huge flat screen with surround sound, we can watch all the games here uninterrupted by wives or kids... or," Finn glanced over at Cross, "others."

Next to Fletch, Crew snorted. "Jamison, are we just going to stand out here and gawk at the building or are we breaking in so we can check out the inside, too? We can't make a solid decision without seeing it all."

The BAMC president dug deep into the front pocket of his jeans, pulled out a set of keys and held them up. "We don't need to break in."

"How the fuck did you get the keys?" Crew planted his hands on his hips and pointed his mirrored sunglasses at Jamison. "Since when does anyone get to inspect a property before it goes up in a forfeiture auction?"

"Since today," Jamison answered with a half-shrug. "I had a connection at the county."

"We *all* have connections at the county. Must be an *extra* special one." Crew, a DEA senior special agent, probably had the most connections out of any of the BAMC members.

Jamison shook his head and went to the windowless metal door. It had a "no trespassing" sign tacked to it, along with the county's auction notice. The forfeiture sale was only three days away, so a decision would need to be made quickly.

Fletch was surprised the place didn't have a "condemned" sticker, too. But because it didn't, it gave him hope that the inside was better than the outside.

After Jamison unlocked and opened the door, no one moved to enter.

"Who's going in first?" Rez whispered.

"The prez," Miller suggested. "This was his idea and he's our leader. He goes in first."

That sounded like a solid plan to Fletch.

"Anyone have a Maglite on them?" Jamison asked.

"Yeah, I keep one right in my back pocket." Miller's words dripped with sarcasm.

"I've got my Fenix on me," Crew announced, digging into his Blue Avengers cut.

They all wore their colors today since they'd been on a run earlier. After breaking for lunch, Jamison had told them he had a surprise and once they left the diner, he'd taken the lead from Finn, the club's road captain. The BAMC president led them directly to this run-down building located on the edge of Rockvale.

"I've got my Fenix on me, too," Cross announced, holding up a compact, but powerful, flashlight law enforcement liked to carry.

Nox shook his head. "The rest of us that failed Boy Scouts will have to use the flashlight app on our phones like normal bipeds."

Fletch could imagine his eyes rolling behind those dark-tinted aviators.

"Normal people don't call humans bipeds, brother," Miller informed Nox.

"Well, there you go. Since when is Bradley *Licks-Windows* Lennox normal?" Fletch planted a hand on Jamison's back and shoved him inside. "We'll follow you."

"You act like it's haunted or something," came from the dark interior. Jamison released a high-pitched, hair-raising scream and everyone froze mid-step. A second later he laughed. "Just fucking with you! Now get the hell in here so we can get this tour over with before the cops come along and charge us with unlawful trespassing."

"Has anyone told him we *are* the cops?" Finn stage-whispered. With the sun setting behind him, Daniel Finnegan's red hair appeared to be on fire.

Fletch wondered if women were into gingers. Maybe, since Finn never seemed to have a problem with snagging pussy. But then, none of the single BAMC members did. The badges they wore or carried tended to be pussy magnets.

Law enforcement had groupies similar to rock stars. Only instead of groupies, they were labeled badge bunnies or holster sniffers.

The problem with hooking up with one of them, even in a pinch, was they were clingy as fuck because they wanted a lot more than a quick bang or to give a blowjob.

They wanted the whole shebang. The ring, the white picket fence and the two-point-five kids. Then when they were sick of being married to a cop—because it was never a picnic—it turned into the same old horror story.

Crew was a good example of that since he lost over half of everything he worked for over the past twenty years. His dreams of retiring any time soon had vanished along with his home, his SUV and more than half of his pension.

"Well, some of us are real cops," Fletch answered. "The rest are questionable."

"I only play one on TV," Finn announced.

"Truth is, you'd make more dough playing the role of a cop as an actor than actually being one," Nox said.

"Ain't that the fucking truth," Rez muttered.

"Who's next?" Fletch asked. It sure as fuck wasn't going to be him. He didn't believe in ghosts, but he also wasn't stupid.

Yeah, screw that, he wasn't taking any risks. If the building was haunted, then let everyone else figure it out first.

Nox answered with, "The sergeant at arms should be next. He should be in there protecting our president."

"From what, spirits? Fuck that. If something happens to him, we can easily replace him," Rez said with a shrug. "It only takes a vote."

"I don't think he's kidding," Finn said.

"Because I'm not," Rez answered.

"I heard that!" came from inside the building. "As your prez, I'm ordering all your asses inside!"

Jamison didn't get the response he wanted, instead he got laughter.

Crew sighed and glanced around the group. "I'll go in. I'm not a pussy like the rest of you."

"At your age, you're closer to death than the rest of us, too!" Decker yelled at Crew's back as he disappeared inside.

"Fuck you. I'm only forty-one. I'm in my prime and not close to being six-feet under," came from inside the door.

"Prime?" Decker released a loud hoot. "I bet your ex-wife would prefer you just lay down and take that eternal rest."

"That's why I refuse to die until I'm at least a hundred. Just to bug the shit out of her. And after that I plan on haunting her for eternity."

Fletch laughed. "Living that long will only mean decades more of you paying alimony." He glanced at everyone else still standing on the sidewalk. "C'mon. Let's go in before Jamison has a fucking meltdown." Since he was second in command, he needed to assist their fearless leader like a good VP would. "Plus, we're standing out here wearing our damn cuts like sitting ducks."

Finn's head turned on a swivel. "Then, it makes sense why Axel chose this particular location over a more populated area."

Finn was right. The building was off the beaten path with no retail stores or residences nearby. It would be a quiet location since most of the industry previously in the area had moved or shut down. They wouldn't catch much attention going in and out with their bikes and cuts, or even with the occasional cruiser or unmarked unit.

Jamison might be smarter than Fletch gave him credit for. "Let's get in there before we lose daylight."

"The windows are boarded up, genius, daylight isn't going to do shit," Rez said.

Fletch slapped his back with, "If we open the doors, it'll help, *genius*."

Yanking off his sunglasses, he stopped short the second he stepped inside. Once his eyes adjusted, he could start to make out basic shapes. Like his club brothers and more solid items that might crack a shin. He only hoped the floors would hold their weight.

After folding up his wrap-around sport sunglasses he

wore when riding, he tucked them into the neckline of his shirt and pulled his cell phone from the back pocket of his jeans. He turned on the flashlight app as did anyone else coming in behind him and not carrying a flashlight.

With phone in hand, Fletch turned in a circle, taking in everything he could see in his immediate radius.

For fuck's sake, the interior was even worse than the outside. And as dark as it was inside, he was afraid of what it would look like once the building had power and they could actually see the details.

Jamison appeared from the shadows. "I went through and propped open every door I could find to give us a little more light."

"How many doors are there besides the front?" Fletch asked.

Jamison counted them off on his fingers. "One out back that leads to a brick patio that's completely enclosed with a six-foot wood privacy fence. I found a second door along the side that leads out to stairs that'll take us to the second and third floors."

"Is that the only way up?"

Jamison nodded. "The exterior metal stairway seems to be the only way to access upstairs."

Rez spoke up next. "We'd have to enclose them."

"Would we?" Decker asked.

Crew stepped up next to Jamison. "It would be smart if we want this place to be on the D.L. Do we really want to advertise that this is our church?"

"Fuck no," Rez answered. "We should avoid any signs at all. In fact, I'd leave the exterior exactly how it looks now so, at first glance, the place looks abandoned. We should fence off the parking area, too. Not only to protect our bikes but keep it under wraps who we are and how many of us are here."

Nox joined them wearing his typical scowl. "Are you that fucking paranoid?"

"It would be stupid not to be cautious, brother," Rez said.

"I agree," Jamison said. "That's why when I got the call about this place and heard some of the details, I figured it would be perfect."

"This place is far from perfect," Fletch muttered.

"You know what I mean. You also know how long I've been looking for the right spot."

Not only the right spot but one at the right price.

Fletch walked to what seemed like the center of the first floor. With one hand on his hip and his phone held out in front of him, he turned in a circle again, this time letting out a low whistle.

Thick dust covered everything he could see. Cobwebs hung like ghosts in the corners. The cheap drop ceiling had missing panels and what remained was either falling down or badly stained. Cracks and holes decorated every wall. The floor was full of missing and broken tiles. Any furniture within his circle of light appeared broken and no better than firewood.

With his mouth still turned downward, Nox scratched the back of his neck after seeing the same disaster as Fletch. "Did this used to be a bar?"

"Sure was," Jamison answered, "but an underground one. PLCB busted it about three years ago, shut it down, the state seized it and it's now finally coming up on the auction block."

"Damn. A modern day speakeasy. Was Frasier a part of the bust?"

Timothy Frasier was both a BAMC member and a liquor enforcement officer. Since he was in the middle of working on a case, he couldn't join them on today's run or the tour. Not that he needed one, since Fletch assumed he'd been in the bar when it was up and running. However, he most likely hadn't seen its current condition.

Though, Fletch was pretty damn sure the bar hadn't been much better then. Illegal bars usually were a hole in the wall, especially since they didn't follow any laws or standards that regulated bars did.

"Yeah, I got the heads up about this place from him. He let me know about it finally coming up for auction. It's been stuck in red tape for the past three years."

"Or... hear me out, Axel," Cross started, "We could raid and take over your brother's clubhouse. I guarantee their church wouldn't take as much work as this."

"Oh yeah, sure. You want to do that just to chap Diesel's ass. And while I'm all for fucking with my wife's asshole cousin as much as possible, I need to consider how that would go over at holiday dinners with the family. You know, since most of my blood belongs to the Dirty Angels. You know, since my *granddad* was one of the founders. Anyway, as we *all* know, SVPD would need a valid reason to raid their MC. And lastly, you know as well as I do, Cross, they've been keeping their noses clean."

Of course Cross was well aware of that since a few years ago he married Nash, one of the DAMC members. Them hooking up caused a lot of issues on both sides of the fence. To the point where Cross was banned from the MC's property—or any club activities—until he no longer wore a badge. Until then, Cross did whatever he could to get under the club enforcer's skin. "Sure they are. They simply outsource their bad behavior by getting the Shadows to do their dirty work. This way, at the surface, their hands look clean."

"They all have families now," Jamison mumbled.

"So does the fucking Mafia." Crew clapped his hands together loudly. "Okay, well, I'm ready for a beer. Or two. Can we get this nickel tour over with so I can go put my boots up, suck down a few cold brews before Sunday Night Football?"

"You don't have your kids?" Miller asked.

Crew shook his head. "Not my weekend. Outside the court-appointed schedule, she only leaves them with me when they get on her last nerve or she has a dick date."

"A dick date? You mean when her date's a dick, or she's getting some dick?"

"A, B or even C, which would be both. I don't give a fuck who she's doing. I only give a fuck about my kids. I love them, I just don't love the vagina they came out of."

"You had to at one point," Miller said.

"Yeah, a really low point," Crew admitted. "Worst mistake of my life."

"You'll be paying for that mistake for the rest of your life, too. Unlike Fletch who escaped before getting trapped two times."

"Can we get on with this tour?" Fletch asked impatiently. He was not in the mood to talk about his failed engagements. Lesson learned. "I also need a beer."

Finn's cough sounded an awful lot like, "Deflection."

Fletch shoved Finn so hard and unexpectedly, his brother laughed and had to catch his balance. "I don't know, Jamison, I'm sticking to my opinion that this seems like too much fucking work."

"It may be, Fletch, but I'm hoping that's why we'll be able to get it for a low bid. All it'll take is a little bit of sweat and elbow grease."

Rez turned to Jamison with a cocked eyebrow. "Are you fucking serious? It'll take major dedication of time and physical labor to get this place to the point it's even usable. Like *months* of back- and knuckle-breaking work."

The BAMC president shrugged. "Okay? Think of it this way… In the meantime, we'll be able to do another fundraiser or two to gather more money to fix up this place. It might not look like anything now but it'll be nice to have a place for us to chill. Instead of me struggling to find an available back room in some restaurant, we'll have our own space for our monthly meetings out of the public eye. Even better, it can be a gathering spot before our runs and, if we do it right, a man cave when we need a break from the fam or work."

"Don't let Monty hear you call it a man cave," Decker warned.

Dani Montgomery was a corrections officer at SCI Greene and the only female BAMC member. However, she was tough as nails and, luckily, not easily offended. She was treated as one of the guys.

"It would be even better, if we turned it into a place to stay when our wives are pissed and we're sent to the doghouse."

"Speak for yourself," Cross mumbled to Miller.

"Oh, right, can't forget about you, Cross," Miller continued. "But just because you don't like pussy doesn't mean you can't get your ass in a jam, too."

"Literally," Crew said under his breath.

"Wait, aren't you the female in the relationship?" Nox asked the only gay BAMC member.

"Fuck off," Cross growled.

"I think they switch out and take turns," Miller said next, adding offensive hand gestures to demonstrate two men switching during sex. "What's that called, Cross? 'Criss Cross, I'm going to fill up Nash with my applesauce?'"

"Christ almighty! Knock it the fuck off," Jamison yelled, a

muscle jumping in his clean-shaven cheek. "Look," he sighed, "in the tradition of MCs, we need a clubhouse. Even if it's only to hang, unwind and socialize. It'll give us more time to bond with our brotherhood than only during our monthly runs. We're supposed to be brothers and it's hard to be that when we're only getting together once a month. I get that not everyone will appreciate this place—"

"We're not a traditional club, Jamison," Nox interrupted him. "We don't follow those old school MC traditions, remember? For one, we don't have prospects."

"But we're all law enforcement and we've all suffered through some sort of academy whether we're a cop or a deputy." Jamison jerked his chin at Crew. "Or even DEA. Our members might not have to prospect, but in a way, going through a law enforcement academy is the initiation."

"What's really bringing this on, Axel?" Cross asked.

Since Cross and Jamison were close due to who they were each married to, Fletch figured Cross knew exactly what was bringing this on. He was simply making a point.

"Because back in 1974 my granddad founded a club that's still strong as hell to this day. Loyal. Close. Family. Blood or not. I want that for us, too."

"And your grandfather's club had a whole bunch of money behind it because of illegal activities. Now that your brother's in charge, the legit businesses they own help support it. We don't have any of that. Do you think our minimal dues and our occasional fundraisers will be able to finance this?" Finn asked. "I'm not talking about the initial cost of the real estate. I'm talking about the ongoing shit. Like utilities and property taxes."

Everyone groaned at the dreaded T word.

"Dues will be increasing," Jamison announced.

"Not without a vote," Finn reminded him.

"We'll vote on it," Jamison assured him. "It's been dirt cheap since we didn't have our own church and had minimal expenses. Now we will. I was also thinking that we could turn the second floor into an apartment and rent it out to help with those costs. We can keep the third floor to ourselves. For storage or whatever we need it for."

"Or make the third floor an apartment and keep the second floor as our space and it'll be a sound buffer for when we get too loud down here," Fletch suggested. Despite it being a shit-hole, the idea of having their own clubhouse was growing on him. He had a say in it since he was VP. However, the building they were currently standing in might not be the best option.

"Who the fuck would want to live in an area that's zoned industrial?" Miller asked.

"Someone who needs a place to live. And think of how damn safe that apartment will be with us coming and going downstairs," Jamison answered.

"If the renter's a single woman, she might not be safe with Fletch around. He's always on the prowl for his next fiancée." Rez snarled like a tiger and clawed the air with both hands.

"Speak for yourself, Alvarez. At least I don't need an app to get laid."

Rez's expression twisted. "I don't need an app. All I have to do is flash my badge and the ladies' clothes fall off."

Snorts and laughter filled the first floor.

"Hate to tell you, Rez," Crew started, "that works for all of us. Except Cross and Monty. But if Monty ever decides to pinch-hit for the other team, it might work for her, too."

"How do you think I have four freaking kids?" Miller asked. "If I walk in the door wearing my uniform, those clothes fall right off."

"You could get snipped," Cross suggested, "then you don't have to worry about having any more rug-rats."

Miller grimaced.

"Okay, we're wasting time here," Jamison said, impatience coloring his tone. "We haven't finished exploring the first floor yet and there are two more to show you."

Cross wandered back to the windows at the front of the building. "I don't think it's smart to have all this glass. Nash told me about the time the Shadow Warriors shot up The Iron Horse Roadhouse during their Christmas party. You were even there during that mess, Ax, remember? They ended up reinforcing that whole place to practically make it bulletproof." He rapped a knuckle on the dirty glass of one of the large windows. "This isn't even close to being bulletproof. You know what this is?"

"Shrapnel," Nox grumbled. "If we're inside, a few blasts will kill us all. If not by the bullets, then by getting our arteries sliced from flying glass."

"Jesus, Nox. Shut the fuck up," Miller groaned. "It's bad enough we're targets while on duty but having to watch our backs off-duty, too?" He shook his head.

Jamison shrugged. "Then like Rez said, we leave the plywood up to disguise this place, and since the windows will be useless, we'll reinforce them from the inside. Or we remove the glass completely and brick them closed."

"Good idea. Even though we might not have any rivals now, we're still a brotherhood and other clubs might see us as a potential threat." Rez's gaze sliced between Jamison and Cross. "Just us being an MC might not make us hated by them, but what we all do for a living could."

"Who doesn't hate us?" Crew asked, slapping Rez on the chest. "Remember, it's the badge not the bike."

"Hey, if we're doing this, we need a karaoke machine,

too," Finn shouted from over near what formerly might have been the bar.

From what Fletch could see, someone must have taken a hatchet to it, turning it into chunks of wood and splinters. That would need to be ripped out and replaced.

"Oh no we don't, brother," Fletch told Finn. "Nobody wants to hear your drunken crooning." The man loved to sing but it was always off-key.

"Women love it."

"The women who *pretend* to love it are probably badge bunnies trying to get under your shield... I mean sheets."

"Speaking of drunken crooning... What about booze?" Rez asked.

Jamison shrugged. "As long as we aren't selling it, shouldn't be a problem. We'll stock the bar ourselves using club funds or, hell, make it BYOB."

"Or make everyone donate a case of beer or a bottle as part of our monthly dues," Fletch suggested.

"I like that suggestion," Jamison said. "And we can get our members to donate used shit, like couches, TVs, tables. We all have stuff lying around we'd like to unload, right? Everything else can be obtained by curb surfing or second hand stores."

"I guess." Decker ran his fingers back and forth over his buzzed hair. "I mean, with the mother club breaking down into six regions to make it more manageable, it does make sense to establish a clubhouse... But, I don't know... Even after we get this place up to snuff, the cost of upkeep, the taxes..."

"We'll figure it out," the BAMC president assured him. "We first need to get the details together and present it to the rest of the members. If there isn't a majority, the whole point of this might be moot."

"But the executive committee needs to vote on it first before we present it to everyone else," Fletch reminded Jamison.

"That's the plan and why I called you all here as well as everyone else available today. I wanted to make sure more than the board members got to see it to make a decision."

"One of us should use our phones to do a virtual tour for everyone who couldn't make it," Rez suggested.

"Before we bring this to vote..." Fletch turned to Jamison. "Are you sure we can't afford anything better?"

"With the way you all hate fundraising? Do you actually need me to answer that?" Jamison asked with a shake of his head.

Fletch sighed. "Then I guess we might be stuck with this shit-hole. Let's go see the rest of it before the sun goes down and three-pound rats come scurrying out."

"Now there's a good reason for us to get a barbecue grill," Miller threw over his shoulder as he disappeared into the dark toward the rear of the building.

Chapter One

Fletch propped his boots on the edge of the propane fire pit as he slouched low in his chair. He gripped a bottle of Corona and balanced it on his thigh. Nox had lit the fire since, being early April, the night had turned a little chilly.

At least it had been warmer earlier in the day when they went on their monthly run. Fact was, nobody enjoyed numb nuts.

He stared across the flickering flames at Nox, wearing his ball cap pulled low and also fisting a Corona. His fifth of the night already.

"You good?" Fletch asked him. Nox had never been super talkative but he was more quiet lately than normal.

Nox lifted his head and Fletch could see the emptiness in his eyes. Along with the faint dark circles under them.

Jesus.

Fletch tried to think of something to say to see some sign of life from him. "It has to suck that Jamison's not only your superior at work but also when you're not working." Fletch threw a hand over his shoulder, indicating their clubhouse behind them.

"Doesn't bother me," Nox mumbled.

"Then, what's bothering you?"

"Nothing."

That was a damn lie.

"There's one more steak left if either of you assholes want it." Finn stood in front of the grill on the other side of the fenced-in brick patio.

"Not me," Fletch said. "My gut's about to bust as it is and that steak has been on the grill too long. It's probably turned into leather by now."

"It's medium."

Fletch grimaced since he liked his steak still mooing. "Like I said, leather."

"Nox?" Finnegan asked.

Lennox shook his head, his lips pressed together so tightly his mouth was nothing but a slash.

Finn closed the gas grill's lid with a clatter and shut off the propane after throwing the last ribeye onto a plate. "I'll take it inside. Someone will jump on it." He disappeared through the rear metal door.

Fletch stared at Nox on the other side of the fire pit. The man lost his wife not even a month after Jamison had been the highest bidder on their building in Rockvale. Losing her was still raw and hitting Nox hard.

A couple of weeks after the funeral—and the long procession of BAMC members on their bikes from all six charters along with everyone from the Shadow Valley PD—he had shown up unexpectedly at the clubhouse and began to work on it at a feverish pace.

Nox working himself so hard worried the rest of them,

but if that was what he needed to deal with his tragic loss, then they let him be.

He'd done more work on the interior of the building than any of them. He still did. And more often than not, he didn't go home and instead would sleep on a cot up on the unfinished third floor.

Even though his excuse would be he'd been too tired to head home, most likely it was because he didn't want to go home to a quiet and empty house.

It would probably be best if Nox sold it and bought something that didn't hold all of the memories.

"I'm going to head out," Nox grumbled, but not making even the slightest move to leave.

Fletch considered the beer in his brother's hand. "Might want to stick around a bit after finishing that one." He jerked his chin toward the almost empty bottle clutched in his tight grip.

Nox turned his eyes toward him, but Fletch only met his gaze and held it because he wasn't backing down. They'd been pussy-footing around him long enough.

Fletch straightened in his chair and leaned forward toward Nox. "Look, I get—"

The back door being shoved open made him swallow the rest.

With a lit cigar clamped between his teeth, Crew's salt-and-pepper head appeared out around the door. "You assholes want to play a hand or two?"

"I'm sorry, what?" Fletch asked, cupping a hand around his right ear. "Did I hear you offering free hand-jobs? If so, I need to know if you have calluses first. I prefer soft palms." He added a jerking motion with his fist.

"I thought you liked it rough, Fletch," Crew answered.

Fletch turned in his chair enough so Nox couldn't see

him widening his eyes and tipping his head ever so slightly toward him. Luckily, Crew picked up on the unspoken message immediately. His gray eyes sliced to Nox and back to Fletch before nodding barely enough for Fletch to catch it.

"Hey, Hard Nox, you need to give me a chance to win back that sixty bucks from you," Crew called out. "Let's go."

"Not interested in playing poker, Crew," Nox said, pulling his cap even lower before draining the last of the beer in the bottle.

"You can come in and listen, then. I've got something to talk about with a few of you. An opportunity you might want to hear. Plus, if you're interested, it might take your mind off..." Crew grimaced. "It'll keep you busy."

Nox surged to his feet and with an underhanded toss, the empty Corona bottle flew through the air and crash-landed in the large metal trash can nearby.

The back gate opened and Rez came through it. "What's up, fuckers?" He glanced around. "Did I hear breaking glass?"

"Nox tossed his empty," Fletch answered, tipping his head toward the garbage can.

Rez's feet stopped moving and he took in the scene, his brow furrowing as he stared at Nox.

"You just get off shift?" Crew asked him.

Rez turned back to Crew, still standing in the doorway. "Yeah. You said to head straight over here."

"That I did. I've got an opportunity for some of you."

"Just some?" Rez asked with a cocked eyebrow.

"Yeah, I'll explain once everyone gets inside. I don't want to have to repeat myself."

"Who else are you waiting for?" Fletch asked, now curious about this so-called opportunity.

"Nobody. Even though I can't offer it to all of you, I would still like all the members to hear it."

"If it has to do with a deserted island, a bunch of hot chicks in string bikinis and an endless supply of cold beer, I'm in," Fletch told Crew.

Crew huffed out a laugh. "Yeah, right. If that opportunity came up, I wouldn't be sharing it with you dickheads. None of you would ever see me again."

"Promises, fucking promises!" Rez shouted, smacking Crew in the gut as he squeezed past him. "What a wet dream it would be not to have to deal with you anymore. Take the rest of your federal fucking buddies with you."

"Tick tock, motherfuckers," Crew warned Fletch and Nox before disappearing inside with Rez. The metal door slammed shut behind them.

"I'm interested in what he's got for us. How about you?" Fletch asked Nox.

"Yeah, fuck it." Nox headed toward the door. "Unless it's painting his fucking house. We still have more to paint here first."

"We're in no rush to finish the second and third floor, brother. You've done more than enough work already."

After purchasing the building last September and while the weather was decent, they worked on enclosing the outer stairs first and then all winter long they worked on the interior until they got the first floor just how they wanted it. Or close to it.

The lower level of the old building now looked like a real MC clubhouse. Only better. It was more like a serious man cave any guy—single or married—would be jealous of.

The way it looked now compared to the way it looked the first time they saw it was night and day. If the front hadn't stayed the same—looking abandoned—no one would know it was the same building. However, they decided to follow Rez's suggestion and left the front exactly how they found it. One of the house rules was that no one used the front entrance. It was kept locked up tight. They only came in or left through the back or side door.

Six-foot high, dark brown PVC privacy fencing now surrounded the parking lot along the side and back of the clubhouse and everyone drove to the back gate into the parking area from an alley at the rear of the building. Since the stairs outside had been completely enclosed—except for the opening at the base of the steps—it provided protection from the weather as well as from prying eyes.

The less people who saw them coming and going the better. Anyone driving by on the street out front wouldn't think twice about the place being in use or occupied. Someone would have to stakeout the location to figure out what was going on inside the building. And if someone was staking out their club's church, too many observant eyeballs would catch them.

Nobody was slipping by a bunch of badges who'd seen a thing or two in their careers.

Even though only a few changes had been made to the exterior, the first floor interior had been completely rehabbed.

Fletch locked the back door behind them and followed Nox down the hallway toward the common area. The men's restroom to the left, as well as the women's room on the right, had been completely cleaned up and restored. In addition to each bathroom having two sinks, the men's had three urinals along with one shitter, while the women's had three stalls.

One bathroom would have been enough for all of them, including Monty, but since they already existed, it was just easier to keep them both since it would've been more work to screw with the plumbing and rip out the toilets and sinks in the women's room to turn it into something else.

Just outside the hallway and to the right, a room had been constructed for the executive committee to meet. It housed a scratched-and-dented conference table someone scored for free, along with six mismatched rolling office chairs.

Unfortunately, due to limited space, the side door leading to the outside steps to the second and third floors was accessed through that room. That meant if a meeting was in progress, anyone wanting to head upstairs had to go the long way around by going through the rear door and the parking lot to access it.

Even with all that, it was the common area that impressed Fletch the most. Endless hours of back-breaking work had gone into it from every member of the Southwest Regional Charter.

Luckily, it turned out better than any of them ever expected.

They had made the two front windows, as well as any windows on the upper floors, bullet-proof by covering them with a clear polycarbonate security shield specifically designed to stop bullets, even from rifles like the AR-15. On the first floor they installed a product called BulletShield over the windows on the inside and left the old graffitied plywood covering the outside.

However, up on the second floor where they planned to turn it into an apartment, they realized no one would rent a place with covered windows. They ended up replacing the glass on the backside with the same type of material, then covered them with blinds. They left the two front windows boarded for now since the space was only currently being used for storage, building material and supplies. They'd deal with the front windows later if and when they got a renter.

Fletch hooked a left to where they had installed a curved counter in one corner. Behind it sat a large fridge and kitchen sink along the outer wall. Under the counter on the backside, shelves held liquor, glasses, mugs, spare six-packs and anything else needed for enjoying a whiskey or beer while watching a game, playing a hand of poker, or even simply chilling.

He snagged a cold beer out of the fridge—purposely not offering one to Nox—before heading over to where everyone else was gathered. They sat either on one of the three mismatched used couches placed in a U to face the ninety-six inch TV hanging on the side wall or at the poker table.

Finn was in the middle of shuffling cards at the old card table large enough for eight players. Rez, Cross, Jamison, Miller, Frasier and Decker sat with him. Fletch pulled out the last open chair and planted his ass in it with a sigh.

Crew hovered between them and the couches, where Monty and North sat with the TV on, but muted, while Nox perched himself nearby on a stool at the counter.

After the Blue Avengers mother club split up, only a dozen members made up their regional chapter. Even so, it was a rare moment when all twelve of them were together in one spot due to their various shifts, special assignments and family obligations.

Today, apparently, the stars had aligned and all of them had made it. Crew most likely had something to do with that due to whatever announcement he was about to make.

Hopefully, it was good news and not bad for once.

Fletch swore the last time the twelve of them managed to be all in the same spot was at Nox's wife's funeral months ago.

"Okay, fuckers, listen up," Crew yelled, clapping his hands together.

"Isn't it Jamison's job to call us to order?" Cross asked the DEA agent.

"I got the A-okay already from the prez to take the reins."

"Is this an official church meeting?" Monty asked from over on the couch.

The woman might be petite at only five-foot-three and maybe a buck thirty in weight, but she was as tough as fucking nails. Any time an inmate tested her, they were the loser.

She wasn't gorgeous or girly, but her solid good looks grew on you, even with her super short dark brown hair. Her striking wide green eyes sucked you in and she could put power behind her voice like no other female Fletch knew. If she commanded someone to do something, their best bet was to say, "Yes, ma'am," and get it done. She could put a hurting on anyone testing her patience or to see if she was weak or a pushover.

Being the first, and currently only, female member of the Southwest charter, she was a BAMC trailblazer.

Jamison prided himself on having a diverse MC. Alvarez's parents had immigrated to the States from Venezuela. Aiden Cross was openly gay. Tim Frasier and Roland North were Black. No one was turned away as long as they were upstanding, sworn law enforcement, active or retired, lived or worked in the region and, of course, rode a Harley-Davidson or an Indian.

They couldn't mind hard work and paying dues, either.

The twelve of them were tight as fuck and Fletch would feel confident if *any* of them arrived to back him up during an incident.

That was what a real brotherhood should be like.

He studied the mural of their club's patch painted on the wall near the poker table. The insignia in the center was made up of a skull and crossbones holding two handguns. "Honor" was engraved on one and the other said "loyalty."

Honor and loyalty. All twelve of them had it.

He'd put his life on the line to save any of them and he assumed they'd do the same for him.

"No, this isn't an official church meeting," Crew answered Monty, "but like I said, I talked to Jamison about this first."

"What the fuck's this about, Crew?" Frasier asked.

"An opportunity to do some good."

"We do good every damn day at our jobs," Miller grumbled.

"This is something a little different," Crew assured them. "A challenge, if you will."

"For all of us?" Monty asked.

"No. Unfortunately, I can't include you all. There are reasons for that and I'll explain once I tell you what it is."

"Then hurry the fuck up, I want to play a few hands of poker before I have to head home to my baby girl," Decker bitched.

Fletch's brow dropped low. "Isn't your mom watching her?"

Decker had been raising his biological niece as his own daughter for over the past two years with help from his mother.

"Of course she is since I can't leave a three-year-old alone, genius. She might be Val's grandmother but it isn't her job to watch my girl twenty-four seven. Especially since my mother thought she was done raising babies after me and my sister turned eighteen."

"She would've been if your sister hadn't—"

Decker cut off Finn. "Right. Old story, new day. Crew, get cracking with your story time so Gingerhole here can deal a hand and I can go home in time to read my Valee Girl her nightly bedtime story before she falls asleep."

"*Aww*. Daddy Decker. How fucking sweet," Finn said on a laugh. He quickly leaned out of the strike zone when Decker took a half-hearted swipe at him.

"You would've done the same. Any of you would have," Decker growled. "Family is family, whether by blood or by bond."

Nobody could argue that fact, so they didn't.

Crew strode over to where Nox was sitting, pulled a stool away from the counter and sat on it at an angle so he could face everyone, including Nox.

"All right, pay attention," Crew started, "there's a few moving parts to what I'm proposing."

Rez grinned. "You're supposed to get down on one knee if you're proposing. And, spoiler, Cross is already married so his ass is literally unavailable."

Cross whipped a drink coaster at the club's sergeant at arms and it bounced off his forehead.

"I'm starting to fucking regret this," Crew muttered, scraping his fingers through his hair.

Fletch smothered a snort.

Finn didn't bother smothering his and slammed the pack of cards face-down onto the green felt. "Okay, let's hear it. We don't have all night."

Crew shook his head and sighed. "I'm warning you now, the next person to interrupt me is getting pepper-sprayed."

Fletch groaned. Getting pepper-sprayed, even accidentally because of being downwind, sucked ass.

"Now you know how I feel trying to lead a meeting," Jamison said to Crew. "It's like dealing with a bunch of toddlers at daycare. And you're one of them. Pepper spray might be better than a gavel."

"I'll do my best to behave in the future," Crew assured him with a straight face.

Frasier released a long, loud hoot from over on the couch at Crew's bald-faced lie.

"Get the fuck on with it! Jesus, Crew!" Nox exploded from over by the counter. "I know you like attention but this is fucking ridiculous."

Crew pressed his lips flat and blew out his cheeks. When he finally released his held breath, he nodded. "Okay... I was tapped to lead part of a special multi-agency task force. The Tri-State Drug Task Force will consist of three groups of fifteen members each. As a senior special agent, I'm being put in charge of group two that will handle the southwest corner of PA. Group one will be concentrating on West Virginia, and group three will be covering the southeast corner of Ohio."

"Who are they going after?" Jamison asked, abruptly sitting up straighter.

"The DEA's ultimate target is a Mexican cartel."

"What cartel is running drugs up here?" Nox asked, rubbing at his creased forehead.

"A cartel isn't. At least, not directly," Crew answered. "And we don't know which cartel is involved yet. That's one of many things the DEA needs to find out."

Fletch shook his head. "Then who's trafficking the drugs up here?"

Crew's gaze swept the room before answering, "An MC."

Silence filled the space around them for several seconds until "Jesus fuck," burst from Cross. He ground the heels of his palms into his eye sockets while asking his next question. "Which MC?"

Chapter Two

"Which MC?" Cross demanded again before Crew could answer.

"Don't worry, it's not the hubby's. It's the Deadly Demons. It's why we'll have three groups of task force members covering the surrounding states. As you all should already be aware, the Demons' mother club is located in West Virginia but they're transporting meth into both Ohio and Pennsylvania. Possibly even into Virginia and other nearby states. However, we're concentrating on the tri-state area since we have proof of that. The intel also shows the Demons trying to expand their territory into both states. My educated guess behind their reasoning is to build a more solid pipeline as well as increase their numbers to keep that pipeline and the cash flowing.

"Normally, no other MC would blink if the Demon's stayed in their own territory, but they *will* sit up and take notice if they encroach on another MC's area." He turned on the stool enough to face Axel. "Not sure if your brother's aware of the territory grab yet or not. If not, we need to try to keep him from finding out about it at this point. We don't want his MC going to war with the Demons while the task force is doing investigations and members are undercover. That could fuck everything up. Plus, I guarantee it'll be messy for the Angels if things go sideways."

Jamison's nostrils flared and his jaw became sharp. "Got it."

"They'll be on a need-to-know basis, because my guess is, we'll be needing them. They just can't know all the details. Cross?"

Cross nodded, even though his light blue eyes were troubled. "Yeah, got it."

"So, what does this have to do with us?" Finn leaned back in his chair and scrubbed a hand down his bearded cheek before crossing his arms over his chest.

"I know you guys well. Even better than a lot of my fellow agents. I'm lucky as fuck that I get to choose my team. Even though four task force members need to be federal agents, the rest can be made up of state and local officers with notable drug arrests, who are trustworthy and also know the area well. None of you are rookies and most of you have quite a few drug arrests under your duty belts."

"Most," Monty mumbled from over on the couch.

Crew turned toward her. "I recognize the fact that your job and Frasier's are just as important as the rest of ours, but they concentrate on different aspects of enforcement. Unfortunately, that means neither of you are a good fit for this particular task force, but that doesn't mean you can't be involved."

"Since they're running meth through our jurisdictions, this does affect us all," Jamison said.

"While that's true," Crew answered, "a couple of you are

no longer working the streets. Like you, Jamison, and also North."

That made sense to Fletch. Jamison was now a sergeant at the Shadow Valley PD and North was a lieutenant with the Pittsburgh PD. They rarely hit the streets like someone lower in rank.

"The rest of you are in if you want to get involved and, of course, your superiors approve it. Because there *will* be paperwork and approvals needed. You know how it is, can't do shit without fighting our way through the red tape. That said, I'm coming to you first before looking outside of our close brotherhood."

"I'm interested." Cross said.

Crew raised a *hold-up* hand and shook his head. "Brother, you and Jamison are automatic no-goes. Even if Jamison hadn't taken that promotion, your ties to the Dirty Angels are what knee-caps you both from this. Since your hubby is a Dirty Angel and that club is full of Jamison's family both by blood and by marriage, they'd never approve either of you for that reason alone. However," Crew shrugged and his mouth pulled up on one side, "that doesn't mean we can't use your connections. You could be our bridge between the DAMC and their allies."

Cross huffed out a sharp laugh. "We're already hated enough. Axel's barely tolerated and I'm *persona non-grata* until I retire. You actually want *us* to ask them to work with law enforcement?"

"If we need them, we'll have to give them a beneficial reason to do so," Crew explained. "But we'll deal with that later when we need to. It's just nice to know the option's there."

"Agreed," Jamison answered.

Cross frowned at him. "You really want to risk the relationship you've rebuilt with your brother?"

"We wouldn't be doing anything to risk that." Jamison turned to Crew. "Right?"

Crew jerked one shoulder up in a half-shrug. "Like everything else in life, brother, there are no guarantees. But basically we might only need a boot to wedge open the door, exactly what you and Cross can provide. After that, some of us can take over dealing with them directly so you don't have to."

Cross scrubbed a hand over his mouth. Fletch assumed he was hiding a laugh at Crew's statement of working with the DAMC.

Of course, Jamison knew the club the best, but Cross knew enough, even though the Dirty Angels kept him at arm's length to the point that he and his biker husband Nash weren't allowed to live in the protected neighborhood where most of the Angels lived. Between Jamison's wife being born and bred in the club, as well as his own strong blood ties to the Angels, he and Bella had a home inside the gated compound.

The DAMC's sergeant at arms, Diesel, hated it, though, and barely tolerated a cop amongst their midst. He loudly and constantly made it known to Axel Jamison's face that he was only still breathing because of his love for his cousin Bella and respect for the Jamison family.

"Well, count me in," Finn announced, back to shuffling cards. He was probably antsy to deal a hand and get a game going.

"Decker?" Crew asked.

Decker nodded. "Yeah. I'm in as long as my captain will approve it."

"Shouldn't be a problem. I'll get the supervising special

agent on that. That's who I'll be reporting to. Fletch? We can approach your captain, too."

Fletch blew out a breath. "Yeah, why the hell not?" It would be a hell of a lot better than doing traffic stops, handling barking dog complaints or dealing with crashes.

Crew twisted his head to look at Nox. "Brother?"

No surprise when Nox answered, "Yeah, I'm in." It would be another excuse for him not to go home to an empty house.

Maybe Fletch needed to approach Jamison about doing an intervention with Nox since something needed to change. He didn't like seeing his club brother the way he was currently.

"Rez?"

"Fuck yeah. Personally, I think it'll be great to work next to you guys instead of only riding beside you in formation. We'll be fighting the good fight as a team."

"Remember to keep that attitude down the road when it gets bumpy as fuck. Miller, you in?"

"Yeah, deal me in."

Crew released a loud, exaggerated sigh. "Not poker, idiot. The task force. Welcome to the conversation. Where the fuck have you been?"

Miller's brow dropped low. "The task force? Fuck no. I've got three kids and the fourth on the way. My wife would crush my balls in her fist for jumping on this. That would mean less time for me to help her with them."

"But think of it... You'll be spending more time away from home, making it less likely you'll have kid number five, you horny bastard. Time to get the old snippety-snip." Fletch did a scissor action with his two fingers.

Miller flinched. "Christ! We're already in negotiations about that. She says if I knock her up one more time, she'll cut them off herself." He puffed out his chest and shook his shoulders. "I can't help I'm such a sexy beast and she can't resist me."

Monty gagged. "Oh, for fuck's sake."

With a grin, Miller turned toward her and drew a hand down over his slightly protruding gut. "You know if I was single, you wouldn't be able to resist all this, Montgomery. Be honest."

"You seriously don't want me to be honest, Miller. You might go home to your wife in tears. But what I will tell you is this... I'd have no problem resisting you or your... *charms*."

"Then you'd be missing out," Miller assured her. "Anyway, you can't see my best feature." He pointed to his crotch and winked.

"Thank fuck I can't!" She began fake retching again.

"Okay!" Crew yelled trying to draw the attention back to him. "Decker's got bedtime stories to tell and I need to win back some cash after I got my ass handed to me at our last poker night. Let me finish this so we can get to that. So, listen up... Besides recruiting three more feds, which I'll handle, we need another six for our team. The more task force members we can recruit from other agencies, the more coverage we'll get. Maybe talk to your chiefs or captains. Or if you know someone who'd fit in, toss their name my way. Here's the thing... Whoever it is needs to be a team player. We already know *we* can trust each other. We're already in a tight brotherhood. Even better, we own bikes and can ride. We'll use that to our advantage to help us fit in and it's one reason they tapped me to lead group two. They know my tie with this club and all of you. They also know of Jamison's and Cross's connections with the DAMC. If we can get the Angels to cooperate, that's possibly a whole other army behind us keeping their eyes and ears open."

"You might be living a wet dream when it comes to my brother's club or even the Dark Knights, Crew," Jamison warned him.

Crew scratched the back of his neck. "Yeah, I get that. It'll be nice if we don't need them. But we might." He sighed. "No, not might. I already have some thoughts, so..."

"You're going to want to use them," Cross concluded.

"Some of us will most likely go undercover for this, so yeah. We'll use whatever we can to our advantage, even if that means some of us having to wear their colors. While some of us might end up wearing Demon colors and infiltrating their club. Bottom line is, whatever we have to do to get the job done is whatever we have to do to get it done. And the job is crushing this meth supply and shutting down their operations."

"I really doubt they'll want to work with us, Crew. We're pigs to them. And do we want to trust them? They're far from choir boys. Even if they are," Finn air-quoted, "legit."

"I get it. But they may be an invaluable asset we can't ignore. Remember, Jamison's grandfather was a founding member, his sister's husband is a part of the club. His brother is the damn president. Even his *wife* was born into the club."

"Don't forget his uncle did life for murder," Nox grumbled from over by the counter.

"If they were still one-percenters like the Demons, I might think twice," Crew said.

"Yo, Jamison, you trust your brother?" came from Frasier on the couch.

"As far as I can throw him," he answered with a straight face.

Chuckles rose around Fletch, including his own.

"Look, he might be my brother, but he's still the president of a club that wants nothing to do with law enforcement. Is the club more legit now than it used to be? No doubt. But that doesn't mean there isn't sketchy shit happening below the surface. Like Cross said, their hands might look clean but they have a team behind them whose hands are painted in blood."

Crew's head tilted and his gray eyes narrowed on Jamison. "You've got proof of that?"

Jamison stared back at him, pressing his lips together. After a few seconds of silence between them, Crew nodded.

Jamison continued, "It's one reason Diesel doesn't allow his Shadows to be members of the club. He mistakenly thinks that draws a clear line of separation between his business and his club."

"Don't forget Diesel's cousin married one of those Shadows," Cross reminded them. "So, D isn't the only direct connection between the club and his crew."

"Well, we're not dealing with those guys. Bottom line is they just need to stay out of our way and our investigations," Crew said. "They stay on their side of the fence and we'll stay on ours."

"Sometimes that's easier said than done, brother," Jamison told him.

"It's going to have to be the way. If they interfere, then..." He shrugged. "The dirt might come out in the wash."

"Jesus, you take down that asshole's crew because of this task force, then," Jamison shook his head, "I'm fucked. Like the stop breathing type of fucked. So, let's make sure that fence is high enough so those Shadows won't be scaling it."

"I hear you," Crew answered. "All right, we'll worry about them later once we have our team together and a better direction. For now, we have a start and something for me to take back to the field office." His gaze swept the group. "Anyone not on the task force will be getting limited info, but that doesn't mean you shouldn't keep your eyes and ears open while going about your normal routine. Any info you can share with us, great. But let's keep this upcoming investigation between us. No one else, not even your brothers and sisters in blue. Got it?"

A chorus of "got its" rose around Fletch.

"Monty, you can't say shit to anyone, but if you hear anything to do with a source of meth or even the Demons at Greene, I want to know about it. You'll be our eyes and ears in the prison."

"You got it."

"Good. I appreciate anyone's help. You might not be a part of the task force but you'll still be an asset. Same with you Frasier, North. Hell, maybe even you, Miller."

Fletch chuckled under his breath. Beside him Finn snorted loudly. Of course, Miller was unfazed.

"One more thing... We'll need space to rent for our task force. So, if any of you have any ideas, throw them out there. Off the beaten path would be best."

If no one else was going to bring it up, then Fletch would since he was the club's VP. "How about leasing our third floor? We could keep a small section of it for storage, if needed, but the rest can be for the team. And even better, we've already secured the building safety-wise, we have it mainly under wraps and it would be an easy way to help with the building's expenses. Since it's in this run-down area, no one will know. Even if the public becomes aware that this is our clubhouse, comings and goings of the task force members could be seen as BAMC members coming in to hang out at our clubhouse. It's the perfect place to have it." He turned to Crew. "Run it past your higher-ups. It would be a win-win situation."

"Great fucking idea, Fletch," Jamison agreed, "but we'd have to vote on it first."

"There's no better time since we're all here now. Let's get the vote done," he suggested.

"Agreed. This way I can approach them with that proposal and my potential task force officer list at the same time. You know how the government likes to be efficient."

Not one person in that common area didn't laugh or snort at Crew's last remark. Even Nox.

If the fastest way to get somewhere was to turn left, the government always turned right. It didn't matter what level of government, either. Red tape and bullshit always bogged down their jobs.

Jamison stood up and announced, "Okay, let's vote then. I'm all for it and the club could use the funds. All in favor?"

Fletch heard a bunch of "ayes."

"Anyone against?"

Jamison's question was met with silence. No surprise.

"There's our answer," he concluded. "This also might've solved another problem."

What the fuck was Jamison talking about?

"We've been trying to come up with a name for our clubhouse," the prez reminded them. "Now we won't have to."

They all shared confused looks at first until what he meant hit them.

A grin spread over Crew's face and he nodded. "Well look at you, Sergeant Smarty-Pants, you're right. We can call it The Plant."

Fletch shrugged since he wasn't so keen on that name. "I kind of liked my suggestion of The Hole." A shortened version of what he called the place when they first bought it. The shit-hole.

"We get it, stud. You like holes. Lots of them. Tight, loose, front, back—"

Jamison cut Finn off. "The Plant makes more sense since we're going to use it for the task force, anyway."

"I don't get it," Monty muttered.

Decker said, "That's because you work at the prison and miss out on this kind of fun shit. For your job, you're locked in a concrete box with those prisoners. You don't have the freedom we do. For the most part, anyway."

"Don't be an ass." She glanced over at Crew. "Explain."

"For a task force like this we need a base away from our stations or field offices to meet and conduct our criminal investigations. We call that off-site location The Plant. I have no idea how that started but it stuck. Usually we rent office space, but I'll talk to the higher-ups involved with this task force and see if we can do it upstairs. This building's more secure than any office space and I'm sure the rent will be cheaper to sweeten the deal." Crew cocked an eyebrow at Jamison.

He nodded. "Yeah. I think it's reasonable to make it financially beneficial for them, too. Like Fletch said, it'll be a win-win situation for both the task force and for the BAMC."

"I doubt anyone will say no to that," Crew concluded. "I'll make sure to lean on them heavily about accepting that idea. That's all I got."

"Thank fuck! Can we finally relax, play some cards and down a few beers?" Rez asked. "I hate talking about work when we're off the damn clock."

Rez had a good point.

"Deal me in, Heat Miser," Fletch instructed Finn. "Time to kick your ass once again. Hope you brought a thick wallet."

"You might beat me at cards, asshole, but I'm better at pool."

"Because you're better at playing with balls."

"You have me confused with Cross. Now *he's* a professional ball player." Finn chuckled.

Fletch ducked because he knew what was coming.

These assholes were nothing if not predictable. And he did not want to be in the path of any flying objects.

Chapter Three

Nova shoved her sunglasses to the top of her head and rushed up the two flights of stairs for a building that appeared abandoned years ago. Located on the outskirts of Rockvale, it sat in a desolate section of an industrial zone.

She'd been part of federal task forces before. None of them had set up their plant in a building like this. She hoped to hell it had utilities, like running water, and the same normal comforts of places they normally rented.

By the time she hoofed it up to the third floor landing, she decided she was going to have a word with whoever chose this spot.

As long as she didn't get shit for being late.

Because she was *late.*

She had texted Crew to let him know what happened, but she hadn't received a text back.

Typical man.

She was sure she'd get it three hours after the fact and when she did, she'd get only a, "K," in response.

She gritted her teeth.

Of course, she had to pick a male-dominated career. What the fuck was she thinking?

She pulled in a breath and hesitated outside the windowless steel door in an attempt to slow her racing heart.

Here she was once again, the only damn female on her latest assignment.

She should've said no when she was approached about joining this task force.

"I should've said no," she whispered, facing the closed door. "I'm going to regret this, I just know it."

With a sigh, she turned the knob and found the door locked. *Jesus.* She glanced at her Apple watch. Yes, she was a little over twenty minutes late, but they couldn't have finished the initial meeting already that involved team introductions and going over the basic details of the investigation.

She was acquainted somewhat with Crew. She'd heard about his reputation from others who'd worked with the DEA agent before. She'd also seen him from a distance at a grand jury proceeding a couple of years ago.

His silver fox good looks had caught her eye. At least until she found out he was married with two kids.

Rumor had it, based on the other women she worked with, that was no longer the case. Like was typical in law enforcement, and it didn't matter at what level, the divorce rate was high.

Every wedding she'd gone to since the beginning of her career, she'd sit in the seats, watch the ceremony and make bets with herself on how long the marriage would last. She also wondered how much money they wasted on a large, fancy wedding.

One piece of advice she'd give to anyone who'd listen and was searching for their *forever* person... Prenups and elopement. Or go to city hall. Don't waste the amount of money that could be used for a down payment on a house for one single damn day of celebration.

For what?

What was left in the end? A wedding album full of pictures with someone's face scratched out, a shaky video of drunk guests doing the chicken dance, two confused kids and crippling alimony payments?

Dogs. That was the answer. Adopting a dog was a much safer bet and cheaper than getting a spouse. Even better, they loved unconditionally. Unlike humans.

Not that Nova herself had a dog.

Maybe she'd get herself a companion once she retired, bought a converted camper van and traveled the country, no longer giving a shit about organized crime or mountains of red tape and paperwork.

She pulled in another breath, lifted her fist and used the side of her hand to beat on the door. She took a step back so whoever peered through the peephole would see both her and the badge she pulled from her pocket and held up to identify herself.

She had no idea if Crew knew what she looked like. If he was a good team leader, he most likely pulled up her photo as well as everyone else's he didn't know personally before letting them into...

The Plant.

Her new home away from home for a while. Unfortunately, so far it looked like a dump.

She dropped her hand and slid her badge back into her wind jacket pocket as soon as she heard the deadbolt click and door knob turn...

When the door swung open, she expected to see Crew. Instead, deep brown eyes surrounded with thick black eyelashes locked with hers. "You're late."

No shit, Sherlock. "I'm aware of the time." She lifted her wrist with her watch. "I notified Crew. Maybe he didn't get the message."

"Since I'm not Crew, I wouldn't know," came the deep rumble that vibrated through her all the way to her toes.

She blinked, tipped her head to the side and stared at him. She reluctantly allowed herself a few seconds to check him out by rolling her gaze from the top of his short dark blond hair, along his clean-shaven face, over his broad shoulders, down his trim torso and his belted waist to his long denim-encased legs. He wore heavy boots that reminded her of what bikers wore.

That would make sense since she'd been told the first floor of this very building was the official clubhouse for the Blue Avengers MC, a motorcycle club made up strictly of law enforcement. She had to assume he rode with them.

When she finally lifted her gaze, she noticed he'd been doing the same thing.

Touché.

She raised one eyebrow when his eyes finally rose enough to meet hers.

"Were you late because you had to do your makeup and hair?"

Damn.

Unless she was undercover, she usually pulled her hair up into a very neat and tight bun while she worked. Since she wasn't sure what this assignment would entail yet, she decided to leave it down and simply finger-comb it.

And yes, she had put on some makeup but that wasn't why she was late.

Typical misogynistic asshole. Unfortunately, that wasn't anything new in her line of work.

"Well, of course. Plus, I had to fix the chip in my nail

polish and pick out the right shoes so they wouldn't clash with my purse. Oh, and make sure my panties and bra matched." She slapped a hand to her chest and bugged out her eyes. "Getting ready for the day as a woman is *exhausting*."

"You're not carrying a purse."

"And you are so damn observant."

"Just so you know, we can't see your underwear."

"And you never will."

A grin spread across his dangerously handsome face and he finally took a step back to stop blocking her entry. He lowered his voice a hair. "That sounded like a challenge."

"Obviously, one you'd never win."

One side of his mouth tilted up even higher and his dark eyes sharpened.

Oh yes, he was going to be so much fun to deal with.

"Think so?"

"Know so," she answered with confidence, stepping over the threshold.

He scrubbed a hand over his mouth and when he was done, his cocky grin was wiped away.

She stopped in front of him and turned until they were face to face. Unlike him, she didn't bother to lower her voice for what she said next. "I bet you're the kind of guy who thinks he can convert lesbians, aren't you?"

She heard a bunch of snickers, groans, hoots and laughs from the large conference table placed in the middle of the third floor. She hadn't taken a good look in that direction yet since she'd been busy dealing with the man in front of her.

Once she was done with him, she'd deal with the rest.

"Is that what you are?"

"You're making me wish I was," she muttered, but loud enough for everyone to hear.

"Damn! What a fucking burn!" came from someone at the table along with a burst of deep laughter.

"Can we fucking get started?" someone else shouted.

Narrowing her eyes just slightly, Nova held his a few more seconds before turning to face the rest of the team already seated around the long conference table.

It was large enough to seat the fifteen members of the task force. Along the walls were four desks with computers, but the room didn't hold much else.

That would have to change. A lot more equipment would be needed than just fifteen bodies and a place to sit. She wondered if Crew had ever led a federal task force before.

But what caught her eye next was a cot in the back corner.

Why would there be a cot? Not only a cot, but one made up using precise military corners. Someone had been to boot camp. Or attended a strict police academy.

Was someone crashing here at night? Or was that only there for late nights?

It didn't matter. She was sure she'd find out the reason eventually.

The floor plan was wide open with wide-planked hardwood floors that had been previously painted white but most of the paint had been worn away. They'd probably be beautiful if they were resurfaced and stained.

Every window she could see was boarded up from the outside and the panes on the inside were either covered in thick dirt or cracked.

While the floor and windows looked like they hadn't been touched in years, in contrast, the smell of fresh paint filled her nostrils. Someone had slapped at least one coat of white on the walls. A blown-up map covering the area the

Tri-State Drug Task Force would be dealing with was pinned to the wall opposite of where she stood.

Their work area had plenty of overhead lights, plenty of open space to work and, as she turned her head back toward the cot, she noticed what looked like a single bathroom in the other back corner.

Sharing a bathroom was slightly better than nothing since she'd have to tolerate urine on the floor and seat since most guys had shitty aim. They could hit a moving target with their service weapon from a twenty-five-yard distance. But a toilet a few inches away? Fucking impossible.

"Take a load off, Wilder," Crew instructed, pointing to an empty conference chair at the opposite end of the table from him.

"Sorry I'm late."

"A little warning would've been nice."

Oh no he didn't. "Do you have your phone on silent?"

"Yeah, because we're about to..." His mouth slammed shut. The group leader grimaced and picked up his phone off the table where it had been placed face down. "Fuck."

"*Mmm,*" she murmured and headed toward the empty seat, eyes and grins following her as she went.

The guy who answered the door trailed her, too, but before he could pull out the chair for her, she grabbed it and did it herself, plopping her ass down and glancing around at the full table, giving her new temporary coworkers a few nods and chin lifts.

The door man ended up sitting three seats away, but his unreadable eyes remained on her.

Her guess was he was probably a pro at cards. He had the poker face down pat.

She ignored him and turned her attention to Crew, now standing at his end of the table. "All right, now that we're all here we can finally get started. You were all chosen for a reason and I'll try to use your strengths where needed."

Admittedly, Crew was even more handsome closer-up. He had to be in his early- to mid-forties. His hair had more gray in it than she remembered, and last time she saw him, he wasn't sporting facial hair. The wiry hairs covering his chin were almost all white, while the rest of his beard was salt-and-pepper to match his hair.

"Distinguished" came to Nova's mind. But she was damn sure that only applied to his looks, he probably didn't act that way.

None of them did. That came with the territory of dealing with the dregs of the Earth on almost a daily basis.

Because of that, similar to doctors and nurses, law enforcement had a dark sense of humor to keep their sanity while doing their jobs. Inappropriate, sure. Necessary, absolutely.

"How about we go around the table and introduce ourselves, then we'll touch on what will be happening from here on out. I'll start... Colin Crew, senior special agent with the DEA. Crew for short. I'll be leading group two." He turned to the man sitting to his left. The one with a face chiseled from concrete.

"Nox. Bradley Lennox. Shadow Valley PD."

He not only seemed closed off, but a man of little words.

They continued around the table.

"Antonio Alvarez, Southern Allegheny Regional PD. Will answer to either Alvarez or Rez. Or, if you're my mom, Tony."

A couple of snorts and snickers filled Nova's ears.

The redhead to Rez's right spoke up next. "Daniel Finnegan. Also from Southern Allegheny Regional PD. I go by Finn."

"Owen Decker—"

"Big Deck!" Finn shouted next to him, slapping him on the back.

"Trooper with PSP," he finished. "Call me Decker."

They kept the introductions quickly moving around the large table.

"Luke Rodgers, DEA special agent."

"Luis Torres. Also a special agent with the DEA."

Then the door man was next. "Fletch. Full name, Shane Fletcher. State Trooper First Class."

A groan came from Decker down the table. "Nobody cares about that First Class bullshit, jackass."

Chuckles circled the table.

Fletch shrugged. "My bank account cares."

Nova's eyes got stuck on his very white, very wide grin. When he noticed her staring, he slowly licked his bottom lip.

Jesus.

Luckily, Crew yelling, "Next!" pulled her attention off the man.

You know better than to eat where you shit, Nova. And haven't you learned your lesson yet about dealing with arrogant, self-centered men?

She jerked her gaze from him and forced herself to concentrate on the next person speaking. "Ian Butler. Corporal with the State Police."

Then it was Nova's turn to be in the hot seat. "Nova Wilder. Special agent. FBI. Call me... Honestly, I don't give a shit what you call me. Wilder. Nova. Doesn't matter to me. The only thing I care about is you treating me as an equal."

She expected some ball-busting over that, but surprisingly, the only responses she saw were shared looks and lifted eyebrows.

She could live with that. As a female agent, she always

had to work twice as much, twice as hard, to prove herself and get the respect she deserved. She doubted this task force would be any different.

They finished going around the table with introductions from Don Mullins, a narcotics detective with the Pittsburgh Police, Ken Proctor from a police department in Uniontown, Warren Reynolds, another corporal with PSP, and another state trooper named Carl Powers. Rounding out the fifteen member task force was Sam Kruger, a corporal with a local PD in Greensburg.

It was quite a group and she would never remember everyone's name. At least not at first. But, of course, one name had already stuck with her... Fletch, the cocky cop who greeted her at the door.

The man who mistakenly thought he was "all that" and a bag of sour cream and onion chips.

She would need to steer clear of him as much as she could. Ask Crew for assignments he wasn't on and make sure she didn't end up partnered with him.

It would be better for her and, of course, safer for Fletch. She was not only an expert with hand-to-hand combat but usually had the highest score during her quarterly firearm qualifications.

While she might be what most men considered "attractive," looks could be deceiving. She was far from clueless or weak. Unfortunately, some men couldn't see past the "pretty."

Crew swept a hand out in an arc, indicating the space that surrounded them. "As you see, we don't have all our equipment yet. Hopefully the rest should be delivered this week. I figured today would be a good time to meet each other, discuss the reason why this task force was formed, plus get some ideas and suggestions from all of you. If we're going to be a team, we all need to be actively involved. If you don't pull your weight, you're out. Any suggestion, no matter how small or how simple you think it might be, I want to hear it.

"Everyone not already a fed should've already been to the Pittsburgh field office, turned in your paperwork, got sworn in as a federal task force officer and picked up your ID. If you haven't, let me know. You'll need those credentials to work outside your normal jurisdictions.

"That said, this might be the only time we're all together in one spot until we're done with what we set out to do. Unless, of course, I need to pull you all in for a meeting. However, no matter where you are or what you're doing, I'll need updates. Report back to me with anything important. This way anything I need to pass on to the supervising special agent, I can. Don't fuck me sideways with my superiors because *you* neglected to tell me something important, no matter how small it is.

"That leads me into my next reminder... You answer to me." Crew tapped his index finger on the table in front of him. "In turn, I answer to my supervisor. Don't make me look bad, got it? If you do, I'll make sure any skid marks left on me will be rubbed off on you. Simply put, don't fuck me and I won't fuck you. Easy.

"All right... Everyone sitting at this table has one damn mission. To stop those fucking Deadly Demons. To choke the supply of meth coming into Pennsylvania from that outlaw MC. Group one will work on taking the members down in West Virginia. Group three will work on stopping the spread of the Demons and flow of meth into Ohio. That doesn't mean we won't be working with those groups. You might be sent south or west. This investigation will be fluid. Meaning, you might be undercover one day, the next you might be stuck in here listening to a wiretap. The next you might be sitting all night in a van doing surveillance while drinking three gallons of coffee and pissing into a container."

"Do we know who their supplier is?" someone down at the other end of the table asked.

"Not yet," Crew answered. "However, our group isn't concentrating on identifying the supplier. Group one is, along with the DEA Houston office. We'll be more focused on the Demons moving into PA and we'll see where that leads us. We know they're dealing on the street because a couple of them got busted doing so but neither biker would cut a deal and give up any info. Until we have something more concrete, our educated guess from some of the chatter we heard is that their MC is a pipeline between two heavy hitters. Both the supplier and possibly another organization with a hand in distribution or possibly even retail sales. Until we identify those bookends and get enough evidence on them, too, we can't go in and start busting the Demons. We want to give them enough rope to hang themselves and whoever they're dealing with."

"How much undercover work are we doing?" Rez asked.

Or at least Nova was pretty sure his name was Alvarez.

"As much as needed. I have thoughts. But then so does the supervising special agent, the assistant special agent in charge, as well as the resident agent in charge." Crew grimaced and Nova understood that pain.

"Don't they always?" she muttered under her breath.

Crew's gray eyes landed on her. "They have a lot to say, for sure. Some good, some not so good. Everyone sitting at this table knows what it's like when we're doing all the dirty work and someone else sitting behind a desk is calling the shots. Especially when it's someone who hasn't done field work in two damn decades. They forget what it's like. Don't worry, I won't mind reminding them." His lips curled into a grin.

Again, a few chuckles circled the table.

"Oh, before I forget... Even though a few of us are certified in wiretapping, Torres has the most experience, so he'll be the Plant manager. I'm not sure how much tapping we'll need to do as compared to group one, but if you have your A-Cert and are asked to do it, you'll report to him. Okay... Right now, that's all I have."

Chapter Four

Fletch pushed away from the table and stood, announcing, "If you're not already aware of it, on the first floor of this building is the Blue Avenger MC's clubhouse. I already cleared it with our president... We're going to give the task force full access to our church. If you need to let off steam with a game of darts or pool, if you need to hide out for a bit for a break, if you simply want a fucking beer, it's all available downstairs. We'll make sure you all get a key. We only ask that you respect the space. The rules are simple. You drink our beer or eat our steaks, you replace it. Clean up after yourself and take care of it like it's your own. We worked our fucking asses off to get our church to where it is now. Don't fuck it up or bring in strangers without permission. If you do and you're not BAMC, you'll lose that privilege. Now, I'm heading down there to grab a cold brew. If any of you want to come down and check it out, you can come with me and I'll give you the nickel tour."

As everyone else stood, too, he heard:

"I'm game."

"Yeah, I want to check it out."

"That's good of you."

He nodded, noticing he hadn't heard a female voice amongst them. He turned to where Wilder had been sitting, but she was already beelining toward the door.

He raked his gaze over her from head to toe once more. Her dark brown hair stopped just past her shoulders and even though it looked like it needed a good brushing, whatever she did to it made it have loose waves that looked sexy as fuck. Fletch imagined that was how it looked after she just had three orgasms back to back.

Her eye makeup was the smoky look women liked to do. Her lips had a shine and a slight pinkish tint to them that kind of matched her eyeshadow.

Her makeup wasn't heavy, but again, like her hair, was sexy as fuck. She would look like a sex kitten if she didn't have that steel edge to her.

But it was her ass...

Jesus.

But then, he'd always been an ass man. If the right ass caught his attention, it didn't matter what the women looked like... at least, to a point, anyway. As long as he didn't have to brown bag it, he was good. Face down, ass up was one of his favorite positions anyhow.

He pursed his lips as he watched the swing of her hips. It wasn't overly exaggerated but tightly controlled as if she knew someone had eyes on her.

When Crew barked out, "Fletch!" he jerked his gaze from Nova just as she disappeared out the door.

Fuck, busted.

He turned to Crew, prepared to get shit for ogling a fellow task force member.

"Stick here for a few. Need to run something by you."

Fletch nodded and Decker whacked him on the arm as he passed by. "I can take everyone down."

"Okay. I'll be down as soon as I'm done with Crew."

"No rush. Maybe some will want to hang around for a bit to shoot the shit or a game of pool."

Fletch walked back to where Crew stood by the conference table and they both watched the rest of the task force members file out the door. With just about everyone wearing boots, it sounded like a herd of elephants heading down the metal stairway outside.

When the door finally closed behind the last person, he turned to the DEA agent and braced, unsure why Crew wanted to talk to him alone. "What's up?"

"Want to run something by you."

Fletch raised his eyebrows and waited.

"It's about going undercover. I know you'd prefer that over a lot of the other shit, like surveillance or wiretaps. Plus, you're good at it. You're like a chameleon and can blend in almost anywhere. I'm going to try to focus on everyone's strengths and clearly undercover work is yours."

"What are you thinking?"

"Using Jamison's brother's MC as cover."

What the fuck? Fletch shook his head. "How?"

"I don't have it all figured out yet because I'll want more input from you, Jamison and Cross. But if we can manage it, want you to go undercover within their MC."

"You shitting me?"

"No. They'll have to agree, of course. Otherwise, you'd have to go in as a prospect without them knowing and there's no guarantee they'd accept you. They might get suspicious since you're thirty-five. No matter how we get you in there, we'll have to create you a whole new identity and background, but I'm damn sure they do some thorough background checks before accepting a new recruit. We really don't want those Shadows, who are tied to their club, digging deep if we can avoid it. Not to mention, the shit they'd probably put you through as a prospect to prove your loyalty could be..."

Dangerous and illegal. But Crew didn't need to say that out loud. Fletch was perfectly aware what he'd have to deal with.

"Right," Fletch murmured. In the past, he had no problem doing what he needed to do to not blow his cover. That didn't mean he didn't have his limits. Some lines he would not cross.

Prospects were basically an MC's bitch during their first year or however long it took for them to prove themselves worthy to earn their full set of patches. It could be anything, even murder. And trying to figure out how to murder someone without actually doing the deed was a pain in the fucking ass. Same way with doing drugs in an undercover situation. Or, *hell*, participating in any felony.

An undercover agent had a pass to do some stuff but not just anything. And anything illegal had to be well-documented and only done for a good reason.

Being undercover wasn't a free pass to commit murder and mayhem.

"So if we can pull it off, you'd go under as a patched member, wear their colors, live their life for a while and we'll figure out an excuse for you to reach out to the Demons. The best part is the Demons would never expect the DAMC to allow a badge amongst them, so it would be a great cover. I may even want someone to go in as a prospect, too. But again, we'd need to limit the shit they'd do for that club. And the easiest way to get around that is by getting the DAMC's cooperation."

"You don't think the Angels will run their mouths?"

"It's a risk. But I'm thinking if we go to them and show how much our investigation will benefit them, they might be willing to work with us. We have to go in with solid info and plead a good case, because if they shut us out from minute one, then we could be screwed."

"We'd also have to look the other way if they're involved in shit Jamison and Cross don't know about."

Crew huffed out a breath. "Yeah, depending what it is. We can let the minor shit slide, but anything else…" He shook his head. "It'll depend on what it is."

"And that right there might cause them to tell us to fuck off."

Smoking pot and underaged drinking was one thing. Kidnapping, aggravated or sexual assault and people disappearing into the ether were another.

"Are you planning on sending someone to prospect with the Demons?" Fletch asked.

"It would be ideal to have someone on the inside. Group one already has a couple of their guys installed inside the mother chapter in West Virginia. But from the intel I'm getting, the Demons are setting up another chapter in our territory and one in Ohio to get a foothold on the local meth market. If we can get someone in their midst while those chapters are still forming, that would be the best time."

"Agreed." Planting a seed while the Demons were still sowing their garden would be the perfect time.

"If we send anyone in to prospect, it needs to be someone preferably in their twenties. Most of us are older than a typical prospect."

"Right. A forty-year-old prospect might catch some attention. Is it possible? Sure. Is it common?" Fletch lifted and dropped one shoulder. "I don't know. Maybe we can find out when we meet with the Angels."

"*If* we meet with them. They have to agree first."

"And if they don't?"

"Then we're going to have someone undercover approach them about prospecting. Another issue is finding someone who can ride. Luckily, you can ride and have your own Harley, so you're familiar with them... Start getting in the habit of calling it a sled. You'll have to get familiar with their vernacular and habits, that's why I'd want to set you up with them ahead of time. Get comfortable with their language and actions before you approach any Demons as an Angel."

"Sounds like fun." He loved challenges like this. Stepping outside the box and working undercover in a situation completely opposite of his normal life. It was like playing cops and robbers when he was a kid. Only then, he always played the good guys. While undercover he'd be playing the bad.

"The good thing about you not having kids or a wife is we can set you up in an apartment in Shadow Valley and get you working in one of their businesses. You'll need to go as deep as possible. Here's the other thing..." He paused. "Since you'd have to live that life for at least a while, I think it would be smart to also send in Wilder with you as your ol' lady. Then we'd have two of you inside that club. And if I can slide someone in as a prospect, that'll make three."

Holy shit. He didn't know what to address first. He decided to start with the easy question. "We'll need that many?"

"We will if the president allows our UCs to deal with the Demons directly. Like buying meth from the Demons. I've got a bunch of scattered ideas that need to be put together to form a more solid plan. But first I need to know... Are you up for it?"

"Fuck yeah. That sounds right up my alley." But... "Do you think Wilder will want to do it?" Especially when it came to shacking up with him and playing the part of his ol' lady, basically pretending to be his wife.

"She won't have a choice. If she doesn't want to pull her weight on this team, she'll need to be replaced."

Damn. That threat sounded cold-blooded but it was necessary. "Plan on her walking, then. I'm not sure she'll be thrilled with living with me. Especially for what might be months."

"Could be weeks. Could be months. Could be even longer. Plenty of time for her to teach you some manners."

Fletch snorted. "Too old to teach this dog new tricks."

"Wilder looks like she's capable of teaching an old dog plenty of new tricks. But warning, she won't use treats, she'll use a damn shock collar." Crew made a zapping sound and laughed.

Fletch winced. "No fucking doubt. Has she done undercover work?"

"Oh yeah."

"Successfully?"

"Hell yes. She went under to gather enough evidence to indict some major players in the Russo crime family."

"Damn. She got her nails dirty with the Pittsburgh Cosa Nostra?"

"That wasn't the first time she made a name for herself among her peers. She's one dedicated and determined agent."

"Was that why she was chosen for this assignment?"

"Yeah. We needed at least one female on the team for undercover work and organized crime is her jam. From what

I heard, she played her part in the Russo organization so well the head of the family was eating out of her fucking palm."

"Wait. Are you fucking talking about Frank Russo, Sr.? *The* top boss? The don himself?"

"Sure as fuck am."

Damn! "I thought that slimy motherfucker was married."

"He is. Or *was,* until someone force-fed him a forty-caliber slug. She went in to target the underboss Frankie Jr. but as soon as the old man saw her, he wanted to claim her for his very own."

"And he got her," Fletch murmured.

Crew shrugged and grinned. "You saw her. Warning though, if this all works out like I hope... She's a chameleon like you. You might think you know what she's made of or who she is, and most likely you'll be wrong. When she's working, she's *working* and she's all in. And when I say all in, I mean *all in.* If she's got a job to do, she'll do it no matter what it takes."

"Is she gray?"

"We're all gray when we need to be," Crew reminded him. "I don't know her personally, I only know what I've heard. So, be aware what you see on the outside might not be what's on the inside."

"Got it. At least I know she won't break her cover no matter what happens."

"She won't break cover. *No matter what happens.*" The last part Crew said slowly and distinctly. Fletch had no problem picking up what the man was putting down.

That gave him a shitload of confidence about working with her. It sounded like she was very good at her job.

But then, so was he. For that reason, he wouldn't expect any less out of a partner.

And that's what they'd be, partners living in close quarters.

Yeah, she was going to fucking hate that.

He grinned.

"One more thing, brother. Start thinking of a good road name. Or if you want, I can pick one for you." Crew smothered a laugh.

"Fuck that. I'd end up wearing a cut with the name Jingles."

"Damn, I actually like that. You can wear a bell around your neck like the Tom cat you are."

"Fuck off." A thought hit him. "Oh fuck! If Wilder acts as my ol' lady, then she'll have to wear a 'Property of' cut."

"Not sure how the Angels' deal with their ol' ladies, but I'd say that's a pretty good chance."

Fletch grinned.

"Just make sure if you two end up on this assignment together, you're still breathing at the end. Don't do shit simply to piss her the fuck off. Underestimating her could be a fatal mistake."

"Do you think she's the one who took out Russo?" Had the Mafia boss done something to her to warrant that?

"No one knows who made him eat lead. It could've been an actual hit or just someone having a bad day."

"Then I'll do my best to treat her with nothing but respect."

Crew snorted and shook his head. "Trust me, you're going to need to do better than your best, because from what I've heard, she won't tolerate anything else."

He'd heed that warning.

For the most part, anyway.

Chapter Five

FLETCH SAT at the table in the first floor meeting room. It might be the last time he sat there for a while depending on whether he went deep undercover or not.

If he did, he'd be scarce when it came to the BAMC. Including the club runs. So, he asked if they could do one right after the executive committee meeting.

Jamison and the rest agreed. Of course, not everyone was available due to their work and home life schedules but most would try to make it.

Depending on what happened in the next week or so, he could be temporarily hanging up his Blue Avengers cut and shrugging on a Dirty Angels cut instead.

It was almost like donning the uniform of an enemy to hide in plain sight.

Hopefully, the DAMC wouldn't look at them as the enemy, but he also wasn't stupid. Unlike fellow military or LEO MCs, they didn't respect law enforcement in any way, shape or form. And while the DAMC was no longer considered an outlaw club, they balanced on that tight-wire and it wouldn't take much to tip them back to their roots.

Since Jamison's brother, Zak, wanted to keep the club aboveboard, Fletch hoped he'd cooperate. If not, they'd have to come up with another way to get their foot in the door with the Deadly Demons.

From what Jamison had reported to Crew, the DAMC didn't have any beefs with the Demons but another club did: the Blood Fury MC. However, one, it was a really old beef and two, the Fury was hours north of where they were. That club wasn't close enough to be convenient.

After all the normal boring shit, like the treasurer's report, was out of the way, Jamison opened the floor to everyone else.

"Anyone have anything else before we adjourn?" Jamison asked once everyone else had their opportunity to speak up.

Fletch knew Crew planned on addressing some task force stuff with Cross and Jamison.

"Yeah," Crew said, leaning back in his seat and folding his arms over his chest. "Any luck on talking with the DAMC prez about a meet?"

"I left him a voicemail. Just waiting on a call back."

"How long does he normally take?" the DEA agent asked.

"When he's good and ready."

"Will that be sometime this century? We need to get some people in place. We're about to get rolling on this investigation and it would be good if they cooperated. For both them and for us."

At the head of the table, Jamison also sat back in his chair and took a slow, deep breath as he considered Crew. "I know that. You know that. Good luck convincing them of that."

Crew shrugged. "All we can do is try. If my method doesn't work, we'll have to approach it another way."

"You mean going undercover without them knowing it," Jamison said flatly.

"I'd prefer not to do that. We're going to need them. It's risky to simply put someone in there as a prospect because the next thing you know that new guy, which would be my guy, is approaching the Demons to buy meth wearing Angels' colors. That's double the risk of getting exposed. Worse, it could start an MC war we want to avoid."

"I'm aware of the list of potential problems, Crew. And I don't want to risk one of your TFOs because of Z being a stubborn fuck. But, truth is, Z *can* be a stubborn fuck, as well as the rest of his officers. Especially the big asshole. The sergeant at arms tends to make decisions that aren't his to make."

"He oversteps?" Fletch asked, surprised.

Jamison's blue eyes turned to him. "Constantly."

"And neither the prez or VP puts him in his place?" Fletch would have no problem telling Rez to remember his place. He might be the club's enforcer, but he was not the ultimate decision-maker. The president was. And Fletch, as VP, assisted Jamison with guidance.

"Depends," Jamison answered. "You have to remember those guys grew up together—for the most part, anyway—so they've been tight for decades. It doesn't matter whose blood's running through their veins, in the end they are true brothers through and through. This bond was established way before they wore their prospect cuts. Zak and I might have been born from the same parents but he's closer to Hawk and Diesel than me. And I don't think that'll ever change."

While Jamison's tone remained level, Fletch knew he had

a lot of regrets when it came to his relationship with his brother.

Fletch couldn't imagine how the DAMC ripped apart one family like it did. Mitch Jamison, the former president of the Blue Avengers, broke free of his father's outlaw club to take the straight and narrow path while Mitch's brother, Rocky, stuck to his roots. Mitch went into the police academy and Rocky went to prison for life. The two brothers couldn't be more different.

It didn't stop there. Mitch's sons took two different paths, too, despite Mitch doing everything he could to prevent that. Axel went into the police academy while Zak went to prison for a decade. Once he got sprung, he went right back to the club, what he considered his home and family, despite the fact doing so would risk him going away again.

That risk was one reason he was adamant about keeping the club clean. On the surface, anyway.

Jamison's next words pulled Fletch from his thoughts. "I can tell you he won't want to meet alone. I doubt Diesel would allow it, anyway."

"Then he can bring his enforcer along," Crew said.

"He might want Hawk with him, too."

"And who is Hawk again?" Crew asked with his eyebrows pinched together.

"His VP," Jamison answered.

Crew shook his head. "Okay. But no more than those three."

"You're asking for them to cooperate with you but you also want to set the terms. That might not go over well," Jamison warned him.

"Tell them what we want to discuss with them is on a need-to-know basis and I'm being generous by allowing three."

Fletch dropped his head and smothered his grin at Crew trying to make demands of an MC he had zero control over.

"Yeah, I won't be telling him that second part because he'll just tell me to fuck off and you won't get a meet with him at all."

"Do we need to twist arms?" Finn asked. "Do we need to bring in one of their guys and hold them in custody until your brother cooperates?"

Axel's mouth became a thin slash. "Look, it took years for us to patch up our relationship to where it is now. And there are still cracks..."

"I told you this might fuck shit up between the two of you," Cross said. "Maybe it shouldn't be you, Axel."

Crew's brow furrowed. "Is it better to get Mitch to approach him?"

"Oh hell no!" burst from the BAMC president. "My relationship with Zak is much better than my father's. Our relationship might have cracks but theirs still has gaping holes. They tolerate each other only because of my mother and the grandkids. That's about it. Mitch hates that Z's still involved with the DAMC, whether it's legit or not. He also silently blames Z for Jayde hooking up with her ol' man. He wanted my sister to stay clear of the club and she's now fully involved because of her husband Linc."

Crew scratched the back of his neck and his jaw shifted. "Yeah, I remember Mitch going off the deep end when that all went down. I thought he came around."

"To a point, he did. But remember, tolerance isn't quite the same as acceptance. So, if you want to do this, I might not be your best bet, but I'm your only bet."

"Got it." Crew turned to Cross. "Can you nudge hubby to get Zak to call Jamison back?"

Cross shrugged. "I can mention it to him. But he'll ask a shitload of questions about it."

"For now, just tell them it's a family matter."

Cross's nostrils widened and his mouth twisted. "No. I'm not fucking lying to him. And, hell, Axel lives in the same neighborhood as his brother. All he has to do is go knock on Z's damn door."

"The fuck if I'm knocking on anyone's door in that neighborhood if they're not aware that I'm coming first. I'll get Bella to talk to Sophie at the bakery. Sophie's good about getting shit done, especially when it comes to our family. I'll tell Bella that it's important my brother get a hold of me."

"You live two fucking streets away from each other. Your kids spend time together. Your wives run a *business* together," Finn said.

"Look, I try not to create waves, since one small ripple can turn into a tsunami. I tread lightly for Bella and our kids."

"Kids you wouldn't have if it wasn't for the generosity of Sophie and Ivy," Cross reminded him.

"And that right there is another reason I try not to stir up shit. I owe both of those women big time. As well as Zak for allowing his wife to be our surrogate."

"And Jag for allowing Ivy to donate her eggs," Cross added.

Fletch had a hard time wrapping his head around the whole Jamison and Dougherty bloodlines. He might have to get it straight if he went undercover with that club.

Jamison released a long sigh. "Okay, I'll work on it and let you know once I talk to him."

"Sooner than later," Crew advised.

"Right." Jamison nodded. "What about the Knights? Once I talk to Zak, I can ask him to reach out if you want them there, too. They're close allies."

"Let's hold off meeting with them for now. I don't want too many people in on what we're doing. Let's take the temperature of your brother and his sidekicks first. If they shut us down and out, then we'll have to come up with another plan. There might not be any reason to approach the Dark Knights."

"It's possible to put someone undercover with them, too," Fletch suggested. "My guess is that they still follow the outlaw ways, unlike the Angels. And if they do, it might be more believable if one of our TFOs wearing Knight colors reaches out and make some deals with the Demons."

Crew ground his hand back and forth against the back of his neck. "One of the requirements to be a member of the Knights is to be Black. That's not negotiable from what I understand. The only two Black TFOs I have are Powers and Reynolds."

"I would think the Knights wouldn't be willing to let your TFOs in their ranks. Voluntarily, anyway," Cross warned. "If you think the DAMC hates cops, the Knights are worse. Because you're right, compared to the DAMC, they still follow the outlaw ways. Even if they were willing to work with your task force—and honestly, I can't imagine they would be—I doubt they'd go as far as allowing a badge to wear their colors."

"Yeah, I get it. I'd rather stick to the Angels for now since we have a connection with them through Cross and Jamison. Keep the Knights as a backup plan, if needed. The Demons are closing in on the DAMC's territory, not the Knights'."

"But they're strong allies," Jamison reminded Crew. "The Knights won't hesitate to join forces with the Angels in a war against the Demons. Even if they weren't strong allies, they'd do it because if the Demons take over Shadow Valley and the surrounding area, what's to say they won't stop and keep marching north. Those two clubs won't wait to be on the defensive, they'll go on the offensive first to squash any territory grab. They'll take out the threat before it takes them out. No one in either club will allow what happened with the Shadow Warriors to ever happen again."

"They'd be afraid of history repeating itself," Crew murmured as he processed that info. "Makes sense. Because of that, we need to be careful. We can't spark a war between three clubs. My ass would be handed to me at the same time I'm handing over my badge."

"And you have child support and alimony to pay." Sitting to Jamison's left, Rez snickered.

Crew shook his head. "Thanks for that reminder, asshole."

Rez grinned. "Anything I can do to help."

Fletch covered his own grin with his hand.

Jamison sighed loudly. "All right. That was more task force business than club business. Any other club business before we adjourn and hit the road?"

Fletch wanted to bring up what had been eating at him for a while now. There was no better time than the present. Especially since the third floor would be getting a lot of traffic soon. "Yeah. Got a suggestion."

"Does this have to do with the task force?" Jamison asked with a frown. "Because if it does—"

"No. The second floor."

Miller, the club treasurer, had been fucking with his phone the whole time they were talking about the Dirty Angels. He finally lifted his head. "We don't have the funds right now to do anything with it."

Fletch sighed just as loudly as their president had. "No shit. We're all aware our reserves are now non-existent from buying and rehabbing this place. But," he pointed toward the ceiling, "that cot on the third floor has been getting a lot of use lately and its current location will be far from ideal for him once this investigation gets rolling."

Something needed to change and it wouldn't if no one confronted Nox.

"We know why he's been sleeping up there. We all know why he doesn't want to go home to sleep in his own bed. We might not like it but we get it." Fletch glanced around the table and got a few nods in agreement. "All of us do. We've even talked about it with and without Nox being present. But he can't keep going on like he has, it's not good for him. He needs to get rid of that house. I'm thinking we should get that apartment done and instead of renting it to some stranger, Nox moves up there. The club could use the rent and he could use the change. Plus, with the task force now on the third floor, someone would always be here, so for the most part, he'd never be alone."

Fletch pictured Nox's eyes. Most of the time they were distant and empty. They would sometimes catch flashes of how the man used to be, but that was few and far between. When his wife passed, it was like he passed with her. She had taken his soul along for the journey. Only his heart kept beating, his lungs kept pumping, and Fletch worried he might do something to stop that.

Keeping the house where his wife died, where he was surrounded by memories of her, was not healthy for him. He stayed either upstairs or on a rack at his station to avoid what he needed to face head-on. Both his loss and his future. Instead, he was simply floating along ignoring it all.

Nothing was going to change if he didn't change it first.

Jamison said everyone at Shadow Valley PD had been nothing but supportive since Nox's wife died unexpectedly. And Fletch knew for a fact that each and every member of the Blue Avengers was and would continue to be there for him, too, for whatever he needed.

That was the power behind both their blue brotherhood and Blue Avengers brotherhood. He was surrounded by brothers willing to bend over backwards to help him.

He just didn't want it.

Fletch hoped Nox getting heavily involved with the task force might give him something to focus on to help get him past his grief, his sense of loss and hopelessness.

Fletch—along with the rest of their BAMC brothers—worried that if he stayed stagnant, or even got worse, he might eat his damn gun. And none of them, not fucking one, would be able to live with themselves if they didn't try everything in their fucking power to prevent that.

"Miller just said the club doesn't have the funds to finish the apartment." Finn's reminder brought Fletch back to the table.

"The club might not, but he would... *if* he sold that house."

"Shit," Finn murmured.

"Now *that's* a damn good idea," Miller said.

"I do have them sometimes," Fletch assured Miller.

"He's not going to like us discussing his business behind his back," Rez warned.

"Too fucking bad. It needs to be discussed," Fletch insisted, "and I want to present this option to him but we would need to vote on it first. That's why I'm bringing it up today."

"Then let's vote," Jamison suggested. "I think it's a great idea and I'm sure you all agree. It would be good for him *and* for the club. All those in favor of letting Nox use the proceeds from the sale of his house to finish the apartment upstairs, say aye."

Of course, everyone at the table voted for it.

Now Nox would have to get on board. It might take a few of them to convince him.

"What about rent?" Miller asked. "If he's using his money, we can't charge him rent until we reimburse him for the construction costs."

"Correct. We can deduct a reduced rent from the amount the club will owe him. And once we finish paying him back, we can increase the rent to fair market value. All in favor of that?" Jamison asked.

Again, everyone was good with that proposal.

"Okay, so who's going to be the one to approach him?" Jamison asked, glancing around the table.

"I'm thinking it should be you, prez," Rez suggested, "since you're his supervisor at work, too."

Jamison muttered, "It was Fletch's idea."

All eyes turned to him. "I'll do it. But I'll wait until after the run. Jamison, it might be a good idea for you to be with me when I talk to him about it."

"I'm okay with that. After Bella heads home, though."

"She's here for the run?" Rez asked.

"Yeah. She should be. She texted me an hour ago and said she dropped the kids off at my parents and was on the way. She's probably out there shooting the shit in the common area with Monty and North's ol' lady."

"Nash coming?" Fletch asked Cross.

"He's on tour right now."

Cross's husband, Nash, was the drummer and lead singer of the band Dirty Deeds. Him being on tour a lot left Cross home alone with their two thirteen-year-old adopted kids.

They had their hands full with those twins. Unwanted because they weren't infants, they spent years of hell passed around in the foster care system. Because of that, they tended to act out. A lot.

He had no idea how Cross dealt with them on his own when Nash was gone for days or weeks at a time. Neither sets of grandparents were involved because they were either deceased or out of the picture due to Cross and Nash's sexual orientation.

Since neither Cross or Nash had it easy as kids themselves, they figured they'd have a better handle than most on helping the twins. Only they might have thought raising them to be productive citizens of society would be a lot easier than it was turning out to be. They were learning the hard way that it wasn't. But both were determined to give those kids the best life they could.

Fletch had nothing but admiration for what they were doing, but he wouldn't want to be in their shoes.

It also had to put a strain on their relationship.

Jamison slammed the gavel on the table.

"That means we're adjourned," Finn yelled and pushed to his feet. "Time to ride, fuckers!"

A few fists pounded on the table in agreement, including Fletch's.

This might be the last run for a while wearing his own club's colors. He would enjoy every fucking second it lasted.

Chapter Six

"If we play our cards right, this might be your new temporary home, brother. Make sure to take a good look around. Get comfy." With a snort, Crew slapped Fletch on the back as Jamison yanked open the steel door.

The door from the rear lot into the Dirty Angels' church had a sign hanging over it that claimed *Down & Dirty 'til Dead.*

Before any of them had a chance to move farther inside, two young bikers created a human blockade as they stood with their arms crossed over their chests and boots spread wide. Prospects from what it looked like. Fletch's gaze narrowed on the patches on their cuts.

Yep. Just what he thought.

The *un*welcoming committee each had two rectangular patches on the front that declared them "prospects" with the names of Nugget and Booger.

Jesus Christ. Someone had fun coming up with those stupid-assed names for their recruits.

Crew hooked a thumb at them and announced, "These

two *still-wet-behind-the-ears, tiny-dicked* little boys think they can stop us," on a laugh.

When one of them began to reach into his cut, that laughter abruptly stopped and all of them went solid.

"You reach inside your cut, that will be the last thing you do," Crew warned him with a growl.

"We should've met them on neutral ground," Cross said, not caring that the prospects could hear him.

"They refused," Jamison reminded him, also acting like the prospects didn't each have two ears. "This was the only place they'd agree to meet."

"They think these two guard puppies will intimidate us," Finn said, making *sure* the two prospects heard him.

"Well then, that's their first mistake," Crew said. "And probably won't be their last."

Fletch was trying his damnedest to keep his trap shut since he was the one who would need to blend in with the club. He didn't want to start off by making enemies in the MC. That would only make his job more difficult.

"They're waitin' on you," the one named Booger announced with a scowl, trying to look intimidating.

"No shit," Fletch responded under his breath.

Nugget picked up from there. "No wanderin' around. No touchin' shit. We'll escort you to the meetin' room and when you're done, straight back out."

With a grin, Finn smacked Fletch's arm. "Escorted just like we're fucking royalty. Can't get any better than that!"

The older of the two recruits frowned. "Let's go."

When Booger swept a tattooed arm out, Jamison took the lead, grumbling, "I know where the fuck we're going." He paused in front of the prospect and went nose to nose with him. "Let me catch you up to speed. My granddaddy founded this fucking club. If it wasn't for him, you wouldn't be wearing those colors on your back."

"Hell, they haven't even earned their colors yet," Finn said. "I wonder if they know that to get their full set of patches, they need to get pegged by all the members first. Kind of like a frat pledge but only kinkier." He began thrusting his hips and humping the air while moaning.

Nugget's eyes widened for a second. "What?"

Fletch turned his head away and smothered a laugh.

"Just ask them to use a lot of lube. It'll make it easier, I promise." Crew added a wink on the end of that.

"They're just fuckin' with you, dummy," Booger told his partner, shaking his head. "That's not gonna happen."

Jamison also shook his head and began to push past them. "Let's go. I'm already tired of being here." When Booger slapped a hand onto Jamison's chest, causing him to stop, he warned gruffly, "Take your fucking hand off me or I'll break every one of your damn fingers. One at a time. Slowly."

The prospect removed his hand but shifted so his body blocked the BAMC president. "Only three pigs are allowed. You have five."

"Oh look, Booger knows how to count," Finn shouted. "Give him his binky for being such a smart boy."

For fuck's sake, they weren't going to make things easier by fucking with the DAMC prospects.

"Two of you have to wait outside."

"That's not going to happen," Jamison announced. "We were told three from the task force. Cross and I aren't on the task force, so we don't count. We're only here to—"

Booger cut him off. "You ain't allowed on this property."

"Who?" Crew asked sharply, even though he already knew full well who'd been banned from DAMC property. It wasn't a secret.

He jerked a chin up at Cross. "That one. The one that sucks dick."

Cross's head snapped up as his spine turned to steel. His wasn't the only one.

Now Fletch was done being silent. He stepped up to Booger, leaned in, curved a hand around his own ear, lowered his voice and asked as softly as he could, "Want to say that again? Didn't quite hear you clearly."

"Said—"

"Nug Nuts, what the fuck's goin' on out there? Think we got all day?"

"Fuck," Nugget grumbled, then twisted his head and yelled, "They got five."

"They strapped?"

When Nugget turned back to them, Crew warned, "Just try to pat us down."

"Fuck Nugget!" came a deep and very loud bellow from what looked like a room on the right side of their church. It had the door cracked open enough to hear, but not see, who was beyond the door.

"Goddamn it," Nugget grumbled under his breath, then twisted his head to yell over his shoulder again. "The cock-sucker's with 'em."

When the prospect turned his head back around, a fist came flying past Fletch, making him jerk out of the way. It nailed Nugget squarely in the nose. It was like smashing a balloon filled with red paint.

Blood flew and the baby biker stumbled backward, landing on his ass. "Jesus fuckin' Christ!" came out muffled as he pressed his hand to his gushing nose.

"Someone forgot to teach you respect, boy. You better learn it quick," Crew told him, shaking out his hand.

"That's probably not going to help my cause," Cross said.

Fletch could see Cross trying not to smile, though. He most likely wanted to dance a little jig on top of the downed prospect. While wearing wooden clogs. With cleats.

"Isn't going to make it any worse," Finn insisted, using his boot to shove Nugget back to the floor when he tried to get up. "Say you're sorry."

"Fuck you!" came from the bleeding prospect. He spat blood on the floor, barely missing Finn's boot.

"What the fuck's goin' on out here?" came another bellow from what Fletch now figured to be the Angels' meeting room.

"Teaching your boy here a little respect," Crew answered the big man standing in the open doorway.

The very tall, very broad biker with a short mohawk and covered in tats, including the sides of his head, took long strides toward them.

Everyone around him instantly went on the defensive. Without meaning to, they might have just started a war.

"What the fuck you do, asshole?"

Fletch quickly scanned the man's front patches. *Hawk. Vice President.*

The older biker named Hawk stopped in front of Nugget, still sitting on the floor and trying to stem the stream of blood coming from his nostrils. The VP's dark eyes flicked from the bleeding prospect up to Booger and then back down to Nugget.

"Nothin'."

"He's disrespecting Nash's husband. I don't think Nash would appreciate it, do you?" Jamison asked.

"Heard 'im," Hawk growled, keeping his eyes locked on Nugget. "Get up an' get gone."

"But—"

"Get up an' get gone," Hawk repeated in an even more

ass-puckering tone. "You were supposed to escort 'em in an' out, you simple fuck, not send shit sideways." He put Booger in his sights next. "Get 'im up, then both of you get gone. I got it from here since you two keep provin' yourselves useless as a fuckin' boar with tits."

Booger offered Nugget a hand and helped to pull the prospect to his feet. No one said a word until both prospects disappeared up a stairway in the back corner of the common area.

Jamison had informed them that the DAMC had rooms above their church. Fletch hoped he wasn't forced to live in one of those. He probably wouldn't be able to sleep without keeping at least one eye open.

And he'd need his sleep to remain sharp. Especially around this MC.

Once the prospects disappeared, Hawk's sharp gaze swept the five of them. It stopped on Cross and hung there for a few seconds before landing on Jamison. "Let's get this fuckin' over with. Don't got all day to waste on you." He jerked his tattooed head toward the open doorway, spun on his heel and strode in that direction.

The five of them shared a quick glance, then followed as Jamison took the lead. As they headed in the direction Hawk disappeared, Fletch took in everything around the common area. The old couches pushed against the wall, the Harley decor and bike parts hanging on the walls, the pool tables, dart boards, the large bar with the large DAMC insignia carved out of wood behind it and what seemed to be custom-airbrushed Harley gas tanks displayed on a shelf surrounded by liquor bottles behind the bar.

He wondered what was so special about those particular tanks that they required a spotlight.

Once Jamison and Cross entered the narrow room, Crew went next, followed by Fletch with Finn bringing up the rear.

"Shut the door," came from the man sitting at the opposite end of the table from where they stood.

The big biker named Hawk made his way around the table to retake his seat to the right of Zakary Liam Jamison, long-time president of the Dirty Angels MC and blood brother to Shadow Valley PD Sergeant Axel Jamison.

Zak sat relaxed in his chair at the head of the hand-crafted wood table. Similar to the wood sign behind the bar, the center was expertly carved with the club's rockers and center insignia.

If Fletch had to guess, a lot of history had gone down in this very room, in this church and on this property. The founders had begun building the clubhouse back in 1974, not long after establishing their club. Decades of murder and mayhem had been discussed, planned and witnessed within these same walls.

While Jamison had given them all a thorough run-down on the background as well as the current situation with the club, Fletch had done a bunch of digging on his own. He needed to know who he'd be living with and working amongst for the next few months. *Hell*, maybe even years.

For fuck's sake, he hoped this particular assignment didn't last that long. If it went past six months, he might ask Crew to pull him and let him do something else, even if it meant spending eight hours a day transcribing wiretaps.

Something he detested.

"You turn our granddaddy's church into a daycare, Z?" Jamison asked his brother as they stared at each other across the long table.

They acted more like acquaintances than actual brothers. Fletch had to guess that was due to who else was in the room because he knew their relationship was much better now than when Zak first got released from prison.

More than eighteen years ago.

Jamison jerked a thumb over his shoulder. "Where the fuck did you find those two rejects?"

Zak took his time brushing his knuckles down his bearded jaw before answering. "They were strays. Adopted them from the fuckin' pound. Decided to give 'em a good home."

If he looked hard enough, Fletch could see the resemblance between the two. The obvious similarities, of course, were the matching brown hair, peppered with a few grays, and their blue eyes. Besides what side of the law they both had landed on, the other obvious differences between them were the amount of ink, the length of hair and, of course, the beard. Zak also had a few more creases radiating from the corners of his eyes. But then, from what Fletch found in his background check on the current sitting president, the ex-con was a couple of years older than Axel.

Zak Jamison did a dime in prison after being framed by the former club president. The man named Pierce had wanted to steal the president's gavel from Zak, so he planted an ingredient used to make meth in Zak's place. Then someone anonymously called in a tip to Shadow Valley PD.

Talk about getting fucked up the ass without a drop of lube.

Fletch considered using that info to convince Zak to cooperate with their investigation, since the Deadly Demons were now trafficking meth in the Angels' territory.

Fletch assumed this club didn't have any knowledge of those actions. Yet, anyway.

But they would.

After a long discussion with the rest of the task force,

they decided it was smart to make the DAMC aware of that and the territory grab before they found out by other methods and took matters into their own hands.

That could get really fucking messy. For both the DAMC *and* law enforcement.

By laying everything out on the heavily lacquered table before them, Crew hoped the task force could control the narrative.

And get their cooperation without too much of a fight.

Hoped being the key word. Any time they dealt with questionable organizations like the DAMC, plans could get jacked.

Speaking of jacked... Axel's older brother was flanked by two very heavy hitters. They might be in their fifties, but they still looked like they could do a lot of damage.

For a second, Fletch was thankful that he had four at his back despite the fact only three bikers sat in front of him. Even though they all had their service weapons hidden on their person, he had no fucking doubt that all three of those bikers were packing, too. Whether they were legally allowed to carry or not.

The big guy to Zak's left shifted in his seat. Fletch didn't need to read his name patch or his title to know who he was.

Everyone knew him and what business he ran. They were also aware of the "security" crew he called his Shadows. What had started out as a simple security business developed into something so much more. The problem was, the Shadows were so damn good, they made it about impossible to pin anything on them.

Without solid evidence to prove any illegal activities, law enforcement was shit out of luck. The Shadows held it all.

But none of Diesel's crew were young bucks, either, and Fletch could only imagine they'd all be hanging up their military gear at any time now and younger blood would take over the business.

"Goddamn lucky we ain't at war," came the deep grumble from Diesel Dougherty, the Dirty Angels sergeant at arms.

Jamison warned them ahead of time that the DAMC enforcer would try to intimidate them, would be difficult "just because" and would do what he could to shut down any negotiations between the two groups.

He hated cops and wasn't shy about letting anyone know it.

Next to Fletch, Cross asked, "For what? Wearing a badge?"

"That's a fuckin' given. For settin' up your church in our territory."

"*Your* territory?" Jamison asked, then laughed.

Diesel slammed his big paw on the table and turned his attention to Axel. "I fuckin' stutter, Axhole?"

Fletch kept his eyes glued to the men sitting at the table, paid close attention to their body language and stayed aware of where their hands were at all times.

Out of the corner of his eye, he saw Jamison shrug. "Sure sounded like it."

Without warning, Diesel surged from his seat toward Jamison in a threatening manner. Every muscle in that room went tight and the air turned thick with tension.

They had expected this kind of posturing, so no one reached for any weapons. They all managed to keep their cool and let the big man whose tiny wife called him the "Beast" play his game.

"Are you going to let your junkyard dog threaten me?" Axel asked Zak.

"Ain't the first time. Ain't gonna be the last." Jamison's brother said all too calmly.

The man was either stoned as fuck or naturally laid-back. Or was really good at acting.

"You know what the fuck is ours," Diesel growled.

"It's only a clubhouse. We don't claim any territory," Jamison informed him, not looking at all concerned that Diesel probably wanted to pound him into the ground.

But then, Jamison was used to dealing with these bikers.

"No?" Diesel barked. "What's that fuckin' patch you're normally wearin' on your tit?"

He was talking about the "Southwest Regional" patch their charter of the Blue Avengers wore on the front of their cuts.

Technically, the beast of a man was right. Their territories overlapped. But when it came down to it, the two clubs weren't the same. One was more of a riding club and a solid brotherhood while the other was a complete lifestyle. The DAMC colors defined their members' lives. They lived and breathed the MC life.

They would die for that life, too.

And that was what made them dangerous.

"We're not in competition, D," Jamison reminded him, not letting the big man get him worked up.

It was hard to believe that Jamison was married to and had kids with this man's cousin. Fletch didn't envy Jamison having to attend family holidays.

"Lucky for you. 'Cause if we were, guaran-fuckin'-teed you'd lose."

As cool as could be, Jamison ignored that threat and returned his attention to his brother. "Z, we didn't come here for a pissing match. We came to discuss an issue that will affect us all, including our families, if we don't do anything about it. We're only asking for cooperation, that's it."

An explosion of "Bullshit!" shook the air in the room.

Fletch mentally flagged Diesel as someone to watch out for if he ended up wearing the Angels' colors. The man was making Fletch's spine tighten to the point it ached.

It would only take a split second and one wrong move or word for shit to go sideways.

The DAMC president turned toward his sergeant at arms and, with a calmness no one else in that room was feeling, ordered, "Sit down. Let's hear 'em out 'fore we kick their asses out."

Diesel's thick fingers curled into fists. "Don't need to hear fuckin' shit about fuck from these pigs."

"Kinda agreein' with my asshole brother for once, Z," Hawk spoke up. "They ain't here to do us any fuckin' favors." The Dirty Angels' VP leaned back in his chair and pursed his lips, his dark gaze running over their small group still standing because they weren't invited to take a seat. On purpose. "We got somethin' they want."

"Then that means we hold the power." Zak turned back to their group and jerked his chin up. "Start talkin'."

Jamison took a step back. "I'll hand it over to Colin Crew. He's a DEA senior special agent and heading this task force."

"Fuckin' task force," Diesel repeated as if trying to spit out a lemon seed.

Crew stepped up to the end of the table. He addressed Zak only and ignored the other two since the president was the most important person at that table. Fletch hoped he was also the most reasonable.

"Like your brother told you, the name's Crew. How do you want to be addressed?"

"Mr. President."

Fletch turned away to hide his amusement and Crew dropped his head and shook it.

When he was composed again, Crew lifted his head again. "That's not going to happen. Try again."

"My house, my rules," Zak said with a casual shrug.

"Z..." Jamison started, ready to step in again.

Fletch caught the slightest twitch in the man's lips. "That'll work, too. But get talkin'. I got shit to do."

Yeah, the men at the table would keep trying to play with Fletch and his brothers. Annoy them to the point it got them riled up and on the defensive. It would either give them an excuse to cause a conflict or kick them out.

They had all discussed about keeping their settings on cool and not allowing the DAMC to spin their dials to hot.

Being a redhead, Finn tended to pop off the quickest. But so far, he was behaving himself.

Fletch risked a quick glance at him. *Oh yeah*, the man was struggling to hold onto his composure. Maybe they should've brought someone else along with them instead.

"We're not here to waste your time," Crew assured them. "We appreciate you giving us a chance to hear us out. But like your brother said, what the Demons are doing—"

"Demons!" burst loudly from Diesel.

"Yeah, the Deadly Demons."

"Know who the fuck they are, pig. That's why you're here? 'Cause of that fuckin' bunch of rejects on two wheels?" His head twisted toward his president. "Why wasn't I told this shit before now?"

"'Cause I didn't know the details. An' if you'd shut the fuck up an' let the man talk, we'd find out those details."

Damn.

No wonder the man had been president as long as he had. Not only did he remain cool, calm and collected, he didn't take any shit. It was probably the same reason why Axel made an excellent president for the BAMC. Their temperaments were the same.

They must have inherited that from their mother because their father and former BAMC president, Mitch Jamison, had never been that level-headed.

Chapter Seven

Crew remained focused on Zak, even though what he said next addressed Diesel's opinion. "You might think they're a bunch of rejects just trying to stir up a little trouble but that's where you'd be wrong. The shit's getting much deeper than that. More dangerous, too. They're doing enough to catch our attention and that's why we formed this task force."

"Just to take down the Demons?" the DAMC president asked, then pinned his lips together and seemed to consider Crew's next words carefully.

"If they were only setting up chapters in both PA and Ohio, we wouldn't give a shit. That would be your problem until both your clubs made it our problem. However, let me first focus on the territory grab they're doing on the down low because that's the part your club will be concerned about more than the issue *we* are concentrating on. What I'm about to tell you are irrefutable facts since we've heard the chatter and witnessed their movements.

"Once they have their churches for these new chapters

established—all of which will report to the mother chapter in West Virginia—they plan on expanding even more. They're going to slowly eat away at your territory before continuing north into the Knights' territory.

"They're not going to come in hot like the Warriors, Z. They're going to spread like black mold and, before you know it, swallow you up. You're living comfortably now because they haven't tipped you off and you think you're still king here. However, that throne will get toppled if you're not careful. We don't want to see you and anyone else in this club go to war again."

"I also don't want to see you end up back in prison, brother," Jamison added.

Zak's dark eyes narrowed and shifted from Crew to his brother. "Shouldn't have been in there the first time, *brother*."

"And you know I had nothing to do with that."

"But you also did nothin' about it, either," Zak sharply reminded him.

Jamison's nostrils flared just enough for Fletch to catch the reaction.

After his chest expanded slowly and then contracted as he released both the air in his lungs and most likely his impulse to defend himself, Jamison said, "You have Sophie and the boys. You have too much to lose to go to war with the Demons."

"So do you," Zak growled. "If it wasn't for us, you wouldn't have Laney an' Liam. Let's not fuckin' forget that."

"You really believe I don't think about that every damn time I kiss them goodnight?"

Zak shrugged.

After being forced to stay quiet, Diesel, looking like someone just dropped a few Mentos into a bottle of Coke, finally couldn't hold it in any longer. "Why the fuck would we work with pigs? Got my own fuckin' *task force* to handle any threats to our club."

"The threat isn't only to your club, Dougherty, it's to all of us. Like I said, this is bigger than them encroaching on your territory," Crew told him.

"My concern's protectin' our territory, our brotherhood an' our families. Don't give a fuck about anythin' else. Got me?"

"You should give a fuck, Diesel. You... Hell, *we*,—whether you want to recognize me or not since I'm Nash's husband and we're raising two kids together—*We* all have families. Kids. Grandkids. Nieces and nephews. Don't you want to protect them, too?" Cross asked him.

He sneered at Cross and slapped a beefy mitt against his chest. "*I* fuckin' protect them. Don't need your fuckin' help, *pig*."

Crew raised one eyebrow. "Yeah? So, you're protecting them from the flow of meth into your territory?" He pointed to the floor. "Right here in Shadow Valley? Right under your damn noses?"

"If that's true, what the fuck you need from us?" Hawk's question was dripping with impatience. "Can we get to your fuckin' destination faster? Not likin' you takin' this long tourist route."

"Agreed. Let's get to the fuckin' point. Why you comin' to us about this?" Zak asked, once again taking control of the conversation. "You can bust 'em for runnin' drugs without us involved. You here 'cause you need assistance from D's Shadows?"

Fuck if that was going to happen. Fletch had no doubt Crew would shut that shit down quickly.

"They have badges?" Crew asked, knowing full well they didn't.

Diesel snorted like a bull facing off with a matador. "Fuck no."

"Then, *fuck no*," Crew echoed. "We're not doing any shady shit. When we take down members of the Demons, we need charges to stick. We don't want them getting off on technicalities."

"Who said they gotta be charged? Plenty of other ways to handle those fucknuts."

Crew tipped his head and stared at the massive man.

Fletch had done a background check on the club's sergeant at arms, too. Somehow the man had only minor offenses on his record even though he probably did enough shit to warrant living in a concrete box for the rest of his life. He was a lucky bastard. But fuck if Crew would let anyone on the task force step over the line like that.

At least step over it too far.

However, Fletch had a feeling they'd be walking that line like a tight rope, including himself. Law enforcement couldn't break the rules like an MC could, but that didn't mean they couldn't bend them a little.

"If you ain't here about the Shadows..."

"Z, we need your connection with the Demons," Jamison spoke up behind Fletch. "That's why we're here."

Zak frowned. "What fuckin' connection? Their MC's no better than a goddamn cluster-fuck. Don't got shit to do with 'em."

"Kelsea had an in with the Demons," Hawk mentioned, leaning back in his chair and letting his gaze land on Diesel.

A muscle jumped in the big man's cheek. "*Had* a fuckin' connection. That thread was snapped clean a long time ago. An' tellin' you right now, it ain't ever gonna be reconnected. Ryder would be fuckin' ragin' right now if he heard you even mention her name along with those dumbfuck Demons in the same breath."

"What connection did she have?" Crew asked.

"A while ago D's cousin got herself a bit twisted an' was seein' one of their members," Zak explained, once again bringing calmness to the table.

"Name?" Crew asked.

Z took a quick glance at D before answering, "Slash."

Crew shook his head. "Doesn't sound familiar."

One side of Diesel's mouth pulled up. "Reason for that."

Crew's gaze sliced to him. "You really think it's smart to be dropping hints about the sketchy shit you've done?"

"What the fuck you gonna do about it?" D challenged, crossing his beefy arms over his chest. "Let's hear it."

Crew raised a palm. "Look. We're trying to be civil here. You cooperating with us would be beneficial to you. We wouldn't want your cousin involved, either. It's too risky. Instead, we would work with your club."

"The fuck?" Diesel exploded from his chair. "The fuck you will. You fuckin' think we wanna work with your pig asses willingly?" He jerked his chin at Cross and Jamison. "Those two motherfuckers ain't supposed to step one fuckin' foot inside this church an' here they are. Actin' like they're welcome."

"D, sit down," Zak said quietly.

The sergeant at arm's dark eyes fell on his president.

"Sit down," Zak repeated with a single eyebrow raised.

Diesel's face twisted and he thumped back into his seat. "Ain't fuckin' likin' this shit. We ain't workin' with no pigs."

Of course that went just as Fletch thought it would.

The whole reason Crew took his time getting to the point was to ease the bikers into the idea. To show them the task force and the DAMC would both benefit from working together and why.

Too bad Jamison's brother had to have his two goons with him.

"Maybe we can use them to our advantage," Hawk suggested.

Okay, maybe the one with the mohawk was sort of reasonable. The other? Not so fucking much.

"Agreed," Zak said. "We really wanna get into a war with the Demons like our club did with the Warriors? That fuckin' conflict lasted for decades. Everythin' we fuckin' do is to make shit better for the generations to follow. Includin' your girls, D. We lost enough to the Warriors. Don't wanna lose anyone or anythin' else. Whether by the Demons or by drugs."

"What happened to the Warriors?" Fletch asked, wondering if they'd fess up. "Seems like those nomads simply up and disappeared."

"Dunno," Diesel grumbled. "Don't give a fuck. Guessin' they got tired of fuckin' with us an' left the area."

Right. They simply "left." Fletch believed that about as much as he believed in the Tooth Fairy.

"Probably all crawled back into their mommy's basements," Zak finally said.

Fletch didn't believe that, either.

He was pretty fucking sure that the DAMC had a hand in the Warriors vanishing from the area, whether they got rid of them or chased them away. However, Fletch found it curious with how that club's name never came up in NCIC, the national crime base, anymore. Not only in Pennsylvania but throughout the rest of the country.

Could they have disbanded and the members went on to patch with other MCs? Sure. Did Fletch think they did?

He glanced at Diesel.

Fuck no.

Zak placed both of his hands flat on the table with their fingers spread wide, like he was about to get up. "Since we got no connection with the Demons, guessin' we're done here."

Damn, for a second there Fletch thought the president was going to be agreeable. Of course, that would've been too easy and the bikers' goal from the second Fletch and his brothers walked into the DAMC clubhouse was to make things difficult for them.

Crew stopped him dead in his tracks. "We want to create one."

Zak lifted his chin. "We don't run drugs."

"Not running. Dealing," Crew clarified.

"Don't do that fuckin' shit, either."

"Economy's tough right now. Some are pushed to do things they normally don't do."

"Dealin' fuckin' drugs."

"Pretending to deal drugs."

Zak sat back in his chair and stared at Crew for a good thirty seconds before saying, "Despite what you probably think, we got a good rep in this community. Don't wanna fuck that up. Could also fuck with the success of our businesses."

"We can have one of your members go rogue and sell drugs behind your backs," Crew suggested.

The president's mouth twisted. "Would never happen."

Fletch bit his tongue. If he started calling them out on every damn lie or stretched truth being told in that room, he wasn't going to make things go more smoothly.

"But it could." Fletch winged his thumb over his shoulder toward the common area behind him. "I'm sure you've had prospects, maybe even members, do stupid shit."

Fletch doubted every DAMC member was a real *angel*, either. More like fallen angels with dirty wings.

Zak shrugged. "An' then we fuckin' handle it like we normally do."

Fletch continued with a possible scenario. "Money's tight for one of your members, he reaches out to the Demons to score some meth so he can make a little extra dough on the side."

"The more I hear, the more I'm not likin' this," Hawk muttered.

"None of your members have to be involved," Crew assured them.

"Then who the fuck will be involved?" Zak asked.

Fletch took a step forward, feeling like a sacrificial lamb. "That would be me."

All six eyeballs at the opposite end of the table zeroed in on him.

Zak's head tipped to the side and his blue eyes narrowed. "How's he gonna do that?"

"By blending in."

"Really not likin' this," Hawk muttered again.

"How's he blendin' in? He's a fuckin'," Zak visibly swallowed down what he was going to say and replaced it with, "*cop*."

"Here we go," Fletch heard Jamison warn under his breath. "Brace."

Zak's eyes flicked to his younger brother before going back to Crew, who explained, "By wearing your colors."

Fletch did what Jamison said. He braced for the detonation.

"By wearin' our goddamn colors?" Diesel roared. "What the actual fuck? Axhole never got to wear our colors. Never will. The fuck if any of you shitbags will, either."

Hawk shook his head. "It's like us holdin' open the door to the hen house an' welcomin' the fox inside. Fuckin' hate the idea."

Zak said nothing. His gaze bounced from Crew to Finn to Cross, then paused on Jamison. It finally landed on Fletch, where it stuck. Fletch met his eyes across the length of the table and held them.

The DAMC's presidents jaw shifted. Then shifted again.

Both of them tuned out the grumbling coming from the men flanking Zak, and instead, remained focused on each other.

Fletch wasn't sure if he was being challenged or if the man was trying to see deep into Fletch's soul. Because of that, he didn't move, didn't blink and certainly didn't look away.

Now would not be an ideal time to show any sign of weakness. Perceived or otherwise.

Zak tapped the length of his left ring finger on the table, his wide black wedding band rapping against the wood. "Whatcha know about MCs?"

"I've been riding with the BAMC for years. Ever since your father was prez. Now your brother's my president."

Tap. Tap. Tap.

"Don't mean goddamn shit! You all are nothin' but fuckin' wannabe bikers who don't got the balls to do it right. Need to hide behind your fuckin' tiny shields."

Both he and Zak ignored Diesel's outburst and remained focused on their own conversation.

Tap. Tap. "How long you been ridin'?" *Tap.*

"Since I got my license at seventeen."

Tap. "What kinda sled you got?" *Tap. Tap.*

"Custom Fat Boy."

Tap. "That what you'd be ridin' with us?"

"Z!" Diesel bellowed like a bull whose balls got slammed in a gate.

"No. Feds will provide a..." *What the hell. When in Rome...* "*sled* for me. One untraceable back to them."

Tap. "A hog?" Zak asked, his ring finger hovering over the table.

Fletch nodded as Diesel bellowed, "You ain't actually fuckin' considerin' this!"

Zak continued to ignore the shitstorm swirling next to him. "Ain't scared of the shit we're gonna give you? 'Cause we ain't gonna spare your fuckin' feelin's."

"If I was worried about that, I wouldn't be here." And there was no lie in that answer.

"We do this, we'll have terms. You don't stick to them—"

"You die," Diesel boomed.

"Jesus fuck," Zak muttered, shaking his head. "Won't die, but might wish you had."

Fletch nodded. "Understood. You give me respect, I'll give it in return."

He did not miss Hawk's amused smirk when Fletch mentioned the mutual respect.

Tap. "You'd come in as a prospect?"

"No. Fully-patched member."

Diesel slammed his hand on the table making the gavel laying by Zak's right hand jump an inch in the air. Fletch was surprised the wood top didn't split.

Since the DAMC president was now actually entertaining the idea of allowing Fletch to go undercover with them, he figured he'd better let him know he wouldn't be alone. "I'll also need a cut for my ol' lady. We can get them made, but we'll need the patches. You'll get those back once we're done with them."

"Ol' lady?" Diesel roared.

Fletch continued as if the big man wasn't thrashing around in his seat, in the middle of having a terrible twos tantrum. "One of our TFOs will be my partner."

"TFO?" Zak asked, now spinning that wedding band with his thumb.

Him fiddling with his ring made Fletch believe Zak Jamison was thinking of his wife and kids. It could be that his first priority was looking out for them, instead of his own club.

If so, that might be what would save this proposition.

"Task force officer."

He nodded. "What's she?"

"FBI."

"You?"

"State trooper."

Zak tugged on his bearded chin as he considered Fletch, while still not paying attention to the two brothers flanking him as they kept trying to interject their opinion on the matter.

It was like he and Zak were the only two in the room. Maybe it would have been better to talk to the man one on one.

Too late for that now.

They already had their boot in the door, now they just needed to keep it there. *And* somehow not fuck it up. Especially when things might be going their way.

Sort of.

"Don't like this," Zak finally said.

"I get that."

"Actually hate it."

Fletch waited.

"But—"

"No! The fuck if this bullshit's happenin'!" shouted Diesel. "No fuckin' way."

"Last I checked *you* wore the president's patch, Z. Did that change?" Jamison asked.

The second Diesel surged up from his seat again, everyone froze once more. "That didn't fuckin' change an' you know it, Axhole."

"You do a lot of talking for someone without that authority," Cross added, having to get his own jab in.

For fuck's sake. Neither of them were helping.

Diesel's dark eyes swung from Cross to Jamison and back. "Remember those tiny tin shields you pigs wear don't protect your fuckin' back."

Jamison blew Diesel an exaggerated kiss.

Goddamn it.

They needed to wrap this shit up before things went south. So south they all landed in hell.

Diesel jabbed a finger at Jamison. "Better hope Bella never leaves your ass. 'Cause the day she does..."

"That a threat?"

"A promise."

Jamison shrugged. "You know where I live."

"Christ! Enough!" Zak shouted, finally losing his patience. "Both of you... All of you... Shut the fuck up!" He twisted toward Hawk. "You trust me as your prez?"

"Of fuckin' course," his VP answered without hesitation.

He turned to Diesel. "You trust me as your prez?"

"Trust you as my brother. A *real* brother. Not like that pansy-ass over there who chose his fuckin' badge over blood."

"Been sittin' in this seat for almost twenty years. There's a reason for that," Zak reminded them.

"Can't make this decision on your own, brother," Hawk

told him. "Gotta go to a vote. 'Specially if you're gonna let the enemy infiltrate us."

"Like a fuckin' STD," Diesel added.

"If enough of the membership votes it down, then we'll tell 'em to fuck off an' find another way. But in the meantime, the Demons might keep marchin' north with their pockets full of a fuckin' drug that could devastate our community."

"We ain't responsible for our community. Axhole is."

"We also got a responsibility to Shadow Valley. Without our community our businesses die an' we don't make any scratch. Without scratch, our coffers go dry. We don't got a full coffer, we end up sufferin', too. Could be a trickle-down effect."

Fletch was pleased Jamison's brother was not only level-headed but wasn't dumb, either. That could be their saving grace.

"Then we handle those dumb motherfuckers in our own way," Diesel said.

"Like you did the Warriors?" Fletch asked.

The club's enforcer turned dark eyes toward him. "Don't got a fuckin' clue what happened to them. Why the fuck you makin' me repeat myself?"

"You can deny it all you want but we both have a *clue* about what happened to them. I'd bet your Shadows do, too. You really want us to dig for that elusive clue?"

Diesel appeared to have a lot to say, but he managed to keep his mouth shut by smashing his lips together.

He might be smarter than what he looked.

Might be. The jury was still out on that.

"Gonna say it again," Hawk started, "if this is what you want, Z, could use them to our fuckin' advantage by lettin' them deal with the Demons. We just need to set the terms, not them."

Zak considered his VP for a hot minute before dropping his gaze to stare at his wedding band. He was once again spinning it when he lifted his gaze to Fletch. "All right. Here's the deal... One, enough of our brothers gotta vote in favor of this idea. Gotta be a majority. Two, you turn a blind eye to anythin' you see or hear when it comes to the DAMC."

Fletch couldn't do shit about the vote but... "Number two would be part of the deal."

"Want that in writin'."

"You're going to have to take our word for it. For... *reasons*," reasons he couldn't disclose, "we can't put that in writing."

"Then no deal," Zak announced with a shrug.

Shit. Fletch quickly pivoted. "To me, a handshake would be just as binding as a contract."

Diesel tipped his head down and only lifted his dark eyes. A scowl twisted his mouth, but Fletch figured that was his normal expression. Grumpy and growly.

He seemed like a lot of fucking fun.

"Can't promise the vote'll go your way. Gonna lay out what you told us an' let my brothers come to their own decision. Ain't gonna make the effort to convince them. They gotta be comfortable with what they decide for themselves an' their families. Not only their own families, but our club family as a whole." Zak jabbed his index finger into the table in front of him. "'Cause this club's our life an' while we wanna protect it, we got our fuckin' limits."

"An' lettin' pigs live amongst us is a hard limit," Hawk said. "Cross knows it. Axel's only got a special pass 'cause of the blood that runs in his, his ol' lady's and his kids' veins. But that pass could be revoked at any time."

"Understood," Fletch answered quickly, before Cross or Jamison put in their two cents and made things worse.

"Again, you're not our target. My partner and I won't be digging around trying to come up with shit to nail any of you. We're a drug task force and the Demons and their distribution ring will be our sole focus. Promise you that."

"Promises can easily be broken," Zak murmured.

Fletch could see the man's reluctance, so he assured him, "Not if I can help it." He stretched his hand across the long table. Zak would have to get up to shake it.

The biker at the head of the table only stared at it, then shook his head. "Too early for that. Once you get the vote. If you don't, then no fuckin' reason for us to cross palms."

Fletch tipped his head in understanding. Zak did the same.

Right now they had each other's respect. But it was extremely fragile and Fletch needed to make sure nothing fucked with it.

Or the task force could be fucked.

Hell, he and Nova could be fucked if they were deep undercover and the club turned on them.

Crew stepped up next to Fletch. "Seems we have a tentative deal, pending your members' vote. Now... I have one last request..."

Chapter Eight

Nova stared through the passenger side window at the 2003 Harley Softail parked in the next spot.

After packing her bags, she had picked up her assigned silver 2005 Dodge Durango with almost two hundred thousand miles on it. How the wheels hadn't fallen off yet, she didn't know. The engine had a bit of a tap, the suspension squeaked and blowing on herself would cool her better than the air conditioning. The interior also smelled like an ashtray full of crushed Marlboro Light cigarette butts.

When Crew had held out the keys, she simply stared at him. He grinned and shrugged. "You know how this works."

That she did.

The Durango was part of the DEA's fleet of seized vehicles, along with the older Harley she had parked next to. Both vehicles were now officially registered to one Terry Parker, formerly known as Shane Fletcher.

She was no longer Nova Wilder, either. Instead, she now went by Sandy Douglas. At least for however long this particular undercover assignment lasted.

She raised her eyes from the Harley to the metal staircase that rose from the side lot of Shadow Valley Pawn to the second floor. A pawn shop owned by the Dirty Angels MC.

New day. "New" ride. New persona.

She sucked in a deep breath and when she released it, she blew out the real Nova Wilder and began her journey into turning into a biker babe. Or biker bitch, more like it.

Either way, an *ol' lady.*

She gritted her teeth at that title.

To prepare, she had done a shit-ton of research on motorcycle clubs, including their structure, terminology and lifestyle. Also on their women, whether they were ol' ladies, sweet butts, house mouses—she couldn't imagine they were called house *mice*—or just female hang-arounds.

She had a hard time wrapping her head around why a woman would want to live in or deal with such a patriarchy. To be involved in an organization where they held no power. Where they were considered property of their ol' man or even the club itself.

But then, she'd dealt with the same type of mindset when she went undercover with the Russo crime family.

Men held the power there, too. The women took care of the domestic duties—even if it only meant managing the household staff—and of themselves, to make sure they looked good on their husband's arm. Just like a fucking expensive accessory.

Nova didn't understand why those women cared so much about how they looked or how they dressed and accessorized. If they did it to keep their husbands from straying, they were wasting their time. While deep in the Russo organization, most of the men she'd been around didn't know how to keep their dick in their pants. The whole reason she had targeted Russo Jr. was to get her borrowed high heels in the door.

If La Cosa Nostra was considered "upper" class, an MC was the exact opposite. No true biker was wearing a thousand dollar suit simply for a lunch meeting. They preferred denim and leather. They also weren't wearing overpriced Clive Christian cologne. They smelled like exhaust, beer and weed with a hint of pussy.

Two different worlds. Same goals.

Power. Money. Territory.

All in the name of their "family."

Like she did before she infiltrated the Russo family, Nova watched hours and hours of video of various outlaw MCs, the bikers and their women. From surveillance footage and interviews to court testimonies. She paid attention to how they moved, how they acted and how they talked.

With La Cosa Nostra, she had to act like she had class. With the MC, she'd have to act crass.

In the biker world, if you got challenged, you handled your business swiftly and firmly. That could mean getting into an actual physical fight.

The word "fuck" was considered a noun, verb and adjective. The wardrobe was simple, the makeup not as much and the more tattoos the better.

While the women of the Russo family worried more about what designer's tag was on their clothing, the women in MCs tended to wear bold statements across their chests, whether on camisoles, tank tops, T-shirts or even inked directly onto their skin.

Personally, Nova preferred the second group. At least for now. That might change after living among them.

She wasn't into expensive or excessive makeup, clothes or jewelry. She also didn't like having to watch everything she said. Peppering the word "fuck" into her conversations wouldn't take much of an effort at all.

The only time she tempered her own cursing was when she was around colleagues she knew would have a problem with it. Even then, she sometimes slipped.

Nova yanked the keys from the ignition and grimaced when she pushed open the driver's door and it squealed like the hinges hadn't been greased since it came off the factory line.

She sighed. She had been hoping to be assigned some really cool car, not one a decade past being sent to the junkyard.

Someone must have gotten their information wrong since she couldn't imagine the ol' ladies of the DAMC drove around in such pieces of shit. In fact, some of the surveillance footage that landed in her hot little hands had shown otherwise.

None of the club members seemed to be hurting financially.

Opening the Durango's rear hatch, she pulled out her large suitcase and two duffel bags. She had to buy some clothes to make sure she fit in with the MC. She actually went to a consignment shop to buy a large selection of tops, jeans and boots so they wouldn't look brand new.

Nothing said a "plant" more than brand-new blue jeans, unworn tops and leather boots not broken in.

Before leaving her condo in Cranberry Township, about twenty miles north of Pittsburgh, she had pulled on a pair of shredded blue jeans snug enough to look painted on, black leather knee-high boots, a black bandana for a belt and a black off-the-shoulder top with a sugar skull on the front and a deep V neckline that emphasized her lack of cleavage.

She had it, it was just difficult to find. To bolster her boobs, she made sure to pack every push-up bra she purchased prior to going undercover with the Russos.

She had been surprised when Frank Sr. turned his attention to her since his type was normally extremely curvy with pouty lips, big eyes, teased hair and even bigger tits.

All of which she didn't have and couldn't fake.

She sighed and dropped the strap of one heavy duffel bag across her body, and then grabbed the suitcase and other bag in each hand. She was determined to get her shit upstairs in only one trip. Similar to when she went grocery shopping since she lived in a second floor condo.

She made her way awkwardly up the metal staircase, her rolling suitcase clunking up and over each step. The weight of her duffel bags almost pulled her backwards a few times, making her heart catch in her throat.

Falling down the steps would take her out of the game before she even got a chance to play.

At the top of the landing she dropped one of the heavy duffels and pounded on the door. As she waited for Fletch to answer, she turned and scanned the pawn shop's parking lot and what she could see of the road out front to make sure nothing and no one looked suspicious.

Since the pawn shop closed at nine, she made sure to arrive at nine-thirty and after dark so no one would witness her "moving in."

Just as she turned to pound on the door again, it jerked opened and the man himself stood in the doorway, only wearing a pair of very worn blue jeans and a grin.

No shirt. No shoes. No...

"Is that fake?" she asked, jerking her chin toward the large biomechanical tattoo that completely covered his right shoulder and extended all the way over his right pec.

"Wanna rub it and see, woman?" he asked, his voice gruffer than she remembered. His grin returned when she frowned at him calling her "woman."

"Just a simple yes or no would work." Admittedly, the tattoo was cool and well-done, real or otherwise.

"No, it ain't fuckin' fake."

She stared at him, then shook her head at the way he was talking before rolling her suitcase over the threshold and past him. She left it by the door along with one duffel bag before going back out and grabbing the second one. She tossed it inside and if he hadn't quickly stepped back, it would have landed on his bare toes.

That was what he would get for not helping.

Not that she needed help since she was capable of bringing in her own stuff. But they *were* supposed to be partners. In her book, a little courtesy could go a long way.

She slammed the door shut and locked it behind her.

Before she could check out her new home, another tattoo caught her eye.

"Wow. You guys are all in, huh?" she asked, stepping closer and pointing at the Blue Avengers tattoo high up on his right bicep. "You'll have to make sure that doesn't show. Not only around the Demons but the Angels, too. It wouldn't be smart to keep reminding them how we don't belong."

"Got it high enough to cover it easily enough with a short-sleeve shirt. With PSP, we can't have tattoos showin' while we fuckin' work. Otherwise, I'd be stuck wearin' a long-sleeve uniform shirt all fuckin' year long."

"That would suck. So..." She plunked her hands onto her hips and tilted her head, trying her best to keep her eyes above his neck. "What's with your speech? I don't remember you talking like that when the task force had our first meeting."

"'Cause I didn't." When he shrugged, her eyes were drawn to his broad shoulders lifting and falling. "Forcin' myself to drop my Gs, speak slang and sloppy English. Also gettin' in the habit of usin' 'fuck' in some form in every sentence."

"Learning a whole new language, huh?" She'd have to pay closer attention to how the DAMC women talked if, and when, she was around them.

"I figured you learned Italian when you were bangin' that motherfucker Russo Sr.?"

Okay then. He wanted to go there. Already. She'd only been in the apartment two damn minutes. "I have a good handle on it."

"Tell me... What's 'Oh, Daddy, fuck me harder?' in Italian?"

Yep, he had to go there. *Asshole.*

"*Oh, Papà, fottimi più forte.* So, which Italian daddy are you trying to fuck? I might be able to give you some pointers."

He cocked one eyebrow. "*Might*?"

"Just so you know, I won't judge you for your sexual preferences. But, warning, the bikers might."

"I'm a straight line without even a slight squiggle, so that's not even an issue. In case you don't know, one of their members is bi. One that I know of, anyway. He's actually married to a Southern Allegheny Regional PD corporal."

"Did you have to dig deep to find that nugget?"

"Fuck no. Cross is a long-time member of the BAMC."

She blinked. "Wait. So, a cop and Blue Avenger is bi and he's married to a Dirty Angel?"

"Aiden Cross ain't bi, he's gay. Nash, the Angel, is bi. Cross and our BAMC president are both married into the DAMC."

She blinked again. *What?* Why wasn't she told any of this? This kind of info was important to know.

"Because of that, those two are who got us in the door with the club."

"They accept badges in their midst?" This was surprising news.

"Wouldn't go that far. Let's just say they got a love-hate relationship that can be tumultuous at times."

Nova could imagine. "Are you always going to speak like that, even when behind closed doors?"

"Gonna try. The more I live it, less likely I'll slip."

She had to give him that. Even reluctantly.

When he dug deep into his front pocket, the waistband of his jeans pulled lower and exposed the sharp V of muscles near his hip bones. A well-defined Adonis belt tended to be crack for some women.

The man kept himself in shape, that was for sure.

She wondered how many real bikers worked out and had distinct abs like he did. She figured they all had a farmer's tan from riding all the time and beer guts from... well, partying just as much as riding.

She figured the only exercise they got was when they fucked.

When he cleared his throat, she slowly lifted her gaze and saw he was holding out a single key. "For the apartment."

She rolled her eyes at his sly grin and snagged it from his fingers before shoving it deep into her front pocket. She'd add it to the Harley Davidson keyring that held the Dodge's keys.

"Crew give you two sets for that hunk of junk you were assigned?"

"Sure did. I'll make sure you get a set. What about the Harley?"

"Nope, since the women don't ride alone. They're only backpacks."

Backpacks.

She fought the urge to roll her eyes again, choosing to breathe out her annoyance instead. She had a feeling she'd be doing that a lot for the next few weeks. She might have to search for some meditation exercises on YouTube.

She glanced around as she pulled on her shirt, flapping it to get air flowing where there was none. "Does this place have air? I'm already getting boob sweat."

Of course, his eyes immediately went to her chest.

And, of course, didn't her nipples immediately stand up and take notice?

"Want me to blow on them for you?"

If she ignored his juvenile sense of humor, he might stop. "The air in the Durango doesn't work, so I'm hot." She glanced around again for a thermostat. "I sure hope this place has A/C." And that it worked.

"It's on. You're just... hot." He jerked his eyebrows up.

Nova groaned. "Let's skip the cheesy pickup lines."

His grin tilted and, *damn*, that made him even more attractive. "Wasn't a pickup line. Was a compliment."

C'mon, Nova. This is work and not play. You need to be close but not that *kind of close.*

You do not need to get caught up in any kind of relationship while working. That never ends well.

"Let's skip those, too. Otherwise, I might have to smother you with your pillow while you sleep."

"I'm sure you're already aware of this but... Prison's not a good place for a fed."

"I would simply need to draw a female judge for my trial and then I'd be acquitted."

He threw his head back and a rich, deep laugh bubbled from him. She was mesmerized by his throat undulating and the flex of the muscular cords in his neck.

Jeeeeesus. That caused something to flex on her and it was not in her neck.

Damn it, her reactions to him might be a problem. She needed to work with someone she wasn't attracted to, someone she didn't react to when he simply laughed. Or showed off his muscular torso with the delicious V.

Not to mention, that tempting line of dark blond hair that started just below his navel and disappeared below his waistband.

"Look..."

Oh fuck me, I am looking...

"These men don't mince words. They say crude shit. They might love their women but they certainly don't temper their words around them. Plenty of shit's gonna be said you probably won't like, whether by me or others that you'll have to deal with."

She hooked a thumb toward the door. "Out there, yes. In here," she pointed at the floor, "you're mistaken. It's simple. Respect me and I'll respect you in return."

Something flashed behind his brown eyes. "Got you."

Got you.

She bit back a sigh. "Good."

"But just a warnin', once I get into character, I tend to stay in character. So, how I act out there," he jerked his chin toward the door, "will most likely spill into here." He pointed to the floor. "Ain't gonna apologize for it." As she opened her mouth to respond, he lifted a palm and continued, "And I'm sure you'll have no problem tellin' me if I disrespect you."

"You're right, I won't."

He nodded. "Good. I can take it as long as it's in here." He once again jabbed his finger toward the floor. "You do that out there, I'm gonna have to react as expected, so don't be surprised if I do and it's ugly. We're playing parts here, Nova, as you very well know. Gonna play my part as best I can."

"As will I," she murmured, glanced around and forced herself to swallow down a response to him about not telling her how to do her job. She knew how to do it and did so successfully. She really didn't want to start off their working partnership with a bunch of tension between them. If he continued to overstep, she'd remind him of who she was. "I'd like to get settled in and change into something cooler than jeans as long as we're not heading anywhere tonight."

"Nope. Scribbled a bunch of notes for us to go over so we're both on the same page. Gonna guess you've done a bunch of research, too, to prepare. I'd like to see what you came up with. But since it's late, we can go over all of that tomorrow. Tonight will be simply to get settled in our new place and maybe get to know each other better since our relationship's gonna need to appear solid and real."

She couldn't argue with any of that. "How many bedrooms does this place have?"

"Two."

Thank fuck.

"But only one shitter."

Shit.

"Try not to leave all your products all over the place in there."

One thing he'd quickly learn about her was that she could give as good as she got. "I guarantee you have more than me, pretty boy."

"*Aww*. You think I'm pretty?" He cradled his chin with the back of both his hands and fluttered his eyelashes.

"Pretty annoying."

He laughed again and rubbed his hands together. "This is gonna be fuckin' fun."

Nova wasn't sure she'd go that far. However, she did enjoy going undercover. To her, it was a challenge to reinvent herself every time she did so. It also gave her a peek into how other people lived and it let her immerse herself into a life she never would have lived normally, even if only temporarily.

Going undercover took skills similar to acting. The best UCs slipped into a completely new skin, making it more difficult for someone else to break their cover. However, once the job was over, sometimes it was difficult to yank the agent or officer back to reality.

Some UCs even fell for their targets. What could be a dangerous and deadly mistake.

Fletch turned slowly with his hand extended. "Make yourself at home in our new humble abode. You want the five second tour?"

Once again his movement drew her attention to his naked torso, but this time the top and center of his broad back where he had another tattoo. A black and gray compass. It might be called a compass rose or a mariner's compass, she wasn't sure, but it had a star shape in the center and a thin line pointing south that was longer than the rest.

Hmm. She wondered what that tattoo meant to him.

That could be a question asked later when they were getting to know each other better, since that was what they needed to do, but first, she wanted to get settled in and unpacked.

And cool off with a shower.

She dragged her eyes from him and back to the apartment. "I can pretty much see most of it from where I'm standing."

The front door led directly into the living room and there wasn't much to it. Basically a dark brown leather couch, a comfy-looking recliner, along with a couple of side tables, a ceiling fan, and below a wall-mounted TV was one of those fake electric fireplaces.

An older Formica dining table with four matching chairs divided the living room from the kitchen off to the left. At the back of the living room to the right was a hallway.

From the size of the pawn shop below, she expected the apartment to be much larger. It could be that a portion of the second floor was being used for storage. Unless there was a second apartment on the other side.

She grabbed her suitcase and rolled it toward the hallway, leaving her duffels behind.

When she heard Fletch on her heels, she glanced over her shoulder to see he had the straps of both heavy duffel bags hanging over his shoulders.

Well, look at that. He's trying to earn some brownie points.

She continued down the hallway, peeking her head inside the first door on the right to see it was a bathroom. About the same size as the hall bathroom in her condo. Like the living room, it contained the basics. A tub/shower combo, a sink, a toilet, what looked like a medicine cabinet over the sink and a narrow linen closet. Nothing fancy but it appeared clean.

That alone was a relief.

As she continued moving down the hallway, she heard behind her, "Since we need to make this look real, your shit needs to be kept in the same room as mine."

"Not a problem since I'm taking the largest bedroom. We can both store our stuff in there." There was a hall closet across from the bathroom and a bedroom to both her left and her right at the end of the hall.

She parked her suitcase in the hallway and wandered into the bedroom on the left first. It was small and the space was tight since it held a queen bed.

"That's your room," he announced, still standing next to her suitcase.

She walked past him to enter the room across the hall.

Much bigger. A king bed. And...

"Nooooo." She glanced up at the ceiling. "What the hell?"

Chapter Nine

"A DAMN MIRROR?"

In the reflection she saw Fletch follow her in and stand behind her. "This is my room. Unless you wanna share."

Uh huh. Sure she did. "How come you get the bigger room with the bigger bed?"

"Because I'm bigger and need the space."

"I know you *think* that may be a valid reason but—" Her eyes caught something else in the mirror and she dropped her eyes to the bed.

Two black leather vests, known in the MC world as cuts, were laid out on the bedspread. Her gaze slid over the smaller one and she slammed on the brakes at her name patch.

What the actual fuck?

Kitten?

"That has to change." She was not going by the ol' lady name of Kitten.

"Too late. The patch is already embroidered and sewn onto your cut."

"I can rip it off and get it replaced."

"But you won't. It's only temporary. And you know you can't use your real name, *Sandy*."

"But I would've picked a nickname a lot better than Kitten. Even the name Sandy would've been better. Who the fuck picked it?" Nova turned her eyes to him, already knowing that answer.

If she hadn't been swamped with wrapping up the reports on another case, she would've been much more involved in the decisions made prior to moving in.

Of fucking course Fletch wore a blank expression. Attempting to be a complete picture of pure innocence.

Bullshit.

She pulled a long breath into her nostrils and reminded herself that this should only be a short undercover assignment. Live amongst the Dirty Angels, learn what they needed to fit in, then reach out to the Deadly Demons and make some deals to collect evidence on the crimes to make a case against the MC.

Easy fucking peasy.

When she picked the vest up off the bed, the back patches caught her eye. She turned it around to get a better look and groaned.

The top rocker was embroidered with "Property of." The bottom one read "Ghost." The large center patch belonged to the Dirty Angels.

Ghost.

She glanced at the other cut and read his name patch. She turned her eyes to Fletch. "Really? Ghost?"

"Badass, right?"

She reluctantly agreed that it was a cool road name, unlike what he gave her. "Much better than Kitten."

"Could've given you the road name of Rider instead." He added an annoying grin onto that.

Rider?

Jesus. Ghost Rider. "In your dreams."

He chuckled and when he did, she stared at the week's growth of facial hair covering his lower face. Typically, he wasn't allowed to wear any in his organization unless he had a good reason, like being undercover. However, right now he wasn't working as a state trooper. At the moment, he was a federal task force officer and those rules no longer applied.

She studied him, remembering how smooth his face had been during that first meeting at The Plant. She was undecided if he looked better with the beard or without. She mentally shook herself when his grin widened and he drew his hand down his jawline.

"Like it?"

"At least it doesn't look like a moth ate it."

"Got enough fuckin' testosterone flowin' through my body to grow an impressive fuckin' beard. Just you fuckin' wait and see."

"Too much testosterone will shrink your balls and give you limp dick," she warned.

"Then, I got the perfect fuckin' amount," he announced, looking proud of himself. "Try it on."

Try on his beard? Was he suggesting she sit on his face?

He tipped his head down toward the black leather vest crushed within her fingers.

For fuck's sake, Nova, get your mind out of the damn gutter.

She loosened her grip and shrugged the cut over her shoulders.

As soon as she did, he slowly circled her, only pausing behind her long enough to say, "My name looks damn good on you."

"It's not your name."

"Sure fuckin' is. For however long we're on this assignment."

She brushed a finger over her name patch. "Just a warning, my claws are much sharper than a kitten's." She added, "So are my teeth."

He stopped in front of her, not leaving enough space between him. But she didn't move back. Instead, she stood her ground.

"I look forward to that."

The rumble of his deep voice sliced through her. She cleared her tight throat and warned, "It might not be a pleasurable experience."

He shrugged. "It might be worth risking it."

"I promise you, it won't."

"We'll see," he murmured.

"Yes, we will."

"Yeah."

She raised her eyes to his. "What?"

"Use 'yeah,' not 'yes.' Tonight will be a good night to start gettin' sloppy with your speech. Also, start usin' more slang. Make sure to color your conversation with curses."

"The last part will be easy."

"You probably had to speak proper English when you were around the Russos."

She ground her molars. "I can't talk about that case." And the fact was, she didn't want to.

"The man's dead." He stated a fact she only knew too well.

"Frank Sr. is dead," she clarified. "Too many other Russos still breathe."

He frowned and his brown eyes suddenly held concern. "We need to worry 'bout them huntin' you the fuck down?"

She lifted one eyebrow. "And why would they want to do that?"

As he stared at her, her heart thumped in her ears. One heartbeat. Two heartbeats. Six heartbeats. Finally, he nodded. "Got it."

"Good. Let's just concentrate on our current job. Not one that had nothing to do with you."

"Just don't wanna be focused on the Demons in front of us when the fuckin' Russos could be comin' at us from the rear."

She understood his concern, and for the most part, it could be valid, but... "They think it was a hit and that's all I'll say about it." That part was leaked to the news. On purpose. Hints of who ordered the hit were planted to throw off the Russos. It had worked as planned.

But that also didn't mean they might not eventually find out the truth.

"A hit that won't come back to you."

He wanted an assurance she couldn't give. "Let's move on."

His hand snaked out and he grabbed her chin, lifting her face and locking his gaze with hers. "You'll let me know if you get word they're lookin' for you, yeah? Need to know if you end up in their sights since we'll be workin' closely together here."

She jerked her chin from his grip and took a step back. "If I'm warned about any type of suspicious activity relating to my UC work in that family *and* it could endanger you, I'll let you know."

She worded it that way for a reason but he wasn't dumb. He obviously saw through it.

"I'll hold you to that. Don't fuck me, Nova."

"Don't worry, I have no plans to fuck you." She might have no plans but then, having actual plans was certainly different than having fantasies. She couldn't guarantee she wouldn't have the second. "All right, I need to shower and change. We can discuss the sleeping arrangements in more detail afterward."

"Ain't havin' no discussion. Wanna sleep in this fuckin' room, then you sleep in the bed next to me."

She set her jaw. "That ain't gonna fucking happen." No better time to slip into her tough biker chick persona.

"Then your room's across the fuckin' hall, *Kitten*."

After her shower, she debated coming out of the bedroom wearing the stuff she would normally wear at home.

She finally decided, since they were now living together, she would have to deal with it and so would he. Plus, she had no doubt Fletch—or Ghost—would be dressing the way he did at home, too. Especially after seeing how he was dressed when she arrived. They might end up sharing this apartment for months and they were supposed to be acting like a real couple. Except for the separate rooms, separate beds and the no sex part, anyway.

Expecting crude comments, she stepped into the living room only wearing a tank top and women's boxer briefs. She was all about comfort when she was kicking up her feet at home to shed the stress from her job. When she had the opportunity, she caught up on her favorite shows or curled up with her iPad and a beer to read the latest book from her favorite authors.

However, tonight she would have company. And she wouldn't be watching TV or reading, she'd be working.

They needed to get to know each other and figure out

everything about their new personas in the next day or so, so whenever they slipped in among the DAMC, they didn't stand out like sore thumbs. They needed to be both knowledgeable and comfortable in their new skins, as well as with each other.

However, it was late, she was tired and her bed was calling her name.

She stifled a yawn as she rounded the couch and heard from the kitchen, "Beer?"

"Sure. As long as it isn't IC Light."

She heard a gag and the fridge door shut. "Fuck no. I've got better taste than that."

"Just so you know, saying that doesn't make it true." She plopped her ass in the corner of the couch and curled her legs under her, deciding she'd give him an hour before calling it a night.

The sound of metal caps being tossed on the counter, instead of into the garbage, hit her ears next. Of course. The trash can could be directly in a man's face and it was still too much effort to throw something away.

When he casually walked into the living room with two open beer bottles hanging from between his fingers and approached her, she couldn't miss what he was now wearing. Or what he wasn't wearing.

He'd changed out of his jeans into loose, gray nylon shorts that almost came to his knees. When he stopped in front of her and handed her a beer, his crotch was at eye level.

"Do you have underwear on?" She snagged the bottle from him and did her best to keep her eyes above his waist. Unfortunately, she was failing.

His brown eyes raked over her. "Do you?"

She plucked at her boxer briefs. "I'm wearing them. It's obvious you're not."

"At home I like to swing free." His lips twitched before he put the beer bottle to them and took a long pull.

Obviously. "Is there any way to talk you into not going commando while we live together?"

"Hard to resist, huh?"

"Don't worry, I have enough control to resist." But that didn't mean she wouldn't be distracted.

He pursed his lips. "I'll consider your request." He settled in the recliner with a groan. "But look, we're now partners for however long this lasts." He tipped his beer bottle toward her. "Know what you're wearin' ain't shorts. And obviously, you ain't wearin' a bra..."

Probably because her nipples decided to pucker up and blow him a kiss at the sight of him swinging wild and free like a monkey in the trees.

"So... How 'bout if we make a deal to learn to live with each other the way that's most comfortable for us both. Anyway, I'm assumin' that motherfucker Russo didn't go to bed in a suit." Before Nova could respond, he shook his head. "Sorry. Gonna try not to mention him again."

"I'm only going to say this once. You assume a lot of shit with that assignment when you don't have all the facts. And you know what happens when one assumes..." She didn't bother to finish since he should know the rest of the saying.

He tipped his head. "That I do. But if you wanna share any stories when it comes to La Cosa Nostra, I'd love to hear them."

Of course he would. "Right now we need to concentrate on this job, not that one."

"And on that, we can fuckin' agree." He tipped the beer to his lips again and once again, she got distracted with his throat.

Nova, this is not good. It's only the first night and he's no different than any of the other badge-carrying guys you've worked with.

Except that wasn't quite true. Most of them did not look like Fletch. Or Ghost.

She needed to start thinking of him by his road name.

"Good. So, let's get started since I'm beat and need to get some rest. What we don't finish tonight, we can finish tomorrow." She took a sip from her beer in an attempt to cool the warmth swirling in her belly.

He set his beer bottle on the side table next to the recliner, got to his feet and snagged a manilla envelope from the old, scratched coffee table placed in the center of the room. He tossed it into her lap, then returned to the recliner, once again settling in and grabbing his beer. "Crew and I created our new identities. I printed out our details. Also in that envelope is your new driver's license and anything else you'll need to become Sandra Douglas aka Kitten. As normal, we're in the system with the info on those papers. Our new names, our new DOBs, new jobs, parents, etc. Nothing you haven't dealt with before."

Her brow furrowed. "Why are you acting like you're in charge of this?"

"Simple. Because you couldn't make those meetings. Just because you're a fed, doesn't mean you outrank me on a normal day. Since we're both TFOs, we're definitely on equal footing."

"I never indicated that I outrank you, Fletch. I know how this works. And by the way, you're speaking like a cop right now."

His lips thinned. "Right. From now on call me Ghost, woman, and I'll call you Kitten."

"Can we make a deal that you don't call me Kitten and I don't have to call you Ghost when we're alone?"

He studied her, his expression unreadable, and after a few seconds, he said, "Fine. Gonna give you that. But if I catch myself slippin', that'll have to change. Expect for you to do the same."

"Then don't slip," she told him simply.

"Easier said than done."

"I have faith you can pull it off. Now... What's our new jobs?"

Before her very eyes, he once again slipped from cop to biker. "Ain't a surprise the DAMC prez limited us to where we could work. Our choice was either the fuckin' pawn shop downstairs or their gun shop. Tried to get you a job at their strip club, but wasn't sure if you could... dance."

"Ha ha," she said humorlessly. "As you've probably noted by now, my tits aren't big enough to be a stripper."

"Not all strippers have big tits."

"*Ah*, so you're a regular patron of that type of art?"

"Let's just say I appreciate the athletic ability, as well as the flexibility."

"Sure you do. You probably watch porn for the plot, too."

He grinned. "Nothin' like enjoyin' a grippin' storyline."

She swallowed her laugh. She was starting to agree with his earlier assessment. This might end up being fun. Her tight muscles loosened a bit. Though, that could be from the beer.

But the man had a sense of humor and he didn't seem to be the typical type A, power-hungry officer, or even arrogant.

So far, at least.

She lifted the envelope. "I'll check this out later. So, who's working where?"

"You're takin' Shadow Valley Pawn and I'm takin' the gun shop."

"They have a range there?"

When he hesitated, she realized he knew more about her than she expected.

"Yeah, but heard how well you score when you qualify. Best you don't use it unless it's after hours. Don't want anyone seein' how well you can shoot. And if you wanna practice there, it's best if I'm with you so we can say your ol' man's teachin' you how to protect yourself."

She nodded. "Got it. Because I'm Ghost's 'property.' Can't do anything without his permission." Bile rose up her throat at the thought of women actually accepting that way of life.

"Wouldn't go that far. Least not with this club as compared to others, but with the Demons that's true, so it's best we play that game so they respect me and will be more likely to wanna deal with me. If they see my woman back-talkin' me or tryin' to take lead on any deals, they'll expect me to put you in your place. So, be prepared for Ghost to react as necessary. Even if that reaction is ugly." He cocked an eyebrow and left the details of what that meant unsaid. "Got it?"

That was the second time he mentioned getting ugly. Her jaw tightened at what he hinted at. She might not like it, but they both knew they were playing roles. She could be mouthy but not to her ol' man and not expect to be 'corrected' for it. Something she had to deal with Frank Sr. "Got it. I'd assume those are two businesses where we might hear chatter about the Demons, too."

"Possibly. But from what I understand, the Demons know which businesses in Shadow Valley are owned by the Angels. Would think they'd steer clear of them to avoid givin' the DAMC a heads up that they've been in the area."

That was a valid assumption. "They could simply come into town not wearing their colors."

"It's not only colors that identify bikers, Nova."

"I'm aware. It could be tats and even their Harleys."

"Yep."

She nodded and considered everything just discussed. "Okay, I'll work the pawn shop. At least I won't have to rely on the fucking piece of shit Crew assigned me to get back and forth to my place of employment."

"Nope. Just gotta head down the steps."

She stifled another yawn. "What else?"

"Every time you leave this apartment, make sure to wear that cut. You don't gotta wear it while workin' since I don't think most of them do. The citizens of Shadow Valley are aware of what businesses the club owns but the DAMC doesn't purposely shove it in their face."

"That way they can pretend a motorcycle club doesn't own the businesses they like to patronize," she summarized.

"Actually, from what Jamison and Cross said, most of the townsfolk don't mind the MC. Now, anyway. How it was back in the seventies and eighties, I don't know."

"Former one-percenters?"

"Oh yeah. Once they started losin' too many members, either by death or by incarceration, they began to straighten up. If their numbers woulda gotten too low, they woulda lost this territory to a rival MC."

Interesting. "Not the Demons?"

"No, an outlaw nomad club tryin' to lay down some roots. They just picked the wrong town to do it in. And once the conflict started, it didn't end for decades."

Damn. She couldn't imagine the local PD and even the local citizens were okay with that. "How did it end?"

Fletch simply shot her a look.

"I guess badly."

"From what I know, some of the Shadow Warriors

ended up behind bars. The rest, we can only assume six feet under." He took a deep, audible inhale and continued, "And that leads me to what I'm 'bout to tell you next in case you ain't already aware... The DAMC sergeant at arms owns a 'security' business called In the Shadows Security. It started out like any typical security business. Puttin' in security systems, providin' bouncers to local bars and private events, normal shit like that. Then he began hirin' mercenaries."

Nova's eyebrows knitted together and the hair on the back of her neck prickled. "Mercenaries?"

"That's what I'm calling them. Former special forces, including a Navy SEAL sniper. After that, the business started to change. Doin' some bodyguard work, private investigations, even illegal wiretappin'. Surveillance. You name it, for the right price, they might do it. And they're experts at it. Not only doin' the questionable shit they do, but not gettin' caught doin' it." He swallowed another mouthful of beer.

"Is that what happened to that rival MC?"

As he held the bottle in his hand, he mindlessly picked at the label with his thumbnail. "We think so. They do jobs other people won't touch and they demand a pretty penny to get it done."

"And none of them have gotten caught for stepping over the line?" She found that hard to believe.

"No. Like I said, they're fuckin' good. Trust me, when I say good, I mean fuckin' brilliant and spotless."

"But you're aware of who they are and what they do."

"Nothin' we can prove. My organization has tried and so have some others. They're nicknamed Shadows for a reason."

"And you're telling me this, why?"

"Just wanted you to be aware of their connection with the DAMC. They also live in the club's compound."

"Compound?" *Jesus*, the DAMC was a more complex organization than she realized.

"Yeah. With all the run-ins with the Warriors, the rival MC, they started buildin' a very secure and gated neighborhood for them to live in."

"*All* of the bikers live in this compound?"

"No, not all, but most of them with families. To help protect them, they keep them all in a central location to make it easier to stomp out any threat."

The club wasn't fucking around when it came to their families' safety. "Got it."

"Wanted you to be up to speed in case you cross paths with any of them. Might end up interactin' with them in one way or another. All the ol' ladies know who they are, you should, too." He finished off his beer, then said, "Surprised the FBI hasn't investigated any of those fuckers. Can't imagine they've never been on the feds radar."

She shrugged. "I'm not privy to all of the past and ongoing investigations. I stick to organized crime."

He huffed out a breath. "Well, these fuckin' guys are organized and they commit crimes."

"Allegedly."

A slow smile crossed Fletch's face. "Right. *Allegedly*."

"Should we be looking for proof while we're dealing with the Demons? Does the state police have an open investigation on any of them?"

"All of 'em." He tipped his head. "That means if we come across somethin', ain't sayin' we should ignore it, but keep it close to the vest. For now."

"Got it. Make note of it and collect evidence, if possible."

"Yeah, but don't go specifically lookin' for anythin'. We promised the DAMC prez we'd look the other way on most minor shit with the club. However..."

"What these Shadows do are not minor crimes," she finished for him.

"Bingo. And here's the loophole, we only agreed to ignore the shit DAMC members do. The Shadows are not part of the DAMC." He smirked. "That makes them fair game."

"Got it," she repeated.

"But keep that to yourself."

"Of course. Who's our main point of contact?"

"The club president, Zakary Jamison. Goes by Zak."

"No road name?" she asked in surprise.

"Not all of them have 'em. They tend to call him Z. He was the one most open to us usin' their club to go undercover. The rest?" Fletch shook his head. "Not so fuckin' much."

"What do you know about him?"

"Got a wife and two boys. His main source of income's a bakery in town, originally started by his wife prior to them gettin' together. He's also our BAMC president's brother."

"Damn. I bet that's awkward at family gatherings."

"Tell me about it. Especially since his dad also was with the Shadow Valley PD before he retired."

"Talk about someone coming to a fork in the road."

"Right. One fork led to his roots, the other led to a new beginning. Zak chose to follow in his grandfather's footsteps."

"He took the wrong path, while his father and brother took the right one."

Fletch shrugged. "Depends on who you ask."

That was true.

It didn't matter if he was a cop or a biker. As long as he was happy with his choice, that was what mattered. And by letting them go undercover in the club, it seemed like he was trying to stay on the right side of the law.

"So you know, when it comes to the meth thing... When he was about twenty he was busted for stealin' and possession of anhydrous ammonia. He did a dime at Fayette for it."

"Damn. Do we need to worry that their club will get involved with trafficking meth along with the Demons?"

"Nope. From what I was told by Axel Jamison and I'm not sure it's the whole story... it was a complete set-up by the former club prez. 'Cause the Demons are distributin' meth, I think that kinda helped sway him to let us go undercover with their club."

Huh. Now that was interesting. "I guess he's not doing it for the greater good of society as a whole?" Her question was a bit tongue-in-cheek, of course.

"An MC has their own society of sorts. Everythin' in their tight-knit community's handled the same way."

"Typical."

"Right. Similar to La Cosa Nostra. Punishment's doled out when needed. Issues are handled in house. Outsiders are kept just that... outside."

"And I'm sure any punishment is handled swiftly."

"That would be my guess."

"But we're outsiders and wear badges and they let us in the door, anyway."

"Yep, but we still need to tread carefully. Need to respect them as much as possible so they don't slam that fuckin' door in our face and then lock us out."

In the years she'd been a special agent, she had seen a lot of shit she had to ignore for the good of the investigation as a whole. This assignment would be no different.

As long as someone wasn't in any immediate danger, she had no problem looking the other way. That didn't mean she didn't file away that info for future use.

"When do we start working?"

"The jobs? On Monday. But Sunday we officially become a Dirty Angel and his ol' lady."

Since it was Friday night, that gave them another day to get used to each other as a "couple" and formulate a plan on how soon they could reach out to the Demons. In her book, the sooner the better.

She unfolded her legs, got to her feet and arched her back to stretch it. "That it for tonight since we have all day tomorrow before we officially become Ghost and," she grimaced, "Kitten?"

Of course that nickname made him grin. *Asshole.*

"One more thing... Sunday they have a club run and after they're havin' a pig roast. It's a normal activity for the club and everyone who can be is supposed to be there. Since we're now DAMC, that means we need to show. It'll be a good opportunity to sit back and observe their way of life so we fit in better."

"A pig roast, huh?"

"You ain't a vegan, are you?"

She rounded the couch, answering, "Nope, I like my meat. In all forms," before heading down the hallway with the envelope.

That would be tonight's reading material before bed.

Chapter Ten

BACON. Hash browns? Coffee!

Her stomach growled at her breakfast dream, waking her up. She blinked. Nope, wasn't a dream. She inhaled the scent deeply.

Yesssss, coffee. It better be caffeinated.

With a moan, she rolled over, jerked her tank top back into place so her breasts were once again tucked safely inside —since sometime during the night they took a run for the border—and sat up. Pushing her messy hair out of her face, she inhaled that glorious scent again.

Please let it be caffeinated.

After rolling from the bed, she plucked her boxer briefs from between her ass cheeks. She must have slept restlessly last night. But then, it was a new place, a new bed and a new partner.

This morning she was glad she took the smaller room so she didn't have to see herself in the ceiling mirror. She could only imagine she had dark circles under her eyes and looked like a zombie.

After leaving Fletch in the living room last night, she had stayed up a while to open the envelope and spread the contents over the bed to sort through them. She had tucked Sandra Douglas's driver's license into a small zippered wallet she had brought with her. Then read through info sheets so she knew, not only Sandra's background, but Terry Parker aka Ghost's.

She planned on skimming it again this morning to make sure she had their new identities down pat but not until her brain had been kick-started by coffee. Lots and lots of coffee.

The only thing she missed about being undercover with the Russos was their damn coffee. It was the best she ever drank. Once she was clear from that assignment, she tried to duplicate it but finally gave up. She doubted they'd appreciate her knocking on their door to beg for a cup.

In the bathroom, she muttered a "Jesus" when she saw her face in the mirror, quickly emptied her bladder and washed her face, then she followed the tempting scent, proving she could be lured anywhere with just a fresh cup of joe.

She was surprised to find the dining table set for two people.

Maybe he wasn't such an asshole after all. To be sure, she'd reserve her final judgment once she had more concrete evidence.

When she entered the kitchen, he was doing something at the stove and as he moved, her eyes were drawn to his ass in those thin, gray nylon shorts.

Someone must do squats. And a lot of them.

Dragging her eyes away before she got caught ogling him, they landed on the coffeemaker next and the almost full pot of coffee.

Thank fuck. "Please tell me that has caffeine."

"It does," he answered, his voice gravelly from lack of use. He glanced over his shoulder and raked his gaze over her. "You normally sleep this late?"

Late? She spotted an old analog clock on the wall. It was eight. "What time were you up?"

"Six. Already went for a run, did fifty pull-ups and showered."

He did what? Already? Hold up... That didn't sound like normal activity for a biker. And the proof was how they looked in all of the videos she'd watched of various MCs. "Do bikers run?"

"From the law." He chuckled at his own joke.

"I'm serious. Do you think it's smart to be out," she swung a hand toward the front door, "there jogging?"

"Probably not. I'll take that into consideration. This club does own a gym, though. So apparently, some bikers don't have an aversion to exercise."

She grabbed the empty mug sitting next to the coffeemaker and filled it up almost to the brim. "The Angels own a gym?" She brought it to her lips and blew on it before risking a tiny sip to prevent it from spilling even one precious drop of the black gold over the edge.

Since coffee was her crack, that one little sip made her want to suck down the whole mug in one shot despite the fact she'd risk third degree burns down her throat. She forced herself to wait because that worker's comp claim would be fun to explain.

He huffed out a breath. "Yeah. Surprising, right? One of their members and his ol' lady runs it. Not everyone uses it but a lot of them do. Including Kat Callahan. Remember her?"

"No."

"She used to be a champion MMA fighter."

Nova knew nothing about MMA. "Used to be?"

"She retired from the cage. Now she teaches mixed martial arts classes to women and girls."

"For self-defense?"

"That and to get them ready for competition. She's also married to one of those Shadows."

"Ah." She sipped carefully at the still-steaming coffee and once that mouthful landed in her stomach, she sighed in satisfaction.

He used the spatula in his hand to point at a mug next to him on the counter. "Get me a refill?"

She nodded, but he had already turned back to the stove and began to serve food onto two plates sitting nearby.

"You know how to cook, huh?"

"I manage."

She leaned closer to check out what he made. She was right. Crispy bacon and just as crispy hash browns along with a mountain of fluffy scrambled eggs. "Who went shopping?"

"I did. And you're welcome."

"Thanks." She hip-bumped him without thinking, then froze. "I didn't mean—"

He hip-checked her back. "Don't worry 'bout it. We live together, Nova. We're supposed to act like more than roommates, remember? Gonna be touchin' a lot more than that to make it look fuckin' real."

She was impressed with how he switched from English to biker-speak seamlessly.

She grabbed his mug and refilled it along with topping off hers.

He turned with the full plates in his hand and tipped his head toward the table.

She followed him over, placed his mug next to his plate and sat across from him. "You'll make someone a good wife," she murmured, staring at the food that smelled delicious. Her stomach growled again.

His perfectly-aligned teeth crunched on a strip of bacon. "I thought so, too, until I had two broken engagements."

"Two?"

He shrugged. "I got the touch, apparently." He shoved the last of the bacon into his mouth.

"Or lack of touch."

"That was never my problem."

"Says you." She took a bite of her own bacon. Perfectly done. Impressive.

"Can prove it to you if you wanna be the judge."

She swallowed her mouthful. "I'll take your word for it. So, you wanted the whole package, huh? Wife, kids, dog?" She picked up her fork and took a bite of the scrambled eggs. Once again, perfect.

She wondered if he could cook anything more complex than breakfast because she sure couldn't. And if he could, she'd be taking advantage of any home-cooked meals he could pull off. Maybe he'd take some menu suggestions.

"Just the wife would've been fine. Maybe a couple of kids later down the road. But at this point I've given up on finding a life partner."

With a frown, she lifted her gaze from her plate to him. "You're too young to give up. You're only in your thirties, right?"

"Thirty-five. Maybe I'm not cut out to be husband material."

"Not every woman is cut out to be with a cop." Neither was every man. Sometimes it was hard to turn off the law enforcement side of your brain once you got home. Being a state, local or federal officer also took a certain type of personality that not everyone could gel with no matter how hard they tried.

"That could be it. Dealing with badge bunnies, the risk that one day I might not end my shift alive, and the fear of your family getting targeted... I guess it could be stressful. Some women can only take the uncertainties for so long before bailing."

"That's why the divorce rate for our chosen career is so high. You also forgot to mention cheating. There's a high probability of that, too."

"I've never cheated." He lifted one eyebrow. "Have you?"

"No." She steered the conversation away from her before he brought up the Russos again. "At least your engagements were broken before getting to the altar. Divorces can be painful, long and costly. Especially when kids are involved."

He snagged the ketchup from the center of the table and squirted the condiment over his two hash brown patties. "Have you been divorced?"

"Nope."

"Engaged?"

"That would also be a negative," she answered.

"An independent woman," he concluded.

"That's the way I prefer it. The toilet seat's always down. The lights are always off in an empty room. Trash actually ends up in the garbage can. Oh, and my T-shirts don't end up shrunken into crop tops."

He shook his head and his warm, rich chuckle made her worry it could get as addicting as her need for coffee.

She sucked down more morning fuel as she shook that from her thoughts. "How long have you been a trooper?"

"Fourteen years. You?" He stabbed a chunk of eggs along with a piece of hash brown and shoved the forkful into his mouth.

"Zero."

His eyes lifted to her, his eyebrows rose and he quickly swallowed his food. "Well, look at that, someone *does* have a sense of humor."

She kept her expression blank. "Who does?"

"Kitten."

She rolled her eyes. "Do badass biker bitches have a sense of humor?"

"If not, you can be the first. I'll rephrase... How long have you been with the FBI?"

"Seems like forever, but actually since I was twenty-three. That's the minimum age to be accepted and I went in as soon as they'd allow it."

"And you're what?" He thought for a second. "Thirty... one now?"

She forced herself to answer "Yeah" instead of "yes."

He smiled. "Good girl."

Her heart slammed to a stop before kicking back into high gear at that type of praise. He was testing her. "Oh no. You do not get to say that to me." Even though the way he said it in his deep rumble almost made her kitty *meow*.

"Only Mafia daddies get to call you that?"

There it was... Proof that making breakfast was not a good litmus test to prove someone wasn't an asshole. "No one gets to praise me like that, period. Not if they like how their balls currently hang."

He winced. "Heard that loud and clear."

On more than one occasion, Russo Sr. had grabbed her by the throat, slammed her against the wall and whispered, "Good girl," into her ear. Unable to break cover, she could do nothing about it except pretend it didn't bother her. She never wanted to hear that type of praise again. It turned her stomach.

"Good." She tried to get them back on track. "Though, before that, I did the FBI Honors Internship Program between my junior and senior years at Pitt." That ten-week program cemented the fact she wanted to become a special agent. And if the FBI hadn't wanted her, she would've found another federal organization that did.

"I'm guessing you had an 'in' to get one of the coveted internship spots?"

"I did."

His brown eyes narrowed on her. "Who?"

"My uncle."

"He was an agent?"

"A senior special agent with the organized crime division. I was fascinated with what he did and some of the stories, or partial stories, he was allowed to tell me. Since I looked up to him, I decided to follow the same career path."

"I bet you make him proud."

"Yeah." Nova's attention was glued to his mouth as he chewed.

"He still working?"

"No."

"He's retired?"

"He was killed in the line of duty." Losing him still hurt to this day. Especially with how she lost him. It was the main factor why she wanted to work in the organized crime division.

"Fuck." He set down his mug and sat back in his chair, watching her intently from across the table. "By who?"

She pulled in a breath through her nose and released it out of her mouth along with, "La Cosa Nostra."

His spine snapped straight. "Jesus H. Christ. The Russos?"

She put down her fork since talking about losing her

uncle always made her stomach twist. This morning was no different. A shame since what she had eaten so far had been damn good. "No. The Parisis."

"*Ah*, so you must have a beef with the Sicilians," he concluded. Wrongly, of course.

She didn't hate all Sicilians, just the ones involved in organized crime and murder. "The only beef I had was with the man who killed my uncle."

"Was," he echoed. "Was it a hit?"

"Cyanide. In his food. He died a slow, painful death." She didn't bother to hide her satisfied smirk.

Fletch grimaced and shoved his plate away, even though he wasn't finished. "How about we divide up the chores around here and I'll do all the cooking?"

"I don't mind cooking," she lied. She actually hated cooking but was enjoying his reaction.

"I mind you cooking."

"I promise not to poison you." She rolled her lips under.

"I don't know you well enough to know if you break promises."

She narrowed her eyes on him. "Just don't do anything that warrants me using cyanide as a spice on your tuna casserole."

"I hope you're fucking kidding."

Nova shrugged. "I most likely am."

"That's assuring."

"You're not speaking like a biker."

"But you are."

"Why? Do ol' ladies tend to poison their ol' men?" she asked.

"Wouldn't put it past them."

She reached for his mug. "I'll get you more coffee."

He snagged it first and shoved his seat back abruptly. "I got it."

She turned her head away to hide her laughter as he grabbed her mug, too, and quickly disappeared into the kitchen.

Her eyes once again zeroed in on his retreating back and that compass tattoo.

Since they were supposed to be using this time to get to know each other... "Why the compass?" she called out, poking at a piece of the hash brown patty. Even though it was now room temperature, she ate it anyway. Her appetite might have waned but she didn't want to waste the food or the effort he put into making it.

He appeared again, carrying two steaming mugs. As soon as he placed one in front of her, she took a long sip, closing her eyes in ecstasy.

"Guess you can't function without coffee."

Unfortunately, with her eyes closed she discovered the rich timbre of his voice affected her even more, so she opened them. "You can?"

"Nope," Fletch answered. "It's the only addiction I have."

"Same. So, the compass?"

"It means guidance, protection and direction. And what cop couldn't use a little more of that? I figured my back was the best place to put it."

It was also a great place to hide it for when he worked patrol. "Do you have enemies and need to protect your back?"

He took a sip of his coffee but remained standing next to her instead of taking his seat. "Merely wearing a badge tends to create enemies."

That was true. Some law enforcement officers made more than others. But then, if you weren't making enemies, you probably weren't doing your job. No one liked getting a citation or arrested.

"Got any?"

She set her mug down. "Yes."

"Yeah," he corrected.

She turned on the ol' lady attitude, even adding a head bob. "Yeah, I got one. What about it?"

He grinned and slipped back into biker mode. "Lemme see it, woman. Need to know everythin' about each other. At least as Ghost and Kitten. Even if it's somewhere no one's gonna ever see it. 'Cause if someone sticks their nose where it don't belong, I gotta have an answer. As your ol' man, gotta know each and every one of your tattoos intimately."

Her first instinct was to roll her eyes, but he was right. "Like yours, it's on my back."

Without asking, he gently lifted up her hair out of the way. "Don't see it." He tucked a finger into the top of her navy-blue razorback tank and tugged it down. "Wait. I see ink, just can't see what it is."

She pushed her chair away from the table and stood. "Pull it up from the bottom." She pinned an arm under her breasts so she wouldn't accidentally be exposed at the breakfast table. They needed to get to know each other, but not that well.

He yanked the chair farther away from the table so he could stand directly behind her, grabbed the bottom of her ribbed tank and lifted it.

The air touched her skin first, causing goosebumps, but it was his touch that caused her nipples to pebble.

Her breath caught as he slowly trailed a finger down her spine while reading the words out loud: *No Fear. No Limits. No Regrets.* She had picked a font that was both feminine but also exuded strength. The ink might be simple but she loved the statement it made.

She'd been told by a couple of lovers that her tattoo sounded like a sneaker commercial, but she didn't give a fuck what they thought. She only cared about what it meant to her. Her body, her message, her reminder.

Opinions were like assholes. Everyone had one. Some stunk, some didn't.

When his warm breath swept over the back of her neck, she tensed to fight the shudder. She failed.

Fuck. He did not need to know how her body reacted to him with his touch or his voice. He might use that to his advantage.

No, he seemed the type who *would* use that to his advantage. She had a hunch he considered himself irresistible. He might be the kind to pull out all the stops if he came across a woman who thought otherwise.

Just to prove her wrong and himself right, of course.

Admittedly, he was hot as fuck. He was also a man who'd understand her job. But she never mixed work with personal pleasure.

Luckily with this undercover operation, she was not in a position where she would have to be intimate with anyone to avoid "getting made." With some assignments, she had to do things not of her choice or not on the up and up to avoid having her cover blown. She made sure to document those instances in her daily report.

For the most part.

There were a few times she had to do things beyond the scope of her assignment. Some she reported, some she couldn't.

She quickly stepped forward and yanked her tank top down, to not only break both his tangible hold on her, but the invisible one, too. "Are we stuck here all day?" *For fuck's sake,* that came out way too breathless.

With heat crawling up her chest into her throat, she remained facing the table so he wouldn't see it.

His arm brushed against hers as he reached past her to grab the ketchup bottle from the table. "Wanna take the sled out later?"

"Sled?"

"Didn't you read through some of the terms they use? I included a list in your packet. That's what they call their Harleys."

She had skimmed it but she'd been too tired last night to retain most of the information because there had been a shit-ton of it.

Even so...

Hell yes, she needed to get out of the apartment. The walls were closing in on her and this was only day one. "Good to know. And, yes, I would love to go for a ride, *Ghost.*"

"Well, *Kitten,* how 'bout you get ready while I clean up?"

She would be stupid to turn down that offer.

Anyway, she could now use a cold shower. A long one.

Chapter Eleven

He had told her to hang onto him while on the club run. That lasted for about thirty seconds.

Unfortunately, the "sled" the feds supplied for this job had a sissy bar on the back and she had no need to hold onto anything, including him. She'd avoided it yesterday, too, while on their solo run. Maybe he should have that crutch removed so she'd be forced to wrap her arms around him like the rest of the ol' ladies riding along on today's run.

She needed to act like she *liked* him instead of only being along for the ride.

Yesterday, they had spent over two hours cruising around Shadow Valley and its outskirts so they'd be seen while wearing their cuts.

He drove by and pointed out all the DAMC businesses and told her which DAMC members ran them. He doubted she'd remember it all, but Crew had included that detailed info in her packet. They also did a drive-by of the DAMC compound. They even stopped in to see Cross and his husband, Nash, and their two kids for a few minutes since they just lived behind the Angels' gated neighborhood.

Later, they stopped at a jam-packed Bangin' Burgers for their famous burgers, seasoned fries and thick shakes. Because the take-out joint didn't have indoor dining, they sat at one of the picnic tables outside to eat. Being out in public, they kept their conversation generic in case someone overheard them while they wore DAMC colors.

A few women scrunched up their faces with disbelief or disgust once they read the patches on the back of Nova's—*Kitten's*—cut. One brave woman actually asked Nova if she was okay.

Of course Nova pulled out all the stops when she slapped back with attitude. "I don't look okay?" She turned and asked Fletch loudly, "Thought I looked pretty damn good today, ol' man, am I wrong?"

The woman's cheeks flamed red. "I just thought—"

"Try not to think so fucking hard next time," Nova snapped. "You think my ol' man's holding me against my will? Fuck no, this man gives it to me good." Then she turned her back on the woman, who skulked away. Finally, when no one else was around, she whispered to Fletch, "I kind of feel bad. I understand why she might be concerned. What woman in their right mind wants to be the property of a man?"

Probably more than either of them would expect. "Yeah, well, you handled it as a biker chick would've. Good—"

Nova cocked an eyebrow, and shot him a warning look.

"Job," he finished, swallowing down the "girl." He valued his nuts and preferred to keep them safely secured in their sac.

Just like on Saturday, he dressed the part of Ghost by pulling on a worn pair of Levi's, a Steel City Harley-

Davidson dealership T-shirt, heavy boots and his cut. Nova dressed similar to the previous day, too, but with a black Harley-Davidson camisole snug enough to push up her tits, making them appear larger than what they were in reality.

After seeing her in the tank top she wore to bed two nights in a row, he had a good handle on their size since she hadn't worn a bra.

Her faded jeans were shredded, her black boots scuffed and she wore a bunch of clunky silver rings on both hands. Around her neck, she also wore a thick black chain with a large O-ring that reminded him of a collar worn by a submissive. That gave him pause since he couldn't imagine she was even close to being a sub, either in life or in bed.

A wide black leather cuff circled her left wrist, a silver hoop decorated her right nostril, silver skull earrings hung from both ears and the dark makeup around her eyes was put on heavy-handed, bypassing the sexy smoky look the first day he met her and now leaned more toward goth. Her dark brown, almost black, hair was covered with a black bandana to protect it from the wind and her brown eyes were hidden by a very dark pair of sunglasses.

With the way she appeared today and if he didn't know better, he never would've guessed she was FBI and not a genuine biker bitch. "Down and dirty 'til dead" was the Dirty Angels' motto and she had slipped into her role as an Angel's ol' lady like a pro.

While he preferred her this morning with her face scrubbed clean versus it being overly done, her whole biker chick look also did things to him he hadn't expected. It made him think she'd have no problem getting "down and dirty" in bed and out of it, too.

He realized the road name Kitten might not fit her. She had warned him her teeth and claws were sharp, he had no doubt that was true. Maybe he should've picked the nickname Lynx or Puma, or *hell*, Wild Cat, for her instead.

He quickly lost his smirk as the long formation hooked a right into the parking lot of The Iron Horse Roadhouse, the public side of the DAMC's church. Since they'd been placed at the back of the pack, and basically ignored the whole ride—when they weren't getting the side-eye—he followed the line of bikes through the open gate and into the back lot behind the building. One of the prospects closed the gate behind them and secured it with chains and locks.

That made the hair on the back of Fletch's neck prickle and Nova tapped him on the shoulder, making sure he saw what happened.

He nodded and found a parking spot along the very back edge of the large paved lot. Once he shut down the Harley with the straight exhaust pipes so he could be heard, he murmured over his shoulder to her, "I'll see about getting a key for those locks."

Leaning forward, she pressed herself into his back so she wasn't overheard. Exactly how she should be every time they were riding together: plastered against him. "Think they'll give you a key?"

"Probably not. I get why they do it, but I don't like being locked in here."

"You're not the only one," she murmured. "If shit goes sideways, we're stuck unless we can somehow escape on foot. But I haven't scaled a fence that high in... Hell, never and there's barbed wire on the top to boot."

"Yeah. Noticed that when we met with their executive committee."

"I'll shoot first and ask questions later," she whispered and used his shoulder to help her dismount.

They both wore ankle holsters since that was the only

good place to hide a weapon. Fletch had a Glock 43 strapped to his right ankle, and a Timber Wolf Tactical knife sheathed in his left boot.

But none of their weapons were sufficient protection if the club decided to turn on them. Not only were they outnumbered, Fletch was damn sure everyone in that club and on the run were packing, whether it be a knife, handgun, brass knuckles, blackjacks, or whatever.

Again, he understood the need to protect themselves, but that still made him cautious. Even though he didn't have anything personal against the DAMC and he gave them no reason to hate him, that didn't mean he didn't feel like an enemy in their midst.

"I'm surprised they didn't tell us to get lost after the run. It's about the optics."

"You and me both," he muttered, getting off the bike. "Let's take advantage of tonight by paying attention and learning their speech and mannerism. Getting to know who's who, in case one of the Demons decides to ask about someone, whether as a test or not, because tomorrow the Angels could tell us to fuck off and we might be on our own. It'll make it a little more difficult if we're kept on the outskirts. The more we know, the better."

"Agreed," she murmured, standing next to the bike. "Should we split up?"

"You comfortable with that?"

She shot him a look.

Of course she was.

"Just be aware, the members and ol' ladies were told who we are since no one simply walks in off the street and gets handed a full set of patches. However, the sweet butts and the hang-arounds weren't, just in case one of them has loose lips or is a plant from any other MC. Once the MC members were told, they weren't supposed to discuss it again. To anyone. But that doesn't mean shit."

"Got it. So, if I get questioned by anyone not wearing a cut, should I just blow them off or should we get a story together?"

"The president told me that if anyone questions it, to say we patched over from the Blood Fury. That club is their ally up north. One DAMC member is married to a former Fury club girl and that couple took in a teen from the Blood Fury, too. So, it's not unheard of for members crossing over, patched or not. It might not be perfect, but it's the best excuse we have."

"Got it. Why'd we move down here?"

Fletch scratched the back of his neck. He should've went over this with her prior to today. His mistake. "Your father's been sick and we came down here to help take care of your parents."

"That's a lame excuse."

"Look, can you come up with anything better? This shit was in your packet." He reined in his impatience and threw an arm over her shoulders, steering them toward a gap in the bushes where everyone disappeared. He had to assume that led to the courtyard where the pig roast was being held. "Kitten's originally from Shadow Valley, so it only makes sense to move home where you were needed. The backstory is, when we originally hooked up you moved north to be with me because you couldn't resist the dick. Now, I've followed you back home since I didn't want to give up such sweet pussy."

He grinned when she shook her head and groaned.

He stopped near the line of tall evergreens that created a natural privacy fence. "Wrap your arm around my waist." As soon as she did, he continued, "Men will move to the other side of the Earth for the right pussy."

"Sad."

"Yeah, well... Men get stupid over pussy, if you don't already know. And don't pretend that women don't get stupid over dick." He glanced down at her. "Ready?"

Once she nodded, they stepped through the gap and into the courtyard.

When they had met with Zak Jamison and his side-kicks, he hadn't seen this part of the property. He had to admit, it was pretty damn impressive and a million times better than the tiny "courtyard" they had at the BAMC clubhouse.

At the far end was a real stage with a roof to protect whoever was using it from the weather. Massive speakers sat at both ends and it even had stage lights. All of it reminded him of a mini concert venue.

To the left was a large pavilion full of wooden picnic tables. And in the middle of the courtyard was a huge fire pit stacked high with wood pallets. The whole area was surrounded by chain-link fencing, topped with more barbed wire to prevent anyone scaling it, as well as privacy screens to prevent spying by the general public, law enforcement or their enemies.

Along the front fence was a commercial-sized smoker and as soon as the smell from the roasting pig hit his nostrils, his stomach growled. Long folding tables were lined up along the fence, too, to hold what looked like a smorgasbord of food and everything else needed to eat and drink. Blue plastic barrels cut in half were full of ice. Some held beer kegs, the rest held what might be water, pop and bottled beer.

Scanning the crowd, he straightened his spine and raised his head as he slipped back into full biker mode. Someone was already lighting the pallet pyre, a few women were beginning to shred the pig for sandwiches, while a couple more were pouring beers. Fletch assumed the working women were sweet butts, women who basically did whatever members wanted them to do, sexually or otherwise, just to have access to the club and, of course, the bikers.

When he pulled Nova tighter into his side, he murmured, "Did you read up on the sweet butts?" into her ear.

He didn't miss her breath catch. He was unsure if it was due to the sweet butt question or if she was just as attracted to him as he was to her.

He reminded himself that this was a job and he needed to keep things on a professional level, even though they wouldn't be acting professional at all.

"Yeah, I know what a fucking sweet butt is and if any of them try sinking their claws into you, the bitch is gonna get punched in the throat."

He grinned. "Nice. That's my sharp-clawed Kitten. Wanna keep all this for yourself."

"Don't push it," she warned more quietly.

He chuckled and when he noticed quite a few eyes turned their direction, he pressed his lips to her temple and gave her ass a squeeze.

"Don't tense, *Kitten*. We fuck like rabbits, remember?" he murmured into her ear.

"I'm not a fan of rabbits, *Ghost*." She sighed, but melted into his side.

That was more like it. He slid his hand from her ass cheek to her hip, giving that a squeeze next. "Hungry?"

"Yeah. But let's wait 'til the line dies down a little."

The screech of an amplifier made them both jerk and turn their attention to the stage. Yesterday wasn't the first time he'd meet Cross's husband Nash, but this evening would be the first time he heard him sing since he was stepping up to the microphone. From what Cross said, Nash could play the drums, guitar and belt out a song like no other.

Fletch looked forward to hearing some great music tonight.

"When Nash was on the run with us, he was alone," Nova whispered, leaning into him. "Where's his husband?"

Fletch adjusted the arm he had hanging around her shoulders. "He ain't welcome to these things." Once the music started, it would be hard to speak quietly, so now was the time.

"Why doesn't he just tell them to fuck off?"

"Supposedly, once Cross hangs up his duty belt, he'll be welcome. So he says, anyway."

"It doesn't have anything to do with him being gay, does it?"

"No. Cross said Nash woulda had his colors stripped if it had to do with that. It's solely based on him bein' a cop. Or... pig. We need to use that term from now on, too."

"Great," she answered dryly.

He shrugged. "Gotta blend in, woman."

She released another sigh. "When we stopped during the run, the women had acted friendly to me. Maybe not completely welcoming since they worry about their men, but nice enough. Their male counterparts? Not so much."

"'Cause we're the enemy amongst them. They don't like us bein' here, Kitten, no matter what the reason. They ain't ever gonna trust us while we got the capability of arrestin' them."

"If they think we care about the pot they're smoking..." She tipped her head to a few guys sitting on top of a picnic table under the pavilion passing a joint.

"Trust me, it ain't about the pot. But on that particular note, they're aware a personal amount ain't worth the paper-work. Normally, if I find it in someone's car or on their person, I ignore it. The only time I don't is if they got enough for an intent to deliver charge."

"Cop speak," she reminded him, elbowing him in the ribs.

"Yeah." He quickly glanced around. "No one's close by."

"I wouldn't be surprised to see the federal law changed soon."

"That's one reason I don't bust someone for that petty shit. But again, it ain't about some pot."

"We need to stop talking shop here."

"Right. And we need to act like I own your pussy."

"In your dreams, Ghost."

"Oh," he purred, "I like a good challenge, Kitten."

She shot him a wicked smile. "You ain't the only one."

"Fuck," he muttered when a huge man wearing DAMC colors lumbered in their direction. Were they about to be promptly evicted from the property?

"Who's that?" Nova whispered.

"Trouble."

The club's sergeant at arms stopped directly in front of them, crowding them with his big body.

Diesel Dougherty locked eyes with him. *Oh yeah,* Fletch liked a challenge but would pass on challenging this particular man. He wasn't stupid. He knew his limits, even if the club's enforcer was about twenty years older. The man might be in his fifties, but he wasn't dead. And his meaty paws were the size of sledgehammers.

"Know you ain't welcome here."

"And you know this was all pre-approved."

"On the run. Now, get gone."

"Your prez said—"

Nova jammed her elbow into his side.

"*Our* prez said we're welcome. Aware of our limits. Gonna respect that."

Diesel sucked snot into the back of this throat and spat a thick hocker at Fletch's feet. "*Respect*. Fuck your respect. An' fuck your asses for tryin' to act like us an' speak like us."

"D..." came from behind them.

Fletch didn't like people approaching them from the rear but he recognized the voice so he kept his eyes on the immediate threat in front of them instead.

Diesel also kept his eyes on Fletch and didn't acknowledge his president.

"Stand down, D," Zak Jamison ordered and came around to stand next to his sergeant at arms, along with a tall kid in his late teens, a lankier carbon copy of the president. Like father, like son. Only the son wasn't wearing a cut. "Discussed this shit already."

The beast of a man was not standing down. "Don't mean I gotta like it."

"Nobody fuckin' likes it!" Zak yelled, then quickly reined it in and lowered his voice. "But you're makin' a goddamn scene an' catchin' eyes. They're supposed to be blendin' in."

Diesel's jaw shifted and his broad chest swelled as he took a deep breath.

"I'll handle this. You go handle that new prospect leanin' all over Vi inside church."

If Fletch thought Diesel looked scary before, he morphed into something even more terrifying. But before he stomped away, he jabbed a finger at Fletch and Nova. "Watch your fuckin' step." Then he was gone.

"Should I go with him?" the younger version of Zak asked.

"Stay out of it. You know he got it covered."

The kid jerked his chin at Fletch. "So, who the fuck's this?"

Zak inhaled deeply and shook his head, his expression clearly showing his annoyance. When he loosened his jaw, he said, "Patched over from the Fury. Go."

"What?"

If the kid didn't believe it, other people might not, either. That could be a problem.

"Get gone, Zeke. Ain't your business."

"This club's my business."

Zak's head jerked back and his eyebrows shot up. "Not yet it ain't. Not as long as I'm still livin', breathin' an' holdin' the fuckin' gavel. You ain't even wearin' a prospect cut yet."

"But—"

"Go! Ain't gonna tell you again." With that, Zak and his son stared at each other in a standoff.

Fletch's gaze ping-ponged back and forth to see who would break first. He was surprised at how long the son challenged his father. Eventually Zeke broke first, looking pissed and stomping off toward the pavilion where he joined a group of older teens, both male and female.

Zak turned back to them, shaking his head. "Fuckin' kids. All sweet an' shit one day and the next... *BAM*... talkin' back an' talkin' shit."

Fletch watched the boys clasp hands and bump shoulders or fists with each other. The girls were smiling and laughing. Maybe even one or two batted their eyelashes at the president's good-looking son.

Fletch figured the kid would end up being trouble with a capital T, if he wasn't already. Especially when a bong appeared like magic and the boy accepted it.

Fletch turned back to Zak and lifted an eyebrow. "He eighteen?"

"Close enough."

"And that makes what he's doin' all right?"

Zak's eyes flicked over the pavilion, his gaze hung there for a second before turning back to them. Fletch could see the man trying to restrain himself. "My kid, so I'll handle it. Said not to interfere with us. You do, our invitation will be revoked."

Fletch raised the palm not attached to Nova's hip. "You got it. Wasn't lookin' for trouble, was just curious since he's over there takin' a hit off a bong." Not just one hit, either. The cloud around him was as thick as a Cheech and Chong movie.

Fletch smoked pot when he was a teen, too, but he never had the balls to do it in front of his parents. Bikers were definitely a different breed.

"Said I'm gonna handle it."

Nova's arm tightened around his waist in an unspoken message. It reminded him that the man standing before them was their only ally in that club. Fletch needed to mind his damn business to stay on his good side and for them to stay undercover. Without them, it would be harder to approach the Demons.

And that was another good reminder. That was the whole reason why Nova and he were where they stood at that moment.

"Stay a bit. Eat. Make some rounds. Be seen. Then get gone. Best not to be here after everyone's pickled 'cause you're outnumbered an' I can't stop anyone from poppin' off. An' my enforcer certainly ain't gonna get your back. Got me?"

"We got it," Nova answered and stiffened against Fletch when Zak didn't even acknowledge her.

Fuck. Fletch quickly answered, "Got you. We'll only stay

about an hour and then we'll split. Tomorrow mornin' we'll head to our work assignments. At least you'll get something out of us for allowin' this."

"Right," Zak muttered. "Us gettin' free labor ain't the flex you think it is to allow pigs amongst us."

"Understood. Gonna do our best to pull our weight and stay outta your hair."

"You do that." With that, he turned and headed toward the pavilion, flicking two fingers over his shoulder as he went.

"At least he didn't give us the middle one," Nova said, watching the man go speak to his son.

"Let's mingle a little bit, try not to cause problems, grab some grub and then *get gone*."

"Yeah, before these bikers get pickled like he said and decide to play a game with us we won't be able to win."

"They just need to see we ain't a threat to them. It might take a while." He didn't have to add that they might not have a "while" to wait. They needed to get working on their connection with the Demons as soon as possible.

"I'm not sure they'll ever see us that way," she murmured, as he steered her toward the smoker and the tables now full of food. "We need to keep our heads on swivels."

"No fuckin' shit," he mumbled.

The tables no longer had lines, so they grabbed some food, much more appealing than expected for a biker pig roast, and once they had full plates in hand, he asked, "Want a beer?"

"Think it's smart we grab one but not drink it."

"Hear you on that, Kitten." He headed over to the beer kegs on ice with Nova slowly trailing behind him.

A couple of women wearing barely enough clothes to cover their tits and ass were handing out red Solo cups full of beer.

A bleach blonde whose nipples were on the verge of popping out of her low-necked top took her time inspecting him up and down. "Damn. Where'd you come from, handsome?"

She might be a good test to see if anyone believed their cover story. "The Fury."

Her bright red lips turned downward. "The Fury sent someone down here? Why the fuck would they do that?"

Nova stepped between him and the woman, ruining his test. "Mind your fuckin' biz."

The blonde slammed her hands on her hips, pushed out her chest even more and faced off with Nova. "And who the fuck are you, bitch?"

Oh fuck.

He would do his best not to step in and let Nova handle it like an ol' lady would.

"Must not've heard me the first time." Nova leaned in, going nose to nose with her. "Mind your biz, *bitch*."

"This is my biz, bitch, since I've never seen him—or you—before."

"Ain't my problem you're stupid as well as blind."

Oh fuck.

He wasn't sure if he should enjoy the show or panic that Nova might get into a brawl. And if she did, that might cause them to get their asses thrown out because he had no idea who this woman was. For all he knew, she could be someone's ol' lady since quite a few of them in this club did not wear their ol' man's cuts. And even more had removed them once they had returned from the run.

The blonde sneered at Nova, reached past her and scraped her long red-painted claws suggestively down Fletch's beard. "Honey, I can be a lot sweeter to you than her. My name is Star and I dance every Monday through Friday at Heaven's Angels. I give great lap dances where touching isn't off limits and is highly encouraged. Dances you'll have a *hard* time forgetting, I promise." She winked at him.

As Fletch opened his mouth to respond, Nova snagged the woman's wrist in a tight grip and shoved her away. "Fuck off, cunt, gonna warn you once and only once. You touch my man again, you'll be forced to breathe through a whole in your neck after I stab you there." Nova chest bumped her, forcing the blonde to take another step back.

Fletch yanked Nova out of her face and back to his side, keeping a firm grip on her arm, ignoring the fact some of the food tumbled from his plate. "Appreciate the generous offer but ain't interested," he told the woman. "Not if you and me both wanna see another day. As you see, got enough to handle right here with my little Hell Kitten."

"A real man can handle more than one."

"Oh, *honey*, he's a real man all right. And I don't mind sharing him, but he's got no interest in skanks like you riding his dick. Or my face." She grabbed Fletch's dick and squeezed, almost making him drop his plate.

For fuck's sake, he hadn't been ready for that.

"Ladies, as hot as it would be to watch you two go at it in a fuckin' cat fight, I'm hungry as fuck. And if my food gets cold, gonna be pissed. Woman, let's go." He jerked Nova's arm.

"I want a beer," she insisted.

If Nova wasn't careful, she'd be wearing one. He shoved his plate at her and she grabbed it. At least her hands would be busy.

"Gimme two beers," Fletch demanded.

Star simply stood there while another woman, similarly dressed, quickly shoved two full cups at him.

He took them and nodded his thanks.

"Don't forget. The name's Star. I'm there Monday through Friday."

Nova's step stuttered as they walked away. "Keep walkin'," Fletch ordered under his breath. "You start a real fight, we're gonna get tossed." He plastered a smirk on his face and said much louder, "For fuck's sake, you just gave me wood, woman."

He heard a few chuckles as they made their way around a small crowd near the now roaring bonfire.

"It's that easy?"

"It's that hard. Now I'm gonna need more than food and a beer."

Nova threw her head back and laughed so loudly it caught the attention of everyone nearby.

She had no idea he wasn't lying. He was hard as fuck that Kitten had turned into a possessive cougar. The rest of the night he wouldn't be able to think about anything but experiencing those sharp claws.

Even if only in his dreams.

Chapter Twelve

THEY PROBABLY STAYED at the pig roast for far longer than they should have. They made a few rounds so they were seen but tried not to interact with too many that might have a problem with their presence. She did have quite a few words with some of the ol' ladies since they were the ones most open to her and Fletch being within the DAMC.

Nova understood why. They were all mothers. None of them wanted meth—or any dangerous drugs, for that matter—flowing into their area, or a war to start up with a rival MC.

When she had broken away from Fletch to spend some time with the ladies, quite a few of them talked about the Shadow Warriors and the havoc they had wreaked on the club. A few of them hinted that some of the DAMC women had suffered badly at their hands but avoided going into details.

Nova got it. She heard their concerns. She heard their painful memories and experiences. And the more she heard, the more determined she was to keep the Demons from hurting them, as well.

Excluding the stripper she went head to head with, all were open, for the most part, and friendly with her. However, they were also cautious. Nova understood that, too.

They loved their men, their families and their lives with everything they had. They were also passionate about keeping everyone safe.

She promised them the task force would do everything in their power to stop the Demons from destroying their area and club family. And by allowing Ghost and Kitten to go undercover in the DAMC would help that goal.

A few times she had caught Fletch simply standing back and observing everyone in the courtyard as the club members drank, ate, laughed and shot the shit. She could see him making mental notes.

She also noticed the longer they were there, the more he picked up on their mannerisms and the better he blended in.

Eventually she worked her way back to him and they sat together under the pavilion for a little while longer with his arm draped over her shoulders as they listened to Dirty Deeds play rock and heavy metal. They also watched some of the women dance with each other, and occasionally with their men when the songs slowed.

One thing made crystal clear by spending time among them, they were all a tight-knit family. Something she never expected with a motorcycle club made up of rough, alpha men whose women wore "property of" cuts. Or had their man's name tattooed on them. She'd seen plenty of that, too.

The obvious difference she noted between the DAMC and La Cosa Nostra was the undercurrent of distrust and disloyalty within the Russo "family." What one could see on the surface was not reality at its core.

The trust and loyalty among the DAMC ran deep and

could not be missed or misconstrued. It was difficult to fake something so genuine.

By the time they returned to the apartment above the pawn shop, she was exhausted. Both her and Fletch agreed it had been a long but very productive day. Tomorrow morning they'd both go off to work at the jobs they'd been assigned. Her at the pawn shop downstairs and him at the gun shop and range on the other side of town.

The plan as of now was to work and live among the DAMC for at least a week, if not two, before reaching out to the Demons. This way they'd seem more established within the club and know the DAMC members better, as well as the businesses. All of that was necessary in case the Demons tested them. One wrong answer could screw them.

It was better to be patient than rush the process. If the Demons caught wind that a task force was on their ass, it could fuck up the whole investigation by making them more paranoid about dealing with anyone new.

The plan as of now was to check in with Crew every couple of days to see what was happening with the rest of the team as far as the wiretaps, surveillance and the rest. The more details they knew about the Demons' activities, the better for her and Fletch when it came time to approach them.

But right now, she needed to get out of the tight clothes she'd been wearing all day, shed the hot leather cut and catch a few winks. Plus, she could really use a beer after watching everyone else enjoy one or two, or even a half dozen, earlier.

As soon as Fletch parked the Harley at the bottom of the metal stairs, she dismounted and headed up. He caught up with her within seconds and, for some unknown reason, stood closer to her than necessary as she unlocked the apartment door and pushed into the cooler interior.

"Beer?" she asked over her shoulder. She shucked the cut and tossed it on the couch as she headed into the kitchen to her left.

Instead of answering, he followed her in, pausing only long enough to shrug out of his own cut and hang it over the back of a chair at the table.

When she opened the fridge, she became aware of his presence behind her, once again crowding her, and tried to ignore his long arm reaching past her to grab a cold beer, too.

His closeness made every cell in her body stand up and pay attention. This unreasonable and unexpected attraction to him worried her.

They had to live together for who knew how long. They had to act like they loved each other and were intimate with each other, too.

She had hated Frank Russo Sr., as well as his son, her original target. That deep down hatred had made it so much easier to stick with her job. Unlike this undercover assignment where she was worried things might get sticky, and not in a law enforcement way. Especially with how her body reacted whenever Fletch was in close proximity.

She had spent hours with him on the Harley both yesterday and today. Each time she climbed on behind him, he insisted she hang onto him, using the excuse that was what ol' ladies did when riding with their ol' men.

She knew he was right. But as soon as she tried it, she immediately regretted it. It would be better if they kept their physical contact with each other to a minimum. Of course, there would be instances where it wouldn't be possible, but she'd do what she could to be prepared for it beforehand.

Her grabbing his crotch possessively in front of Star had been a spur of the moment reaction. She'd only done it because she figured a possessive ol' lady would stake her claim quickly and firmly. However, he hadn't been lying when he said Nova's minor cat fight with the stripper made him hard.

The evidence had been *hard* to ignore.

He was attracted to her. She was attracted to him. And that was why she worried.

Also, any attitude she had thrown his way to deter him, he quickly knocked it aside. He didn't get angry. He didn't get insulting. He saw it more as a challenge instead of taking it as a personal insult, like so many men did.

While she had always been attracted to strong men, she avoided over-the-top alpha-holes. Most men *said* they preferred strong, independent women until they dealt with one. Nova was as far from a "yes, dear" type of woman as one could get.

She had played an "obedient" role while undercover with the Russos. Forced to dress to impress, plaster on a smile, make sure she looked good, and say "Yes, dear." She hated every damn second of it and it had left such a bad taste in her mouth, she still had it to this day.

She didn't *need* a man to make her a whole person. She was that on her own, thank you very much. However, that didn't mean she wouldn't consider being with a man who'd complement her.

If and when she found her partner in life, she wanted to be an equal. She would need someone just as accomplished as her. Someone who understood her need to be strong. A partner to stand by her side and would bend over backward to defend her right to stand where she did.

A man who'd support her career and the choices she made in her life. No questions asked.

She had her own thoughts, feelings and desires. The man

in her life would need to respect all of those. In turn, she would do the same for him.

She had zero interest in being the "property of" any man. To be his puppet. To be under his thumb. To be forced to obey or face consequences.

While most of the DAMC women wore one of those cuts on the run today, none of them, not one, had come off to Nova as a simpering, weak female. Not one of those women seemed to have a spine made from anything but steel.

In truth, she'd been impressed with them all.

While she didn't ask them—mostly because she didn't want them to have to defend their choices—she figured wearing those cuts only came down to the biker culture and long-held traditions. If she had to guess, none of them were forced to wear them and they did so of their own free will. That decision alone gave those women more power than someone outside of the MC would see.

If you explored it even deeper, what was the difference between wearing one of those cuts and a wedding band? Wasn't a ring worn on your left hand telling others that you "belonged" to someone else?

Maybe.

And maybe she was overthinking it.

"Are you just going to stand there letting the cold air out of the fridge?"

His deep rumble behind her jerked her from her trance. She usually didn't let her thoughts get the best of her unless she was alone or with people she trusted. Getting lost in her head otherwise could be dangerous.

She shut the door and took a step back, abruptly bumping into Fletch.

His arm shot out and around her, most likely out of instinct, to keep them from getting knocked over. From the unexpected contact, the beer fell free from her fingers, a grunt escaped him and a gasp from her as the bottle hit the linoleum, luckily not shattering.

She stared at it for a second and as she went to pull free, to put space between them, his arm tightened around her middle.

Holding her against him.

Her heartbeat went from zero to sixty to one-hundred-sixty in a flash.

"Nova..." came way too close to her ear and in a way that shot sparks flying through her.

Her breath seized. Her breasts became heavy and her nipples pebbled like the traitors they were. "Let me go," came out way more breathless than it should.

For fuck's sake, at least she didn't moan.

"I just want to make sure you're okay."

"I'm fine." She was *not* fine. He tempted her and that made her far, far, *far* from fine.

He immediately released her and snagged the beer from the floor, setting it on the counter. "Let that settle before you open it or it'll give you a shower."

Nova swallowed her pounding heart back into her chest and nodded. Cursing her shaky fingers, she grabbed the beer, put it back into the fridge before selecting an unshaken one.

"You sure you're okay?" he asked, taking the beer from her and twisting off the top.

"Yes." She needed to pretend the contact with him didn't bother her. With a schooled expression, she pressed a hand to her thumping heart before turning and accepting the opened bottle from him. "Are you?"

"No, Nova..." His deep rumble swirled through her, causing the fine hairs on her body to stand on end. "I'm not."

She lifted her eyes from her beer and met his, her fingers now choking the bottle.

Heat. Interest. That was what she saw in his. She wondered if her own reflected the same, if her attempt to hide it had failed.

In what seemed like slow motion and without breaking eye contact, he pried the beer from her fingers and set it on the counter behind her along with his. "Not even close."

She licked her lips and swallowed again, trying to loosen the tightness in her throat and chest.

"This isn't smart," he murmured.

She clung to her self-control by her fingernails, pretending to not understand what he meant. Fooling herself by believing if she acted as if the attraction between them didn't exist, it would go away. "What isn't? Having a beer?"

His bearded jaw shifted, his nostrils flared and just as she started to step away from him so she could breathe, his hand snaked out to grab her behind the elbow and yank her into him.

The second her mouth opened, his lips collided with hers, driving his tongue inside and stealing her breath.

Stealing her resolve.

His fingers drove into her hair at the back of her head, fisting it, while his other hand curled around her hip, keeping her tightly pressed against him, against his hard body and even harder cock.

As if someone lit a match and threw it onto a gas-soaked pyre, her body exploded into a firestorm. The white-hot flames licked along her skin, singeing her everywhere they touched. Everything on her body pulsed in time with her heartbeat, including her pussy. Blood rushed in her ears and her pulse raced in her neck. The tight control she normally kept was unraveling more with every second.

She needed to end this. To gather her wits and think straight. To break free from his hold.

This *wasn't* smart.

It was careless and could create a huge mess.

A noise bubbled up her throat, but he swallowed it. She went to push him away but did the exact opposite by gripping his face and holding him there. He took her tongue tangling with his as encouragement and deepened the kiss. Claiming her mouth.

Using his hips, he bumped her backward until her ass pressed against the counter behind her. And when she couldn't go any further, when she was pinned between him and the cabinets, he slid his hand from her hip to her ass to heft her up and onto the edge of the counter.

With a moan that rose from deep within her chest, she spread her thighs and wrapped her legs around his waist, pulling him into her even closer.

Until his hard cock was hot and heavy at the apex of her thighs.

Until trickles of wetness turned her clenching pussy slick.

Everything inside her screamed for her to rip off her clothes, rip off his, too, to urge him to take her. To fuck her hard and fast until they both came.

In contrast, her brain kept whispering warnings about them needing to stop. To keep their relationship professional. That this was only the beginning of a long road ahead of them. That this was a start of an in-depth investigation and if they went any further, and if they followed their carnal desires, working together could get awkward. It could even cause it to fail.

She tried to drown out those whispers, but they persisted. They grew and became louder. Got demanding.

They had to live together. Work together. Be a team.

Not get distracted.

Sex was always a distraction.

Every damn time.

But she couldn't pull away. Not because he was holding her, but because she hadn't felt this alive in months. Maybe even a few years.

She'd been forced to pretend to love someone, to be attracted to someone, to be submissive for over a year.

And now... Finally...

Finally she was free from that. Free to choose. Free to enjoy what she hadn't enjoyed for so long. To be herself once again.

When his hand squeezed her breast over her camisole and his thumb lightly strummed back and forth across her aching nipple, her back automatically arched, a clear signal for him to continue.

She dug her fingertips into his cheeks and tilted her head to give them both better access for their tongues to spar.

It had been a long time since she'd enjoyed a kiss. He was so damn good at it and she couldn't get enough.

His kisses were like enjoying a thick, juicy porterhouse steak, meaty and satisfying, versus a dry beef patty left on the grill too long. Not the sandpaper kisses she had been forced to endure on her last assignment.

When he began rocking his erection against the V of her jeans, she matched his energy. Matched his pace. Shifting her hips against his.

She shouldn't encourage this. She should stop this.

But she was caught up in a whirlwind of not giving a damn at this very moment. Because...

She wanted more. She wanted it all.

She wished their clothes would simply vanish. No

barriers existing between them. Nothing stopping them from taking this further. From taking this to the very end.

He ground his cock against her over and over. Even with them both still wearing jeans, he quickly took her to that tipping point. It wouldn't take much more for her to come.

Gripping his ass, she tried to pull him closer, even though it wasn't possible, urging him to rock harder and faster against her. She needed that release.

At any second, she expected their jeans to ignite from the friction, from the heat.

She was so close.

But still too far...

Before she could urge him to take this further. To shove her over the finish line...

He turned solid against her and pulled his mouth from hers.

Damn. She had been teetering on that narrow edge. She had been only one tiny push away from falling over.

Disappointed, she opened her eyes. His face was turned away, his eyes squeezed shut, his chest heaving. The line of his jaw sharp enough to cut glass.

Most likely, he'd been about to come, the same as her.

But he stopped.

He'd been stronger than her.

When he turned back, when his eyes opened, still full of heat but now mixed with confusion, he pressed his forehead to hers as both of them continued to pant.

"Jesus fuck," he breathed. "This is a bad, *bad* idea, Nova. We can't do this."

She didn't bother to respond. Because if she did...

She'd encourage him to forget this ever happened, then turn around and encourage him to continue.

Reality and desire warred within her.

Her head warned her this was a terrible idea. Her body told her otherwise.

He had awakened something inside her that had been lying dormant for months, if not the last couple of years.

Everything she did with Russo, so her cover wouldn't be blown, forced her to detach her body from her mind to deal with it. Russo was too selfish and narcissistic to even be aware of her lack of presence and response. Even the pure hatred in her eyes.

She despised every fucking second of it. And when it was over...

When the job was over...

She rid herself of the ball of disgust and rage with revenge.

She brushed off those moments and vowed to never deal with anything like that again.

Succeeding in her career, getting those hard-earned accolades, was not worth her sanity and self-respect. It was not worth the long, hot showers and raw skin when she scrubbed away his touches. It was not worth all the makeup she had to use to cover the bruises.

When Fletch finally stepped back, freeing himself from her hold, he avoided her eyes. "This is a bad, bad, *baaaaaad* fucking idea."

"Of course it is."

"Tell me you don't want me."

He was asking for the impossible. "I... can't. It would be a lie."

"Tell me anyway." He demanded in a voice rough and raw, a tone mixed with anger and frustration.

Lying was a part of her job. She could do it. For him and for her.

To keep this undercover assignment on track.

Just say it, Nova, say it. Then convince yourself that your lie is the truth. "I don't want you."

She gave him the answer he wanted but also, in truth, the one he didn't.

"I don't want you, either. It would be a huge mistake. One that could fuck up everything."

"And what you just said wasn't a lie."

"We both know that."

"Yes."

"This can't happen."

"Agreed."

"It was a moment of weakness. That's all." He dropped his head and rubbed at his forehead. "I'm going to take my beer and go to bed. Forget this ever happened."

Another lie. Neither of them would forget it. "That would be for the best."

He tipped his head back and with his eyes tipped upward, he ground a hand back and forth on the back of his neck. "That's what I'm going to do. You should do the same."

"I need to shower."

"Give me five first."

She wasn't sure if he saw her nod.

Still avoiding her eyes, he snagged his beer, turned and took long, quick strides out of the kitchen.

Nova stayed where she was and slowly drank her beer, giving him more than five minutes. She kept an ear open and when she finally heard his bedroom door close, she waited a little longer to make sure he didn't change his mind.

Once she drained the rest of her beer, she tossed the bottle into the trash and went to take a very cold shower.

Nova couldn't sleep. Instead, she stared up at the ceiling wide awake.

The cold shower she took did little to stop the replay of that kiss in the kitchen. It did little to slow the rush of unadulterated hunger every time she remembered the thrust of Fletch's cock against her. It did little to cool the smoldering heat at her center.

It did little to tamp down her imagination of what would've happened if Fletch hadn't been strong enough to veer off the dangerous path they'd been barreling down.

Thank fuck he did.

It had been a moment of weakness for her. Well, quite a few moments. And she hadn't been proud of how she reacted to him.

Stay on course. Stay professional. Stay focused.

That needed to be her mantra.

Along with "keep a cool head and keep him an arm's length away."

For her own good.

For his, too.

He was probably in his bed across the hall unbothered by the whole thing. Most likely, he'd finished his beer and instantly fallen asleep.

Unlike her.

Maybe if she took matters into her own hand, she'd be able to dull the sharp edge she'd been skirting and she'd finally get some rest.

She would need it. Tomorrow morning she was scheduled to report for duty at the Shadow Valley Pawn. Keeping her eyes and ears open would be difficult to do if her ass was dragging.

So, yes, she needed to finish what Fletch started and finally get some sleep.

Slipping her hand into her tank top, she brushed her palm over both nipples and slid her other hand down her stomach and into her boxers.

Despite her shower, her pussy was once again slick. All because her thoughts about the man on the other side of two closed doors. It wouldn't take much to get up and go across the hall, climb into his bed and finish what they started.

Would he push her away again? Or would he jump on her offer?

Don't move from this bed, Nova. It's safer this way. If you go to him, all you'll feel tomorrow is regret.

With her middle finger, she slowly stroked along her slit, occasionally dipping her finger inside.

She closed her eyes and twisted one nipple between her fingers, then the other. Imagining it was his hands squeezing, his fingers tweaking. His mouth pulling on her breasts, his teeth scraping over the very tips.

She cried out as she pinched one nipple harder and slid two fingers deep inside her. Driving them into her own wetness.

She plunged her fingers in and out, smashing her clit with her thumb. Pressing, circling, over and over.

This would be quick and dirty. The goal only to bring her to orgasm.

To wipe her mind free of how much she wanted the man asleep in his bed.

Her back arched as she began to fuck herself in a frenzy.

"Yes... yes... *yes*... Oh please... *yessssss*," she moaned.

Chapter Thirteen

"YES... YES... YES... OH PLEASE... YESSSSSS."

No.

No.

Goddamn it. No!

Why the fuck was she doing this to him? Didn't she know the walls were paper thin? That he could hear every gasp, every moan and every damn cry? He could hear the fucking bed squeaking?

This was worse than torture.

It was fucking criminal.

Wrapping his pillow around his head, he attempted to drown out the sound.

Of Nova touching herself.

Of her bringing herself to orgasm.

He was so damn hard, it was excruciating.

Should he go over there and finish what she started? Would she want that or would she tell him to fuck off?

He hadn't been lying when he told her, as well as himself,

that hooking up would be a huge mistake. It would create problems. Possibly even interfere with their investigation.

He'd been right to break up what they'd been doing in the kitchen. Even when every cell in his body vetoed him doing so.

Now she was being the smart one and taking care of business on her own. He needed to take a page from her book and do the same. Maybe if he pulled one off he could finally get some sleep. Forget about the woman across the hall and how hard he was for her.

With a frustrated groan, he whipped the pillow and it landed somewhere in the dark.

Without hesitation, he shoved his boxer briefs down far enough to fist his pulsing cock. A string of precum clung to the pad of his thumb for a second before it broke and he rubbed the natural lubricant over the crown. Then he began to pump, holding his breath so he could hear her race toward her own orgasm.

He imagined her making those same noises as he drove his cock into her over and over. In his mind's eye, he could see her meeting him thrust for thrust. Encouraging him to fuck her harder by using her words, her fingers, her teeth.

Soon he couldn't hear her over the roar of his own racing pulse. He had no idea if she came yet. When his lungs began to fight for his next breath, he released the one he was holding.

He stroked his rock hard length from root to rim in a frenzied pace.

Jesus fucking Christ. He didn't want to fuck his fist. He wanted to fuck her.

He wanted that greedy little mouth on him everywhere.

He wanted his all over her, too. He wanted to taste her

pussy. He wanted to pull those tightly puckered nipples into his mouth and suck them as hard as he could.

He wanted to lick down the line of her tattooed spine all the way to her ass crease and then continue even further.

He wanted to taste her everywhere.

Touch every fucking inch.

Leave marks along her flesh.

Bury himself deep and once she pulsated around his cock, fill her with cum.

That was what he wanted. That wasn't what he was getting.

Instead, it was his own hand on his own dick in his own room.

Because he was trying to do the right fucking thing.

And the right thing meant not touching Nova and only touching himself.

He switched his grip on his cock from underhanded to overhand and stroked even faster.

The pressure built and he didn't slow down until he was right there...

At the breaking point.

With one last upstroke, he scrambled to cup his other hand around the pulsing head and, with a grunt-turned-groan, captured the warm, silky strings of cum in his palm.

When it was over, his head flopped back to the bed and he lay there with a palmful of warm DNA until his breathing went back to normal, until his heart slowed, until sanity and reality returned.

With his eyelids now heavy and sleep beginning to pull at him, he rolled to sit at the edge of the bed, pulling tissues from the box on the nightstand. He wiped his hand, then used another tissue to clean off his now deflated cock before shifting his boxers back into place.

He needed to go clean up because despite using tissues, his hands were sticky and jerking off had made a mess.

He fought the urge to curl up in the sheets and let his exhaustion pull him under. He wished like fuck that this bedroom had its own bathroom.

Listening carefully again to make sure she wasn't up and about, he heard nothing but his own breathing.

Crumpling the used tissues into a ball, he rose to his feet, didn't bother to turn on the light and carefully opened the door. He took another second to listen, but all was quiet and Nova's bedroom door was shut completely.

Thank fuck.

With no threat of running into her, he relaxed a little and padded barefoot quickly and quietly down the hallway to the only bathroom in the apartment. He paused when he noticed light spilling out into the hallway from the slightly ajar bathroom door.

She must have forgotten to turn it off after her shower. He reluctantly admitted that Nova had been right when she bitched about men leaving the lights on. It was in their DNA. But, apparently, she had the same bad habit.

Or maybe she left it on as a "night light" to assist finding the bathroom in a dark apartment that neither of them were overly familiar with.

The only saving grace with wasting electricity was the fact that neither of them were footing the bill. The government was.

He shoved the door open and froze with one foot over the threshold.

. . .

WITH BOTH HANDS braced on the sink, Nova jerked sharply when the bathroom door was suddenly and unexpectedly pushed open.

She had been staring at herself in the mirror, not only contemplating life in general, but what happened in the kitchen and how to avoid that happening in the future. Especially since they'd be working closely together for weeks, if not months.

Now she stared at Fletch in only a pair of snug boxer briefs as he stood there, his eyes wide and his mouth gaping at finding her in the bathroom. "Shit."

"Shit" is right.

"Sorry," he mumbled. "Didn't know you were in here. I thought you left the light on."

"Usually when the light's on, it's a good indicator that someone is occupying that space," she told him needlessly.

"What are you doing?"

"I was..." *Washing my hands after masturbating.* She choked down that explanation and finished with, "I had to pee. What are you doing up?"

"I have to piss."

"Then, I'll leave you to it." When she turned to leave, her eyes flicked down to the wad of tissues balled up in his hand before they returned to his poker face. She tipped her head to the side and held his gaze. "Allergies?"

"They've been acting up lately."

"You haven't sneezed or coughed all day."

"I was just blowing my..."

She lifted one eyebrow. "Load?"

"Nose." He pushed past her and tossed the tissues into the toilet, flushing it quickly.

"Flushing the evidence, huh?"

"Of my allergies?"

She laughed at his tightly schooled expression. "My allergies were bugging me, too."

"I heard."

What? Oh shit.

"Your allergies caused mine."

She must have been too loud. *Damn it.* "I didn't know allergies were contagious."

"It's kind of like a yawn. One person starts and everyone else around them gets sucked in."

She nodded at his comparison like she was taking it seriously. "Got it. Don't have allergies out in public, otherwise it might cause a rash of them."

"It might cause a flash mob of people suddenly sneezing."

Her eyes flicked to the toilet. "Is that what you call it? Sneezing?"

He grumbled, "I need to wash my hands," and used his hip to nudge her out of the way.

When she had leaned her ass against the vanity to stay out of his path to the toilet, she had ended up blocking him from the sink. She shifted just enough to give him some room but didn't move away completely. "You must've been sneezing a lot if you got it all over your hands."

He shook his head and continued washing.

"I'll be quieter next time," she promised. "I didn't mean to disturb your sleep."

"You didn't disturb my sleep, Nova." He shut off the water and turned his head until his brown eyes met hers. "You disturbed my sanity."

She raised both eyebrows. "I didn't realize I had that much power."

"Women have more power than we give them credit for."

Wasn't that the fucking truth? She snagged the hand

towel hanging next to the sink and gave it to him. "Well then... I'll let you finish up in peace."

He quickly dried off his hands. "I'm not sure how much peace I'm going to get living in the same apartment as you."

She crossed her arms over her chest and leaned her ass against the vanity again as she considered him and his words. "The truth is, Fletch, Ghost doesn't need an ol' lady. Not all DAMC members have one. If you'd rather I pull myself from this assignment and have Crew put me elsewhere, I can do that. Neither of us can be distracted." And she didn't want to be blamed for putting him at risk for being the cause of his distraction.

He shifted enough to go bare toe to bare toe with her. Only, being this close had caused the earlier combustion in the kitchen. She reminded herself that she should be keeping him at arm's length.

"Do you think I'll be less distracted if I don't know where you are?"

She stared up at him. "What are you talking about?"

"I'll repeat it slower." He leaned in closer. So close that she could see the gold flecks in his irises. "Do you think that not knowing where you are or what you are doing will be less distracting for me?"

He wasn't kidding when he said he'd repeat it slower. The second time, the question had come out as thick and as slow as chilled honey.

Her heart skipped a beat, then began to thump heavily. Her eyes dropped to his throat and she spotted his pulse pounding, too.

He said she disturbed his sanity. Well, that was only fair since he also disturbed hers.

They'd only worked together for two full days so far. They were only at the beginning of what could be a long investigation and if they were having an issue already, she had no idea how this would work for the next few months.

It wouldn't.

Some kind of chemistry existed between them they couldn't deny. This wasn't something they'd be able to simply set aside and pretend it didn't exist. So, either they had to accept it and possibly even act on it... Or they needed to go in different directions.

Like her extracting herself from this particular job.

Because, as she reminded him, they needed to concentrate on the task at hand. Distractions could be dangerous. One slip could even be fatal when dealing with an outlaw MC trying to protect themselves and their illegal enterprise. A very lucrative source of income the task force was trying to take away.

"I've been a special agent for almost eight years, Fletch. Why do you think I'd need anyone worrying about me now?"

"I didn't say *you* would need it, but that still doesn't mean *I* wouldn't worry about you."

Her eyebrows pinned together. "I don't understand why."

He closed his eyes for a second and inhaled deeply. When he opened them again, he confessed, "For fuck's sake, I wish I knew why. I've never had an urge to," he shook his head, "protect someone before, especially someone who I know damn well can take care of themselves."

"See? There's no reason to worry about me."

"I know there's no sane fucking reason, Nova, but my brain isn't being reasonable right now."

That made two of them. Since they were standing so closely, she had the urge to taste his lips all over again. Of course, this was after she told herself over and over that they needed to remain professional with each other and nothing more.

"So, the question remains... do you want me to pull myself from this assignment?"

He stared at her and his chest slowly inflated, then deflated just as slowly. "That's not what I want."

"What do you want?" she whispered, watching his Adam's apple slowly slide up his throat and then back down when he swallowed.

"I want to work with a partner I trust. A partner I respect. A partner who knows what the hell she's doing."

"And for you, I'm all that?"

He nodded. "That's not the problem."

She waited.

"The problem is that's not all I want."

She asked, "What do you want?" even though she already knew his answer.

"You."

"Then the next question is: What do we do about it?"

"It's impossible to ignore."

That wasn't a good enough answer. In fact, it was a deflection. "This is the last time I'm going to ask this: Do you want me to extract myself from this particular assignment to make it easier for you to do your job?"

"I won't be able to stop thinking about you, Nova, whether you're here or elsewhere."

That confession seemed to be painful for him. Maybe even a bit frustrating.

Her fear was, if she walked away from this assignment, this apartment and even Fletch, that she wouldn't be able to stop thinking about him, either.

How can two people get caught up in each other so quickly?

It made no sense to her.

Plain and simple, it had to be lust. But acting on it could make it worse.

"Then, tell me the solution."

"This is my solution..." His hand shot out and curved around the back of her neck, closing the slight gap between them.

Him taking her mouth, just like he had in the kitchen, caused her to groan. She wrapped her hand around the back of his head, holding him, encouraging him to take the kiss even deeper.

But he didn't. Instead, he quickly ended it, hooked his thumbs into her boxer briefs and shoved them down her thighs until they free-fell to her feet.

"I can smell your hot, sweet scent and now I can't fucking wait to taste it."

Jesus. The rawness in his voice shot a shiver through her.

With a very determined look in his eyes and without another word, he grabbed her waist and set her on the edge of the vanity, shoved her thighs apart and dropped to his knees.

Was he going to...

Oh yes, he was...

Pushing her legs apart even wider, he licked a line along the inside of one thigh until he got to the apex, then shoved his face against her pussy, his mouth clamping onto her clit. Her hips jumped as he sucked it hard, not even close to being tender.

The man was on a mission.

He was taking what he wanted with zero apologies.

She had no plans on asking him for one, anyway.

This was what she had thought about earlier as she masturbated. Maybe not doing it in the bathroom, but everything else...

Oh yeah.

She curled the fingers of both hands into his hair, and fisted them tightly to keep him there. Tilting her hips, she gave him even better access while also encouraging him to lick more, suck harder and fuck her with his tongue.

He did that and more.

Sliding two fingers into her wetness, he drove them in and out. She had just done this herself not long ago, but, admittedly, him doing it was so much better.

Especially with his lips on her.

That was the icing on her cake.

He sucked each labia into his mouth so roughly, she whimpered, but did not tell him to stop.

Clearly, this was a man wanting to pleasure her first before he took his own. He didn't *have* to drop to his knees on the bathroom floor.

He *wanted* to.

He wasn't making this all about himself. She was a part of the equation.

What he was doing made her realize he was the type of man who got pleasure out of giving it. That shouldn't be a novel concept when it came to sex.

She had no choice in choosing her last "lover." And she was so damn thankful he never ended up being an actual lover at all. What she had to do to keep from having her cover blown had been completely involuntary and part of the job.

If she hadn't, she would have failed. And for her, failure was not an option.

But with Fletch, having sex with him was *her* choice. She craved him.

Even if it would make a complete fucking mess when it came to them working together.

Even if the bathroom wasn't the most ideal situation for what they were doing.

Even if...

No. None of that mattered. What Fletch was doing to her was the only thing that mattered right now.

And what he was doing was...

Her head dropped back, her mouth opened and...

An orgasm tore through her, curling her toes. Her cries making him dig the fingers of his left hand into her thigh even harder, to the point of pain.

He slipped his other fingers from her still pulsing pussy but kept stroking her with his tongue, more gently now to capture the results of his handiwork, until the last wave of her climax faded away.

When it did, he rose to his feet. She opened her eyes and they stared at each other. She only imagined his look of surprise, bordering on shock, was mirrored on hers.

She whispered the only thing that came to her because that single word said it all. "Damn."

His lips and the short wiry hairs surrounding them were shiny and she was sure if she kissed him, she would taste herself. But her mind wasn't on kissing him right now. It was on the hard length pressing against his skin-tight boxer briefs.

And the dark spot forming on the fabric where the tip was.

When she lifted her eyes, he said, "Know this is fucking wrong."

"Of course it is, but we're going to do it anyway." Unless one of them found the strength to walk away like he had earlier.

A tortured expression crossed his face. "Tell me no, Nova. Tell me no so I can walk out of this bathroom and avoid this mistake."

Yes, it most likely would be a mistake but no, she didn't want anything else. "I won't."

"You want this as much as me."

Untrue. Because she didn't want this as much as he did, she wanted it... "More."

"Impossible."

"Prove it to me, then," she challenged him.

He nodded slightly and when a look of concern crossed his face, he reached past her to pull open the mirrored medicine cabinet. "Oh, thank fuck."

When a strip of three condoms appeared in his hand, "thank fuck" also whispered through her head. She might be on birth control, but that didn't mean she wanted to fuck a man she hardly knew without more protection than what her Pill provided.

"They're not expired, right?" Because who knew when they were put in the cabinet or by whom.

He scanned them. "No. If they were, I have more in my bag."

A bag in another room. And if he left the bathroom right now, one or both of them could come to their senses and stop this whole scenario in its tracks.

On one hand, she was thankful the condoms weren't expired, on the other... It might have been better if they were.

But the truth was, she wanted to be with someone of her choice. Not someone she had to for her job. She had only sold her soul to the devil so she could turn around and defeat him.

Which she did. Successfully. But the win had been bittersweet.

So yes, she was ready to selfishly have sex and enjoy it. Even if it was in a bathroom while perching on a vanity and could very well cause complications because of the man she was about to do it with.

Deep in her gut, she knew if it wasn't tonight, and she remained undercover with Fletch, it would happen eventually. They might as well get it out of the way, so they could concentrate on their assigned task.

That was what she told herself as Fletch tore a wrapper free from the strip and set it on the vanity next to her.

"Second thoughts?" he asked, setting the other two condoms aside on top of the toilet tank.

"No. You?"

"Of course you're having them. So am I. But that's not going to change the outcome, is it?"

She lifted her gaze from his erection and smiled at him. "Apparently not."

Chapter Fourteen

Tonight, she was reclaiming her sexuality. She was taking back what she had set aside in the last couple of years because of her job. So, to hell with the risk when it came to having sex with Fletch. It was better to take a risk now than later regret not taking it at all.

Yes, afterward, she might want him even more. On the other hand, it might get him out of her system and she wouldn't want him ever again. But she wouldn't know that answer until they moved forward.

"Let's do this," she whispered. She was so fucking ready.

"Let's do this," he echoed with a softness his brown eyes did not hold. They were intense as he stared at her still waiting on the edge of the vanity.

Still naked from the waist down. Her thighs still parted, her pussy still slick.

All because of him.

She picked up the condom sitting by her hand and held it between them.

He shook his head. "In a sec."

She didn't want to wait. She wanted him now before she ended up talking herself out of it.

If she did that, she'd end up lying in bed kicking herself for walking away and not taking what she wanted. She'd remain restless and wanting when, instead, all she had to do was...

Well, all she had to *do* was Fletch.

"What are you waiting for?"

"I'm not waiting," he murmured, focused on her mouth. When she licked her lips, the heat flared in his eyes.

"Then, if you're not waiting, what are you doing?"

"This..." Once again he took her lips like military troops rushing a hill needing to be conquered.

After exploring every recess of her mouth, he pulled back only enough to suck on her bottom lip for a few seconds before releasing it, leaving it swollen and throbbing. Because once again, he was not gentle.

Not that she wanted him to be.

She didn't want it to be safe or boring. She wanted it rough, raw and on the edge. To kickstart her dormant desires.

Nipping along her jawline, he occasionally caught her skin with his teeth as he went. When she tilted her head back to give him better access, he traced the tip of his tongue down her neck, then sucked at the hollow of her throat, vibrating the delicate skin there with his groan.

He didn't stop there, though. No, he kept moving, biting along her left shoulder, pausing here and there to sink his teeth deeper into her flesh, causing her to gasp at the pain sending an avalanche of endorphins through her.

He kept going, drawing his tongue along her left clavicle, then running his skilled lips along the right side until he once again dipped his tongue into that very vulnerable spot at the base of her throat.

While he did that, he slipped one side of her ribbed tank top off her shoulder, then the other, before hooking a finger in the loose neckline to draw it down slowly, his mouth now following along as it lowered. He didn't stop until both breasts were exposed and his warm breath swept over the aching, puckered nipples.

His lips plucked at each tip before surrounding them, sucking and pulling. Causing her back to arch and shoving her breast deeper into his mouth while he cupped the other, kneading and pinching.

Her breath caught and she shuddered when his teeth sank into the top curve.

That bite would leave a mark.

After he did the same with the other one, she groaned, sliding her fingers into his hair, an unspoken request for him to do it again.

He did.

When she tipped her head down, he raised his eyes to meet hers, and did it once more. All while watching her reaction she didn't bother to hide.

With a satisfied smile, he bared his teeth and slowly sank them again into her tender flesh. She twitched at the sharp, but pleasurable, pain, then he ran his tongue over each bite before standing and studying his handiwork.

She squeezed her breasts together as best as she could and stroked her thumbs over two of the red marks.

"You like that." His pleasure was apparent in his low voice and thick words.

"I don't dislike it," she whispered.

He took a half-step back and in no rush, shoved his boxer briefs down his muscular, lightly-haired legs until they joined hers on the linoleum floor.

A glistening pearl of precum clung precariously to the

very tip of his thick cock. His erection bobbed when he leaned closer and plucked the condom from where it was sandwiched between her palm and her breast. After tearing the latex disc free from the wrapper, he took his time rolling it down his hard length, adding a few extra strokes with his fist.

Adjusting his position once more, he pressed the head of his cock against her slick folds before hesitating. "You can say no, Nova. We can stop right here."

"If I wanted that, I would've stopped you before you went to your knees."

"Don't think this is a case of *quid pro quo*. You owe me nothing."

Damn, she'd been wrong by initially pegging him as a cocky asshole. Tonight he was proving otherwise.

She wrapped her legs around his hips and tilted her own. "I do, since you're giving me my desire back."

She wasn't sure if desire was the right word, especially when his brow furrowed.

Not surprising, he opened his mouth to question her. She gave her head a small shake and pressed her fingertip to his lips. Because, *for fuck's sake*, she didn't want to explain right now how she had tucked away her sexual desires for longer than she liked. Solely for her career.

"I want you. That's all you need to know," she said simply and hoped he'd accept that answer.

While the wrinkles in his forehead smoothed out, the concern still remained in his eyes.

"Enough talking," she said.

"Is that my signal to get to it?"

"No, this is..." Wrapping her hand around the back of his neck, she pulled his face closer, until they were practically nose to nose. She demanded slowly and very clearly, "Fuck me."

His crooked smile was sexy as hell and he wasted no time shifting slightly to realign his cock. "You don't have to tell me twice."

She certainly didn't. She was wet enough that when he thrust forward, he was met with no resistance. A sigh slipped from her as he filled her completely, his eyes locked on hers when he stilled for a second.

He took one breath. Two. Then...

He moved.

With one hand gripping her hip tightly and the other curled around the back of her neck, his hips flexed smoothly as he drove himself like his cock was the hammer and she was the nail.

"Yes... That's it," she moaned, accepting and savoring every inch.

His fingers dug deeper into her neck and hip, holding her in place as he pounded her over and over, a soft grunt escaping him with each thrust.

Fletch was a man on a simple, but determined, mission. To bring them both to orgasm.

His eyes lifted and he looked beyond her. She didn't need to turn to see what he was looking at.

The mirror behind her.

He was watching himself fuck her.

With flared nostrils and bared teeth, his pace didn't slow once as he powered in and out of her, her body jerking with each slam of his hips.

This was what she needed. *This* was what she desired.

This was what she had missed.

She needed a good fuck. Needed to get her blood rushing, her juices flowing. To feel alive again but to also lose herself for a short time.

To forget everything else outside of their self-made

bubble in the bathroom. Of course, the bubble wouldn't last. It would quickly burst and real life would rush back in, but she wanted to enjoy it while it remained whole.

Except that he slowed. Was suddenly no longer so frantic or demanding.

Worse, without warning, he pulled out.

"What—" she started, worried he'd had a change of heart.

He pulled her off the vanity and to her feet. Without a word, he spun her around and she realized why.

The mirror. Smaller than the one above his bed but large enough to see themselves from their hips up.

He brushed the head of his cock back and forth through her folds and then held it in place. "Brace yourself," he warned.

She planted her hands along the edge of the vanity and tipped her ass up, preparing herself for his next onslaught.

With a thrust forward, he once again filled her completely.

Now they could both watch him fuck her.

Seeing his larger body behind her made her pussy squeeze his cock.

"Like a tight cocoon made of hot silk," he murmured when their eyes locked in the mirror.

He began to move again. This time not so quickly, not so demanding.

He took his time, watching her face. Watching his own movement.

She snagged her bottom lip between her teeth and with hooded eyes, she watched his face, watched his movement, too.

This would be so much better in his bed and under that huge mirror. But having sex in his space might seem too personal. Unlike what should be a quick fuck in a neutral zone, the bathroom.

This should've been short, dirty and intense. Simply a fast, satisfying scratch for their itch.

Over and done within minutes.

Instead, he was unexpectedly drawing it out with his current pace. She wanted to complain, but honestly, she couldn't. He was good with his hips, even better with his cock and his lips...

She couldn't get enough of his mouth. So much better than those dry, condescending kisses Frank Russo, Sr. had continually pressed to her cheek, her temple, her mouth.

A patronizing pat on the ass, a kiss to her bare shoulder, or a painful squeeze to her hand to remind her to be seen but not heard.

He did not like her speaking up or asking questions.

She learned quickly to keep her mouth shut and only listen.

But then, that was the reason she remained in his presence. To listen. To witness. To learn. To make notes and collect evidence.

He was the boss. Her opinions were unneeded and unwanted. She learned quickly to keep them to herself or she'd pay for being outspoken.

The less she said, the better.

The less she said, the more she was forgotten.

The less she said, the more she blended in with the background.

A fatal mistake for Frank Sr.

She was treated as arm candy. A trophy. A way to prove to his "family" that the don was still capable of bagging an attractive mistress almost forty years his junior. One willing to be intimate with him.

Even though that was farthest from the truth.

Secrets and lies were the foundations of the Russo organization.

Loyalty among them only smoke and mirrors.

In the end, she did what she needed to do. Smile and act empty-headed. Appreciate all the "gifts" he bought her. Simper and fawn over him when he was generous. Bite her tongue when she was degraded, insulted or treated like property.

In the world Frank ruled, side-pieces, like children, were meant to be seen, not heard. They had no valuable opinions and if a woman in his presence had one, it would often be beaten out of her. She would be "reminded" of her place.

The Russos liked their women meek and mild. Quiet and subservient.

Nova had been considered nothing but decoration.

Decoration who also kept many secrets and told just as many lies.

In the end, her patience and tolerance paid off...

She ripped herself free from her spiraling thoughts and forced herself to come back to the present. To the bathroom and to Fletch.

"Lost you for a minute," he grumbled.

She wanted to tell him it was because he was going too slow, giving her time to think and not only act.

But the truth was, even though she had stepped out of her head and the game, her physical response had not. She had learned to separate the mental and physical a long time ago. That skill came in handy when she had become Russo's *goomah.*

It also made that particular undercover assignment successful because it kept her sane. It prevented her from killing Russo Sr. during the night as he obnoxiously snored on the pillow next to her because he was too fucking proud to wear his goddamn CPAP.

However, sex with Fletch wasn't a part of the job. It wasn't needed to keep from blowing her cover.

Having the ability to be able to choose what to do—or not do—might seem simple enough and even be taken for granted, but when that decision was stripped from someone and they were forced to live under someone else's thumb, it left behind a feeling of powerlessness. Even helplessness and hopelessness.

"With me," came the gruff order.

Gripping her hair, Fletch used it to yank her head back, arching her neck, exposing her throat. The pull on her hair rough enough to make her scalp tingle.

A flush rose from her chest and climbed up her throat. Her tank top had gathered at her waist, leaving her breasts completely exposed. She certainly didn't need the mirror to see how puckered her nipples were. They were beaded to the point of discomfort.

"Nova." Her name rumbled from deep inside him and spread goosebumps along every inch of her skin. He pinned his cheek to hers and their eyes met once again in the mirror. "Keep them open. You need to stay with me. Otherwise, I'm ending this right now."

Why would he care if she was fully present or not? He was getting what he wanted. Wasn't he?

Even so, his comment surprised her. "You could just end this now?"

He paused and removed his cheek from hers. "I want to have sex with you. Not some random body. *You*, Nova. And if you're somewhere else mentally, you're only going through the motions. That's not what I want."

She frowned at the tinge of annoyance in his voice. She assured him, "I'm not. I want this, too."

"That's what I thought, but something changed."

"I got lost in my head for a second, that's all. I'm back."

"Are you going to be one hundred percent present?"

It hit her then that she'd never been with a man before who actually cared about that. As long as they were getting what they wanted, they pretty much assumed she was getting the same. "Yes."

He stared at her in the mirror for a few seconds and when she didn't avoid his gaze, he gave a single nod, adjusted his stance and began to fuck her once more.

When her heavy eyelids began to droop, he demanded sharply, "With me."

She wanted to get lost in what he was doing but he was worried she'd only get lost. Again, something she never dealt with before.

She gritted her teeth and demanded, "Fuck me. Give it to me hard and fast. Give me everything you've got."

"I can't give you everything. We're in a goddamn bathroom."

She could see his anger and frustration surfacing but she had no idea why since this was only supposed to be a quick, *let's-get-it-out-of-the-way* fuck. "Then give me whatever you can."

"Fine. You want it hard and fast? I'll give it to you hard and fast. Told you to brace. Better heed my warning."

Before she could, he slammed into her so hard, she jerked forward, almost smacking her forehead into the mirror.

She quickly adjusted her grip on the counter and tipped her ass up even more to take the brunt of him. He pounded her so hard the slap of their skin filled the small room, accompanied by their heavy breathing.

The rhythmic sound became hypnotic and she began to lose herself again. But not in the past this time...

In what Fletch was doing. What he was pulling from her.

"That's it. Like that," she groaned. "Make me come."

The added guttural grunt on the end of each thrust caused searing white heat to sweep through her like a fiery tornado.

With a grimace, he wrapped his hand around her throat, sliding it up until her head was tipped all the way back. She still managed to keep her eyes on the mirror so she could watch them.

Because watching them fuck was stoking that fire inside her even more. The same as it was him.

After releasing her hip, he slapped her ass cheek sharply before sliding his hand around to her belly and then down to her pussy.

He grabbed her mound like he owned it, squeezing it roughly before he touched where they were connected. After gathering some of the wetness with his thumb, he began to circle and press on her pulsing nub, driving her to distraction.

She matched his movements by rocking back and forth and occasionally grinding against him to drive him even deeper.

His breath shuddered and, even though his hand wasn't gripping her throat tightly, his fingertips dug into her neck. "Fuck, Nova," he groaned. "Fuck. You have to come soon."

"Keep going," she encouraged him. "Keep... going."

"No shit, but you need to fucking come. This isn't a drill, this is a real emergency."

She would've laughed if he didn't look and sound so damn serious.

When she pushed away from the counter, she shoved him back a step. She quickly disengaged from him and turned around, once again perching her ass on the edge of the small counter surrounding the sink. "Fuck me."

Without hesitation, he speared his rock-hard cock into her again. But this time he wrapped an arm around her back and held her close, shoving his face into her neck, his rapid pants sweeping over her heated skin, causing goosebumps.

She grabbed his ass, feeling his glutes bunching beneath her fingers, and spread her thighs even more. His other arm curled around her hips and he drove deep once more, grinding his cock, smashing her clit. She threw her head back and cried out his name as she began to race up the mountain as her orgasm built.

"You're so fucking wet," he groaned into her neck. "I want to feel you soaking my cock."

To do that he'd need to remove the condom and that wasn't going to happen.

But she was so damn close to coming... With a tug on his ass, she smashed her pussy against him and his balls against her anus.

Then she was there... She reached the peak and flung herself over the other side. Her climax not only rippled around his cock, the intense waves ripped through her like a tsunami. "Yes. Fuck yes."

With a low groan, Fletch pulled his face from her neck and captured her mouth once again, while stabbing his cock into her one... two... three more times. And on the third, he yanked his mouth from hers, pinned their damp cheeks together and stayed fully seated as his cock pulsed inside her, almost bringing her to another orgasm.

When he was done coming and when the last wave of her orgasm faded away, they remained wrapped in each other's arm while trying to catch their breath in the bathroom of an apartment being used as a cover for their task force assignment.

The second he jerked sharply against her, she knew that wasn't a result from him coming, but because reality had hit him and hit him hard.

The same way it was hitting her.

Like a sledgehammer to their chests.

They had let their sexual attraction take over instead of using their damn heads and following common sense.

She worried that if sex was this satisfying with him against a bathroom sink, all she'd be thinking about in the days, even weeks, to follow was how much better the sex would be in an actual bed.

They were doomed.

She was doomed.

She knew it had been a risk.

The problem was, they were here for an important reason, not to play naked romper room. As she feared, having a sexual relationship with her partner might end up being an unneeded distraction. Even if this ended up being their only time together.

But she couldn't imagine he wouldn't want to do this again. Because even though both of them had just come, she was already thinking about that big bed of his with the large mirror over it.

Not good, Nova. You're not a teenager with some crush. It was dick, not crack.

"Fuck," he finally mumbled, slowly pulling out and releasing his hold on her.

"This was not a good solution," she forced up her throat. Because she needed to be clear they were partners, not lovers, even after what they just did. One of them had to be strong enough to prevent this from happening again. "This was a very bad idea."

His brow furrowed, his lips turned down at the corners and his jaw tightened at her words.

To her, that proved he didn't agree. But it would be better if they kept their relationship strictly professional. At least until the assignment was over.

Yes, that would be for the best.

For both of them.

Even if he didn't agree.

He avoided her eyes as he removed the condom, knotted the open end and tossed it into the small trash can next to the toilet. "Thought it would be a mistake. Guess I was right."

He snagged his boxers from the floor and, without another word or taking the time to pull them on, left the bathroom.

She remained where she stood until she heard his bedroom door close down the hallway. Once she cleaned up again, she headed to bed.

But after what just happened, she doubted she'd get any sleep.

Chapter Fifteen

When the front door buzzer sounded, Nova looked up from cleaning the glass display case at the back of the store near the checkout area. From where she stood, she could see the majority of the pawn shop and keep an eye on customers as they browsed. It also gave her a direct view of anyone entering the store.

She didn't get involved when customers brought in items to pawn since that took a certain knowledge she did not possess. Instead, she did menial stuff like cleaning the smudges off the glass cases and ringing up customers' purchases.

Ivy, Jag Jamison's wife and ol' lady, normally worked in the office behind the counter area, doing whatever she did for the business. The stunning redhead told Nova she maintained the websites for all the DAMC businesses and did most of the basic bookkeeping for them, as well.

She only filled in on the pawn shop floor and dealt with customers when necessary. Her brother Dex and some other club prospects also worked the floor the same as Nova.

Because of her vantage point, she had no problem seeing the man entering Shadow Valley Pawn.

One Shane Fletcher, aka Ghost.

Even dressing his part as a member of the DAMC, including wearing the club's colors, the man drew eyes wherever he went. Including Nova's, especially since she knew what he looked like underneath those clothes.

He was certainly nothing to "sneeze" at.

After spotting her, he took long, smooth strides down the wide aisle that ran from the front entrance of the pawn shop and split the rows of shelving that held everything imaginable that could be pawned.

Before he made it halfway to her, a redheaded girl, almost an exact clone of her mother, stepped out from one of the rows and blocked his path. He abruptly came to a stop to avoid running into her and glanced down in surprise at Ivy and Jag Jamison's not quite sixteen-year-old daughter.

"Hi! What can I help you with?" Alexis Jamison stared up at him with a gleam in her eye a girl her age shouldn't have when it came to a full-grown man in his thirties.

Honestly, Nova couldn't blame the girl. Fletch was hot as fuck, even though she'd been trying to ignore that fact for the past week. An almost impossible feat.

Fletch raised one eyebrow at the girl, then jerked his chin toward the back of the store. "I'm here to see Kitten."

"Oh! You're Ghost!" she said a little too loudly, poking his name patch on his cut. "Kitten talks about you."

His brown eyes lifted from Lexi and found Nova again. "She does?"

"She was right."

Nova could hear his low rumble from where she stood. "'Bout what?"

"How damn *hot* you are. Too bad you already have an ol' lady."

Clearly, Fletch hadn't been prepared for that statement, but he recovered quickly and smoothly with, "Even if I didn't, you're too young to be an ol' lady."

"I won't be young forever," Lexi assured him with a wink and a whole lot of sass.

Nova groaned under her breath, then turned and gave Ivy a pointed look through the window separating the counter area and Ivy's office. With raised eyebrows, she tipped her head toward Fletch and the woman's very ambitious daughter.

Ivy shot up from her seat and peered out of the office window. Her lips pressed together, she shook her head and, with an annoyed expression, came around to the open office door.

"Lexi!" Ivy yelled.

Fletch's eyes flicked from Ivy to Lexi and back to Ivy. "Gonna take a wild guess that you two are related."

"That's Ivy," Lexi said, flipping a dismissing hand over her shoulder toward her mother.

"Already met her," Fletch informed the teenager, amusement tinging his response.

"You mean *Mom,*" Ivy corrected her with a sigh.

Lexi turned to where Ivy now stood next to Nova, who struggled to keep her own amusement from her face.

The teen rolled her eyes. "That's my *mom,* Ivy."

"That's better," Ivy said. "Now, go back to whatever you were doing. And if I find you hiding in a corner on your phone, I'm taking it away again. For a whole week this time. We're not paying you to make TikTok videos."

The huge smile she previously pointed toward Fletch fell into a tight frown. "I wasn't."

"I'm going to check your account to see what you're posting and when."

"I didn't, Mom!"

"You better not be lying. If you want to earn spending money, then you need to actually *earn* it."

Lexi sighed, slapped on a tight smile, not so flirtatious this time, and said to Fletch, "See you around, Ghost." She disappeared between two rows of shelves.

"Jag needs to remind me again why *he* thought it was a good idea to have kids," Ivy muttered and disappeared back into her office.

Nova rolled her lips under and watched Fletch as he finished his journey to where she stood without being sidetracked again.

"What are you doing here?" she asked him.

"Can't come see my ol' lady?"

Nova lifted her eyebrows in answer.

"You done for the day?"

She glanced up at the clock on the wall. *Damn*, she'd lost track of time. "I guess I am now. Is there something we need to do?"

He tapped his fingers on the display case, leaving marks behind. "Yeah."

She sighed, sprayed the spot with glass cleaner again, making him jerk his hand away, and wiped away the fingerprints with the cloth.

"Anal much?" he grumbled, drying off his wet hand on his jeans.

"No, I haven't done it much."

"N— *Kitten*."

At his tone, she realized maybe teasing him about sex wasn't smart. "It was a joke."

He stared at her, definitely not finding her answer funny.

The past week had been a bit awkward between them. Luckily, the morning after they had sex, Nova had started working at the pawn shop and Fletch at the gun shop, so they were apart most of the day. In the evenings, they would head over to the DAMC's clubhouse to hang out there for a bit, grabbing dinner and some drinks at The Iron Horse Roadhouse. It was the perfect spot to be seen together and, more importantly, wearing their cuts. But they tended to have more conversation with other people than with each other. And, of course, taking the Harley there and back made it impossible for them to talk while they rode, too.

Nova guessed Fletch was still out of sorts after what she said in the bathroom on Sunday.

He had assumed she'd been disappointed in the sex when that was the farthest thing from the truth, but it had been easier to resist him by not dispelling that notion. Plus, with him thinking she didn't want to have sex with him again, he had placed an invisible barrier between them.

Nova glanced around to make sure no one was standing close enough to overhear their conversation. Just to be safe, she lowered her voice anyway to ensure what she said was for his ears only. "By the way, I never told her you were hot."

No way would she tell a girl, only fifteen-and-a-half years old, how hot an adult man was. That was just weird and a bit icky.

"Figured she was stretching the truth, since apparently you don't think I'm hot."

It always surprised her how fragile men could be when it came to their sexual prowess. "I never said that. I just think it's smarter if we don't get involved in that manner." At least while on the task force. "We need to remain professional."

"Then you should've said no, *Kitten,* and not let it get that far."

Of course, he made it her fault. "I thought we were just getting it out of our system so we could think with clear heads," she hissed.

"And we both knew that might be a complete failure." His nostrils flared and his brown eyes became sharp. "Obviously, it was."

"It's only a failure if we allow it to be."

"That why you've been freezin' me out since the bathroom incident?"

The bathroom *incident*? "Look, I'm trying my fucking best here. I'm here to do my damn job, Ghost, not do you."

"Wasn't good enough?"

She sucked in a sharp breath. "Where the hell did you even get that idea?" She lowered her voice. "During... *the incident*, you were even commenting on how," she leaned closer to him, whispering, "wet I was."

She leaned back after getting a whiff of a mix of Hoppe's No. 9, used for cleaning firearms, and a pungent gun oil. Two scents she was very familiar with.

"You kept disappearin' into your head. Coulda been thinkin' 'bout someone else like—"

"If you say Russo, I'm going to kick you in the damn nuts."

"A past lover," he finished.

Are they really going there? Here? In the pawn shop where they were supposed to be a biker and his ol' lady who slept together regularly and not task force partners who shouldn't? "I guarantee you there's not one lover from my past living in my head. And do you seriously need me to prop up your ego?"

One side of his mouth pulled up. "So, you're sayin' I fucked you good."

She released a long sigh, and somehow managed not to

roll her eyes. She deserved a medal for that feat. "Yeah, Ghost, you fucked me good," she whispered sharply. "That doesn't mean we should do it again. It wasn't that you sucked, it's that things between us could get complicated."

"I disagree."

"Then we'll have to agree to disagree."

"What's the major issue with us doin' that again?"

She bugged her eyes out at him. "Do we really need to be talking about this *here*?"

"You're right. We shouldn't. You're done with your shift. Let's go." He grabbed her arm and, even though they were on opposite sides of the display case, he began to pull her around to the end.

When she tried to jerk her arm free, he only tightened his hold. "I have to tell Ivy I'm leaving."

"Ivy, Kitten's leavin'," he yelled, not stopping until he had dragged her through the store and out into the late afternoon sun.

Since the pawn shop had no windows, she blinked at the shock of brightness as he kept pulling her through the side parking lot toward the apartment stairs. She had to walk faster to keep up. If she didn't and she stumbled, he probably wouldn't care and she'd end up with road rash.

"Slow down, Ghost!"

"Keep up, Kitten," he growled.

"Why are you in such a damn rush?" She tried to slow him down by leaning back. She failed.

"'Cause I want a fuckin' answer."

"Another thirty seconds isn't going to change that answer."

Without warning, he released her wrist at the bottom of the stairs and with jerky movements, hiked up them, jammed his key into the lock and shoved the door open.

She took a calming breath at the bottom of the metal stairway and shook her head before following him up and inside.

As soon as she shut the door behind her, he spun on her with his hands clamped on his hips and his expression not showing any kind of happy. That made two of them. "What's the major issue of us doing that again?"

"You know why, so I shouldn't need to answer that, but I will since you're purposely being obtuse. I need to focus on being Kitten. You need to focus on being Ghost. We both need to focus on gathering intel on the Demons."

"And you can't focus because we fucked? Why?"

"Because..."

"Because what happened in that bathroom keeps replaying in your head twenty-four seven." That wasn't posed as a question, he stated it as fact.

A fact she couldn't deny. She slowly pulled in a breath through her nostrils.

"Wouldn't it be less distracting if we don't withhold what we want? *That's* what's making me lose my damn mind, Nova. I fucking want you and I'm not afraid to tell you that I can't fucking stop thinking about what we did and how much I want to do it again. *That's* my fucking distraction. Not the sex part. The *not* having sex part. If I knew I would get to fuck you later tonight, maybe I wouldn't be so goddamn obsessed with you and this whole fucking thing. Ever think of that?"

Hold on... Did he just admit he was obsessed with her?

Who admitted that kind of shit?

He ignored her gaping mouth and continued, "We've been dancing around each other all week. We've been avoiding this discussion. But we need to move on so we *both* can focus on our jobs."

"And you think moving on is having sex again?"

"Yep."

Of course he would. "You also think by doing that it will help us focus, despite the fact we both worried having sex would be the actual distraction?"

"Yep."

Okay, he had a point, but... "Here's my concern... If we keep having sex, are you going to get possessive? Are you going to get overly protective of me? Because I've dealt with that shit before and I'm telling you now... I don't like it. I don't need it. I am my own woman. I can also take care of myself."

"Yeah, Nova, I got that. I can't say I won't be protective because I would be that way with any partner of mine. I would expect for you to have my back, too."

"Having your back is different from you stepping in when you think I can't handle a situation solely due to me being a woman. I'm warning you now, that won't fly with me. I didn't get to where I am in my career because I need some man to rush in and save me. That's a problem I've had in the past. We sleep with a guy and suddenly they believe we can't function without them. That getting dick turns us into helpless simps."

"The confidence you ooze is what caught my attention, Nova. Some men might not like it but I think it's sexy as fuck. Some men want a doormat and 'yes' woman, while some get hard over one who's kickass. I'm in the second group. Maybe that's why my two engagements failed. I needed a woman with a spine of steel able to handle the day to day challenges and risks that came along with my job. I needed a woman who understood why, when I got home, I needed to grab a beer, go out back and spend some time alone to decompress from the bullshit I deal with on the job. They couldn't understand it because they didn't live it day in and day out. Like you do. You get it."

Nova lifted her palm. "Wait. That's a helluva lot of explanation just to try to convince me to have sex with you again."

"You're right." He shook his head and scrubbed both hands down his face. After a few seconds, he blew out a breath and nodded. "You're right. Let me make this simple. I'm Ghost. You're Kitten. Let's live as if we really are them. Everything Ghost and Kitten would do if they really existed, we should do, too. It'll make our identities much more authentic. Then once this assignment is over and Ghost and Kitten no longer exist, we no longer exist, either."

She wasn't sure she liked his proposal, but she didn't dislike it, either.

She needed water and a moment, so she headed toward the kitchen.

"For fuck's sake! I've never had to convince a woman to fuck me before," he said to her back as he followed her.

Maybe she needed something stronger than water. She opened the fridge and grabbed a bottle. Once she shut the door, she saw him leaning back against the counter, with his nicely sculpted arms crossed over his broad chest.

"Never?" She cracked open the lid on the water and guzzled a third of it. She needed to cool off the heat in her belly at the pitch Fletch was making to convince her to have sex with him again.

She wanted to. She did.

"No. Not when the woman acts interested. If she isn't, then I simply walk away." He shrugged. "I know you're interested, Nova. That's fucking clear. So, yeah, this is the first time I've ever had to plead my case."

She smothered a smile. "Plead your case? Are you sure you're not just trying to soothe your bruised ego?"

He pulled the water bottle from her fingers and took a long swallow. And of course, her eyes were immediately glued to his corded neck as his throat moved.

"Backwash."

"I ate your fucking pussy, Nova. You think I'm worried about a little backwash?"

"I meant from you." She wrinkled her nose and didn't accept the bottle back when he held it out to her. "Look, I'll consider what you said."

"You'll consider it," he repeated flatly.

"That's the best answer I can give you right now, Fletch. It's not a no. It's also not a yes because I need some time to think about it." What she really needed to do was change the subject because she was tempted to go along with his plan without giving it much thought. And that would be reckless. "Now, what's the reason you came to get me from downstairs? Does it have to do with the task force? You know, the reason we're together in the first place?"

"Nice deflection." He crossed his arms over his chest again, and of course, she was distracted by the way his shirt sleeves pulled snugly around his bulging biceps.

"Fletch, I said I'd think about it."

He considered her with his lips pressed tightly together. A few seconds later, he shook his head like he was shaking something free.

Most likely his annoyance.

"Crew called me and told me about a biker bar where some of the Demons hang out. But it's not only them, the bar welcomes anyone wearing colors as long as they don't cause issues. Figured we could go there wearing our cuts and hang out for a bit. Maybe make some conversation and contacts. Keep our eyes and ears open."

"Where's it at?"

"Just outside of Uniontown. A little dive called the Hawg Wild Saloon. It seems it's becoming a regular drinking hole for some of the Demons. Especially since they're looking to establish themselves in that area."

"When are we going?"

"Now. So, go do what you need to do to get ready. You're going full biker bitch tonight. Plus, you'll be wearing my name on your back."

"No, Kitten will be wearing Ghost's."

When a grin spread across his face, she wondered if she should be worried about what it meant.

Chapter Sixteen

Fletch sat back in his chair in a dimly lit corner watching Nova do her thing. Playing pool, making conversation, throwing her head back and laughing loudly. Anything to attract attention from the bar's patrons.

His eyes continually scanned the interior. It was dark, dank, and full of bikers overdue for a fucking bath. He needed to smear some Vicks under his nose to drown out their B.O., the pleasant aroma of stale vomit and eye-stinging cigarette smoke.

When they first walked through the door, Fletch had spotted the empty corner table. A perfect spot to see and be seen. He had slipped his hand under Nova's cut and onto her lower back to steer her over there and settle his ass in for the evening.

Taking a page from the outlaw biker's handbook, he ordered her to fetch two beers, making sure to do it loudly enough so anyone nearby heard him. He had noticed her head jerk back at his order before she took a visible breath and slipped into her role.

When she turned to head to the bar, he smacked her ass sharply and gave her a cocky grin. "Takin' that later," he called out to her.

He focused on the "Property of Ghost" patches on her back as she made her way to the busy bar, all eyes on her as she moved with an over-exaggerated swing of her hips and badass bitch attitude seeping from her pores.

Of course, that tempting rock and roll made his gaze slide from her cut to her ass.

Fuck. He really *did* want to take her ass later.

Then he realized he wasn't the only one sitting in that bar thinking the same thing.

He needed to concentrate since they were in enemy territory. Enemies to both law enforcement and possibly the DAMC. As far as he knew, the Angels didn't have any current rivals now that the Shadow Warriors MC disintegrated into thin air, but that didn't mean other MCs weren't out there with a beef against them.

Either way, he needed to stay on top of his game. So did Nova.

He kept his eyes on her as she squeezed her way between two smoking bikers with big beer guts sitting at the bar so she could place an order.

And wasn't one of those fuckers brave enough to touch her damn ass?

Fletch dug his fingers into his thighs and forced himself to keep his own ass in his seat.

She could handle it.

She could.

He needed to let her handle it like a biker chick would.

For fuck's sake.

This bar might end up being a regular hangout for them

until they could make the right connections and earn the Deadly Demons' trust.

If he fucked it up tonight by punching that bastard in the throat, effectively making enemies within the first five minutes, they'd be dead in the water with this particular lead.

If that happened, he'd never hear the end of it from Crew.

Nova said something to the guy as she leaned into the bar and planted a boot on the bottom rung of the handsy motherfucker's stool.

Whatever she said had the man taking a closer look at the rockers on her cut and then glancing over his shoulder at Fletch before shooting him a grin that needed to be wiped off his unkempt bearded face.

Fletch unclenched his jaw, forced his own grin and yelled out, "Sweet, huh?"

The fucker gave him a nod and a thumbs up.

Fletch wanted to shove that fucking thumb deep into the dude's eye socket.

He internally screamed, *"He touched your fucking ass!"* when she returned to the table with two draft beers. Somehow he managed to swallow it back down since he could safely guess she wouldn't appreciate his response and after that, probably would never have a shot at seeing her naked again.

Unfortunately, his reaction was more proof that fucking Nova had been a bad idea. Because, *fuck him*, he was already becoming possessive. One thing she was concerned about.

Not good.

But, *hell*, Kitten belonged to Ghost. No one should be putting their hands on his ol' lady. And get away with keeping all of their fingers.

Fucking goddamn.

He took a slow, deep inhale.

Nova took a sip of one beer before setting the pint glasses on the table, immediately climbing onto his lap and hooking one arm around his neck. "The guy playing grab ass bought our beers."

Great.

"He also told me he'd buy all our rounds tonight if I went out back with him and sucked his dick."

He unlocked his jaw. "And your answer was..."

"I told him I wasn't his personal ball washer and since my ol' man doesn't like sharing, he wouldn't have any fucking balls at all if I did that."

"Good," he once again swallowed down *girl*, "answer."

A grunt escaped him when she shifted in his lap.

"Are those your keys in your pocket, or are you happy to see me?" she asked, raking her short nails through his beard.

He lifted his chin, hoping she'd scratch him there. He wasn't used to growing a beard and it was still itchy as fuck. Unfortunately, she didn't, but slipped her hand into his cut and planted it on his gut instead.

"Keys," he murmured. "You got firsthand knowledge I'm bigger than that. But if you're lookin' for a reminder, keep squirmin' in my lap and pressin' that hot pussy against me."

He reached around her, grabbed his beer and guzzled a mouthful hoping to cool off the still searing fury caused by that guy groping Nova's ass. When he was done, he turned his head away and purposely belched loudly. Of course, he had to play his part of Ghost. He wasn't sure if Nova would call him out on it, but since she was now fully cloaked in Kitten's skin, she acted as if it was no big deal.

He lowered his voice just enough so he could be heard over the blaring '70s rock music coming from the old jukebox on the opposite side of the bar. "See any Demons?"

"Nope. And I searched on my trek to the bar while trying not to be too obvious."

"Haven't seen any, either. Don't mean they won't come in here later. Here's the plan—"

An unexpected burst of loud laughter came from her, drawing some interest from surrounding tables, and then she leaned in, whispering, "Do I have a say in this plan?"

"If you disagree with what I'm about to say, I'm sure you're gonna let me know."

She sucked on his earlobe for a second before leaning back and giving him a heated look that made him want to throw her over his shoulder, beeline it right out of that damn bar and not stop until he was sandwiched between her thighs.

However, he wasn't sure if what she did was as Nova or Kitten. It would be smart and safer for him to assume anything she said or did while at Hawg Wild was strictly Kitten.

"Work your magic. Be seen. Maybe start a little conversation, even flirt. But try to avoid these guys pawin' you. They might do it to test me or to cause trouble since I doubt bikers usually ignore that shit when it comes to their ol' ladies. If I gotta make a stand against one or more of them, then we might blow our cover, get our asses tossed or I just might get my ass royally kicked. Would like to avoid any and all of the above. So, side-step when you can, brush it off with a laugh when you can't. Warn them when you need to but don't say anythin' to them that's gonna fuck this up."

"Basically, you want me to work the crowd. That's easy enough. What are you going to do?"

"Sit here and observe. I don't plan on approachin' anyone tonight. Don't want it to look suspicious by bein' too friendly. We're new here and unknown. This ain't a typical DAMC hangout so, again, they might test us. Thinkin' if we come here enough, they might let their guards down and then I'll start makin' small talk to get info."

"Well, I can't argue with any of that. But it would be smart if you interact next time by shooting some pool or playing darts. You good at that?"

"Yeah, can hold my own on both accounts. Will do that, just not tonight."

She nodded, then gave him a heated look that made his cock take notice.

When her lips curled slightly, he knew he was in trouble.

And he certainly fucking was when she smashed her lips against his and drove her tongue deep into his mouth.

What he thought was a show for the bar, to let them know who she belonged to, quickly became a whole lot more.

As she continued to thoroughly claim his mouth, he drove his fingers into her shoulder-length hair, curled them into tight fists and captured her resulting gasp. Nudging her black leather cut open to make sure, if anyone was watching, they could see what he was doing when he squeezed her breast roughly.

That made her rock her ass against his cock, grinding against him, until he was hard as fuck.

He finally had to grab her hips to stop her motion. If she kept at that, he'd come in his fucking jeans and they'd have to leave. Because fuck if he was sitting all night with a wad of cum in his boxers.

When she finally pulled back, the pupils in her eyes had expanded to the point they were mostly black.

They stared at each other for a few seconds, both breathing heavier than they should be if the kiss had only been for show. Then without a word, she rose from his lap and turned to walk away. He snagged her wrist and yanked her back to him.

He lowered his voice so only she could hear him. "Was that you or Kitten?"

Her expression gave him nothing. "Does it matter?"

Fuck yeah it did. He closed his eyes for a second, then released her wrist. "Be careful. Gonna keep an eye out. If you need to scrape someone off, head back over here."

That exchange had been over an hour ago.

So now here he was, sitting by himself in the corner, nursing his second draft, puffing on a cigar he'd tucked into his cut at the last minute. Trying to look relaxed as he both scanned the crowd and kept an eye on Nova working the bikers.

She was damn good at it, too.

He had no idea what she was saying and the music was too loud to actually hear the exaggerated laughter coming from her whenever she threw her head back, but whenever she did, it drew more than Fletch's eyes.

Yeah, Kitten was a meal on more than one biker's menu tonight.

He lost track of how many games of pool she played, but even when she lost, one of the many men gathered around the billiards area would give their turn to her.

She didn't have to leave the pool table once. One biker or another was constantly bringing her a fresh beer or a shot. In fact, full glasses were stacking up on a high-top table nearby.

Occasionally she'd go over and fake taking a sip—most likely out of concern with her beer being spiked—but by keeping busy playing pool, it was a good excuse not to drink too much, anyway.

In game after game, she moved smoothly around the table, knocking her target ball into the pockets like she'd been playing pool all her damn life. Every time she bent over to line up a shot, she had a crowd, either behind her to watch her ass or practically next to her to give her unneeded "advice."

Since the majority of patrons in the Hawg Wild Saloon were bikers, he took note of the MCs names displayed on their backs. One or two of the club names seemed to be familiar, but the rest he'd never heard of.

While the majority were also one-percenters, every last one of them—outlaw or not—could be trouble.

But, *for fuck's sake,* he still hadn't seen one damn Demon yet. Not only was that disappointing, he hated wasting time in this bar if their club members no longer made Hawg Wild a regular stop.

Leaning back in his chair with the stub of his cigar clamped between his teeth, his eyes sliced through the bar one more time before landing back on Nova just in time to catch a man wearing a Twisted Steel MC cut lean into her and say something into her ear. Her answer to whatever he said was to fling a thumb over her shoulder in Fletch's direction.

Fuck.

When the biker glanced his way, Fletch acted like he didn't notice it when, in truth, he was paying careful attention.

When the TSMC member said something again to Nova, she turned toward the man and leaned on her cue stick. Whatever she was saying to him, she was not being nice. Her expression was hard, her eyes sharp, her body tense.

No mistake about it, she was serving him up some attitude.

As to be expected, the biker didn't like it.

Fuck.

When he went to grab for her arm, she pulled it away in time and stepped out of reach, gripping her cue stick like she was about to enter into combat.

Fletch started to rise from his chair but plunked back down when Nova jerked her chin toward his table, still giving the man shit. She then shut her mouth, tilted her head and stared the guy down with her fingers flexing on her makeshift weapon.

Even from where Fletch sat, he could see the biker's tight jaw start popping as he stood there for a few seconds more, his expression showing a whole shitload of unhappy.

As soon as Nova turned and went back to the game, the Twisted Steel member left the pool table area and headed in his direction.

For fuck's sake. What shit did she stir up?

Fletch forced himself to appear relaxed and unbothered while he took a few puffs on his cigar, but the heavyset man lumbering toward him was blocking his view of Nova.

He reminded himself for the umpteenth time tonight that the FBI agent could handle herself.

The stringy-haired man with solid tats, not only up both arms, but also completely covering his neck, halted in front of him. The name on his patch said Wire. "Don't keep your woman on a leash? She got a smart fuckin' mouth."

Fletch took his time raising his eyes to meet his and just as slowly said, "You that fuckin' blind you don't see the collar she's wearin' 'round her neck?"

Tonight she had worn the black choker chain with the large O-ring like she had last Sunday during the DAMC run and pig roast.

The man with the long, shaggy beard glanced back over his shoulder. Fletch presumed at Nova. "Yeah. Saw it."

"My leash snaps onto that. But she's been a good girl

lately, so tonight she's got her freedom as a reward. She steps outta fuckin' line, she'll pay later."

The man lifted one bushy eyebrow as he considered Fletch's warning before a yellow-toothed grin slid across his face. "Like your thinkin'. She don't fight that?"

Fletch gave him an answering smile, while silently thanking his parents for teaching him good dental hygiene. "Fuck yeah, she fights it. Makes doling out her punishment all the sweeter. Anyway, what fuck ain't better without some fight to go along with it? That ain't no fun."

"Fuck yeah," the man murmured with his eyes glued to the subject of their conversation. "Looks like she can get really fuckin' feisty." He turned back to Fletch, his eyes even darker now. "Wanna sell her?"

The fine hairs on the back of Fletch's neck instantly stood at attention and it took everything he had to remain in Ghost's persona. "You can't afford her."

"Try me."

He sucked on his teeth in annoyance. "Look... She ain't for sale, brother. Spent too much time trainin' her."

"Train a new one. Will make it worth your while."

"Don't got another one to train right now. I sell her to you, then what am I supposed to fuck tonight? My fist?" He scraped a hand down his beard and shook his head.

"How 'bout rentin' her to me, then. Just for an hour. She like it rough?"

"Loves it rough. Blood. Bruises. Loves for me to squeeze her fucking neck 'til she blacks out. She eats that shit up and begs for seconds. But she ain't for rent, either, brother. Let one of my club brothers borrow her one night and she was returned to me broken. Took me a while to fix her. Wasn't easy and ain't goin' through that shit again. The only acceptable damage on my woman will come from me. Got it?"

The hungry look in the man's eyes was becoming a bit fucking scary. "Yeah, brother, got it. Damn." He reached down and squeezed his crotch. "You ever need extra scratch, willin' to pay good for some of that. Most bitches cry when you show 'em who's boss and she don't look like she'd shed a tear no matter what's done to her."

Fletch forced down the bile rising up his throat. "Know how it is, my man, went through a few of 'em 'til I found Kitten. When you find the right one, you gotta fuckin' hold on to 'em. That's why she's wearin' my name on her back. Also got it branded on her ass. This way she don't get lost, if you know what I'm sayin'."

"Lucky fucker."

"That I am. So, you can look, you can fantasize while you jack off... But you can't fuckin' touch. I own that fuckin' ass, that mouth and that tight cunt."

Wire scratched the back of his tattooed neck. "Can respect that."

Fletch sure as fuck hoped so.

"Keep me in mind if you ever get bored of her or you take her past her breakin' point and need to find a fresh challenge."

Jesus H. Christ. He swallowed down Fletch's response and responded as Ghost would. "You a regular here?"

"Yeah."

"Then, know where to find you. You mind a little damaged goods?"

"Fuck no. Not if I get a motherfuckin' discount and she still got some fight left in her."

Fletch gave him a nod. "Then, I'll keep you in mind."

Wire answered with his own nod and yanked on his long, thick beard that looked like it hadn't been maintained in decades.

When he reached down, Fletch stared at his extended hand for a second before slapping his palm in it. They clasped hands and shared a chin lift before the biker lumbered away.

Fletch watched him go and noticed the man's attention remaining on Nova as he worked his way through the bar. Thankfully in the opposite direction from her.

He'd have to keep an eye on the guy. Sometimes when men were told no, that spurred them to go after what they couldn't have even more. And worse, some men would do anything to get it. Including using force.

Another hour passed with still no fucking sign of a Demon. Fletch needed to piss but he didn't want to leave Nova alone while he did so. Maybe it was time to go. They could stop on their way back to the apartment to grab late-night grub and for him to relieve his screaming bladder.

He ground out his cigar directly onto the table and tucked it back inside his cut, but before he could rise and retrieve Nova, he noticed from the corner of his eye another biker approaching him.

While conversation with random bikers was helpful, it distracted him from keeping an eye on Nova and the men crowding her despite her wearing a "property of" cut. He figured bikers would have some silent code between them in regards to fucking another biker's woman, but then maybe that only counted within their own brotherhood.

He'd have to ask Zak or Dawg, the gun shop manager, since it would be good information to have. There had to be some kind of known, or even unspoken, rule.

Of course, the biker stopping in front of his table was once again white. The obvious lack of diversity in this bar shouldn't be surprising. For the most part, it seemed as if bikers stuck with their own.

In fact, some of the patches he saw tonight on cuts were clearly white supremacist symbols, including swastikas, SS bolts and imperial eagles.

He was actually surprised to find a man with Native American blood, as well as an openly bisexual member amongst the Dirty Angels. Fletch wondered if that club had always been accepting or if that changed once Zak Jamison earned the gavel.

When his newest visitor extended his hand, Fletch clasped it and gave the man a chin lift the same as he had with Wire.

"Boz. Tainted Souls."

"Ghost. Dirty Angels."

While he hadn't planned on chatting up anyone tonight, these random approaches were turning out to be even better. Maybe that was the key. Let them come to him. He just wasn't sure if he'd have the patience to do that every night when they came to Hawg Wild.

Because they would be back. Every Friday and Saturday if possible, unless he got word the Demons rolled in on a different night. If that happened, they'd pivot.

"Whatchya doin' down here? This ain't your territory." Boz pulled out a chair, swung it around and straddled it backwards.

"Same as you. This ain't your territory, either, is it?"

"Nope. But the Angels usually stick close to home."

"Not all of us. Nothin' wrong with checkin' out new landscape."

"Heard the Demons are lookin' to claim this area. Figured that's why you're here. Know your territory starts just a cunt hair north of here. If the Demons end up takin' this bar, the rest of us might not be welcome to hang here any longer."

Well, someone didn't like the fact that the Demons were on the move. That could work to Fletch's advantage.

"True that. But we ain't worried about the Demons encroachin' on our territory. They know better. Ask the Warriors. They learned their lesson for fuckin' with us." He took another sip of beer, pretending it wasn't flat and warm. "Was on a ride with my ol' lady. Figured this would be a friendly place to take a break. Likin' the atmosphere and so's my ol' lady, so we might be back since we're also lookin' to make some new... *friends*."

Boz's bloodshot eyes narrowed. "What kinda friends?"

"Ones with a hookup."

"What kinda hookup you talkin' about?"

"My ol' lady likes a little pick-me-up now an' again."

The biker studied him, his expression closing down tight. "Can't help you there."

That was a fucking lie. "Know anyone who can? Our club don't deal, so we always gotta look elsewhere. My ol' lady would be really fuckin' grateful if she could score tonight. *Really* grateful, if you know what I mean." Fletch was reeling out the line hoping to hook a big fish.

Boz twisted his neck to check out Nova. He stared for longer than Fletch liked.

"Yeah, she looks like a keeper. 'Specially if she's wild as fuck in bed. She give good head?"

"The fuckin' best. Can suck the ball off a trailer hitch. And when she's flyin' high, she lets me do all kinda shit to her. If I keep her happy, she keeps me happy."

"Damn. Lucky bastard. Last bitch I face-fucked kept gaggin' to the point she puked. Can't help I'm hung like a horse." He grinned, showing off a mouthful of what might be six teeth at the max. Fletch wasn't going to waste the time counting. But once again he was glad he was very familiar with a toothbrush and toothpaste.

"Hear that, brother," Fletch said. "If you know anyone who can help me out of a jam, send them my way, would ya?"

Boz shrugged. "Sure. If I know where to find you."

"Right here." Fletch tapped his finger on the scarred and pitted table. "Plan on spendin' some time down here 'til we find a regular connection since my old one's spendin' a 'lil R and R in Fayette. Like I said, if I keep her happy, she keeps me happy."

"I find someone to hook you up, I get a finder's fee?"

"What kinda finder's fee?"

"Said she can suck the ball off a hitch. Would like to test that claim."

Shit. Fletch needed to avoid further talk about a finder's fee. He was not offering up Nova's mouth in exchange for info. He'd find it another way if he needed to.

"She's real particular with what she likes."

"You talkin' dick or drugs?" Boz asked.

"Both."

"What're you lookin' to score?"

"Cotton candy." Fletch hoped like fuck the biker before him knew the slang for crystal meth.

He glanced over his shoulder toward the pool tables. "Damn. No wonder she's so damn skinny. Even without any meat on her bones, she still looks damn good for an addict."

Maybe Nova was skinny for this guy's taste, but Fletch knew firsthand what was under her clothes. The woman was in fucking shape and not once had she held back on eating. She ate almost as much as he did.

"Never said she was addicted. She got an occasional sweet tooth, that's all. Eatin' cotton candy's fun for her, fun for me, too. You got me?"

"Sure do, brother. About that finder's fee..."

Fuck. "If she was just a side-piece, wouldn't give two shits about sharin' her, but she's my ol' lady, brother. Ain't willin' for you to bust a nut down her throat."

Boz grinned and nodded. "Hear you on that. Wouldn't want another man humpin' my ol' lady's face, either. Maybe we can watch our women go at it instead."

Fletch pulled on his chin, pretending to give serious consideration on that offer. "Now *that* I can live with. Nothin' better than watchin' two bitches eatin' each other's snatch. Fuck, that gets me goin' just thinkin' 'bout it." He grabbed his crotch and adjusted himself, even though his dick had gone into hiding with this conversation.

Boz's grin stretched across his face. "Same here. I find a good source, I'll send 'em your way."

"Appreciate it, brother. Just make sure it ain't some undercover pig."

Fletch didn't like the way the man chuckled. "Any undercover pigs 'round here tend to go missin'. Anyone I send your way's gonna be legit."

"Will hold you to that. Now," Fletch stood, "need to fetch my ol' lady. She's spent enough time with other men tonight. Time to remind her who she belongs to."

With an approving nod, Boz also rose to his feet and clasped hands with him again, but this time they bumped shoulders.

Yeah, he damn sure had enough of this shit for tonight. It was time to do what he said, fetch Nova and get them the fuck out of there while they could leave on a good note.

Because, sure as fuck, in a place named Hawg Wild it wouldn't take much for shit to go sideways.

Chapter Seventeen

They stopped to fill their empty tanks on the way back to the apartment. While they ate in an isolated booth in the back corner of a twenty-four-hour diner, they discussed what each of them heard earlier at the bar.

They both agreed they should return to Hawg Wild since it seemed the easiest way to make contact with the Deadly Demons without raising red flags. Especially after Nova had scored info that the outlaw club did indeed use that bar as a regular hang-out. She also heard they were having a huge club party at their church in West Virginia and that was the reason none of them were there tonight.

That important tidbit made sense and also verified the intel Crew had provided about that bar.

As they swapped tales, he decided not to hold back on telling Nova how interested those bikers were in having their way with her. She needed to be aware of that danger—if she didn't already know it—so she'd be prepared tomorrow night when they went back.

"Seems like we caught a lot of flies with your honey,"

Fletch said after swallowing another mouthful of homemade chicken pot pie. His favorite kind with the pastry crust, not the Pennsylvania Dutch kind made with the noodles.

Nova's face scrunched up. "Gross."

"I'm just saying... You were the perfect bait. Two of those fuckers approached me solely because of you, not because they wanted to be besties. At least with me anyway, it was debatable even with you."

"What did they want?"

He raised one eyebrow. "What do you think they wanted?"

"I know the shit they said to me, just wondering if the shit they said to you was similar."

Most likely it was worse. "The one you had words with wanted to buy you, Nova."

Her head jerked back and her mouth gaped open as that sunk in. "He what?"

He tipped his chin down while keeping their eyes locked. "Yeah. And if he couldn't buy you, he wanted to rent you by the hour."

She burst out laughing.

What the fuck? "You think that's funny?"

He focused on the slide of her throat as she tipped her water glass to her lips and guzzled it. When she was done, she wiped her thumb across her bottom lip. He would've gladly done that for her, if she had asked.

"Don't you?"

"Fuck no, I didn't find anything funny about that. Jesus, Nova, it's sick."

She shrugged like it was no big deal. "Of course it's sick. But what the hell do you expect? These guys have the mindset that women are their property to do with what they will. That includes selling them. They treat anyone with a vagina as a commodity. Are you surprised? I'm not."

His nostrils flared. "No. But I guess it hits differently when it comes to you."

"Why? Because we fucked?"

Of fucking course, but that wasn't the only reason. "Because you're my partner."

"Bullshit." Her brown eyes narrowed on him and her mouth twisted. "They might not know you can't make money off me, but I do. So, I'm not worried about it. Besides a few of them touching where and when they shouldn't or saying ignorant shit because their pea brains are stored in their fucking balls, they behaved as expected. Would I want to be alone with them in a dark room? Fuck no. Not unless I had my Glock with me, along with two full mags."

"Well, at least your brain isn't in your balls and you see them for the threat they are. I'm thinking when we go back tomorrow night, we'll play doubles." With him partnering up with her at the pool table, the risk of inappropriate touching should be reduced or even non-existent.

"Why? Are you worried about me?"

Of course he was. "Nothing to do with that," he lied. "I just think we should mix it up every time we hang out there so it doesn't appear as though we're there for a specific reason. For example, you play darts while I play pool or you sit at the bar and start up some conversations while I'm playing pool. Shit like that."

"All right. I'll allow it."

He huffed. "You will, will you?"

She pushed her empty salad plate away and leaned back against the booth's red vinyl seat. "Do I have to remind you *again* that you're not in charge here? Suggestions are one thing, orders are another. Here's a fun fact in case it's not clear... Anything you can do, I can do just as well, if not better. Unfortunately, as a woman in this career, I have to constantly prove my 'worth.' I guarantee, since you have a dick, you don't." She lifted a palm and shook her head to stop his response. "I've already experienced it firsthand more than once, so don't even try to deny it."

"I wouldn't, because I agree. Believe me, the state police has plenty of enlisted members who don't believe women should be in law enforcement. Their twisted opinion is that women aren't as capable. Not strong enough. Not fast enough. There's always some bullshit reason. And usually the assholes complaining the loudest are the slugs." He wondered if the FBI used that same term for lazy as fuck agents.

"It's like that at every level of law enforcement. So yeah, women need to constantly prove themselves. While men can do the bare minimum and get the same amount, if not more, recognition and respect."

He grimaced when he thought about how he treated her the first day they met. But then, he was an equal opportunity ball-buster. "Sorry you have to deal with that."

"Don't be sorry. Just respect and value us as a coworker doing the same job. It's that simple. The capability to do our job, and do it well, does not come down to gender."

If she was looking for an argument, she wasn't getting it from him. "True that." He sighed. "You ready?"

He wanted to get out of there before dinner struck him like a brick over the head. It had already been a long day and unlike Nova being smart about eating a salad, of course he had picked a heavy meal. Hopefully it would help him sleep good tonight. However, they were still only about halfway home...

The apartment, not *home*, he reminded himself. Their

temporary residence.

Either way, he didn't want to risk nodding off. And it wouldn't be a good look if Ghost ended up being Kitten's backpack. *Hell,* he wasn't even sure if Nova knew how to drive a motorcycle.

He studied her as she gathered her stuff and stood.

Of fucking course she knew how to operate a bike. She could probably drive an eighteen-speed semi.

Hell, maybe even a tank.

When he snorted, she lifted her head. "Problem?"

"Nope. Just thinking about how much more of a badass you are than me."

Her eyebrows pinched together. "In regards to what?"

"Everything," was the safest answer he could give before slipping his hand under her cut and using it to steer her toward the lone waitress behind the counter. He paused long enough to toss a twenty to their server before they headed out into the warm night.

The DAMC ladies had warned her before the run last Sunday but she had brushed it off as a joke, thinking they were screwing with her. That was, until she had a tiny orgasm later that afternoon on a long back stretch of road. Nothing Earth-shattering but enough for her to take notice.

The best part about it, no one else had a clue it happened.

Including Fletch.

But tonight with a full belly and after putting in a long day, she let the Harley's vibrations overtake her and lull her into a deeply relaxed state.

When she sat across from Fletch at dinner, she'd been

more than hungry for food. She was hungry for him.

Some of that was caused by the occasional glances she shot his way while he sat in the corner at Hawg Wild like a king expecting his subjects to come to him. His confidence, as well as his good looks, not only kept drawing her attention, but some of the other women in the bar, as well.

Nova was actually surprised he hadn't been approached by any. But then, it had been their first night at the bar and maybe most of the regular patrons were wary about anyone new in their midst.

Some of the bikers hanging out near her at the pool tables had lobbed some hard-ball questions at her about the DAMC and Ghost. She had answered when she could, deflected when she couldn't.

Of course, they had every right to be cautious since law enforcement had infiltrated MCs in the past. Because of that, it made sense for her and Fletch to return tomorrow night and every weekend after that until the bikers and their women got used to seeing their faces and stopped giving them the side-eye.

However, that didn't mean Ghost and Kitten wouldn't continue to be tested to make sure they were who their patches said they were. Nova would be more surprised if they didn't.

But now, they were only about five minutes out from Shadow Valley Pawn.

It might be late, but her body was low-key humming. And, of course, her mind was spinning with possibilities and the question of whether it would be smart to knock boots with Fletch again.

She could let the Harley's vibrations draw another orgasm from her or...

She could let the man driving it do that.

Nova was sure if she asked for his assistance, he wouldn't say no.

To test that theory, she slipped her arms under his cut to encircle his waist in a tight hold. He turned his head, most likely in surprise since she'd been avoiding holding onto him on every other ride. If he said something, she didn't hear it over the wind in her ears and the loud exhaust. Plus, she couldn't see if his mouth moved since he wore a bandana over his lower face to avoid choking on suicidal bugs.

She probably shouldn't be distracting him, but he was certainly distracting her, even if he didn't mean to.

She wiggled closer until her pussy, throbbing due to the mix of vibrations and anticipation, was pressed against his ass.

He covered one of her hands planted on his gut with his own and nudged it lower, but not all the way to where she was sure he wanted it.

After giving her fingers a slight squeeze, he removed his hand and wrapped it around her left calf, giving that a much firmer squeeze. She took his action as a sign he was open to her touching him intimately. She did so by sliding her hand lower and finding how hard he was.

Had he been thinking about sex, too?

Of course he had. What man didn't constantly think about sex? It seemed to be a part of their DNA, like leaving the lights on.

When he leaned back slightly, she curled her fingers around the hard line in his jeans, just as possessively as his grip on her calf. His erection was a clear indication he'd be up for the task of bringing her to orgasm. At least once. Hopefully twice. Maybe even three times. She would be a fool to place a limit on it.

Leaning into him, she pressed her lips against the back of

his neck, causing him to jerk and the bike to wobble at the unexpected contact. She grinned at his reaction.

Licking his skin, she found it slightly salty due to the warm weather. She dragged her tongue up and down the center of his neck before sinking her teeth in gently. Not hard enough to leave a mark but deep enough to remind him of her warning that Kitten had sharp teeth and claws.

While slowly sliding her palm up and down his hard length, she kept one eye on the road to make sure he was keeping the bike between the lines. She wanted to orgasm, not end up in a damn ditch.

She was sure he'd agree with that.

When he twisted the throttle hard, the bike shot forward and the engine screamed as he sped through the streets of a sleepy Shadow Valley. When he finally turned into the pawn shop's lot, she was a little worried when he didn't even slow down.

Obviously, someone was in a rush.

She slammed into his back when he stopped suddenly in the spot next to the Durango.

He quickly shut off the bike and ripped the bandana down. "Get off."

Well, that *was* the plan.

With one last teasing nip to the back of his neck, she threw her leg over the seat and before she even had both feet planted on the pavement, he was off the bike, too, latching onto her arm and hauling her up the steps.

Of course, his enthusiasm was ramping up her anticipation.

"Hurry," she breathed as he jabbed the key at the deadbolt. It took him three times and a whole bunch of grumbling before he was successful. She hoped he had better aim when it came to jabbing his cock into her.

As soon as he shoved open the door, he fisted her cut and practically flung her inside, before slamming the door shut and pinning her against it.

"For fuck's sake, Nova," came out of him a split second before he took her mouth. *Jesus.* He wasn't just kissing her, he was practically eating her face like a starved man.

Their tongues twisted together, a struggle over who was in control. One second it was her until he yanked it back from her just as quickly.

A game of tug of war. That was what it reminded her of, only the adult version.

Slipping a hand under her cut, he squeezed her breast so hard she gasped, then captured his lower lip in her teeth, clamping down hard enough for him to actually chuckle.

A weird reaction but she'd go with it.

While he twisted her nipple through her shirt, she groaned into his mouth when his lips claimed hers once more.

Then, suddenly, his hand was gone, but only for a split second before he clamped his hands on her ass to haul her up and against him. She wrapped her legs around his hips and her arms around his neck, clinging to him while rubbing her pussy against his denim-covered cock.

Without breaking their kiss, he turned and carried her through the living room area and down the hallway, not stopping until he kicked his partially open bedroom door wide enough for them both to fit through.

He didn't stop until he got to the bed where he let her slide down his body until she was once again standing on her own two feet.

"Naked. Now."

That sounded like an order and not a suggestion but she'd

let it slide this time because she was in total agreement and it wouldn't be to her benefit to argue.

They stepped apart, both of them panting and watching each other slip off their cuts and their shirts. She left on her bra as they both sat on the edge of the bed, unlacing their boots and tugging off their socks. They mirrored each other's actions when they once again stood and faced each other, unbuckling their belts, unfastening and shoving their jeans to the floor.

Now they both stood in their underwear, staring at each other.

"Take them off." Another order, this time with his voice rough and raw.

A fire burned in his eyes as he stroked himself over his cotton boxer briefs, watching her slowly unfasten her bra and letting it drop to the floor.

Then she did something he didn't expect. She turned around and made a show of pulling down her panties. She did not let them drop to her feet, instead she wiggled them slowly over her ass checks, then her thighs and once she hit her knees she bent over, giving him a clear view of her bare ass and pussy. Once her panties were around her ankles, she straightened and stepped out of them.

"Fuck, Nova," he groaned.

"Yes. Fuck Nova," she repeated in a murmur. "I hope that was your plan."

"You have any doubt? I told you I wanted this. You were the one who resisted."

"Because I wasn't sure it would be smart."

"And now you are?"

"I still think it'll complicate things. But, Fletch..." She closed the gap between them.

"What?"

She lifted her face to his. She had so many things she could say to answer his question. Yes, things would get complicated. Yes, it might risk their investigation. No, she wasn't willing to find someone else to have sex with. Not when the man she wanted was within her reach.

Selfish? No doubt. But at the moment, she didn't care. That might change come morning like it had last time.

"You're not naked," she finished instead. She grabbed the waistband of his boxer briefs and yanked them down, freeing his bobbing erection.

His hips jerked when she wrapped her fist around the base of his cock and without breaking eye contact, she slowly lowered herself to her knees. Once she was in position she licked her lips and stared at the thick, glistening crown.

Her pussy clenched in anticipation and from the memory of the two of them in the bathroom last weekend that was now replaying in her head.

"Nova," he murmured. He brushed the hair away from her face and tipped it up to him, using two fingers under her chin.

When their eyes met again, she caught the slight widening of his before he could hide his reaction. She wondered what that was about but then, she was a bit surprised by how much she wanted Fletch. Maybe it was the same for him. An undeniable attraction both had tried to initially fight but kept failing at.

Whether that was the reason, or whether it wasn't, didn't matter. Both of them were naked and they were doing this. Smart decision or not.

Keeping her eyes tipped up, she took him into her mouth and witnessed a complete change to his expression as she did so.

While the skin on his neck had tasted salty, his cock had a

tang to it that she hadn't experienced in quite a while and surprisingly missed. She kept watching his face as she drew him in and out of her mouth.

With his hands gripping the sides of her head, his fingers tangled in her loose hair, using it to guide her, but not forcing her to take him faster or deeper.

At least, not yet.

She scraped her short nails down his lightly-haired thighs before cupping his soft sac, pulling and kneading his balls gently within her fingers.

"Christ, Nova," came out on a long groan.

Her cheeks hollowed out when she sucked him with force, while pumping him at the root with her fist and increasing her pace with both her hand and her mouth.

She was playing with fire. She knew what she was doing could send him over the edge before they even had a chance to fuck.

She didn't want that but she also was enjoying his reactions to her giving him head. She must be doing something right. Confirmed by the deep, low groan that filled the air around him and made her want to double down.

She scraped her teeth lightly over the swollen head and ran the flat of her tongue down the thick ridge, sucking at the spot where the root met the delicate skin of his sac. She reversed the action and once she encircled the crown with her lips again, she took her time swallowing his length until she reached her limit.

"Fuck... fuck... Fuck, Nova, you gotta stop..." Releasing her hair, he grabbed her elbows and hauled her to her feet.

She wiped the back of her hand over her mouth. "I wasn't done."

"No shit, but I was. As much as I want you to suck me off 'til I come, I'd prefer to finish inside you."

She wanted that, too. "Then let's get to it."

"You wet?"

"You have to ask?" She grabbed his hand and pressed it between her thighs.

"Fuck yeah, you are," he whispered, his Adam's apple sliding up his throat, hanging for a split second before dropping back into place.

He drew his middle finger through her slick folds and then dipped it inside her. Once he pulled it free, he lifted his hand between him and Nova couldn't miss the shine on his finger.

"Is that from the bike or you giving me head?"

"Both. Plus, the anticipation of what we're about to do next."

A smile crept across his face. "I'm one lucky motherfucker. All those fuckers at that bar that wanted you, Nova, they don't get to have you, but I do."

"Less words, more action," she suggested. "Condom?"

He jerked into motion and rounded the bed. When he bent over buck-assed naked to dig through a duffel bag on the floor against the far wall, she appreciated everything he was pointing at her.

He had a hell of an ass. She couldn't decide if she wanted to bite it or slap it first. Despite that, she remained where she was. Tonight, she decided she'd leave scratches in those perfectly shaped globes instead.

When he turned and he lifted his eyes to her, he came to an abrupt halt. "What?"

"Nothing. I'm waiting."

"Nova, you've got a look on your face that makes me wonder if I should be celebrating or worried."

"No reason to worry. I'm just thinking about everything I want to do to you."

Chapter Eighteen

"I've been doing that every fucking night," Fletch admitted. "We've got a lot of catching up to do if we do everything I imagined us doing."

He was a little surprised when she answered, "I'm game."

But was she only game for tonight or for the rest of the time they'd be living together in this apartment? Even if she didn't want to share a room and a bed and only stopped over for nightly visits.

He wouldn't be against morning wake-up calls, either.

And maybe they could even meet back here during their lunch breaks.

He was getting ahead of himself.

As soon as he came back around the bed, she plucked the condom from his hand, tore it open, threw the wrapper on the nightstand closest to them, then stepped back in front of him so she could roll it down his length.

He bit back a groan when his cock pulsed and flexed within her fingers. Her touch was nice, but being inside her would be even better.

"One good thing about condoms is it'll help keep me from embarrassing myself in thirty seconds flat." He made it come off like a joke, but he was hardly joking. After fucking her in the bathroom last Sunday night, doing it again was all he could think about.

"If you finish in thirty seconds, you'll have to make it up to me in other ways," she warned.

"I can think of plenty of ways, don't worry." He had a whole mental list full of them. In fact, that list was so long, if anyone actually saw it...

Yeah, not a good idea.

"I'll hold you to that." She grabbed his arm and yanked him back to the bed, repeating, "Less words, more action."

"You got it, Kitten."

He wanted her to be on top so he could take full advantage of the mirror on the ceiling. He climbed onto the mattress and once he was settled onto his back, he held out his hand. "Mount up, Kitten, you can ride me like my sled."

She ignored his hand and straddled his hips. "Do you vibrate like one? I orgasmed on the run last Sunday."

He stared at her. "What?"

She smiled. "Yep. The ladies warned me that it could happen, but..." She shrugged.

Damn. He had no clue that happened. "You need to share that shit with me."

"Is that a suggestion or an order?"

"It's a plea. Do me a solid and tell me."

"I'll consider your request. Now..." She grabbed his cock from where it laid near his hip and held it straight up.

He lost his train of thought as she lifted up, hovered over it then, with her bottom lip tucked between her teeth, she slowly... oh, so fucking slowly... sank down and he watched it disappear. Her lips parted as she ground down against him to seat it even deeper, until his cock was completely encased in her wet heat. And, *fuck*, it felt so damn good.

His first instinct was to grab her hips and begin thrusting up and into her like a wild man, but he forced himself to relax and look up into the mirror. To take the time and appreciate a very naked, very sexy Nova.

Fucking perfect.

She was perfect. This was perfect. Having a mirror to watch what was about to happen was absolute perfection.

She curled over him, licking a long line from his stomach, up between his pecs, around both nipples and up his chest. She brushed her lips along his strained throat before her mouth hovered above his. Simply taking the time to breathe each other in for a moment before she closed the gap between them.

Her every little move, every little shift, made him want to jam his cock into her over and over, but he forced himself to lay still and wait. He would let her set the pace, let her control what happened next. At least until he couldn't bear it anymore and took over.

He wanted to watch her. In front of him. Above him. He wished there were mirrors on the walls, too, so he could see her lithe-like movements from every angle.

She was thinner than the women he normally went for. Not actually skinny, but lean muscle. He wasn't into gym bunnies more concerned with zero body fat and thigh gaps. *Hell no.* He appreciated a woman with enough flesh to dig his fingers into, curves to hold onto. Breasts big enough to smother him until he had to tap out.

Nova had none of that. She was almost the complete opposite of the women who normally caught his eye. But something about her drove him fucking insane with wanting her. Not just with wanting to fuck her, but more. He had this crazy urge to claim her, to make her his. So no one else could have her.

He didn't understand it, this unexpected pull toward her. But now was not the time to question it. Now was the time to appreciate her and to accept what she was willing to give him.

Especially after she planted her hands on his chest, sat back up and began to rock back and forth. Her pussy ground against him, her hips circling and driving his cock even deeper inside her.

He couldn't pull his eyes from the mirror. She reminded him of a ballet dancer, her motion flowing and graceful. "Look at us. That's hot as fuck."

She tipped her head back to see what he did, to watch herself rising and falling on his cock at a steady, lazy pace. Sliding up to the rim, dropping back down to the root. "If that mirror could talk..." Nova murmured. "Let's just hope it's not a two-way mirror with a hidden camera."

"Jesus fuck, if it is..."

Nova's movement stuttered when she couldn't contain her laughter. "You've been a busy boy." She pinched his nipple in a teasing manner.

He grinned, not caring about the secret he was about to spill. "Surprised I don't have blisters. But then, living with you for the past week has driven me a little insane."

She shook her head. "I don't know why."

"Look at you," he said, jerking his chin up toward the mirror. "Just look, Nova. Like I said, I'm one lucky fucker right now."

"I'm just a woman."

He huffed out, "Hardly. You are not *just* a woman. You are so much more."

She paused and dropped her head to stare down into his face, a crease marring her brow. "Fletch..."

"It's the truth."

"You've only known me for—"

He grabbed two handfuls of her ass and lifted his hips. "Long enough."

"No, not long enough to know that."

"Bullshit. Sometimes you just know. I trust my gut. Don't you?"

I TRUST MY GUT. *Don't you?*

Of course she did. Women's intuition. A gut feeling. A natural instinct. Whatever someone called it, she followed it. She'd be stupid not to.

Even so, while she initially thought he was an asshole during that first task force meeting, once she moved in with him, she immediately felt comfortable in his presence.

She didn't trust just anybody, but with him, she had dropped her barriers faster than normal. It could take months, even years, for her to let her guard down around a person she didn't know. Not until they proved themselves to be trustworthy.

Respect. Honor. Loyalty. Honesty.

In her book, all of that was important. It also was hard to find.

Yes, it had only been a week, but she trusted her gut and believed Fletch would have her back no matter what. If she needed him, he'd be there.

That meant a lot to her. It was also one reason she decided not to pull herself from this assignment after the bathroom sex last Sunday.

But enough of that. They were having sex right now.

They shouldn't be analyzing anything deeper than what was currently happening.

They were naked. He was hard and she was wet. That was all that should matter right now. Nothing else.

The rest could wait.

"My turn."

His eyes flicked from the mirror to her face. "Your turn for what?"

Her answer came in the form of rolling off of him, hooking his waist with her leg and then dragging him along with her, until he ended up on top.

No surprise he didn't fight it. "You want to watch me fuck you."

"You wanted to watch me fuck you," she tossed back at him.

"Who wouldn't? All those motherfuckers at the bar would've paid a hefty price to be where I am right now. To see what I'm seeing. To feel your pussy squeezing their cock. Feel the scrape of your nails, the bite of your teeth, the press of your mouth."

She didn't want to think about those guys at the bar. She wanted to forget about them and concentrate on the man propped on his arms above her. He had his knees anchored into the mattress between her legs and his hands bracing himself on either side of her head.

But he wasn't fucking her. He was studying her instead.

"Less words, more action," she reminded him again and slapped his ass.

He jerked from the sting, then chuckled. "Such a demanding woman," he murmured with a grin, shifting enough to align his cock. "I like it."

Fortunately, he didn't need any more urging. He began

rolling his hips, smoothly sliding in and out of her, whisking away any thoughts of the bar or those bikers.

Of anything or anyone but Fletch.

She focused on him. Both before her and in the mirror.

Now she understood the appeal of it. That ability to observe the two of them. Watching the flex of his muscular ass and the pump of his hips stoked the fire at her core.

She scraped her nails up his back. Too short to do any kind of damage, they still left faint red lines in their wake. His compass tattoo came alive as his back flexed and bowed as he curled over her. She dug her nails deeper into his ass, leaving scratches behind that wouldn't disappear as quickly, unlike the ones up his back.

She left her mark on him. Even if only temporary.

Nova was here.

She came, she saw, she conquered.

Their rapid breaths merged into one when he lowered his head and kept his parted lips right above hers.

He continued to move in and out of her. Taking his time, drawing this out tonight to the point she lost track of time because she became lost in his eyes. Until a bead of sweat rolled down his temple and landed on her chin.

He wiped it away, then ran the back of his fingers down her cheek and tucked his thumb between her parted lips. After swirling her tongue around it, she snagged it between her teeth and grinned.

As soon as he pulled his thumb free, he drew it down her chin and circled his hand around her throat, but didn't squeeze. Instead, he kept it there with just enough pressure to remind her that was one place where she was vulnerable.

But her throat wasn't the only place crushable. So was her damn heart.

Luckily, since she hardly knew this man, she wasn't

worried about having to protect that vulnerable organ. The one she had never given to anyone. Because in the past, no one had been worthy enough for her to take that risk.

She was also in no rush to find someone who was.

She was in no rush to find someone who was.

She was in absolutely *no* rush.

But *if* she was looking...

If she found someone with everything she was looking for...

Could it be the man above her? Watching her watching him in the mirror?

A week. It had only been a week.

She reached up and grabbed his bearded chin, tipping it down. "Fletch..."

"Yeah?" he whispered.

"Make me come." And wipe out those disturbing thoughts in her head that certainly didn't belong there.

"Working on it."

"Work faster."

"Demanding," he murmured with a grin.

That grin quickly turned into a grimace when he began to power up and into her, fucking her faster and harder, adding a sharp tilt every time he hit the end of her.

She was about to bitch when he paused, worried he'd leave her hanging, but he only stopped long enough to lift up her hips and shove a pillow beneath them.

Then he was right back at it, the angle of his cock hitting all the right spots.

He pounded her over and over, shoving every thought out of her head as she held on tight, gripping his ass, encouraging him to keep up the pace.

Then she lost herself.

Totally lost herself.

Her head fell back, her mouth opened and she cried out his name as an orgasm overtook her, dragging her under, tumbling her around and taking its time to spit her back out on the other side. Where she landed...

Boneless.

Weak.

Shaky.

Absolutely and totally satisfied.

He didn't stop since he wasn't done. He chased her to the finish line and she spurred him on by drilling her fingers into his ass and whispering encouragement.

But she didn't expect what he said next.

"Those assholes might want you, fantasize about you, but they will never fucking have you," he growled, driving into her over and over. "Never, Nova. Not as long as I'm breathing."

Was that a claim of some sort? And why would he feel the need to put that out into the universe?

A week, she reminded herself again, it had only been a week.

Finally, with a grimace, he threw his head back and his pace was no longer smooth and steady, but choppy and frantic.

With one last thrust, he stiffened and stilled, his face buried against her neck, his breath beating a tattoo against her throat. His heart pounding against her chest. His cock pulsing deep inside her. His long grunt-turned-groan muffled against her skin.

Without lifting his head, he lowered most of his weight, pressing her deeper into the mattress, taking her mouth.

It wasn't a quick "thank you" peck, but a slow and thorough kiss as he clung to her. And when he was done, he slipped from her and rolled to her side with a loud, satisfied sigh.

While he was removing the condom, she rolled off the bed because she was afraid he'd want to curl up with her. To take her in his arms and actually cuddle. Because something happened during sex. Something changed.

It was no longer just a physical or sexual attraction. They had made a deeper connection somehow, some way. It had snuck up on her.

"I'm going to go clean up," she announced, avoiding looking in his direction.

"Nova..."

She paused as she picked up her discarded clothes off the floor. "I'll see you in the morning." She quickly resumed gathering her things.

"You're not sleeping in your room." Not a suggestion, but a clear cut order.

She lifted her head and finally glanced over at him, lounging on the bed with his brow furrowed and the used condom still in his hand.

She asked it anyway... "Is that an order or a suggestion?"

"If you don't come back here when you're done in the bathroom, I'll come get you. Was that clear enough?"

Yes, the shift between them had definitely snuck up on her. So unexpectedly, she hadn't had time to put her walls back in place. Fletch had managed to breach her barriers.

Normally she would just tell a man who said something like that to fuck off. Instead, she answered, "Crystal," placed her clothes down on top of the dresser, tagged his T-shirt from the floor and pulled it over her head.

She didn't wait to see if he had a response before making her way out of the room and down the hall to the bathroom.

She stopped in front of the sink and a woman she didn't

recognize stared back in the mirror. A woman actually willing to let the man in the next room into her head. Maybe even into her heart.

She shook herself mentally.

Since when did she like demanding men?

Never. That macho alpha bullshit had always been a huge turn-off for her. Even more so after dealing firsthand with the Russos blatant misogyny.

So, why now? Why Fletch?

Why, when he made demands, did it turn her on?

It could be just the mood she was in tonight. That had to be it.

The next time they had sex, she'd most likely hate it.

The next time they had sex...

She wasn't going to fool herself and pretend it wouldn't happen again. Or that she wouldn't want it.

But one thing she needed to make clear with him was, what they did during the light would be as Ghost and Kitten, what they did in the dark would be as Fletch and Nova.

Keeping both their professional and personal lives separate might prevent their developing relationship, along with the job they were tasked with, from going sideways.

Or at least she hoped so.

Only time would tell.

Chapter Nineteen

Last Saturday night had been a complete fucking bust. At least for Ghost and Kitten since, again, they didn't see hide nor hair of a Demon at the Hawg Wild Saloon.

What wasn't a bust—at least so far—was what was happening between Fletch and Nova.

Sex and a lot of it.

Last Friday night, the connection between them seemed to have shifted a bit to what Fletch thought was more than sex. But despite his order for her to come back to his bed, she slipped quietly back into her own room after cleaning up.

He figured she did it out of spite since the woman was quite clear about not taking orders from the likes of him. Even though in the last week she'd end every night by heading to her own room, as soon as he'd call out her name, she'd come to his. At first she was testing him—no fucking doubt—but then it turned into a little game between them. Or a challenge, more like it.

Yeah. If Nova didn't want to fuck him, she wouldn't and he could do nothing about it. Luckily, she did, but still wanted to play the *hard-to-get* game. He didn't mind the game she was playing as long as he was hard and he "got" her in the end.

Every night after they had sex, she went to clean up, then climbed in her own bed to sleep. Despite him telling her every damn night to come back to his.

Not once had she even lingered afterward. Not fucking once.

She was making a point.

She was not going to be forced to do something she didn't want to do, even if it was simply sleeping next to him all night. A clear indicator of how headstrong she was.

It was also a good reminder of how much her strength and stubbornness turned him the fuck on. If she had given up easily and listened to any order he tossed her way, he might actually be disappointed.

Tonight he had to remind himself to get his mind out of his bedroom and back to the task at hand, even though he certainly couldn't wait to get back to their shared apartment later so they could make use of that ceiling mirror again.

That mirror made it the... Hottest. Fucking. Sex. *Ever*.

He actually considered getting one for his own place. But again, that was later, this was now and he needed to pay attention to his current surroundings.

After deciding to play doubles, he picked a pool table and placed a quarter on the rail to get in "line" for a turn at playing the winner of the game that would be played before them.

Being Friday night, the bar was hopping, full of bikers and their babes. That meant there was a long wait at the pool tables and also the dart boards.

Smoke, of both the legal and illegal variety, clouded the air, the smell of stale sweat and unwashed bodies filled their nostrils and the number of those bodies was higher than Fletch would like. Being in the midst of so many one-percenter bikers and their ilk in such a compact space made him a bit wired. Especially since he and Nova would be considered the enemy to every single patron in the bar, if they were outed.

Because of where he currently stood at the edge of the billiard area and, with a sea of people blocking his view of the bar, he lost sight of Nova.

He wasn't comfortable with that. Not one fucking bit. But not one biker in that place got their own beer or booze if a woman was with them, whether ol' lady or otherwise. He only hoped that Nova wearing Ghost's cut would keep most hands off her.

When he finally spotted her elbowing her way back through the crowd and returning to him, he blew out a held breath. Even though he knew she could take care of herself, that didn't mean he didn't worry about her. That instinct was impossible for him to shut off.

His relief was short lived when he saw what she carried. Two bottles of fucking Budweiser. He guessed bikers weren't picky as long as their beer was cold, wet and, of course, cheap.

The woman joining him definitely wasn't cold or cheap. Now wet on the other hand...

He grimaced when she reached him. "Bud?"

She rolled her eyes and shoved one of the bottles into his chest. When he went to grab it, she tightened her grip and went up on her toes, putting her mouth to his ear.

He automatically palmed her ass, pretending she was whispering something dirty when she was actually telling him she'd seen four Deadly Demons MC members at one end of the bar.

"Thank fuck," he murmured. He didn't want to waste another damn weekend in this dump without any results.

She scraped his earlobe with her teeth and her short nails over his beard as she lowered herself back to her feet. "My reaction, as well." She scanned the busy billiard area. "Any over here?"

"No."

"You put a quarter on the table?"

"Yup."

She nodded and tipped her bottle to her lips, taking a tiny sip. "I think next time I'm up at the bar, I'll grab a couple of waters and head to the restroom to refill our bottles with that."

"Smart," he murmured, keeping his head on a swivel and constantly scanning the bikers for any threats or possible issues since it was much more crowded tonight than it was last weekend. He had no doubt some scuffles, maybe even brawls, would break out. They needed to stay vigilant.

Unfortunately, it was hard to hear his own damn thoughts over the rock music blasting from the jukebox. Not to mention, the drunks singing along at the top of their lungs—off key, of fucking course—to a George Thorogood song.

"Tell me something I don't already know."

When he dropped his eyes to her, Nova was smiling up at him. And, *damn*, if that didn't catch his breath.

He couldn't get over how gorgeous she was, even dressed as Ghost's ol' lady in torn jeans, a T-shirt with the neckline she cut out in a V, so low it showed the top half of her push-up bra, and a wide black leather belt cinched around her waist, emphasizing how narrow it was.

Like last weekend, she had put on her makeup heavy-handedly, donned the black chain collar around her throat, added a wide black leather cuff on one wrist and a few silver and turquoise rings on her slender fingers.

He was not one to wear jewelry, but since he had an ear pierced already from a previous undercover assignment, he had a silver skull hanging from his left ear and wore a couple of typical bulky biker-type rings Nova had borrowed from Shadow Valley Pawn.

The amount of the side-eye he kept getting from members of other MCs made it apparent that the Dirty Angels didn't step out of their territory often. Maybe the DAMC wasn't the best option for going undercover but it had been the easiest and smartest. They never would've slipped into another club without a lot more work and even more worry about being made. Being outed as undercover law enforcement in a hostile MC would be dangerous, possibly even deadly.

Tugging on Nova's cut, he drew her off to the side and out of the way. He found a spot for them over by a lone stool since every table in the bar was packed solid tonight. He perched on the edge of the high wooden stool, angling himself to make sure the back of his cut could be seen.

When he tugged Nova between his spread thighs, she leaned back into him, appearing more relaxed than she really was. Like his, her gaze constantly sliced through the throng of bar patrons as she pretended to chug her beer.

Hooking an arm under her breasts, he pulled her even tighter against him so when they talked it would be less likely anyone could overhear them. He nuzzled his nose against the back of her head for a second. At least her hair smelled a lot better than everything else around them. By the end of the night, that would change and both of them would need to shower to shed themselves of the funk.

He grinned into the dark silky strands. They could help

save the Earth by conserving water if they showered together. She'd more likely agree to join him if he made it a suggestion and not an order.

Fuck. He needed to stay on track. Sleeping together had definitely distracted him. Something they both had wanted to avoid.

"Since I planted a few seeds last weekend, let's see if those have sprouted and one of the Demons comes to us first so we don't gotta go to them."

"Smart," she said.

"Tell me somethin' I don't already know, woman," he echoed her from earlier.

He couldn't hear her soft laughter due to the din surrounding them, but he could feel her shaking with it before she pinched his arm.

He dropped his voice even lower so no one could hear him say, "As much as we need to be here, would rather be home fucking you."

He barely caught, "We're working."

"Yeah, workin' on gettin' me hard as fuck, Kitten," he said much louder, hoping he *was* overheard this time.

He slid his right hand up to clamp onto her left breast and gave it a rough squeeze. That move caught the attention he hoped it would. He figured he'd leave it there for a bit as long as Nova didn't elbow him in the nuts.

When she didn't complain, he took a quick sip of his beer, then held it out in front of her so she'd take it from him and as soon as she did, used his left hand to cup her pussy over her jeans while mouthing the word "mine."

He got the reaction he was hoping for when more eyeballs turned their way. The interested parties could be watching them out of either curiosity or horniness. Since most bikers and their women were not shy and since Hawg Wild was full of them, he figured anything went.

His ultimate goal, of course, was to catch the Demons' attention. With so many different club colors in there tonight, he needed to do something to stand out for them to notice. Other than telling Nova to get on her knees and suck him off. Something they witnessed right in this bar last Saturday night.

No matter what, they had time before he had to do anything more drastic to stand out since it was only eight and that was early yet for this type of drinking hole. Bikers tended to party later, longer and harder than the average bar goer. Evident from the nonstop hoots and hollers that rose around the pool tables and dart boards, shouts and cursing heard from various areas around the bar, along with loud, boisterous laughter and the occasional sound of breaking glass.

Yeah, this weekend was definitely rowdier. Tonight he noticed a lot of cuts from MCs he hadn't seen at all last weekend, including the Rabid Dogs MC. An outlaw club from the western end of Maryland, well-known within the law enforcement community and flagged as extremely dangerous and volatile.

As they sat there waiting for their turn at the pool table, the chatter he heard was that most of the MC members in the bar were in the area for a poker run to be held the next day. But neither Fletch or Nova could catch what club was holding it and where.

It would be a good idea to get that info and if things didn't work out tonight—or, *hell*, even if they did—they could join in tomorrow in hopes to rub shoulders with more Demons and possibly start gaining their trust.

Remaining on the stool with Nova sandwiched between his legs, he kept one hand possessively clutching her breast for a good half hour as they nursed their beers. Every few minutes, he'd strum his thumb back and forth over the pebbled tip without one whispered complaint from her.

He'd been prepared to spend most of the night at Hawg Wild, but with every minute that ticked by the crowd was becoming rowdier and louder. Because of that, he wanted them to be out of there before shit hit the fan and they both got splattered.

"Baby, go see how long before our turn, then go fetch me a cold fuckin' beer," he ordered loudly over the music.

She straightened, turned into him, gripped his face with one hand and gave him the deepest, dick-hardening kiss with lots of tongue. He lost himself for a few seconds until he remembered this was Kitten, not Nova, and realized she had only done it for show.

But before she could pull away to go do what Ghost instructed, a biker about half as broad as he was high bull-dozed his way through a thick of people and headed in their direction with dark eyes pinned on both him and Nova.

Well now... Maybe the line he'd thrown out had landed him just the fish he was trying to catch.

Unfortunately, Fletch couldn't tell if the approaching biker was a Demon without seeing the back of the guy's cut, but he sure as fuck hoped that was who he was reeling in. The big man got a few back slaps along the way, so he must be well known in the bar. That could be a good sign.

As he worked his way over to them, Fletch noticed a scar split his right eyebrow and a longer one marred his left cheek. He narrowed his eyes on the man's name patch.

Wolf.

With as shaggy as his face and hair was, he did kind of remind Fletch of a wolf. A mangy one that smelled as if it rolled around in a dead animal carcass. And not just once, either. The funk was so bad his eyes burned and he wanted to plug his damn nostrils.

Holy fuck, didn't these assholes take showers on the regular? Or was it that they didn't do laundry and wore their clothes until they were fucking ripe and could walk away on their own?

He couldn't imagine a sweet butt or even an ol' lady being forced to suck their dicks and not have them gagging.

Fletch wanted to gag at that thought.

If his nostrils had to be assaulted, this man better be a fucking Demon.

The Big Bad Wolf took his time eye-fucking Nova first and Fletch fought to keep his upper lip from lifting into a sneer.

He gave the biker a chin lift. "Ghost. Dirty Angels."

"Wolf," came the grunt along with an answering chin lift. "Deadly Demons."

Thank fucking fuck. Now they were getting somewhere.

Fletch grabbed Nova's pussy over her jeans. "See you checkin' out my ol' lady. Like what you see?"

"Yeah. You lend her out?"

Jesus fuck with these people. "Ain't offerin', just askin'."

"You askin' made it sound like you were offerin'."

"Don't share her outside my own brotherhood."

Fletch forced himself to stay loose when Wolf reached out and drug a thumb over Nova's bottom lip. The fingers she had clamped on his thigh dug painfully into the muscle but that was the only indication that Wolf's touch bothered her.

"Fuckin' shame," Wolf grumbled. "Looks like she could do some damage."

"Damn right she can. Name might be Kitten, but she's more of a fuckin' wild cat. Got the scratches and bites to prove it."

Wolf's nostrils flared with heat and interest as he took a closer look at Nova. Maybe Fletch needed to dial it back some before he got another offer to purchase her. Or even rent her for an hour.

"Said she ain't no kitten. Guessin' she likes it rough."

"Not just rough, begs me to choke her the fuck out. And she comes just from me slippin' my belt off 'cause she knows what's happenin' next. Why she's wearin' my cut. Also why she ain't sittin' down. Her ass got stripes on it right now that won't go away 'til next week."

When Wolf slid a hand over the zipper of his jeans, Fletch noticed the biker sported an erection.

Christ, he needed to back it down before the Demon decided he wanted to claim Nova for himself and plugged a bullet between Fletch's eyes right there in Hawg Wild.

Wolf stared at Nova for far too long before finally lifting his bloodshot eyes and narrowing them on Fletch. "Never see you Angels in this bar. Why ain't you hangin' out at The Iron Horse?"

With a casual shrug, Fletch explained, "New to the area. When me an' the ol' ball an' chain went explorin' last weekend, came across this biker friendly bar an' stopped in for a cold one." He paused before challenging sharply, "Got a problem with us bein' here?"

"I say that?"

"No, but sure actin' that way. Ain't here to make fuckin' trouble. Just enjoyin' the atmosphere." *Holy fuck,* he hoped that lie came off as truth. "This is more our kinda place. The Iron Horse gets borin'. More action here than there."

The Demon's dark eyes narrowed again and suspicion colored his next question. "New to the club, but got your fuckin' patches already?"

"Ain't new to the life, new to the DAMC."

"Whataya mean?"

"Was up north with the Blood Fury for the past few years. Ol' lady's pop got cancer an' we hadta come down here to take care of 'im. He passed, so we're gonna get his house once the estate's settled. Since the Fury's an ally with the Angels, they let me patch over. Can't be livin' as Fury in Angel territory. Angels want their dues." He needed to redirect Wolf. "What about you? Thought the Demons were in West Virginia but your patch says otherwise. Last I checked, Uniontown ain't in your home state."

Wolf's eyes hooded and it took him a few moments to respond. "Prez got me setting up a chapter here."

"For what reason?"

Wolf's head jerked back and his already big body suddenly seemed to expand. "We fuckin' need one?"

Fletch lifted and dropped one shoulder, trying to appear unthreatened. "Guess not. Don't you think you're gonna step on some toes settin' up so close to Shadow Valley?"

Wolf's dark eyes shuttered. A clear sign he didn't want to share the Demon's true intentions on creeping northward. "Tell your prez we ain't movin' in on their territory. Might kiss it but we ain't fuckin' it. You get what I'm sayin'? Don't need them on our backs."

"I'll pass on the word, but ain't sayin' he'll be okay with that."

"He ain't got a choice."

For fuck's sake. Zak Jamison and the goons who flanked him weren't going to like that news. Fletch yanked on his chin. "Ain't for a nobody like me to decide. Like I said, new to the club. Got no power. Got no say. Best I can do is pass it on."

Wolf nodded. "You do that. Ain't lookin' for war. Just

need a neighbor that minds their own business. They mind theirs, we'll mind ours."

"Will pass that on, too."

"Speakin' of business... Heard you're lookin' to score for your ol' lady." Wolf flicked to Nova and back while thumbing his nose.

"Yeah, she got a slight sweet tooth, but it ain't only for her."

"Thought she was addicted to sugar an' that's why you're lookin'."

Fletch's eyebrows shot up his forehead. "She look like a sugar addict?"

Of course that had Wolf doing a slow, thorough roll from Nova's head to her boots again. "Just repeatin' what I heard."

Nothing like talking about a woman like she wasn't right there listening. That had to piss Nova off. But thankfully, she wasn't interjecting and only biding her time. "That's only what I told that Boz guy. Didn't want him knowin' the real fuckin' reason. Ain't his business, an' better that way."

"How much you lookin' for?"

Fletch scratched his bearded chin and pursed his lips. "How much you got?"

When Wolf hesitated and his eyes sliced through the immediate area around them, Fletch pivoted quickly. "Just need a sample for now. If it's good shit, might be lookin' for more."

Wolf frowned. "Angels don't run drugs or guns. They're a fuckin' stain on the rest of us since they wanna be squeaky fuckin' clean. A buncha wannabes pretendin' they're pit bulls when they're nothin' but a buncha kicked puppies."

Fletch pulled his head back and stared Wolf down. "The fuck we are. My prez is fuckin' smart enough to make sure our club flies under the pigs' radar." He cocked an eyebrow. "Unlike some others with more members inside than out."

"Now that I think about it, you kinda look like a fuckin' pig."

"Last I checked, a pig's pink, fat and tasty. Ain't none of those things."

Nova purred, "Oh, you're tasty, baby. I can vouch for that." She reached back, grabbed his crotch and squeezed.

Fletch grinned. "Yeah, baby, ain't nothin' better than when you deep throat my fuckin' dick. So fuckin' good at it." He added a wink. "My woman gives the best head I ever fuckin' had. Gotta hang on tight to a bitch you can face fuck without her gaggin'." He sucked at his teeth. "Enough about snatch. Need to finish talkin' business 'fore it's our turn at Eight Ball."

When Wolf's gaze remained stuck on Nova, Fletch coughed sharply, drawing the man's attention back to him. That seemed to shake him free enough to say, "Can hook you up with a sample. You like it, then what?"

"If it's good shit, gonna be lookin' for a steady supply."

"What're you talkin'?"

"Enough to make it worthwhile. Need to bring in some extra scratch on the side. What the club pays me is shit. Practically fuckin' slave labor. Need to start a little side hustle to make life a bit sweeter for me an' the ol' lady. I keep her happy, she keeps me happy. Get what I'm sayin'?"

"Hear you on that. Whether you get it from us or not, you can't be sellin' in our territory. Gonna hafta stick in your own."

"Plannin' on it. Wouldn't want to step on any other club's toes. Know better than that. Also need to keep it on the D.L. from my own prez."

"You goin' against your prez's rules can cause some shit we don't want blowin' back on us."

"That ain't a worry. Know how to handle it."

Wolf tilted his head and studied Fletch. He made sure to keep his expression blank because the fucker was searching for a reason to tell him to fuck off. "You deal for the Fury?"

Fuck. He didn't know much about the Blood Fury. He wasn't sure about what that MC did for money. But whatever answer he gave, he'd need to own it. "Not for the Fury. Again, for myself. What my prez don't know, don't hurt 'im and it puts a nice wad of scratch in my pocket. Hopin' to make enough to upgrade my sled, too, now that we're down in Shadow Valley."

"Wantin' one of those Jag Jamison customs?"

"Fuck yeah. Who don't? An' if you know anythin' about his work, that shit ain't cheap."

"That's for damn sure."

"Speakin' of sleds... Heard chatter 'bout a poker run tomorrow. Know who's holdin' it?"

"Rabid Dogs."

"Anyone welcome?"

"Guessin' so. Plenty of 'em here tonight to ask."

"Will do that." Fletch nodded. "You gonna be there?"

Wolf tipped his head toward the crowded bar behind him. "Most of us will. Pretty big fuckin' deal 'round here. Why so many clubs are in the area tonight."

"Look forward to it. Be good to rub elbows with other like-minded people. Bring that sample then?"

Wolf's jaw shifted just enough for Fletch to catch it. But the Demon said nothing for the longest time and only stared at Fletch. Yeah, the man wasn't sure about dealing to someone he didn't know. Fletch couldn't blame him.

The biker might look like shit and smell like it, too, but he wasn't a complete dumbass.

When Fletch began to fear that Wolf would just up and walk away, the big man finally spoke. "No reason to wait 'til tomorrow."

Well, damn. But that could be good or bad. Fletch decided to wait him out.

He was relieved when Wolf dug deep inside his cut. He could barely see the tiny plastic baggy in his fat fingers and couldn't tell if the meth was in rock or powder form, but either way, they were scoring like he hoped.

Things were going better than expected.

Unfortunately, his relief was short-lived and quickly turned to annoyance when Wolf leaned close and reached out to Nova.

Fletch couldn't stop himself from tensing when the man made a show of tucking the tiny zip-lock baggy, no larger than a dime, into Nova's pushed-up cleavage. He didn't just tuck it and go. He pushed it deep into her bra and he fucking lingered.

The fucker was copping a goddamn feel.

Fletch was impressed that Nova kept her shit together. However, he couldn't help but suck a sharp breath in through his nose and growl, "Brother," in warning.

Wolf took his time pulling back. When he did, he puckered his lips and blew Nova a kiss before giving Fletch a shit-eating grin, adding on his own warning. "Wouldn't mind takin' her for a ride."

"Ain't gonna happen, brother, and don't like you fingerin' my woman without permission."

Wolf shrugged, still wearing the grin Fletch wanted to wipe off his face. "You wanna play, you gotta pay. And with the way she reacted to me touchin' her, shows she liked it and wants more."

Fletch ground his teeth, grabbed Nova's hair in his fist before ripping her head back far enough that their eyes met. He bared his teeth and growled, "That true?"

Her brown eyes were wide and held worry. "Only want you, Ghost. Swear it."

Damn, she was good.

"Good answer. Otherwise, I'd whip your ass with my belt right here in this fuckin' bar. Fact, would even make you bend over the bar to do it. That would teach you a fuckin' lesson you wouldn't soon forget."

"Now that I'd pay good money for," Wolf said with a chuckle. "Pay even more to be able to do it for you."

Christ almighty. They needed to get the fuck out of there. And a fight breaking out near the bar was the perfect distraction and an even better excuse to leave.

"Nobody leavin' marks on my woman but me. All right, gonna let her try that sample tonight. Will let you know at the poker run tomorrow whether it's the quality I'm lookin' for."

"It's good shit."

"That's what they all say," Fletch grumbled. "Don't take lightly to gettin' screwed over. Happened once and that motherfucker regretted it."

With his eyes on the fight that seemed to be spreading in their direction, Wolf reached into his cut again, pulled out a folded piece of paper and held it out to Fletch.

He took it and opened the flyer to see the details of the poker run. It said right across the top in big fucking letters that all clubs were welcome.

The fucker had known that info and held out. No surprise.

Fletch nodded and flicked the flyer with his finger. "We'll be there." He folded it back up and slipped it into his back pocket.

"No loss if you ain't." With that, Wolf then headed toward the fray.

As soon as he was out of sight, Fletch jumped to his feet and grabbed Nova's arm. "Got what we wanted, now we're gettin' the fuck outta here. Don't trust any of these fuckers to not try and distract me so they can grab you. We're so fuckin' outnumbered here. The worse it gets, the tighter my asshole is puckerin'."

She got up on her toes again and with her lips against his, she murmured, "Agreed. Let's go home."

"Best fuckin' thing I've heard all goddamn night."

With a hand gripping the back of Nova's neck, he steered her toward the exit. Just in time, too, since just as they reached the door, someone was thrown into a table nearby, causing a whole new tussle to break out.

They got out while the getting was good.

Chapter Twenty

After getting a "taste" from Wolf the night before, they met Crew on their way to Saturday's poker run in a parking lot to hand over the tiny bag of powdered ice they scored.

The task force leader would test the sample to confirm the meth was the same shit the Demons were selling on the street and to confirm Wolf wasn't selling his own stash for his own side hustle.

They weren't looking to bust a small-time dealer, they wanted to get to both the source and the major distributer the Demons were sandwiched between. Crew had newly discovered info that the Demons weren't keeping all of the meth they hauled from the border. They were transporting it for someone else, a much bigger organization who was financing the purchase and then the MC was keeping a kilo in payment for each run.

Saturday was a long fucking day surrounded by too many asshole bikers he couldn't trust. He was tense for most of it and didn't let Nova out of his sight at all, even though she reminded him more than once that she could take care of herself.

He had no doubt she could, but she was supposed to be his ol' lady and as her ol' man, she "belonged" to him. That responsibility included both protecting her and keeping her in line, whether she liked it or not.

Halfway through the tortuously long poker run, Fletch finally got the text from Crew with the go-ahead to make arrangements with Wolf to buy more. They all agreed they should only buy a small amount to start until a solid relationship was built between Wolf and Ghost.

Once they did that, they'd start making bigger buys, then work on finding out who they were transporting for. It would just be a matter of time and patience. For now they only needed to concentrate on the outlaw MC.

As soon as he caught up with Wolf at one of the stops, they set up a time and date for a buy. Soon after, Fletch and Nova slipped away when no one was paying attention and headed back to Shadow Valley.

On the way back to the pawn shop apartment, they picked up a large take-out order at Bangin' Burgers, and not even a minute after hitting the front door, they both stripped down to their skivvies, enjoyed the cool air conditioning and stuffed their faces and stomachs.

Then after a shared shower, they had a late "afternoon delight" for dessert and Nova actually fell asleep by his side for a few hours.

All in all, even though the poker run was miserable as fuck, the day ended better than expected and he, Nova and Crew were satisfied that their part of the investigation was going smoothly so far.

At least until Wednesday night when Wolf didn't show up at the agreed upon buy location.

They'd been waiting on the metal bleachers at an empty baseball field just south of Uniontown when a Harley pulled in twenty minutes later than the scheduled time. Fletch had already been annoyed for being left hanging like that, but then to see someone else show up made all the fine hairs on his body stand on end.

He didn't like this change of plans. Not one fucking bit. Neither did Nova.

"Keep an eye out to make sure this isn't an ambush or anything sketchy," he muttered under his breath.

"Yeah, I'm not liking this," she said. "Did Wolf tell you he wasn't coming?"

"No." Fletch had even given the fucker the number to his assigned task force cell phone. "Okay, let's go deal with whoever this is. Just watch my back."

"You got it," she answered.

As they climbed off the bleachers and headed toward the stone parking lot, he called out, "Who the fuck are you?" to the biker dismounting his sled. "You a Demon?"

The unknown man, about as unkempt as Wolf, turned and hooked a thumb over his shoulder at his back patches. In the shadowed parking lot, Fletch could barely make out the Deadly Demons' rockers. That still didn't mean it wasn't a set-up.

As they approached the man, Fletch purposely didn't hook an arm around Nova so they'd have both hands free and be prepared to act, if needed.

Since they needed this biker's name for their task force daily report, he asked, "Who the fuck are you?" again as the short, heavyset guy turned around to face them.

"You Ghost?"

Fletch pointed to his own name patch. "That's what the fuck it says, don't it?" He purposely squinted when searching the front of the Demon's cut. "Your name's Bitch?"

"Ain't Bitch. It's fuckin' Stitch."

"Got it. Poor lighting."

"He sure looks like a bitch," Nova snickered, standing right behind Fletch but off to the side.

"Who's that?" he asked, jerking his chin at her.

"My ol' lady."

"Why the fuck you got your ol' lady with you to do business?"

Because she can shoot your fucking ass dead in less than three seconds flat, that's why, asshole. "'Cause we're makin' it look like we're out for a damn Sunday drive. Never know who's watchin'. Not just the pigs, but the nosy fucks in my own club. Prez don't want anyone in our brotherhood sellin'. I get caught, my colors will be stripped. Or fuckin' worse."

Stitch's eyebrows jumped up his forehead. "Your prez don't know you're here?"

Fletch sucked on his teeth. "Does yours?"

"He don't need to know. This shit's between Wolf an' you."

"Then, why ain't Wolf here?" Fletch barked with annoyance.

"Yeah, Wolf was supposed to be here," Nova added, unhelpfully.

Stitch answered, "Had shit to do," while shooting Nova an annoyed look.

Bullshit. "Why the fuck didn't he tell me you were comin' instead?"

"'Cause he don't fuckin' answer to you."

Fletch bit back a sigh. "But you answer to him?"

Stitch spit on the ground, avoiding his question.

"He asked you a fucking question," Nova insisted.

What the fuck was she doing?

No matter what, she was right, Fletch needed answers. "You sellin' your club's stash behind your prez's back? Don't need that sorta trouble."

"And you need to keep your bitch on a shorter leash. Ain't doin' nothin' our prez don't know about, so don't you fuckin' worry 'bout shit that don't concern you. Wolf's gotta sell a certain amount with..." Stitch shook his head, his expression showing that he'd already said more than he should. That sucked because the more he ran his mouth, the more new info Fletch might be able to obtain.

"What, your prez divvies up your stash an' you all gotta sell?"

"Somethin' like that." His eyes narrowed on Fletch for a second, then his gaze flicked to Nova. "How do I know you ain't some undercover pig tryin' to fuck me hard?"

"How the fuck do I know you ain't some undercover pig?" Fletch countered.

"Yeah!" Nova shouted.

"How 'bout showin' me the colors inked onto your back?" Fletch suggested.

The other biker answered, "Long as you do the same."

Damn. He fucked up.

Before he could come up with an excuse, Nova stepped up next to him with her hands on her hips and attitude rolling off her before she even opened her mouth. *Again.* "He ain't got 'em. He's—"

With a deep scowl, Stitch cut her off with, "You always let your slit speak for you?"

"Slit?" Nova screamed, spreading her legs in a defensive stance. "You're calling *me* a fucking slit, you fat fuck?"

Goddamn it. Fletch knew biker chicks weren't afraid of

running their mouth, but, *for fuck's sake,* she needed to dial it back some so this deal wasn't fucked.

"Shut the fuck up, Kitten," Fletch growled, shooting her an unspoken message that, of course, went ignored.

"Fuck that." Nova flung a hand toward Stitch. "I'm not gonna let this motherfucker—"

Fletch sucked in a breath to steel himself for what he was about to do, then before he could think twice, he swung, backhanding her. Hard enough that her head jerked back and the sound of the impact against her cheek filled the space between them.

Goddamn it!

He jabbed a finger in her direction. "When I tell you to shut the fuck up, woman, you shut the fuck up. You fuckin' know better than to run your trap when the men are talkin'."

Nova blinked and her mouth gaped slightly.

Fuck. He had knocked her right out of her role for a second.

He breathed a little easier when he saw her mentally shake herself and slide back into character.

The second she did, she screamed, "You're a fucking asshole!" while palming her red cheek.

When Stitch grinned, Fletch wanted to backhand that motherfucker, too.

He forced himself to stay in character, despite the fact he was pissed she had gone over the top, in turn, forcing him to respond in the same manner. "An' you're a fuckin' cunt. Go sit on my sled and if you don't listen, leavin' your ass here. Your twat is tight but sometimes it ain't worth dealin' with your goddamn mouth."

With a set jaw and fury—whether real or fake—filling her eyes, Nova flipped him the bird and stalked toward his Harley, bitching under her breath the whole way.

He watched her go, hoping like fuck she wasn't truly pissed at him for his knee-jerk reaction. Nova also had to know she'd been playing with fire by being mouthy in front of Stitch. She'd done enough undercover work to know he'd have to stay true to his character that, in this case, was an asshole biker who treated his woman like property. His property.

He turned back to Stitch and shook his head. "Fuckin' bitches."

"Sometimes a quick, to the fuckin' point lesson's all it takes."

"Problem is, she tends to enjoy those lessons. The rougher, the better. An' sometimes she pushes me just to get one."

Fletch ground his teeth when Stitch licked his lips. "Yeah?"

"Yeah. Any-fuckin'-way, ain't got my colors inked on my back yet, since I'm new to the DAMC. Gonna get them soon. Crow's been booked solid lately." Name dropping was always beneficial.

Stitch's brow dropped low. "Can't be new if you got your full setta patches."

"Already explained that shit to Wolf. Ain't wastin' my breath explainin' it again. Don't wanna trust me, then let's end this right here, an' I'll have a few words with Wolf about not dealin' with anybody but him in the future."

Stitch pursed his lips and scratched at his shaggy beard as he considered Fletch's low-key threat. "Guess if Wolf trusts you, gotta trust you, too."

"Don't give a fuck if you don't trust me. Only here to do a fuckin' exchange. You got what I want, I got what you want. Simple shit you're makin' difficult."

Stitch tilted his head and studied Fletch.

Fletch threw up his hands. "You don't wanna sell to me, then I'm fuckin' out. You're the fucker who's gotta explain it to Wolf. But, brother, ain't gonna stand here all fuckin' night playin' the whose dick is bigger game. Already waited twenty fuckin' minutes longer than I shoulda 'cause your ass was fuckin' late.

Stitch huffed out, "Twenty minutes ain't shit."

Fletch shrugged and started toward Nova, where she waited for him at his sled. She was leaning against it with her arms crossed over her chest and there wasn't one smidgeon of happy on her face as Kitten glared in his direction.

Or he sure as fuck hoped it was Kitten glaring and not Nova.

"Hold the fuck up," Stitch called out when Fletch was about fifteen feet away.

Fletch paused but didn't turn around. He made Stitch come to him and when the biker appeared in his sights, the man was already digging deep into his cut. He palmed a bag, holding it close to his gut, most likely to hide it from anyone unexpectedly rolling into the baseball field parking lot.

"Lemme see it. Ain't gonna get fucked. I do, then I'm goin' to my prez an' tellin' him the Demons are dealin' in Angels' territory. You got me?"

"Only fuckin' you're gonna get is from your pissed off ol' lady. Sleep with one eye open tonight," Stitch said with a chuckle and held it out but kept it low and out of sight.

Fletch had expected to get an ounce broken down into gram baggies and ready for sale. Not an ounce of slightly yellow shards of ice. "You don't got this shit broken down? The taste he gave me the other night was powder. What the fuck!"

Stitch sniffed hard. "Processin' costs extra. Now you can cut it however you want. Endless fuckin' possibilities."

Fletch grabbed at the baggy. "Whatever."

The Demon quickly pulled it out of Fletch's reach and shook an open palm at him. Grinding his teeth, Fletch dug into his cut and pulled out a tight roll of marked hundred dollar bills.

He made sure to exchange the money for the product at the same time. Crew would be pissed if the feds' money disappeared and Fletch didn't have anything to show for it. And he sure didn't trust the fucker standing before him.

He tucked the drugs into a hidden pocket inside his cut. "That'll get me started but what if I want a pound?"

Stitch was thumbing through the roll of cash, making sure it was all there. Once he was satisfied, he hid it in his own cut and lifted his gaze to Fletch. "A pound sure's a fuckuva lot for a street dealer like you."

"How the fuck would you know since you don't know shit about me? And you didn't answer my fuckin' question."

Stitch shrugged and spit on the ground. "Talk to Wolf."

He would've done that if Wolf had showed the fuck up like planned. He bit back a sigh. "Will do that."

With a nod, Stitch headed over to his sled and straddled it. His Harley roared to life a few seconds later and within a minute he was gone.

Leaving Fletch alone to deal with the fallout of that unexpected backhand to his partner's face.

Nova's eyes tracked Fletch as he returned to the Harley. She forced her jaws to unclench as he stepped boot tip to boot tip with her. He ground one hand against the back of his neck and planted the other on his hip. "Fuck, Nova. Sorry. You pissed?"

She lifted a single eyebrow. "Do I look it?"

"Yeah, you've been fuming over here the whole time."

"Do you blame me?" Not breaking their locked gazes, she pushed off his bike and stood, making him take a step back. "That was bullshit, Fletch. I wasn't expecting it."

He sighed and scrubbed a hand down his beard. "Know it. It was the only quick way I could think of to convince that motherfucker we aren't cops."

"I'm aware we need to remain in character and act appropriately but that doesn't give you a pass. I wasn't prepared."

"I know and I feel like a fucking dick about it. If it'll make you feel better, you can hit me back. Just be careful of my pretty face." He grinned in his lame attempt to lighten the mood.

"Glad you think this is humorous."

His grin flattened. "Nova, I was just doing what I thought needed to be done to be convincing. I certainly didn't want him leaving with the product. Just in case you have doubts and I need to clear them, I don't fucking hit women. I don't get my kicks abusing women."

"I didn't say you did, but there are plenty of fucking men who do." She blew out a slow breath.

She was damn sure plenty of bikers knocked their women around. Luckily, she hadn't seen it with the Angels and hopefully she never would because, without a doubt, she would step in.

His eyes narrowed on her and when he reached out to touch the cheek he struck, she leaned out of his reach.

She shook her head. "No."

"I was playing my part, Nova."

Of course he was. "I'm well aware of that. That doesn't mean I have to accept what you did or even forgive you."

She would but she didn't have to.

Of course she expected him to be physical with her.

Playing grab ass, cupping her pussy or squeezing her breasts were one thing. Backhanding her...

That was a whole different ball game.

Of course she knew it was Ghost hitting Kitten, not Fletch hitting Nova. Because if it had been the second scenario, all bets would've been off and she would not have hesitated to strike back and defend herself.

But she still let it get to her because it dragged back memories of dealing with Russo Sr. The man was a damn monster, but she had stuck with that assignment because she had successfully integrated herself into the organization. Not an easy feat. And no one in the FBI had gotten that close to the head of the family. She alone managed it and she wasn't going to possibly fuck up the only chance to bring the Mob boss down.

Because of that, she took the hits along with the successes.

"Swear I won't do it again. Ever. I went with my gut and, clearly, my gut was dead wrong."

She closed her eyes and sighed. He said he had gone with his gut, and if she had to admit it, she would've done the same. "It wasn't."

"Whether it was or wasn't, it won't happen again, Nova. I regretted it the second I did it."

Her eyes opened when his long fingers splayed over her cheek. The one that didn't throb.

He brushed his thumb across her bottom lip and then tipped her face up to him. "Let's go home so I can make it up to you."

Sometimes dark clouds *did* have a silver lining.

But only sometimes.

Chapter Twenty-One

Fletch wasted no time taking them back to the pawn shop and their temporary residence.

During most of the ride he kept a grip on her knee.

Whether that was to reassure her or himself, she didn't know. But she got it. He felt guilty.

And at first, she was shocked when he struck her, but by the time they dismounted the Harley and climbed the stairs, she was mostly over it and had forgiven him. That didn't mean she wouldn't make him suffer a little for it.

Being undercover, sometimes you were forced to do things you normally wouldn't. It went with the territory. She had no doubt he would never get physical with her in that manner if they hadn't been playing their roles.

So, yes, after the initial surprise, the longer she thought about it and the way he acted and his look of regret afterward, she forgave him but it would be hard to forget.

But not because of him.

He peered over his shoulder at her as he unlocked the front door. "You okay?"

"Yes, fine." She followed him into the dark, cooler interior and immediately shrugged out of her hot leather cut.

While he locked up, she went into the kitchen to grab a beer and ice for her still smarting cheek. When she closed the freezer door after grabbing a tray of ice, she jumped when she backed up and bumped into Fletch.

He grabbed the tray from her and twisted to crack the ice loose. "Grab a towel."

She pulled one from a drawer along with a plastic, sealable bag.

He plucked those from her fingers, too, filled the baggy with the ice, wrapped it in the towel, then crooked his finger at her. "I said I'm going to make it up to you."

"I figured you meant when we were naked."

He scratched at his chest. "Well, I thought that was a given."

He must have been anxious to shed his cut, too. She glanced down. And his boots.

"You want a beer?" she asked, before taking a sip of hers.

"In a minute. C'mere," he urged softly.

She studied the man before her, now leaning back against the counter with the ice in his hand.

She realized at that moment they'd slid from simply being undercover partners, fellow task force members and even sex partners into something much more solid. She had no idea when that deeper connection happened, but she guessed it could've been that first night in his bed when she felt a slight shift.

Or it could've been sometime during all those late nights when they kicked up their feet in the living room and shared stories about their careers. Or the mornings she'd roll out of bed to find breakfast already waiting for her on the table with a mug of freshly brewed coffee, prepared just how she liked it.

Or when she finally gave in and began to wrap her arms around him every time they rode the Harley.

Or the way he whispered her name when he was deep inside her.

Or the way they looked so perfect together in that ceiling mirror.

She hadn't thought too much about it until now. She could no longer deny it did happen, and when she wasn't expecting it.

Maybe she'd been avoiding the truth because this was only supposed to be an assignment and nothing more.

But when she stepped between his legs and he hauled her against him, pressing the ice to her aching cheek and studying her face, she knew without a doubt things had changed.

At least for her.

She tried to imagine coming home at night to an empty apartment and she no longer could.

Yes, they hadn't slept together all night. Not once. But that was because she had been trying to avoid any kind of attachment. To prevent their working relationship from moving into one more personal.

But not staying in his bed all night hadn't hampered that. It was the time while they were awake that grew the connection.

"You okay?" he asked softly again.

She snapped herself free from her surprising—and a little bit disturbing—discovery. "You already asked me that."

"Yeah, and you told me 'fine.' Coming from a woman, that word isn't as reassuring as it should be. I want you to be honest with me."

"I have no reason to lie."

He studied her face. At least the part not covered by the ice pack and his big hand.

When she avoided his eyes, he used her chin to turn her to face him. "What's going on?"

"Nothing."

"Bullshit. I've seen you naked, Nova, now I want the naked truth. I'd be stupid not to expect a reaction after what I did but not quite the reaction you gave me when we were both playing a part."

"You thought I was overreacting?"

It took him a few seconds before he answered. "I wouldn't call it overreacting but I saw something on your face that caught me off guard."

"Your handprint?"

His lips thinned. "No. Something deeper than that. And you're trying to avoid talking about it."

"If me wanting to avoid a certain discussion is true, then you should respect that."

"You just confirmed my suspicion."

She raised her gaze to his. "Of what?"

"Here's the thing... I expected you to get pissed and you had every right to be. What I didn't expect was you to be hanging onto that anger the way you did. Especially after you were pushing both me and Stitch. I figured you were trying to distract him from asking too many questions, so I added to your distraction with something even bigger. I apologize."

And, of course, what he did worked. "Fletch, I've already let it go."

"It's still lingering since it's coming from a deeper place." He tapped gently on her chest with his index finger.

She sighed, grabbed the towel-covered ice and pulled

away from him, giving him her back, so he could no longer analyze her reaction. "No woman likes to be hit."

"No shit."

"It's worse when you can't protect yourself."

"I'm sure plenty of ol' ladies crack their ol' men upside the head when they step out of line. Stitch probably wouldn't have blinked if you had hit me back."

"I'm not talking about bikers, Fletch."

He grabbed her arm and spun her around. "Family?"

"Not the family you're thinking of," she murmured before downing the rest of her beer and putting the empty bottle aside.

It only took that long for Fletch to read between the lines. The man was far from dense. He was sharp and had already proven to her that he was damn good at his job. So, of course he'd easily pick up on what was only an insinuation.

The fact was, she trusted him. She'd never trusted anyone in her line of work as much as she trusted Fletch. It actually surprised her that she wanted to tell him something she'd kept from everyone else, including her co-workers, her superiors, even her friends and family.

Because of having to prove herself in her line of work, she never wanted to fail at an assignment, especially with one so big and important as the Russos. She was embarrassed with how far she had to go to prevent that failure.

However, she could see her personal relationship continuing with Fletch even after this assignment was over. And if so, then what she was about to reveal would come out eventually anyway. Whether tonight or another night when they were lying next to each other in bed and sharing secrets in the dark. Because she had a feeling that was where they were headed.

Fletch had asked her to stay with him in his bed every damn night, and every damn night she left and slept alone.

She hadn't wanted to fall for him.

She had resisted as best as she could.

She had to face the fact that was one "assignment" she failed.

"Talk to me," came his murmur.

She turned to face him again to find his head tilted and him trying to read her. Both her body language and her expression.

Her first instinct was to lock everything down, but she didn't, especially after he said, "I want to know everything about you, Nova. The good, the bad, even the ugly. It doesn't matter. Honestly, I'm having a difficult time figuring out what makes you tick beyond being an agent. And your career doesn't make up everything about you."

"Maybe that's because I don't have much beyond my career. Since becoming an agent, my focus has always been doing the best I could. Proving to myself and others that I *could* be the best. Because of that, relationships have suffered. To be honest, I've slept with you more in the limited time we've worked together than the past five years combined."

His eyebrows rose. "Should I take that as a compliment?" He wasn't being cocky, his question was truly genuine.

She nodded. "Yes, you actually should."

His surprise turned to satisfaction. "Then I'll accept that compliment and give you one back. I have not wanted to be with anyone as much as I want to be with you. That's a straight fact. Your dedication to your job... Hell, your strength in general impresses me. You're sexy as fuck. You're smart. You're good at thinking on your feet. You're everything I've ever wanted in a woman—hell, in a partner, too—whether career- or personal-wise."

Holy shit. She did not expect that kind of confession from him. "I'm hardly perfect."

"Of course not. But who the fuck is? Anyone who appears perfect on the outside is usually far from it on the inside. It's usually a false front. The bottom line is, no matter how long this assignment lasts, I want you by my side."

"You mean during."

"That's a given. But—and I'm not sure how you feel about this—even afterwards."

"What are you saying?" Her pulse began to race at what he was implying. Could they want the same thing?

"This job is only at the beginning. We still have a long way to go. That gives us plenty of time for us to see if this... *connection* building between us will remain true. And not only because we're forced to live and work together." He pushed away from the counter and closed the space between them. "But here's the deal... if you're interested in that, we need to be completely open and honest with each other." Before she could agree, he added, "About everything."

He wasn't the only one who could read between the lines. She knew exactly what he wanted from her. He'd been curious about her undercover work with the Russos and hadn't hidden that curiosity. Every time they had shared stories—whether "war" stories or humorous ones—about work, he always hinted around at that particular job and she always avoided discussing it.

If they'd only remain as work partners in the task force, what went down with the Russos wasn't his business. But if they became more, something they both seemed to want, then it needed to be said. Because after what she told him, he might change his mind about wanting anything further with her.

It was better to be upfront with him now, than later, if they ended up deeply involved.

"What I tell you goes no farther than the two of us," she finally said.

"Okay."

He said that too quickly. "I need more than an okay. I need a promise, Fletch. The risk is much greater than only losing my job."

"It's about losing your freedom."

"That and," she inhaled and breathed out, "possibly my life."

"You used your position for personal gain," he surmised.

"I didn't *gain* anything."

"Payback for your uncle, then."

"Sure, I wanted payback for my uncle, but I had no legal way to access the Parisis."

"The Russos were the next best thing."

"Basically, I wanted to destroy La Cosa Nostra from the inside out. Even though that was an impossible task for me to do alone, I did what I could and how I could. I couldn't do as much as I would've liked, but it was something. It wouldn't bring my uncle back but at least it kept me from feeling totally helpless about his loss. I couldn't just sit back and accept what they did to him and live with myself."

She still wasn't absolutely sure she wanted to tell him everything. Either now or ever. She was putting a lot of trust in his hands if she did. She'd also be handing over enough power to him that he'd easily be able to crush her.

His voice was a low rumble when he said, "No secrets, Nova. Not between us."

It was instinct to protect her secrets. Just like it had been instinct for him to strike her earlier to protect their undercover assignments as Ghost and Kitten.

"Why? Because we're fucking?" slipped from her before she could stop it.

His expression sharpened and his spine snapped straight. "For fuck's sake, Nova, after what I said, you still think it's only fucking?"

She had already determined they were way past that. But admitting it only made her more vulnerable and she didn't like feeling exposed.

He set his jaw. "Damn."

His apparent disappointment made her sigh and admit, "No, you're right. It's more and because of that we have to completely trust each other. It's the only way both this," she swept her hand out around them, indicating their assignment, "and this," she waved it between the two of them, "will work. I know that. I just..."

"I swear I won't tell a fucking soul, Nova. Not one. Whatever you tell me I'll take to my grave."

Funny, normally she'd hear something like that and think, "Sure you will." But with Fletch, she actually believed it. By keeping it to himself, he'd be protecting her from what could happen if it got out.

It was one reason why she felt completely comfortable with him. Why she wanted to keep building their relationship.

They shared more than a physical and sexual attraction, he had her complete trust and she needed his.

She sucked in a deep breath to start at the beginning, hoping like hell her gut instinct about him wasn't wrong. Because if it was, she could be making one of the biggest mistakes of her life.

"When I first made contact with the Russos, my target

was Francesco Jr. I made sure to make myself seen at his birthday party being held at a high end restaurant in the city. Long story short, I did manage to catch his attention, but as soon as he introduced me around that night, I found myself separated from Frankie and on his father's arm instead. They were slick when it came to manipulation. I recognized what they were doing, but of course, I let it happen because Frank Sr. was a bigger fish than Frankie at the time. In actuality, I couldn't believe that opportunity was falling into my lap, so I went with it." She shrugged.

"But did you have to fuck Sr. to get in good with him? And if so, did the AUSA frown upon that or did you get prior approval?"

Of course he'd want clarification on how she got in so deep with the Russos. Fletch had suspected she'd fucked Frank from the moment he found out she'd been undercover with that crime family.

Of course, the Assistant U.S. Attorney preferred she didn't actually have sex with either Frank or Frankie Russo. She had lucked out because if Frank Sr. hadn't taken a sudden shine to her and if he hadn't had his prostate removed in secret due to cancer—*thank fuck*—then it might have gone that far and she *would* have needed approval from the AUSA first or at least tried to extract herself from that situation. And if she had to back out of the undercover assignment, she would've wasted all the gains she achieved in a short amount of time within the Russo family. To end up on the arm of an actual Mob boss was a major score inside a criminal organization. Few achieved it and lived to tell about it.

She had.

"Luckily, no. He had health issues with his prostate he kept hidden because he didn't want to appear weak. Because of that, he wanted everyone to believe we were having sex and having it often. I was instructed to lie about it and brag often and loudly about how virile he was. In actuality, I ended up being his constant companion. Because of that, I heard things I never would've heard otherwise. More than I would've by being with Frankie. Did I hate every minute of having to sleep beside the head of the Russo family almost every damn night? Hell yes. Did I do whatever was necessary to gather evidence against him? Of course. I was in the perfect position to do so. When I first targeted the son, I never expected to get that deep within their organization. Once I did, I did whatever necessary to stay there, even sliding between Frank's sheets every night." She forced down the bile rising into her throat at the memory. "I even put up with his kisses and him groping me in front of others. I told myself it was only until I had enough to take his ass down. In some ways him getting physical with me was more motivation to gather as much information as quickly as possible."

"You were with him for over a year, right?"

"Yes." For more than a year of her life she had to tolerate a man she hated on a daily basis. She rarely had time away from him. Unlike a normal job, she didn't have weekends off and couldn't go on vacation to take a break. Working twenty-four-seven had taken a toll.

"What about his wife?"

Nova let out a sharp laugh. "Please... You think she fucking cared he had side pieces? I certainly wasn't his first. Gianna Russo got the financial benefits of being married to a very wealthy and powerful man without having to deal with the rest of the bullshit. She fulfilled her 'job' by giving him three heirs and expertly maintaining his household. After she did what was required, she only wanted to enjoy the spoils. And believe me, she made him pay because she had very rich tastes."

His eyes narrowed on her. "Would you have had sex with him, or even Jr., if you had to?"

"Not by choice. Only by necessity."

"To further your career or because of your uncle?"

"The truth?"

"Truth is required for trust," he said simply.

He was absolutely correct and she would require nothing but the truth from him, too.

"Both. My thirst for La Cosa Nostra to pay in one way or another had seeped into my bones. Unfortunately, I couldn't get that satisfaction with the Parisis. So, I jumped on the chance for revenge when it came to the Russos."

"Damn, Nova. When you went under, the father wasn't your target. You might have had to fuck Jr." An unrecognizable emotion crossed his face. It couldn't be jealousy, could it?

"Of course they knew that might be required when they wanted me to target the son. Before I went under, it *was* cleared, with reluctance, by the AUSA for Frankie. I was advised by my supervisor it was acceptable as long as I was willing to testify about having to go that far to avoid my cover being blown. Or to avoid death, of course."

She was glad she wasn't the one required to get that particular permission. That had been decided for her. She could only imagine how that conversation would've gone if they came directly to her, especially once her target changed from Frankie to his father.

Are you willing to testify to the fact you had to sleep with Francesco Russo Sr., the notorious don of the Russo crime family?

Oh sure, sir. I'll sit on the stand so everyone in that courtroom can stare at me knowing I fucked a sixty-nine year old crime boss just to get all the accolades.

Let's also not forget, for a twisted sense of revenge.

If it had come down to that, she would've kept the last part to herself. The FBI tended to frown upon their agents seeking personal vengeance. For good reason.

"In case it came down to an indictment," Fletch stated flatly. "*Oooor* you could've walked away and refused to do it at all."

True. Those would've been her choices. The FBI had heard whispers of Russo Sr.'s prostate cancer, that was one reason she had been told to target Frankie. No one expected Frank Sr. to be looking for a new "girlfriend" when he couldn't even get it up.

But then, no one considered the fact that both Frank and Frankie regarded women as accessories. It wasn't always about sex with them, but more about impressing the people around them, as well as their business partners.

Having a beautiful, sexy, well-dressed woman on their arm made them appear more successful. Power and money were always the ultimate goal, sex was simply a residual benefit.

"I wasn't going to walk away, Fletch. No matter what I had to do."

"Even if you had been forced to go that far to keep from getting made, he was dead before any indictments ever came about, right? So, you might not have ever had to admit that on the stand."

"Even so, it most likely would've come up as a defense tactic from their attorneys in future indictments. Since taking down Frank Sr. was just the beginning." The Russo organization wasn't a house of cards, where if you removed one card, the rest would collapse. There were plenty of other cards to shore that teetering house back up.

"Is the FBI working on detonating that whole organization? Both the boss and underboss are just the tip of the whole Pittsburgh Sicilian mobster mountain."

"Of course there's a lot more to do, but without me, obviously, since I'm now here. With you."

"Makes sense. There was no reason for you to stick around after he was taken out. And I'm glad that fucker got his due so you could be here." He took the ice pack from her and held it to her cheek. "With me."

She had no idea if the feds had managed to slip another agent inside, whether male or female. Since she was off that job, she wanted to concentrate on the one at hand. After Russo's death, she could do nothing more with the organization and not risk being made.

She was actually surprised she had made it more than a year with them as it was.

"Right, my job was done since I had been nothing more to them than a fancy accessory, like the gold chain Frank wore around his fucking neck. His wife was his immediate heir and he had adult children to help run the organization."

When she stopped talking, Fletch's lips flattened out and his eyes searched her face. "There's more to this story, Nova. You're holding something back."

"And you're very observant."

"The best cops are. But the whole fucking reason we got into this conversation was because of your reaction to me backhanding you."

"You've been bugging me about my time with the Russos," she reminded him.

"Yes, but you finally relented to talk about it because of what happened earlier. What you just told me had nothing to do with that, Nova. So, what fucking did?"

"I might have been spared from having Russo pumping between my legs, but I wasn't spared anything else."

She let that sink in. Again, he was smart and observant. He was already on the track he just needed to keep chugging forward.

She saw it in his expression before it even left his lips. "He hit you."

Bingo. "Yes."

"Fuck," he barked.

"I said that silently to myself every time he did it along with some other choice words."

"But you had to keep your mouth shut. That had to be difficult. To not fight back. To not protect yourself. To go against your very grain. Because I know damn well if I had hit you and not Ghost, I'd be looking worse than you right now."

He was spitting out facts. "If I didn't want it to make the abuse worse, yes. And, you're damn right, it was a struggle. Every fucking day." And every night she fantasized about smothering him with a fucking pillow. Sometimes slicing his throat or balls. Or, *hell*, both.

"Exactly like a fucking abused wife. Knocking you around was a power play to make him feel and appear strong when we all know the truth. An abuser like him is really weak as fuck because fear is what drives it. He was afraid of losing the power he had. Striking women, putting fear into them, made him feel like a big fucking man. The same way as making you lie about all the banging you guys didn't do."

"Yes. But in a way it worked against him. Every fucking shake, slap, backhand or punch only made me more determined to bring that fucker to his knees. Staying and taking everything he dished out only helped guarantee that I would succeed."

Chapter Twenty-Two

"Jesus Christ. You basically took one for the team."

More than one. It was almost a daily occurrence and when a business deal went wrong, putting Frank in a horrid mood, he struck out even more.

It was safe to say that was why his wife never complained about him taking *goomahs*. It was also most likely the reason Frank Sr. had gone through so many of them. Nova wouldn't doubt that some ended up "swimming with the fishes."

"Truth? I would've taken more. I would've done whatever was needed to take that fucker down."

"For fuck's sake, Nova, I don't know if that was better or worse than having to fuck Russo. Both are equally fucked up. And he's lucky he's dead because I would've wanted to take out the fucker myself."

"Now you know how seriously I take my career."

"I already knew before that fucking story. I take my career seriously, too, but I have my limits. You don't see me out fucking lot lizards at the truck stops."

Her face twisted.

"That reaction you just had? That's the same I'm having even *thinking* about you fucking any Russo."

"Well, I lucked out in that department."

He sighed and scrubbed a hand across his forehead. "Right, but you let him use you as a punching bag instead."

"We're trained to deal with physical altercations, Fletch. That training and my instincts helped mitigate some of the damage."

"*If* you saw it coming. Sometimes abusers strike out for no reason. Even if it's only about something wrongly perceived. It could be as simple as an insult from someone else earlier in the day. The anger over that embarrassment could build until it explodes and you just happen to be in reach and the recipient."

"Most of the time I saw it coming. Unlike when you back-handed me."

"And I said you could hit me—" He suddenly became so still, Nova thought he morphed into a statue. Just as quickly, his brown eyes widened and he jolted back to life. He pulled the ice from her cheek and locked gazes with her. "Jesus, Nova. Was I right all along and Russo's demise wasn't a contract hit?"

She pressed her lips together. This was the part she had wanted to avoid and the reason she never discussed her time with the Russos.

But she didn't have to respond, her hesitation was enough of an answer for him.

"*Hoooooly* fuck," he groaned. "It was because of *being* hit." He stepped away from her and threw the ice pack into the sink.

Yes, he had been on the right track, but he finally pulled into the station.

Anger rolled off him in waves when he stalked back to

her and growled, "Why the fuck didn't they pull you? Why would they allow you to remain in that situation?"

"Because I didn't tell them about it."

"You didn't—" His head jerked back. "Why the fuck not?"

"No one had gotten that far into the inner circle before. I had achieved what others couldn't. I wasn't going to walk away no matter what I had to do. I didn't want to risk getting pulled from the job, Fletch."

His nostrils flared and he sucked in an audible breath. "You left it out of the reports."

"Yes."

"He could've fucking killed you, Nova."

He was stating the obvious. "That's one of the hazards of the job. I knew that before I got sworn in. You did, too. You risk the same every damn day when you put on your uniform. You said that risk ruined two engagements."

He blinked. "But the difference with me is if someone gets physical, I can fight back or at least do what I can to protect myself. You couldn't. Or wouldn't. Either way..." He shook his head like he was clearing it. "You took the head of the Pittsburgh Cosa Nostra out. Jesus fuck."

She lifted one eyebrow and said slowly and carefully, "I don't know what you're talking about. Everyone assumed it was a hit from a business deal gone wrong."

He planted his hands on his hips, dropped his head and shook it.

He stood that way for far too long with his chest expanding and contracting. When he finally lifted his head, she couldn't read what was in his dark eyes. Was he impressed? Concerned? Nervous?

"Do the Russos have *any* fucking clue that you took out Sr.?"

"If they did, I wouldn't be standing here." She said that with more confidence than she should. Organizations like the Russos tended to be paranoid. They didn't hesitate to squash even *perceived* threats to protect themselves and their businesses.

"You've got some fucking balls, Nova."

"I know you think that's a compliment but as you know, I have a pussy and they can take much more of a beating than balls. Just one direct tap and you guys can be taken to your knees."

His lips twitched. "That's true, our damn balls are our weakness. Okay then, I'll correct myself. You've got *some* pussy."

"You've said that before but we were naked when you did."

"Then let's get naked and I'll correct my mistake."

"Not yet."

His brow dropped low. "Are you not done talking about this shit? Impressing me with how fucking far you'd go for not only your job, but for a roundabout type of revenge? Because if I was any other guy, I'd be shitting my pants right now. I'm not sure if I should admit this, but... knowing you took out that motherfucker while no one was the wiser, turns me the fuck on."

"Does it?"

"Fuck yeah. But I'm concerned, too, because you were right. This isn't just about losing your job if anyone finds out. It's about losing your fucking life. If they knew, the Russos would not let Daddy Dearest's death slide even if it cleared the path for Jr. to be crowned head of the family. Simply out of principle alone. They never let a slight slide."

"I'm well aware of that. This is why you are now the *only* one who knows."

He lightly touched her cheek, now mostly numb from the ice. "Thank you for trusting me," he murmured.

Since she didn't want him dwelling on the truth she just revealed, she needed to find a way to lighten the mood.

One side of her mouth pulled up. "Okay."

His turned down. "Okay what?"

"Tit-for-tat." Maybe it wouldn't "lighten" the mood but it would distract him from his concerns with the Russos and the fact that she lopped off the head of a very powerful snake. She could use a distraction herself. Even better, he'd been the one to suggest it.

He shook his head. "Tit-for-tat? You'll show me your tits in exchange for me showing you my tats?"

"You've seen my tits and I've seen your tats. I'll take you up on your offer."

He frowned. "What offer?"

"Don't act like you've forgotten, especially now that you know what I'm capable of."

He released an exaggerated sigh and took a step back. "*Fine*. I'm a man of my word. I told you I'd give you a free shot."

"It wasn't free, I already paid for it."

He tipped his head. "You're right. You did. And I guess now it's my turn to pay."

"You can back out if you want, *pussy*," she teased.

His brown eyes widened. "You just said pussies are tougher than balls."

"That's a known fact. If I got kicked in the crotch at the same time you did, who do you think would be back on their feet first, if I even went down at all?"

She swore he paled a little. Oh yes, his face definitely got whiter and maybe even green around the edges.

She shot him a smile. "It's also why men could never have

babies. Humans would go extinct. You guys can't even handle a simple cold."

"Unfortunately, I heard no lie in what you just stated. I've helped with some roadside deliveries. They were..." He grimaced. "It... The head... The stretching... The... Yeah, you women deserve medals."

Fletch's chest expanded and he stepped back, spread his boots wider, loosening up a little by shaking out his arms, bouncing on his toes and stretching his neck to the left and to the right like a prize fighter.

She shook her head and rolled her eyes. "Really?"

He grinned and shrugged. "Well, yeah, I have to 'mitigate the damage.'"

"You really think I have that much power behind my hit?"

"I don't know, do—"

She didn't wait for him to finish before making contact with his jaw using her fist. Hard enough for the impact to twist his neck, his whole face to shift and a grunt explode from him. She held back just enough so she wouldn't break her fingers, or his jaw. She didn't want either of them landing in the ER.

Plus, it would suck explaining those medical bills to Crew.

He grabbed his jaw and worked it. "Damn," he groaned. "I didn't tell you I was ready and you could've hit me where I wouldn't have a damn bruise to explain. And, to be fair, it should've been open-handed."

"Fair?" Nova didn't fight her grin. "There are no rules in fight club."

He snorted, then groaned again. "That's not the saying and this isn't fight club."

She shrugged. "You say potato, I say too fucking bad. You offered, I accepted. Now quit your whining."

He continued to move his jaw around to test it. "Man, you have a mean right hook."

"I actually held back and to be honest, I'm much better with my Glock."

"Let's not test that theory."

She tipped her head to the side. "Smart choice."

He tipped his head back. "Is my nose bleeding?"

"I didn't punch you in the nose."

He pulled his lips back to show her his teeth. "Any missing?"

She shook her head. "No."

"Good. I didn't need you fucking up my pretty face."

She rolled her eyes. "Don't worry, it's still pretty."

"So," he grabbed her hips and pulled her into him, "are we even now?"

With a twitch of her lips, she answered, "I guess so."

"That means you forgive me?"

She stared up at him and noticed his brown eyes held a spark. "I'm still working on it."

"What will get you there faster?"

"Oh, I don't know. I'm sure you can come up with something that involves us getting naked. Otherwise, I can make a list."

"I have my own naughty list, thank you very much." He laughed but he quickly sobered as he brushed his thumb back and forth lightly over her still sore cheek. He whispered, "Sorry you dealt with that shit."

She didn't know if he was talking about Russo or him backhanding her. Either way, it sounded like he meant it, and anyway... "Fletch, it's over and done with. Let's put it behind us and move on to better things."

"You mean *bigger*, better things." He grabbed her hand and pressed it to his zipper.

"Let's not get carried away."

He dropped his head until his mouth hovered just above hers. "Okay, *fine*. Better things like this?" He crushed his lips to hers.

His tongue slid along the seam of her lips demanding entrance, which, of course, she granted. The tips of their tongues touched tentatively at first. When he twisted his head to take the kiss deeper, their tongues began an intricate tango.

A dip. A swirl. A slide. All done with flawless execution.

Their hearts kicked, mouths melded, breaths mingled. Creating a true and in-sync partnership.

When his fingers curled around the back of her neck, they didn't stay there long. He slid his hand up until his fingers tangled tightly in her hair, holding her just where he wanted her, giving him control to lead this dance.

Not that she fought it.

She found, unlike with other men in her past, she didn't mind handing it over to Fletch in the bedroom. All because of that solid trust that had built between them. The way he made her feel comfortable without even trying.

They were equals. Partners.

And the best part was, the power switched easily between them during sex. He never forced it on her and because of that, she never demanded the same.

But they weren't having sex. Not yet, anyway, since he was busy taking her mouth like a conqueror claiming a new land.

And she was *here* for it.

His other hand gripped her jaw for a second before his

long fingers slowly glided down her throat, where they gently collared the base for another heartbeat or two.

Then he continued on. His tongue and lips clashing with hers, his warm fingers leaving a trail of goosebumps behind wherever they went.

A moan slipped up her throat and they shared it between them.

After his hand slid down her spine and cupped her ass, he jerked her tighter against him. His erection strained against his zipper, the hard length pressing into her lower belly, causing her pussy to clench and her core to ignite like throwing a match on dry tinder.

Her nipples beaded so tightly, she wanted to rip off her shirt and bra and push his head down to encourage him to use his mouth to relieve the deep ache.

They'd get there.

Not once had he disappointed her. He'd proved his prowess again and again. Sometimes making her orgasm so many times that when it was over, she could hardly gather her wits and strength enough to make her way back to her own bed.

There had been plenty of occurrences where she thought about giving in and staying with him all night. But she had been trying to avoid the truth. To avoid what ended up happening despite resisting it.

They both ended up there anyway.

A strong connection between them. An unexpected bond.

Unbreakable? Not yet. But she could see it heading in that direction. If they allowed it.

Love? Possibly. She hadn't been looking for it. Her career had always come first. But he was a man able to deal with her strength and her dedication to her job, as well as the dangers that went along with it.

Just like she could do the same with him.

A rarity for her and maybe with his two failed engagements, a rarity for him, too.

They were two sides of the same coin. With a natural understanding of how each were built and what drove them.

Keeping their lips locked and their tongues touching, he managed to unbuckle his belt and unfasten his jeans using only one hand before drawing hers down into his boxer briefs and wrapping her fingers around his erection. She circled his hot length, the silky precum smearing across her palm.

She began to stroke him slowly.

Not to get him off, but to keep the white, searing flame he had sparked burning bright.

Sliding her fist up to the rim and back down to the root, she pumped and squeezed, then thumbed away each silky pearl she milked from him.

With a deep, low groan, he decided to stoke her flames, too, when he also expertly unbuckled her belt and undid her jeans with one hand before wedging it into her underwear. Where he found her center with his skilled fingers and discovered how wet and wanting he made her.

Her swollen clit pulsed against his thumb as he drew it across the sensitive nub. A gentle strumming quickly turned to rough grinding while he plunged his long middle finger in and out of her center at the same time.

Her hips twitched every time he buried his finger to the last knuckle, drawing another moan from her. He shared that one, too, before giving her another of his own.

He sucked her bottom lip into his mouth, tugging on it, before snagging it sharply between his teeth.

She thought once he released it, he would pull away and

be in a rush to the bedroom, but she was wrong. Instead, he captured her mouth completely once more, taking his time to explore and taste every inch until they fed off each other frantically.

As if they were afraid they'd starve if they stopped.

She wasn't expecting it. Her climax didn't creep in on her. *Hell no*, it didn't. It rolled over her like a damn rogue wave, making her pussy pulse and causing a riptide around his finger.

He took the cry from her intense orgasm hostage, not allowing it to escape by keeping his lips sealed tightly to hers.

She pumped him as fast as her heart pounded. As quickly as her pulse rushed. Until finally his hips stuttered and he quickly pulled his throbbing cock free from her grasp.

She recognized the signs. He'd been close to coming, but, unlike her, he wanted to hold back. To be fair, she wanted him to hold back, too. Otherwise, she'd have to wait too long for him to fuck her.

She was too impatient right now to wait.

He slipped his hand from her underwear and pinned his forehead to hers. With his eyes closed and his jaw tight, his chest heaved.

"I'd say that was an okay start, Ghost." Her whispered words had a bit of a shake as she struggled to control her own breathing.

Clearly, she could've hit him harder if he was still capable of kissing her like that.

Because *damn*... That was the hottest fucking kiss she was ever a part of.

Evident from the way he was still gulping down air, he might agree.

"Only okay, Kitten? How about we finish this somewhere

other than the kitchen? A place you can unsheathe those razor-sharp claws."

Of course, she had no desire to resist when he grabbed her arm and dragged her through the apartment directly to his room.

That night ended up being the first of many she no longer rolled out of his bed and went to sleep in her own room after they got "down and dirty."

Just like the Dirty Angels motto...

She hoped to get down and dirty with him many more times, even possibly until she was dead.

Chapter Twenty-Three

Fletch blinked open his eyes, then dragged a hand across them to bring the mirror on the ceiling into focus.

In it was the view he now saw just about every morning.

Nova.

Totally fucking naked and sprawled across his chest.

He grinned at that sexy as fuck sight.

Sometime during the early morning hours, the top sheet had been kicked down to the end of the bed since both of them overheated from sleeping skin to skin. That problem could be avoided if they each slept on their own side of the bed but for some reason, that never happened.

They went to bed touching, fell asleep touching and woke up touching, too.

He dragged his fingertips lightly up her spine and over her tattoo.

No Fear. No Limits. No Regrets.

He couldn't argue those words didn't fit her perfectly.

Just like she fit him perfectly.

And, of course, he fit *inside* her perfectly.

One side of his mouth lifted higher and he brushed a knuckle down her smooth cheek. He usually woke before her since he was naturally an early riser but didn't find it a hardship to remain in bed until she woke, too.

He lifted his head to listen more carefully to what disturbed his sleep. "What is that?"

"What?" she murmured sleepily, her eyelids still pinned shut. With a groan, she snuggled closer, nuzzling her nose against his chest.

"That noise. Listen. Is that a phone?"

"Could be my vibrator."

Unless her sex toy was haunted, it was not her vibrator. She still had to be half asleep to give that answer. "I sure as hell hope not. Because if you've needed that lately, I'm slacking in the satisfaction department."

She lightly patted his chest as if that was supposed to appease him. "Sounds like a phone."

He frowned. "Whose?"

She finally blinked her eyes open and raised her head. They heard it again. "It could be mine."

"Your task force phone is on the charger on your nightstand. Mine is on my nightstand. It's neither of them."

The vibrating stopped. "Probably my personal one. Who the fuck would be calling me at this time in the morning?" With a loud yawn, she rolled out of bed completely naked and still appearing half asleep.

She was *not* a morning person. Actually she didn't become half human until she finished her first mug of coffee. It took a second mug to complete the transformation into a living, breathing woman.

But even as a zombie, her being naked was a breathtaking, dick-hardening sight. That was if he didn't already sport morning wood.

Admittedly, he'd never tire of seeing her rolling naked from his bed. *His* being the important part. "It's not as early as you think, Nova."

With another huge yawn, she stood next to the bed, interlocked her fingers and stretched her arms over her head. He couldn't tear his eyes away but his fingers did do a little stroll down to his hard-on while he watched.

It had been a whole month of this.

For the last month she'd been sleeping by his side all night. It had taken him weeks to convince her and now that he had her there, he wasn't letting her leave it.

Except to answer her phone.

Or piss.

Or work.

These last few weeks had been full of late nights at Hawg Wild, with getting in good with Wolf and meeting his little biker crew at various locations for discreet buys. While dealing with those assholes was getting old and tiresome, they were at least getting somewhere.

While he was weary of dealing with those Demons, at least he had this time with Nova. It was the only saving grace with this whole damn thing.

He'd done some long undercover assignments before but none this fucking boring. He might as well be out doing patrol and writing citations. But he understood a foundation with the Demons had to be laid, buys had to be documented, info had to be gleaned and all the rest of that happy task force crap.

This wasn't a shock and awe mission, it was a slow and steady undertaking.

Gather info, gather evidence, build a solid case.

He yanked on his beard. The length was now out of control and it was looking almost as raggedy as some of the

Demons. Even though it didn't look as flea-bitten or mangy as some of those outlaws, he still hated it and so did Nova. He needed to dig out some clippers and at least give it some shape sometime soon.

He'd have Nova do it, but she'd "accidentally" slip with the clippers and leave a bald spot on purpose.

The only good part about letting it grow was not having to shave every damn morning. Luckily, Nova didn't mind the roughness between her thighs. Thank fuck she didn't because he had his face buried there a lot.

"Whoever it is probably left a voicemail. I'll grab it on my way back from the bathroom. My bladder is telling me not to do business before I do my business."

"Well, hurry the fuck up, because I also have important business to attend to."

She glanced over her shoulder at him as she headed toward the open bedroom door. Most of the time she was too grumpy to have early morning sex so they usually made up for it at night.

Actually, they more than made up for it. He was surprised his balls hadn't shriveled up into BBs.

"Do you have to drop the kids off at the pool?"

"No," he called out after she disappeared down the hallway. "Ghost wants to make Kitten purr."

"Kitten might need to find a warm, sunny spot to curl up and go back to sleep." He heard right before the bathroom door shut.

She was back in less than three minutes. Skirting the bed, she went directly to the closet to dig around in her bag stored at the bottom.

Of course, she was bending over in all of her fucking glory, making sure to point that juicy temptation in his direction.

Jesus. The woman didn't have a shy bone in her body.

He grabbed his own rock hard bone and shook it. Then, neither did he.

"Nova," he growled, anxious to pet and stroke that kitty.

"What?"

"Hurry up, grab your fucking phone and get back in bed. We have important business to take care of that has nothing to do with your damn phone."

She straightened with her cell phone in her hand and faced him. "Is that an order or a suggestion?"

"Didn't it sound like a strongly-worded suggestion?"

"Sounded like an order to me. But you're welcome to reword it and tweak the attitude a bit."

"Are you trying to kill me by causing a lack of blood to my brain?" he asked.

"If I wanted to kill you, you'd already be dead."

No fucking doubt.

She approached the bed. "But if you were dead, I would lose access to that dick you're holding."

No doubt about that, either. "Well, there you go. One good reason to keep me breathing and my heart pumping."

"You were doing a lot of heavy breathing and pumping," she hit the power button on her cell phone to check the time, "only about three hours ago. Damn. I knew I needed more sleep."

"What time are you supposed to be downstairs?"

"Ten."

"Then you can take a cat nap after I fuck you again. Or a Kitten nap." He huffed out a laugh.

"Was that supposed to be funny? Because if so, it missed the mark by a mile." With a loud sigh, she climbed back on the bed and settled next to him by sitting cross-legged against the headboard.

He rolled into her, trailing his fingers up her bare thigh as she tapped on the phone's screen. After putting it to her ear and listening for a few seconds to the voicemail, her brow furrowed.

With a look of confusion, she lowered her phone and stared at it.

He didn't like the expression she wore. "What's going on?"

A crease marred her forehead as her gaze landed on his face pressed against her hip. He was tempted to put his mark there.

"That was the office at my condo complex," she answered, sounding distracted.

"Did you forget to pay your HOA?"

"No, my condo fees automatically get withdrawn from my account every month."

He sat up. "Okay then... What's the problem?"

"The message said there was a bad leak in the condo above mine yesterday and the maintenance men, along with the insurance adjuster, need access to my place to assess the damage. Fuck. I wonder how much of my shit was destroyed. What a fucking pain in the ass."

"At least you weren't home and have a place to stay if any major repairs are needed. Your upstairs neighbor's insurance should cover any damage. Are you going to call them back and see how soon you need to be there? Did they say how bad the leak was?"

"No. Only that there was a leak and they indicated there *could* be damage." She drug her hands down her face and sighed. "They want me to let them in before noon and gave me the direct number to the maintenance guy. I'm supposed to text him as soon as I arrive on scene."

Arrive on scene. Such a typical badge's response, even to

a personal issue. Cop speak was hard to break, even when it was a necessity to avoid it while undercover.

"The office doesn't have a key?"

"I could leave one with them in case of emergency, but fuck that, I don't want anyone having access to my place when I'm not there. Especially with my job."

Made sense. He wouldn't give anyone he didn't know or trust a key to his place, either. Especially since he owned weapons other than the state police issued ones he carried on the job. Plus, he didn't want anyone digging through all his personal and financial info. Even though all that shit was kept in a large gun safe, he would never risk it. Nova might not have the space for a big safe if she lived in a condo.

"So, when do we leave?"

Her eyebrows knitted together. "We?"

"I'm going with you." That shouldn't even be a question.

"You have to work at the gun shop today," she reminded him needlessly.

"Kitten, I don't *have* to do shit. I'm only an extra pair of hands that they're not even paying, remember? This isn't our real life." Well, except for the sex part. That was pretty damn real.

She rolled her brown eyes. "No shit. But still..."

"I'm going with you," he insisted again. "I'm curious to see how you live, anyway. You can tell a lot about a person by their place."

"It's not much since I'm hardly there. I could've rented but I figured buying was a better investment."

"Come on, it will give me a peek into Nova Wilder's life."

"Why? To see if I pass muster to be fiancée number three?"

Hold up. "Do you want to be fiancée number three?" *For fuck's sake,* his voice actually cracked asking that.

"It was a joke."

"Was that supposed to be funny? Because if so, it missed the mark by a mile," he echoed her from earlier.

She sighed and combed her fingers through her messy hair. "None of this is funny, Fletch. If my place needs any work, I'm not there to let a construction crew in to do the repairs. I'm stuck here in Shadow Valley and it's at least forty-five minutes one way. I really don't want to give strangers a damn key."

"Then don't. We'll figure it out. But there's no point in worrying about that until we get there and see what the fuck is going on. It might be only water stains that can wait."

She chewed on her bottom lip. "Maybe."

He squeezed her knee. "Ghost is gonna make his feral Kitten some coffee to domesticate her and a quick breakfast while she showers. 'Cause I sure as fuck know you can't function properly without a heavy dose of caffeine."

"Fill travel mugs, too."

"How the fuck you gonna carry that on my sled?"

"Fuck!"

They were not driving that untrustworthy piece of shit Durango all the way to Cranberry Township and back. They had taken it to meet up for a buy with a Demon one night during a thunderstorm and they were lucky he didn't wrap it around a damn tree when it fishtailed because the tires were so shitty.

He'd have to talk to Crew about switching it out with something more reliable. And safe.

Especially if they were still undercover come winter because fuck if that death trap was making it anywhere in the snow, sleet or freezing rain.

And if he was going to die, it certainly wasn't going to be in a damn Dodge.

Even though she'd been living in Shadow Valley for over two months, strangely, it didn't feel like "coming home" when Fletch pulled the Harley into her assigned parking spot in front of her building.

They had decided to leave their cuts back at the apartment since they didn't want anyone tying her to the Dirty Angels MC. No one in the complex knew what she did for a living and she preferred to keep it that way. She liked living in anonymity and it also kept her safe. She would greet her neighbors if they crossed paths but she never took the time to get to know them.

Fletch had also considered their safety by not only taking main roads and highways to her place in Cranberry Township, but secondary roads, too, despite it making the trip take a little longer. Again, being cautious didn't hurt. She hadn't asked him to do it, he decided on his own. She also caught him checking the mirrors many times to make sure they weren't being tailed.

It was definitely a lot easier to be with a man with the same mindset, unlike the civilian men she'd dated in the past who couldn't understand the reason for not allowing them to hold her dominant hand, the need for her to keep her head on a swivel in any public space, and her inability to sit with her back to the door.

If they insisted she was being paranoid, that was the last time she went on a date with them. It proved they didn't care enough to understand her reasonings even after she took the time to explain them.

The only problem she'd have with Fletch—if they ever went on an official date together—would be how to sit in a restaurant so neither had their back to the entrance. The night they ate in a diner, they had found a booth where both could keep their eyes on the door. Unfortunately, that wasn't always possible.

As soon as Fletch shut off the loud bike and heeled down the kickstand, she dismounted but he remained straddling the Harley. He yanked the bandana used to cover his mouth and nose down to his neck. "You going to text the maintenance guy?"

"I wanted to see the damage first, but I guess I can do it now so we're not stuck here waiting too long." She quickly sent a text while she waited for him to swing a leg over the bike. After pressing Send, she glanced up to notice he hadn't moved. "You coming?"

"In a few. I have to make a quick call to the gun shop so Dawg knows I won't be his bitch today. And I want to do a quick check-in with Crew to let them know where we are and why. What's your condo number?"

She rolled her lips inward when she pointed at the large number painted in bright white on the pavement in the spot where they parked.

Fletch snorted. "Message received. See you up there."

"No rush. I have a feeling we'll be here a while."

Chapter Twenty-Four

As SHE CLIMBED the stairs to her second floor condo, she made a mental list of personal items she wanted to bring back with her to Shadow Valley. Stuff they could haul on the bike, at least. Since the investigation was going so slowly, she had a feeling she and Fletch would remain as Ghost and Kitten for a while yet.

Not such a hardship since she was actually getting used to living and working with Fletch. Not to mention, sleeping beside him.

They made a good team and she was worried the strong bond they had might break once the assignment was over and they no longer worked so closely together.

So, yes, right now she was okay with the investigation going at a snail's pace. The longer it went, the longer they could avoid a possibly awkward discussion about what should or would happen between them afterward.

The longer they played Ghost and Kitten, it might be easier to determine if Fletch and Nova had a chance at developing their personal relationship into more than lovers.

Look at her, actually considering getting involved in a long-term relationship. A *real* one this time.

Not with Frank Russo, Mafia don. Not with Ghost, the biker. But with Shane Fletcher, PA state trooper.

She shook her head and huffed out a breath as she stepped out of the stairwell into the second floor hallway.

Her phone dinged in her hand and she paused to read the text from the maintenance man. *Be there in about 15. Currently inspecting another condo.*

That was a fucking relief. Now they wouldn't be waiting around half a day while twiddling their damn thumbs.

When she reached her door, she dug out her key from the front pocket of her jeans, but as she soon as she tried to plug it into the deadbolt, it tumbled from her fingers and fell to the floor.

With a muttered, "Fuck," she bent over to retrieve it and wrinkled her nose when she noticed the condition of the hallway carpet. She never paid attention to how filthy it was until she had to touch it. Making a mental note to mention the condition to the maintenance guy when he arrived, she straightened, plugged the key into the lock and turned it.

Before she could open the door more than a crack, she was hit from behind with a force so great, she body-slammed the door, expelling all the air from her lungs.

As the door banged open, she fell forward and tried to lessen the impact by twisting her body to keep from face-planting.

She failed and hit the floor hard, anyway.

What the fuck!

If Fletch thought this was funny...

Before she could rise enough to figure out what the hell was going on, two men—*not* in maintenance uniforms—were on her. One grabbed her arm, to keep from being punched, and a handful of her hair to keep her down on the floor. The other tackled her legs as she tried to kick free.

She growled as they both drug her farther into the condo and slammed the door shut.

Fuck!

Her stomach churned, her heart slammed in her chest and her mind spun as she tried to figure out who these fuckers were. She didn't know them. She'd never seen them before. They didn't look like bikers, so she doubted they were Demons and the possibility that this was a random home invasion was even slimmer.

But deep down she knew.

She. Fucking. *Knew.*

Dread filled her chest and narrowed her throat as she stared at two of Russo's soldiers.

She quickly assessed the situation.

She'd been set up. And she fell for it.

She fucking fell for it!

She tried to scramble away from them on her elbows and knees. She needed to roll onto her back and go for her concealed weapon. But as soon as she reached toward her ankle, a boot pinned her right wrist to the floor. With the amount of pressure he was putting on it, if she struggled, she might find herself with a broken wrist and unable to shoot with her dominant hand.

While she was accurate with her left hand, too, the chance she'd miss might be slim but enough of a risk she'd prefer to wait until the moment was right.

Not only did she need to shoot to stop the threat, if she was going to pull the trigger, she wanted it to be worth the hassle that went along with an agent-involved shooting. Even if it was justified.

Right now these assholes didn't know she had her Glock

or they would've removed it from her. If luck was on her side, she also might not be aware of what she did for a living. If she was *really* lucky, they only knew her as their late boss's *goomah.* A woman who kept her mouth shut and did only what she was told.

Them being in the dark gave her the upper-hand. As would acting like a scared woman unable to defend herself.

"Who are y-you and w-what do you want?" she cried out, fear thick in her voice, when in reality she was fuming. She hoped by being loud when Fletch approached the door, he'd hear her tone of voice and at least have some warning.

The last thing she needed right now was him walking into this situation unknowing and unprepared.

Her eyes flicked to the door. *Fuck,* they had locked the damn thing. And one of them must have pulled the key from the deadbolt because she spotted it on the floor just outside her reach. Not that it would do her any good.

Fuck. Fuck. Fuck!

With the door locked, Fletch wouldn't be able to slip in unnoticed to help her out of this jam.

The shorter, older *soon-to-be-a-dead-man* jabbed the gun in his hand toward her and ordered, "Sit up!"

From what she could see, the man she immediately labeled as Asshole was palming a Sig Sauer P226. If she was right with the identification, she knew that model didn't have a traditional safety, similar to her Glock.

She sat up and held out her palms in surrender, making sure they shook. "Don't h-hurt me. *Please.* I'll do anything... *anything* you want, just don't hurt me." She tried to squeeze out a tear to make her fear look genuine, but her anger was running hot just below the surface, making it impossible.

It was anger at herself for failing to realize the call was a fucking trap, anger at Frank Russo for pushing her to the point she had reacted in a way she never should have and anger at the two rancid turds standing over her.

Both of them needed a double flush to rid the world of their stink.

Dipshit, the taller, heavyset goon warned, "You try anything fucking stupid, you'll regret it. Our only order was to bring you back alive and able to speak. That's it. Believe me, we know how to keep you just alive enough to do that. You don't need to be pretty or in one piece to answer questions. That means I strongly suggest you cooperate. If you do, this will go easier for you."

Oh yeah, like she believed that fucking lie. Her middle finger was itching to spring into the upright position.

Instead, she pulled in a long breath and whined loudly, "C-can you... put the guns down? I... I c-can't think when you have them pointed at me." She sniffled like she was about to sob. "Please. I'll cooperate. I swear!"

"Stop fucking yelling! Bring it down a few notches before you attract the neighbors' attention. I promise you don't want that. It wouldn't be good for you or them."

"S-sorry, I'll... be more quiet." No, she wouldn't. "But you're making me nervous with those g-guns. They scare me."

Asshole ignored her plea and kept his gun pointed directly at her forehead. "The boss wants to see you, Naomi. Or... is it Nova Wilder?" His bushy eyebrows lifted.

The blood drained from her face at hearing her real name but she managed to keep her expression fearful and not surprised. How the fuck did they find out her real identity? "Why would Frankie want to see me? I was his father's g-girlfriend, not his."

Some skill was needed to hit a moving target. If she dove for her ankle holster, he'd most likely miss her. But Dipshit had his gun drawn, too, even though he now held it down at his side. Despite that, if he was a good shot, she'd be dead not even a second after she plugged a hole in Asshole.

She had to think clearly and plan carefully in hopes that Fletch would arrive soon, even if only as a distraction so she could put these two fuckers down. Humanely, inhumanely, it didn't matter to her as long as they both stopped breathing.

"He thought it a little suspicious when after his father died you disappeared at the same time. He wants to ask you a few questions since you didn't give him that chance before you left."

She blinked quickly, still trying to drum up some tears. Just one, that was all she needed, *damn it.* But the fury licking inside of her was making that impossible. "Why now? It's been months."

Scared, Nova, act scared. Not like you want to punt his balls toward the one-yard line after slicing out his tongue.

"You didn't make it easy to find you after you vanished. Not only did you use a fake name, which we found quite interesting, your cell phone was disconnected. It's almost as if you purposely went underground. He wants to know why."

If they didn't know why, that definitely meant they didn't know who she worked for. That also meant they wouldn't expect her to be armed. Two things in her favor.

Actually, three. Fletch should be coming up to the condo at any time. That meant she needed to keep speaking as loudly as possible—without getting gagged—and to keep Asshole and Dipshit talking and focused on her.

Unless... *Shit.* If he heard voices, he might think it was only the maintenance men discussing the non-existent water damage.

She needed to use key words Fletch might recognize as a red flag. Maybe he'd hear them and realize whatever she was saying weren't things she'd ever discuss with a condo complex employee.

"You don't need to take me anywhere to find out why I left. I can tell you and you can pass the message on to Frankie. The reason was simple. After getting slapped around by Frank, I no longer had an interest in staying and letting the son take up where the father left off. That's exactly why I left. It wasn't anything nefarious like Frankie might think. It also made sense that if someone had put a hit on his father's head, that Frankie would be their next target since he, as the underboss, was next in line. Who in their right mind would stick around and risk becoming collateral damage? I did it purely out of self-preservation and no other reason."

Asshole shook his head and sneered, "Nice try, but we know you were involved with whoever put a contract out on Frank Sr. Who were you working for?"

They didn't know shit. They were fishing. Because if they knew anything concrete, she'd already be dead.

"Nobody!" burst from her with an added bottom lip quiver for good measure.

Asshole jabbed his gun toward her. It pissed her off even more since he had his damn finger on the trigger. Proof that La Cosa Nostra didn't require their soldiers to follow gun safety protocol. *Stupid fucks.*

"Bullshit. Who hired you to infiltrate the family, Nova Wilder?"

Where the fuck was Fletch? "Nobody! I swear!" She wasn't even going to try to come up with an excuse for using a different name. In the end it wouldn't matter.

"Keep your secrets for now. We'll hear them soon enough. And if you're not willing to spill them, then we have ways to make you willing. We need to go. The boss is waiting to hear everything you have to say. The longer we make him wait, the more impatient he'll be and the tougher he'll be on you."

Great.

Whatever happened, she was not leaving her condo with them. She'd rather die quickly by a bullet from one of those dumbfuck douchebags than go through a long, torturous interrogation at the hands of Francesco Russo Jr., a chip off the old block.

However, Frankie wouldn't get his manicured fingernails dirty or risk stains on his Gucci button-down dress shirt. He'd have his soldiers do the dirty work for him while he watched from a splatter-free zone.

A hierarchy existed in La Cosa Nostra for good reason.

"It'll be much easier for you if you came with us willingly. Otherwise, we'll gag you and tie your hands. What's your choice?"

"I'll go with you. He just wants to talk, right?"

"Right," Dipshit answered.

"And as soon as he realizes I don't know anything, he'll let me go?"

"Of course," Asshole assured her.

Motherfucking liars. "Will someone bring me back here when we're done?"

One side of Dipshit's thin lips pulled up. "We'll make sure you get home safely."

Sure they would.

Did anyone ever believe their bullshit?

She nodded like she was too stupid to live. "Fine. I'll speak with Frankie. He'll see I had nothing to do with it." As she went to stand, she cried out in pain. "*Oh!* I must've twisted my ankle when I fell."

She reached forward, rubbing it for a split second before

quickly pulling her Glock, lifting it and taking two shots center mass at the one closest to her. The one with his fucking gun still pointed at her.

Or did.

She didn't bother to wait to see if the fucker was down for the count before turning her Glock on the second one, who was definitely still breathing and raising his own weapon after staring in shock at his downed partner.

Before she could pull the trigger, the door crashed open, causing fragments from the wood frame to fly. Fletch, already with gun in hand, fired twice in quick succession, striking Russo's soldier in the back.

Nova kept her weapon pointed at Dipshit's chest when he, with wide eyes and a couple of extra orifices he wasn't born with, folded to his knees in slow motion with his mouth gaped open. When he fell forward, he crashed to the floor face first.

Ouch. That would've hurt if he wasn't dead.

She slipped her Glock back into its holster and took Fletch's offered hand. Once he yanked her to her feet, she kicked Asshole with her boot. "Think I should check for a pulse?"

After holstering his own gun, he wiggled his fingers in his ears and worked his jaw. It would be a while before their ears stopped ringing. Shooting a gun in real life was nothing like the damn movies. "With the size of that puddle of blood, if he has a pulse now, he won't soon."

"Yeah, but you know someone had to have dialed 9-1-1 by now and I'd prefer the EMTs not be able to revive him." She leaned over and pressed two fingers to the vein that ran along Asshole's throat.

Nothing.

Fletch squatted next to Dipshit and did the same.

Their eyes met and both gave a shake of their head.

"Good shoot," he said, rising back to his feet.

"I'd say." It was a good shoot if out of the four people currently in her condo, the two still breathing were the only two that mattered.

"You okay?"

"I am now," she answered.

Fletch's brow furrowed. "So, who are these fuckers?"

"One guess."

"Jesus fuck, Nova," he exploded, scraping a hand down his beard. "You said they had no reason to hunt you down."

"I didn't think they did."

"Did they accuse you of taking out their boss?"

"It sounded like they thought I was working for someone else. My guess is Frankie thinks I was a mole for another crime family. One with a beef with them."

"How the fuck did they figure out where you live?"

"They found out my real name but I don't know how."

"They don't know you're FBI?"

"No, thank fuck. They gave no indication of that at all. Because if they knew, I'm sure I just would've been dispatched when I wasn't expecting it. Instead, they wanted to take me to Frankie for his special type of questioning."

"Christ. They would've tortured you for answers."

"Yeah, I don't think they were inviting me to a tea party and a cozy chat."

"Thank fuck I came along with you."

She ground her teeth together. "I was handling it."

He stared at her with a look that said it all.

She released a slow breath and added, "But I appreciate you being my backup." More than appreciated it.

He continued to stare at her silently.

She tacked on, "And for taking out Dipshit."

"I know that must've been painful, but thank you for the recognition," he said sarcastically and with a deadpan expression. He sighed. "Well, the bright side of this clusterfuck is they don't know you're FBI."

"But that doesn't mean Frankie won't keep looking for me if they suspect me of being a plant for an enemy. The Russos certainly like their revenge."

"Great," he said dryly. "Well, good thing we have that apartment in Shadow Valley for now. They'd never expect you to be living and working with the Dirty Angels. They think you're part of La Cosa Nostra, not an MC."

"I just hope like fuck I'm not pulled from the task force. That could happen, Fletch. We both know that. They might consider me compromised."

"Then you'll have to convince them otherwise."

That might be easier said than done.

Fletch brushed his fingers over his hair and shook his head. "For fuck's sake, I just got off the phone with Crew, too. I guess I need to hit redial and see how he wants to handle this fucking mess."

"And I'll need to call my supervisor before the local uniforms get on scene. I'm expecting to hear sirens at any minute now."

"Yeah, well... We're going to be making a bunch of calls and it's going to be a fucking shit show."

It would be worse than a shit show with all the paperwork and interviews. Plus, most likely being sidelined until they were both cleared to go back to active duty.

And she wasn't including the mess in her apartment from two men bleeding out from gunshot wounds. "I guess I'll never be able to live here again."

"Thank fuck we have the apartment above the pawn shop for now. And even if we get pulled from the task force and put on desk duty with our respective departments, there's always my place."

His place?

Before she could respond to that, he had her pulled into his arms and smashed against his chest. She could hear and feel his heart thumping against her ear.

She was still a little too tense to appreciate the embrace, but she wrapped her arms around him anyway, squeezing him just as tightly. If this was what he needed, then she'd give it to him. Though, he was a man. Most likely he thought she was the one who needed consoling.

"You okay?" he asked again and pressed his cheek against the top of her head, burying his nose in her hair.

Some of the tension she'd been holding onto began to disappear. Admittedly, him holding her was a bit comforting. "You asked me that already."

"Jesus fuck, Nova," he breathed into her hair. "I thought I was going to fucking lose you. I almost busted the door down without a thought and came in guns blazing."

She pulled her face away from his chest and tipped it up so she had a clear view of his face. "Um, Fletch?"

"Yeah?"

"That's exactly what you did."

He shrugged. "But I thought about it first."

"For how long?"

His lips twisted. "Less than a heartbeat."

With a smile, she pressed her face back into his broad and very warm chest. "I had everything under control."

"Yeah, you're right. You would've done just fine without me."

While that might be true, that didn't mean she didn't appreciate him being there and for doing what he did.

Everything worked out mostly because of who he was

and what he did for a living. If any other man had been with her, the situation might not have turned out the way it had. She might've ended up bleeding out on her condo floor instead of Russo's two soldiers.

She whispered, "Thank you for coming with me."

"Wouldn't want to be anywhere else, Nova. No matter what shitstorm's about to come next."

Yeah, they'd both be put through the wringer until they were cleared and allowed to go back to doing what they did best.

However, one important thing was now apparent after today's clusterfuck and staring death in the eye.

Fletch was no longer only her task force partner. No longer just a convenient sex partner.

He truly was so much more.

Chapter Twenty-Five

As THEY WAITED for Crew to show up, Fletch paced the pawn shop's side parking lot in an attempt to loosen his *tight-as-fuck* muscles. He really needed to go for a run to clear his head, but that would have to wait until they saw what their near future held.

He wasn't worried they wouldn't get through the investigation. An investigation they were now the subjects of, not the one they were supposed to be a part of. He had confidence they would.

It was a good shoot for both of them. Despite that, there'd still be plenty of red tape to hack their way through.

What worried him the most was that one or both of them might be pulled from the task force. And if that happened, that meant he and Nova would no longer be living together.

Yes, he fucking knew it was only supposed to be while they were undercover with the Dirty Angels. However, over the last few weeks they had settled into each other's lives like a real couple.

They were no longer only playing Ghost and Kitten, a biker and his ol' lady.

They had become "Fletch and Nova." A true team in more ways than one.

While at first it had been a work arrangement out of necessity, their personal relationship had fallen in sync more naturally.

Professionally, they worked well together and, personally, they simply clicked.

Now he couldn't imagine waking up every fucking morning without Nova by his side.

It was crazy. After two failed engagements to women unable to handle his career, fate, luck, or whatever it was, had brought Nova into his life.

He thought they were simply having fun in bed but earlier this morning, after the potential of losing her, he had a wake-up call. He realized she was the perfect woman for him.

He also realized there would be no other.

Nova was it.

She was the type of woman he'd hoped to find as a life partner and failed. Twice.

Maybe the universe had dropped her into his path out of pity.

Or maybe it had only been dumb luck.

He wasn't going to question it, but he did question how Nova felt about him.

The woman reminded him of lava. A cooler, thick crust on the outside, but molten just under the surface.

In the past few weeks, they had never talked about anything beyond their current living and working situation. They mostly focused on what needed to be done on the task force, in Shadow Valley and with the Demons. That was it.

They were at the point now where that conversation was

needed. Because if Crew showed up and gave them the bad news that one or both of them were being pulled from the task force, he didn't want what developed between them, so far, to end.

He had just found her, he didn't want to lose her.

He hoped she felt the same.

But that conversation would have to wait until after speaking with Crew.

In Cranberry Township, while waiting at her condo for the local uniforms and the coroner to show up, they both made their required notifications to report their agent- and officer-involved shootings.

Then Fletch contacted Crew before anyone else could.

Of course the task force leader advised them to not say shit to the locals, to simply let them babysit the crime scene and start their reports, and for Fletch and Nova to head back to the apartment to wait.

Crew advised he would call the Assistant U.S. Attorney and do what he could to speed along the process. The DEA considered the Demons' case a priority because of the amount of meth being trafficked and he was afraid the investigation might stall if they had to pull Fletch and Nova and put others in their place. If that happened, they'd be restarting from scratch to build a relationship with the Demons. Attempting to do so could raise some red flags with the outlaw MC.

With Nova upstairs on a video call with the FBI's Pittsburgh Field Office special agent in charge, he had decided to step outside so he wouldn't distract her. He also figured they might not want him hearing their discussion about the Russos, in case some of it was classified.

The other reason, besides to try to relieve his pent-up energy, was to wait for Crew. It wouldn't hurt to talk to his fellow Blue Avenger and the task force leader alone to get a read on what might go down.

He heard the Harley long before he saw it turn onto the side street and then the lot. He had to step out of the way so Crew wouldn't run his ass over since the man was coming in hot.

The DEA agent wore his signature mirrored sunglasses. What wasn't typical for him was his dirty, worn jeans and the holey Harley T-shirt. The only thing missing for him to look like he belonged in an MC was a cut. Of course he wouldn't wear their BAMC colors deep in DAMC territory. That could raise all kinds of suspicion, especially with him meeting with Ghost and Kitten. And they already had enough shit going on.

As Crew swung a leg over the seat, Fletch approached him. They bumped fists but neither said a word before scanning the lot to make sure no one was in earshot.

"We going up?" Crew asked, jerking his chin toward the metal staircase.

"Not yet. Nova's in the middle of a video debriefing with her SAC."

Crew scraped his fingers through his short salt-and-pepper hair. "No surprise. It's routine. Well, not by video but at least they didn't force her to go into the field office. If we want to keep her undercover, it's best she doesn't go strolling into an FBI building." He sighed and slid off his sunglasses, folding them before hanging them from the neckline of his T-shirt. "Truth, brother, do you think your covers are blown?"

"Told you they weren't."

"Yeah, but you called me right after shit just hit the fan. Now that a few hours have passed, I'm assuming you and Nova had a chance to go over what went down and compare the smaller details. Do you think there's *any* fucking chance?

I don't want either of you compromised and then blowing this investigation by being outed as UCs."

"No," Fletch answered with confidence.

"Not even Nova's?"

"Nope. I heard some of what those fuckers were spewing before I kicked in the door, but while we waited for the locals, she went over everything they said to her, from the second they showed up to the second they stopped breathing, so we could both analyze it. Those motherfuckers had no idea she's FBI. They had no clue she was undercover when she was with Russo Sr."

"Thank fuck. Now I can fight to keep you as part of the task force. I'd hate to have to replace you both since you did a damn good job getting right where I needed you with the Uniontown chapter of the Demons. And who the fuck knows, if we had to replace you, whether the Angels would be willing to cooperate again."

"If I had to take a fucking guess? No. Remember when we were all surprised as fuck when they agreed in the first place? Now after being around them, I can say that approaching them a second time would probably be met with more resistance than the initial ask."

"Yeah." With his hands on his hips, Crew tilted his head and his gray eyes locked with Fletch's. "Then, if she wasn't made, why the hell did those motherfuckers show up and want to take her to Russo Jr. for a little chat?"

"Jr. thinks she was working with another crime family."

Crew's brow furrowed. "What the fuck? The Russos think whoever took out a contract on Sr. planted Nova on the inside?"

"Yeah, isn't that some shit? They couldn't be more wrong."

"Who did they think she's connected to?"

Fletch shrugged. "We don't know. They never said. And, of course, dead men tell no tales." One side of his mouth curled up in a half grin. He hated the situation they were in now, but he was glad those fuckers were no longer breathing.

"Isn't that the fucking truth. I don't know, brother... Unfortunately, this all made shit sticky."

"Dispatching two men can do that. But it would've been stickier if they had lived."

"True." Crew studied Fletch's face carefully. "Gotta ask... You okay with what you had to do?"

Some officers struggled with having to kill another human being, but Fletch had no qualms with taking down someone threatening Nova's life. He would've had a harder time dealing with it if something had happened to her because he *didn't* take that action. "Yeah, brother, I'm good."

Crew nodded, then smirked. "PSP might make you sit down with a therapist so you can get in touch with your feelings."

Fletch snorted. "Yeah, I was told it might be required. But it's not me I'm worried about, it's Nova. And not because of any emotional damage due to the shoot. She thought she was done with the Russos. They made it clear she's not. That's one of the things she's currently discussing with her SAC. Crew," he said more solemnly, "she was fucking badass this morning and how she reacted was proof she was an excellent choice for this task force. Throughout these last few weeks, she's impressed me time and time again."

"Not surprised. Her rep is why I chose her, brother. Know you might find this hard to believe, but I do know what the fuck I'm doing."

"Sometimes," Fletch said with a smirk.

"Not sure if she told you—my guess is she didn't since I heard she's not one to brag—but... she earned the FBI Shield of Bravery for a job she was on right before she went under with the Russos. Not many agents earn it."

Fletch's eyebrows shot up his forehead. "No shit? Damn. She didn't say a fucking word. Hell, I'd be wearing that medal on a damn chain around my neck with a spotlight on my belt pointing up at it. But, seriously, it's no surprise. She kept her cool, played her part as a scared woman like a fucking boss and then took out one of Russo's soldiers without blinking. She would've taken the other one out, too, if I hadn't crashed the party."

"And if we're sharing some truth, I wish like fuck you would've stayed clear, because now I might lose two task force officers, when it could've only been one."

"Crew, look, there's something you need to know..." Fletch sucked in a deep breath but before he could confess to what was going on between him and Nova, the older man shook his head.

"Yeah, figured you were both playing naked slap-and-tickle on the government's payroll."

"Should we have put it in the daily report?" Fletch joked.

"Only if you described everything in detail and even drew instructional diagrams."

Fletch snorted. "It would've been stick figures, well, except for my large cock. I would've drawn that realistically and to scale."

"Do I need to ask your partner if you're exaggerating?"

"Not unless you don't mind being jealous or depressed."

"I'm sure I'll survive. I've never had any complaints." He held up a palm. "At least about the size of my dick. I can't speak for the rest. I'm sure my ex-wife has a list of my faults longer than a CVS receipt."

"So, what's the plan for now?"

"Well, lucky for you, I already convinced the AUSA to

let you remain undercover while you both get cleared by their office and PSP's internal affairs. But you need to lay low. No dealing with the Demons, no task force business at all. Until I get the go-ahead, you two will do nothing but go to your assigned jobs at the DAMC businesses, since we need to stay on their good side, and come home. That's it. It's going to suck but you need to suck it up and wait it out."

"We can do that."

Crew arched an eyebrow. "Are you speaking for the both of you? Are you that far in your relationship?"

"Ask her when you go up. I'm sure she'll agree."

"Believe me, I plan on it. But, Fletch, if it turns out they want her pulled, she won't have a choice. She won't be able to stay here just because you two want to continue to bang on the DEA's dime."

"They might have to make an exception, because right now she's safer living here in Shadow Valley and in this apartment. Now that the Russos know where she lives, she'll need to put her condo on the market. Or at least once that whole clusterfuck is cleaned up. But until that happens she's got nowhere else to go."

Crew's eyebrows rose. "A hotel. But then, that wouldn't be so convenient for you, would it?"

"I'm more worried about the Russos hunting her down than my sex life drying up."

"Look at you, asshole. That's the first time I've ever heard you put something else above getting your dick wet. But you're right, she can't go back to her condo, it's been compromised. A hotel might be her only option if they pull her and don't approve of her remaining here and playing house with you. Or here's a fucking thought... you could sublet your place to her while you stay here."

Crew thought that Nova living in his place would make

Fletch panic. It didn't. Even so... "I prefer you do what you can to keep her here, whether she's pulled or not."

"I've already planted that seed and I'll continue to water it. I got your six, brother." Crew slapped Fletch on the back. "Plus, I wouldn't want that monster cock of yours to shrivel up from neglect. But let me just say this before we get upstairs, especially since my nuts don't need a violent adjustment... You are one lucky bastard, Fletch. If I was ever going to tie myself down again, I'd want someone like her. Brave, highly intelligent, driven and hot as fuck. She might not be perfect—who is?—but she's pretty damn close."

He couldn't disagree with Crew, he *was* a hell of a lucky bastard.

Hopefully, Nova felt the same way about him.

Chapter Twenty Six

Fletch was sprawled on his back in the center of the bed. Every light was on in the bedroom so he could get a very clear view in the mirror.

Unable to do task force business had made them stir-crazy so they spent a lot of time trying new things both in and out of bed.

Having copious amounts of sex was definitely a huge hardship.

Said no one ever.

Or at least that would never come out of his mouth. And it didn't seem like Nova had an issue with it, either.

If he wasn't still working at the gun shop five days a week, this down time would feel like a staycation. Or a sexcation.

If it was up to him, that would be an official thing.

He skimmed his fingers along Nova's arm, following it all the way to her hand. Her thumb was pressed to her own clit, grinding and circling, while her fingers touched where they were connected. With every tilt of his hips, her fingers brushed over his cock as it slid in and out of her tight heat.

With her head resting on his collarbone and her soft dark hair spread over his shoulder, her hooded eyes remained focused on the mirror above them, just like his. The flush that started at her chest had now spread up her throat.

He covered her hand with his. "Want me to take over?"

"I've got it handled. Find something else for your hands to do."

He could do that.

He flashed her a grin, but it quickly faded away as he continued on his path up her lower belly, his fingers drawing invisible lines all the way up to her breasts where he traced each dark pink areola. While her breasts weren't large, there was enough soft flesh to fill his palm. He squeezed and kneaded both while strumming his thumb over the tightly beaded tips.

With the way her lean legs were spread wide and draped over his thighs, it gave them the perfect view of his cock appearing and disappearing every time he lifted his hips to drive deep.

Tonight, neither were in a rush to come. Unlike when they had sex earlier at a more rapid pace.

He'd been waiting for her to return from working downstairs at the pawn shop. When she came through the door, the first thing that greeted her was him sitting on the couch wearing only a smile and pumping his hard-on with his fist. She matched his smile as she stripped her clothes off piece by piece while taking her time approaching and watching him jerk-off. By the time she finally got to him, he had gloved up and was more than ready for her to straddle his lap. Without a word between them, she lined him up and sank down until he couldn't be any deeper.

What started out leisurely, quickly turned into a frantic

race to orgasm as she rode him hard and fast, using her teeth and nails everywhere she could reach.

It was one of the rare times he was unable to wait until she came first. Not only because he was already locked and loaded before she had walked through the door, but seeing her bouncing on his lap with abandon and her head thrown back as she clawed at his shoulders and chest, made him lose his shit. The cries and whimpers escaping her parted lips didn't help the situation, either.

Luckily, he managed by the skin of his teeth to stay hard long enough for her to finish by grinding her pussy against him.

They had fallen into an almost daily pattern of one frantic, quick bang and then later, a slow sex marathon.

Exactly what they were doing now.

Keeping it slow and steady. Taking their time to appreciate the view. Appreciate each other. Appreciate the fact they worked well together. Whether in bed or out of it.

He would fucking miss this if either of them were pulled from the assignment. If that happened, it might be best if they were both pulled so they wouldn't miss out on more of these moments.

Because he needed them. He needed her.

They would both still be eligible to work for the task force, just no longer undercover. And she could stay with him in his place until she sold her condo and found a new one.

Or, *hell*, if she was willing, she could just move in with him. They were already living together in an official capacity and they hadn't killed each other yet or even gotten on each other's nerves, so he knew cohabitation between them could work.

But that was a discussion they hadn't had yet since they were still waiting for the final word that they were cleared. It should be any day now, but the square, lopsided wheels of government turned way too fucking slowly.

"Look how goddamn beautiful you are when you're getting fucked." Pulling both of her nipples, he stretched them as far as he could, then rolled them between his thumb and forefingers.

With a moan, she arched her back and drove his cock deeper into her pussy. That hot, silky cocoon pulsed and her inner muscles clenched and unclenched around his cock, almost driving him to flip her over to take her hard and fast. And continue to do so until they both lost their minds.

But he forced himself to stay where he was and to continue at a lazy pace.

Slipping his hand from her breast up to her throat, he pressed his thumb against her racing pulse for a moment, then collared the base of her neck with his fingers. His hand looked so fucking big curled around her long, slender neck.

Proof one didn't need to be huge to be strong. This woman was the epitome of strength.

Seeing his hand wrapped around her throat also hammered home the fact she trusted him as much as he trusted her.

Her fingers working her clit sped up to a blur and when she clamped tightly around his cock, he knew she was almost there.

At least she'd come before him this time.

Using his nose to nudge her hair away from her neck, he traced the outer shell of her ear with the tip of his tongue before licking a long line down to that tender spot at the junction of her neck and shoulder.

"You're mine, Nova."

Even though her eyes were hooded, she kept them open and they both watched him bare his teeth and slowly sink them into the nape of her neck. An exclamation point on his claim.

She cried out, not from pain, but because she was coming.

Now all bets were off.

With an arm draped over her jumping hips, he pinned them down, planted his feet and drove up and into her with as much power as he could muster.

For fuck's sake, she felt so good, so right. Too damn good. Too damn right.

This woman belonged to him.

Nova was his.

Nobody but his.

Never again would she be anyone else's.

Not as long as he breathed.

But he belonged to her, too.

She had stolen his heart, body and soul.

She owned every damn piece of him.

Because of that, he'd do his fucking best to give her everything she asked for and accept everything she was willing to give him.

"Nova," he groaned as he thrust up one more time and grunted, his cock pulsing as it filled the condom.

They'd have to discuss that, too.

Because if things between them kept moving in the direction they were, he wanted nothing between them.

Not a damn thing.

No condom.

No secrets.

Nothing.

True fucking partners with every bit of their life open and shared.

Once he was empty, he dropped his hips and melted into

the bed. She remained sprawled boneless on top of him, totally relaxed with a soft satisfied smile curving her lips. She reached back to drag her fingers along his beard and into his hair before cupping the back of his head.

Once their strained breathing no longer filled their ears and the sheen of sweat began to dissipate, he took a chance by asking, "Do you agree?"

No more hiding. No more wondering. It was time to get everything out in the open. It was time to get serious.

"Agree with what?"

He tucked a lock of her hair behind her ear, knowing what he said next would spark a conversation they'd been dancing around. "That you're mine."

She shifted enough so they disengaged. She reached down, carefully pulled the full condom from him and knotted the end.

She rolled toward his nightstand to tuck it into a tissue until he could dispose of it properly, but she didn't slip to his side like she normally did. Instead, she remained lying on him, this time face down, giving him all her weight since he'd voiced a few times how much he loved the press of her body against his. She was heavy enough for it to be comforting, but light enough for it not to be smothering.

It wasn't until she went practically nose to nose with him that she asked, "Am I?"

"Do you want that?"

"I'm neither an ol' lady or a mafioso's piece in real life, Fletch. I have no desire to be owned or claimed by anyone. Or even dictated to."

"Dictated, never. Claimed, maybe, but not owned. And by claimed, I mean wanted. You'd belong to me and no other."

"Listen, I have no doubt you want me. You make that

very clear, even without words. And I'm sure you know I want you, too. But do we need to stake our claim? We already have each other."

"We have each other for now, but what about after this?"

"Are you asking what will happen to us if our job situation changes? Don't you want to wait until that time comes before we consider our options?"

"It could be soon, Nova."

"That could simply mean we'd need to give up our DAMC cuts and move out of this apartment. It could mean we move on to other assignments, whether in the task force or with our respective departments."

"Nova, if you're pulled from the task force, as a fed you could be sent anywhere for your next assignment." He didn't think he could bear being apart from her for a year, maybe even more.

She considered that a moment. "That's true, but I don't think that'll happen. I'm not getting that vibe from my supervisor."

"But it's a possibility. We need to consider our options now in case it does."

Her eyebrows knitted together. "What do you think are our options?"

"For one, you moving in with me."

"You mean until my place sells and I can find another one?"

"No."

She blinked. "You mean us living together... permanently?"

"Living together would be the first step."

"We're already doing that. You mean us living together somewhere else."

If he was going to put shit out there, he was going to put it all out there. He wasn't going to hold back. She needed to know how he felt and what he wanted. Either she wanted the same as him, or she didn't. And if she didn't, he needed to know that now, not later when he was too far gone. "That's what I mean. This place is temporary. I don't want us to be temporary, too."

"I know you have this thing about getting hitched. Anyone who's had two fiancées must. Clearly you don't have a fear of commitment like some other men. But I've never really given a shit about the whole walking down the aisle thing, or the white gown, exchanging rings and vows and all the rest of it. While that might have been some girls' dream, it was never mine."

That didn't surprise him. He imagined she'd been the kind of little girl who said fuck Barbie and society's stereotypes and played spy wars with G.I. Joe instead.

And that right there made him realize he'd been chasing the wrong type of women and why none of them ever stuck. He needed one who broke the typical mold.

Nova was certainly that woman.

A rarity who would be hard to find again, if not impossible.

Not that he wanted to try. He found the woman he was meant to be with. She was lying on top of him right this very fucking minute.

"It's not about the ceremony and all that other bullshit," he explained. "I don't give a fuck about that. It's about the commitment."

"Commitment," she echoed. "But not love?"

Fuck. Now they were digging deeper into the very conversation they'd been putting off. Or at least one he'd been putting off. "I didn't say that."

"But shouldn't you love someone before committing to

them? Unless it's some sort of business or family arrangement, of course. Situations like that certainly happen."

What he was about to reveal next could change everything. If his gut instinct had been totally off, it could send their partnership off the rails. It could either get really fucking awkward... or solidify it.

He was about to take a leap without a fucking parachute and hope she cushioned his fall. "Who says I don't love you?"

She went solid against him. "Umm..."

Fuck. He was in a free fall, spinning and barreling to the ground.

He hooked a leg around her and twisted until she ended up on her back with him over her. She stared up at him with wide brown eyes.

With a frown, he dug his elbows into the mattress and brushed her tousled hair out of her face so he could see it more clearly. "Why do you look so fucking shocked?"

Normally, he'd be amused by her *deer-caught-in-the-headlights* expression since much didn't shake her, but right now he wasn't. While he didn't expect her to declare her undying love—not yet, anyway—he hadn't quite expected *that* response.

"I... I just wasn't prepared for that. You hadn't said a fucking word."

"You're right. I hadn't. But, holy fuck, Nova, I figured it was obvious. And I didn't want to come out and say it until I was sure what I discovered that morning in your condo was actually real or only an emotional reaction from seeing you in that situation."

Her lips gaped open for a second before she pinned them closed. She swallowed so hard, he could see it. Now he was starting to doubt *everything*. Did he just make a fucking fool out of himself?

He never should've said shit. He might have fucked up a good thing.

"And now you know for sure?"

He could lie and lessen the damage or he could say "fuck it" and continue marching down this disastrous path. "Yep." *Jesus Christ*, that was a fucked-up way to answer an important question. "Yes, I do."

"Fletch," she breathed.

With their chests pressed together, she could probably feel his heart thumping heavily. "By your reaction, I'm assuming you don't feel the same."

"I didn't say that," she whispered. "But you haven't actually told me. We're discussing it like we're discussing how shitty the Steelers played in their last game."

"Yeah, well... I'm not the most romantic guy. That's one of my many faults."

She snorted softly. "Do I come off as a woman who needs romancing?"

"No. I guess we're a lot alike in that respect."

"That could be good or bad."

"With us, I think it works. I respect and appreciate everything about you, Nova. I assumed you felt the same way about me."

"I do."

"Well, there you go." Problem solved. Easy fucking peasy, right?

"While that's needed for a solid relationship, that's not love."

Fuck, he might have shot his load too quickly. "Then what is?"

He braced himself when she took a deep breath before saying, "How I realized just how much I missed you every time I walk through the door and see you after we've been apart for hours. How quickly my heart beats when I watch you getting undressed. How it swells and tumbles with the way you look at me."

Now his mouth was probably hanging open. "Damn, Nova. You just said you aren't romantic, but that sounded romantic as hell."

"It wasn't meant to be romantic. It was one way to tell you how much I love you."

"Fuck," he whispered.

"Yeah. Fuck."

He cocked an eyebrow. "Wait. Are you fucking with me?"

She laughed. "No. You want to know when it hit me?"

"I'll admit, sometimes I can be a dumb fuck but I'm not dumb enough to say no to that."

"Like you, in my condo that morning. The second you kicked in my door I knew you were perfect for me. It's not taking me out for a romantic dinner. It's not flowers. It's not sweet words. Or opening a door for me. It's kicking down a fucking door and plugging a hole into a threat about to take me somewhere to be tortured. But... I've never been in love with anyone before and also like you, I wanted to make sure it wasn't simply an emotional reaction to that situation."

"Neither of us said a fucking word," he groaned.

"Did we need to?"

"I guess not. But the validation is nice."

"That I agree with. But, Fletch, I'm not a woman who will need to hear it. I'm the kind of woman who believes actions speak louder than words."

"Then you should've known I loved you for a while now."

Her eyes flicked to the mirror for a few seconds, before coming back to him. "Now that I think about it, I saw it in the way you looked at me, but at the time I didn't recognize it for what it was."

"Well, now you know," he whispered.

"Yes, now I know and now you know, too."

He grinned. "Now I know, too."

It was a relief he wasn't such a damn fool after all. His gut instinct hadn't failed him yet.

She lifted her head and brushed her lips lightly across his. "Well, I'm glad we finally figured that out. Now all we have to do is figure out where the hell we go from here."

"No matter what happens and as long as you're willing, we'll figure it out. Together."

"That sounds like the perfect plan."

Yes, it did.

Epilogue

FLETCH'S HEAD was thrown back on the pillow but his eyes were tipped forward as he watched Nova just about eat his cock whole. His fingers dug deeper into her hair, guiding her mouth up and down his hard as fuck length.

She'd only allow that for so long before she'd knock his hands off and continue at her own pace. Truth was, he didn't care how fast or slow she sucked him off, he was only glad she loved to do it.

As soon as she was done, he'd turn the tables and bury his face in her pussy. And as soon as she came, he'd be sliding into her wet heat to finish off the night.

She had a habit of using her mouth to take him to that very fucking edge and just when he was about to blow, she'd stop so he could fuck her.

Of course, bringing her to orgasm with his own mouth beforehand gave him the much needed time to step away from the edge a bit so he didn't come the second he slid inside her.

Because that was something he never wanted to repeat

again. Ever. She burst out in laughter when he had sworn her to secrecy.

The warm, wet suction of her mouth, the way she squeezed her fingers around the very base like a cock ring, the way she cupped his balls.... And, *fuuuuuuck*, the way she locked gazes with him as she did all that...

"You already have me locked and loaded. Now you're getting close to switching off the safety and pulling the trigger," he warned with a groan, gripping her hair tighter and lifting his hips.

She smiled around his cock and lifted a lone eyebrow.

Yeah, she knew *exactly* what she was doing.

With a wet pop, she released him from her hold and crawled on her hands and knees up his body. She drew her tongue across his bottom lip and then nipped it hard.

"I'd like for you to get farther than the tip this time."

"It happened once!"

She twisted her face.

"What-fucking-ever. Twice, then. Anyway, now that you've given me emotional damage, do you want to ride A, my face, or B, my cock?"

"C. Both."

"Excellent choice. But my only requirement is that we do A first." Especially now that they no longer used condoms. He was not into the fetish where men ate their own loads out of their woman's pussy.

Fuck no, that was not for him. And never would be. His stomach churned just thinking about it.

He groaned when the "I'm a Barbie girl in the Barbie world" lyrics blared from his nightstand. He knew exactly who he'd assigned that ringtone.

Crew.

"What the fuck," he muttered.

Nova's eyebrows were pinched together. "He's calling now?"

"The asshole's got perfect timing as always."

Crew tended to wait until very late at night to call, since during the day he and Nova were working for the DAMC and it was difficult to talk task force business without being overheard. He also avoided the evening because they might be actually *doing* task force business.

The only problem with all that was they tended to be in the middle of more important business when he finally did call. The task force leader was becoming a regular cockblock.

He snagged his phone from the nightstand and glanced at the time. It was just after one in the morning.

That was because they had completed another successful buy earlier with one of Wolf's crew. A half pound of meth. Uncut. With an approximate street value in the Pittsburgh area of over twenty-two thousand dollars.

"Don't move. As soon as he's done running his trap, we're continuing where we left off."

Without waiting for her response, he stabbed the phone harder than necessary and put it to his ear. "What?"

"How'd the buy go?"

"Like clockwork. I already told you that by text. So, why are you calling?"

"Got news," the task force leader announced.

"That couldn't wait?"

"Nova with you?"

"What do you think?"

"Were you two in the middle of fucking again? Switch me over to a video call. You both need to hear this."

"I'm not putting you on video."

A snort came through the phone. "That answered my question."

Fletch sighed and hit the speaker phone icon instead. "Okay. She can hear you."

"We found out who the Demons are transporting for."

It was about fucking time since they'd been undercover for about four months now. Fletch had been trying to find out from Wolf but didn't want to ask directly since that would raise a huge red flag. He was only supposed to be a biker trying to make some extra scratch, not someone who'd care where the product came from or where the bulk of it was going. "Who?"

"You're not going to fucking believe it. Or... maybe you will."

"Crew," Fletch growled. The longer the DEA agent delayed Fletch and Nova having sex, the crankier he would get.

"Brace yourselves..."

Nova slipped to his side and laid an arm across his chest, using it to prop her chin as she focused on the phone.

"The Russos."

Silence surrounded them.

Fletch's eyes flicked to her to see her reaction. It turned out it was the same as his.

Surprised as fuck.

"Nova, did you have any clue that they were dealing in meth?" came from the speaker.

"No, but Russo had a lieutenant running each of his main enterprises. Typical Mob shit. You name it, they're doing it: racketeering, gambling, loansharking, extortion, money laundering, fencing... The list is endless. Their organization is a thick web of RICO violations and other crimes. But I never once heard Russo talk specifically about trafficking drugs. Keep in mind, I didn't get to sit in on all of his meetings. There were times when Frank didn't want me with him and other times when some of his lieutenants didn't want me in the room."

"This might be a newer enterprise for them and if they were distributing drugs when you were undercover with them, it was on a much smaller scale," Crew said.

"Do you think Jr. decided to expand in that direction once he took over?" Fletch asked her.

"Could be," Nova answered. "Once Frank set his sights on me, he kept me close. He didn't want me catching Frankie's interest, so maybe it was already in the works."

"That's what we're assuming at this point," Crew said.

"So, now what?" Fletch asked him.

Jesus. When the fuck was Nova going to get free from those motherfucking mobsters? This news just pulled her back in. In a way, anyway.

They'd have to make sure Nova was never involved with that end of the meth investigation. Because if anyone in that organization recognized her...

The vision of her on the floor in her condo with Russo's soldier ready to kill her blinded him for a second.

"Want you two to keep doing what you're doing, if you're up for it. Already cleared it with the DAMC president. Since we're paying them hefty rent for you two to shack up in that apartment, they're okay with you staying there. For now, anyway. Keep making contact with Wolf, keep doing buys. Maybe the more comfortable the Demons get with you, the more they'll trust you and possibly run their mouth. Nova just needs to stay away from Pittsburgh and even farther away from the Russos. We don't want her cover blown because one of them recognizes her. No one's going to believe she went from Russo Sr.'s side piece to a biker's ol' lady."

"Agreed."

"You all right with remaining on the task force, Nova?" Crew asked. "If not, I can probably find a replacement."

A replacement? "As my ol' lady?" he practically squeaked. He cleared his throat quickly. Nobody was replacing Kitten.

"No, dummy, as a member of the task force. If she wants out, we could have her leave Ghost's cheating ass."

"Ghost doesn't cheat, asshole!"

Nova burst out laughing and patted his bare chest. "He meant as a cover story."

"I knew that."

Crew's loud snort filled the space between Fletch and Nova. "Good thing you have the brains, Nova, because him being pretty isn't enough."

"Hey! I graduated at the top of my academy class."

"That's not saying much, brother. We're talking the state police here, not much brain power needed, unlike us special agents. Right, Nova?"

Nova pinned her lips together. "Mmm hmm."

"Don't agree with him," Fletch muttered. "Especially if you expect me to..." He stuck out his tongue and licked the air.

She whacked him and shook her head.

"Expect you to do what?" Crew prodded.

"Nothing," Fletch answered.

"I'll just use my imagination, then."

"How about visualizing me giving you the middle finger instead?"

"Okay, I'll keep you updated, but for now, I'm keeping you two with the Dirty Angels for as long as they'll tolerate you. Want you to keep buying from the Demons for at least a few more weeks."

"I'm good with it." Fletch turned to Nova. "You up for it?"

"I had to give up my place because of those fucking Russos. So, hell yes. I want to be involved with taking those fuckers down. Whether directly or indirectly."

Fletch hit mute. "That's the only reason you want to stay?"

She rolled into him.

"Nova..."

She grinned. "What?"

"Yo, asshole! Do you have the phone muted? I can't hear shit."

Fletch unmuted the phone. "We're good with it."

He stabbed at the End Call icon and the call disconnected as Crew was starting to say something else.

He tossed the phone back onto the nightstand, then rolled toward Nova until they both lay on their side, facing each other.

He buried his fingers into the hair above her ear. "I wouldn't want to be doing this with anyone else, Nova. I've never trusted anyone as much as I trust you and believe me, I trust my MC brotherhood a fuck of a lot. Most of us have been together a long time. So, that's saying something."

"I trust you completely, too, Fletch. And if anyone's going to be at my back, whether with the Russos or the Demons—or, hell, in any situation—I'm glad it's you."

Damn, that sounded like fucking music to his ears. "Partners for life?"

"Partners for life." She smiled with a wicked gleam in her eyes.

He returned the smile and tackled her.

He still owed her an orgasm or two.

And he always paid his debts.

The adventures with the Blue Avengers MC and the Tri-State Drug Task Force continue in **Beyond the Badge: Finn (Blue Avengers MC, book 2)**
Turn the page to read chapter one!

Sign up for Jeanne's newsletter to learn about her upcoming releases, sales and more! http://www.jeannestjames.com/newslettersignup

Beyond the Badge: Finn

ABOUT THE BOOK:

When an undercover assignment ends up literally under the covers...

As part of the Tri-State Federal Task Force, Daniel Finnegan, road captain for the Blue Avengers MC, is investigating the Deadly Demons, an MC trafficking drugs into Pennsylvania.

When he reluctantly goes undercover as a dancer with an all-male revue at a club recently purchased by the outlaw bikers, he comes face to face with Melina Jensen.

As manager of The Peach Pit, Mel could be an important asset for the drug task force with her unfettered access behind the scenes. Unhappy with the way the Demons are destroying the business, it doesn't take much for Finn to convince Mel to work with him as a confidential informant. Even though becoming a CI for the task force isn't without risk, Mel's willing to help in any way she can.

To give Finn better access to The Peach Pit and the illegal dealings without raising any red flags with the MC, they start to "date." Only, what starts out as a fake relationship ends up being anything but. Until eventually, neither can no longer dance around the truth.

However, once Mel's safety is threatened, it's up to Finn to find a way to protect her without blowing the entire investigation.

TURN THE PAGE TO READ CHAPTER ONE...

Beyond the Badge: Finn (Sneak Peek)

UNEDITED

CHAPTER ONE

"What the fuck!" Finn screamed at the ninety-six inch TV. "That was clearly holding! You refs are fucking blind!"

"Jesus, dude, you're going to stroke out," Monty warned as she bumped his leg with her knee.

He lifted his legs out of the way, only enough for her to get to the other couch."Seriously, you couldn't go around?" He dropped his boots back onto the scarred and battered coffee table.

"I could've. But I didn't." The twenty-six year old prison guard sank down onto the empty couch to his left, cracked open a can of IC Light and took a long swig.

Three large couches were set up in a U and he had sprawled out in the center one so he could see Pittsburgh Steelers game perfectly. This afternoon they were playing the Baltimore Ravens and he hoped his team gave their rivals a bad spanking.

Finn wrinkled his nose at the beer she was drinking. "There's better beer in the fridge."

Danielle Montgomery rolled her green eyes. "If I wanted another brand, I would've grabbed other brand, genius."

"I wonder about you sometimes," Finn informed the only female member of the Blue Avengers MC.

"Well, I wonder about you *all* the fucking time."

Finn pointed the top of his beer bottle at her. "Do men like that short hair of yours?"

Her dark hair was kept pretty damn short, but then keeping it that short prevented the max security inmates from grabbing a handful and ripping her around by her hair.

"Do men like that short hair of yours?" she echoed.

Finn grinned and flapped his eyelashes. "I get my fair amount of the male gaze."

Monty almost choked on her crap beer. She pounded her chest and coughed. When she could talk again, she said, "I heard gingers are spicy."

"I'm super spicy. Do you want a taste?"

"Eww. No. You're an asshole. I don't like spicy asshole."

"To know that means you've tasted one."

"I get my fair share of the male gaze."

"Do they tend to wear orange jumpsuits and identify as an inmate?"

She grabbed the pillow tucked in the corner of the couch and whipped it at him.

He laughed and ducked. He snagged it from where it landed next to him and tucked it behind his back. "Thanks. I wanted that pillow for the past fifteen minutes but was too lazy to get up to grab it."

Monty shook her head.

"Can you two shut the fuck up? I'm trying to watch the

game," Nox bitched from the couch on the right side of the U.

"That's right, we're crashing in Nox's living room right now since he's made himself at home here," Decker said as he joined them, dropping on the couch next to Nox and throwing a thick arm over the man's shoulder. With a scowl, Nox shrugged off his arm.

"If you need to cuddle, go do it with Monty."

Decker looked across the TV area and asked, "Monty?"

"Don't even try it," she warned.

Nox finally sold the home where he and his late wife had lived. Since that house held too many memories for him, a deal was struck that after the closing he'd take the equity and use it to finish the second floor of The Plant as an apartment. This way he could live upstairs at the clubhouse, something he'd already been doing anyhow. However, he was still in the middle of working on his new digs.

The floors were now refinished, the plumbing and bathroom fixtures installed, the walls and trim painted, and the primary bedroom framed out. Eventually, Nox would build a second bedroom, but that would be the last thing on his long to-do list. A kitchen was his next priority.

He was still sleeping on a damn cot up there. But he'd moved it from the third floor—since that was now home to the Tri-State Federal Drug Task Force—to the second floor, where he had more privacy.

Since the apartment wasn't completely habitable yet, he was using the first floor of the Blue Avenger's church as his living room and kitchen until appliances were installed and he furnished it, since he ended up donating all the furniture he'd owned with his late wife.

"What's going on, fuckers?" Antonio Alvarez called out, appearing from the back hallway.

"You're missing the game," Finn informed their club's sergeant at arms.

Rez shook his dark head. "I was listening to it on the radio on my ride over. I'm not sure I want to watch this slaughter." Keeping his eyes glued to the game on the huge TV, he stepped behind the curved counter in the back corner of the common area and grabbed a cold beer from the fridge. "Fucking dirty birds!"

A grumble went up from all of them at the nickname they called the opposing team.

"What do you expect? They're always tough to beat," Axel Jamison said, also coming from the back of the building since they only used the rear or the side door to get into The Plant, their club's church.

"Did you just get off shift?" Monty asked the BAMC president.

"Yes, unfortunately. I came straight over."

"Where's Bella?" Monty asked about his wife. "With the kids?"

"No. She's doing something with the Dirty Angels sisterhood. I think they're all helping plan some fundraiser Ellie Walker's foundation."

The Walker foundation was a worthy one. She had set it up to provide prosthetic care for amputees who couldn't afford it, since her husband was a vet who'd lost his leg while serving in the military.

"Who's got the twins?" Rez asked.

"My parents. My dad's dropping them off here soon." Axel said, joining them over by the TV.

With beer in hand Rez shouted, "What the fuck!" at the TV when he came over to stand at the end of the couch where Finn had his ass planted.

Finn flung a hand toward the big screen and bitched,

"Right? They're playing like shit. They might as well just fucking forfeit this game and go home."

"Don't count them out yet," Nox grumbled.

"There is no way they're pulling off a W with this shit show," Finn told him.

"Where's Fletch when we need him?" Rez asked. "He probably didn't do his ridiculous pregame routine." He twisted his face and flapped around his arms and almost spilling his beer as he emulated Fletch that time they caught him doing his superstitious routine. Now the state trooper only did it where no one could see him.

"Guess it's not so ridiculous if you think it helps," Monty huffed and shook her head.

Finn grabbed his phone from the cushion next to him. He texted their VP.

Hey, asshole! Did you do your Steeler's pregame routine? If not, you better do it. They're playing like they belong in the pee wee league!

The reply came with thirty seconds. *Like I'm going to fucking tell you that. I don't want to be blamed for this embarrassing loss.*

Finn quickly texted back, *Too late. Your fault. You didn't do it because you're embarrassed to look like an idiot in front of the FBI.*

You mean Nova, you dumb fuck?

Finn growled, tossed his phone back down on the couch and shouted, "Don't fucking run it! Pass it! Pass! Pass! *Noooooo*!"

"Yo, arm-chair coach, you're going to burst a blood vessel and I don't want to have to replace you on the task force," Crew yelled as he emerged from the room where their executive committee met.

"Were you upstairs?" Axel asked him.

"Yeah, I was checking to see who's up there already since we have a task force meeting."

"And?" Decker asked.

Crew answered, "Powers is up there transcribing some calls and Torres is listening to some dirty talk."

"Dirty talk?" Monty asked, her dark eyebrows raised. "I should've became a cop. That sounds like fun."

"He's listening in on wiretaps. It can be boring as fuck. In fact, ninety-nine percent of the time it's a snooze fest."

"Transcribing those fucking calls are even worse," Nox mumbled.

"We're all taking turns doing it," Crew said. "Because, yes, it fucking sucks."

"Anyone else up there?" Rez asked.

"Not yet. Reynolds, Butler and Rodgers can't be here. Kruger and Mullins will be here after the game."

"Yeah, that was dumb to schedule a meeting on a Sunday," Finn told the task force leader.

"It was actually smart." Crew tapped his finger against his temple. "How many of us are already here on Sunday? If not for a club run, then for football?"

Finn couldn't argue that point, so he didn't. Instead, he downed the rest of his beer and watched the next play.

And of course the Steelers got a penalty! When he whipped his empty beer can, it pinged off the TV, leaving some splatter behind.

"Hey!" Monty yelled at him.

"What the fuck are you doing?" Nox asked.

Jamison shook his head. "You want to replace that monster out of your own pocket?"

"This season is fucked!" Finn yelled in frustration.

"It's only the first game of the regular season. You know it takes them a bit to get their shit together," Crew reminded him.

"Yeah," Decker agreed. "They're always better the second half of the game and the second half of the season. It's the Steelers way."

It sure seemed to be. They always spiked his blood pressure.

"Aww shit. Better straighten your asses up," Rez announced. "The old guard just walked in."

"That means little ears are in the building," Jamison reminded them.

"They're almost twelve, Jamison. And they're around bikers all the time, especially since you *live* in a neighborhood full of them. You don't think they hear worse shit than what we say?" Decker asked.

"But you all are supposed to be upstanding citizens," their president reminded them with a completely straight face.

Not one person in that room didn't laugh.

Even Mitch Jamison chuckled as he escorted his grandchildren into the common area. "I wish it was different, but it isn't. They might hear it but that doesn't mean they can repeat it until after they're eighteen. It's the Jamison family law."

"Eighteen? Good luck with that," Nox grumbled.

"Hi, Dad!" Laney ran up to her father and practically tackled him. "How was work?"

Jamison wrapped his arms around his twelve-year-old daughter, squeezed her tight and planted a kiss on the top of her head. When he straightened, he smiled down at his daughter. "Work."

She giggled and pulled free, then fist-bumped Crew on her way over to throw herself on the couch next to Monty, grabbing the potato chips from the table and shoving her hand deep into the open bag.

Hell, those chips were probably stale. Finn had no idea how long they'd been sitting out on the table with the bag gaping open. Around there it could be weeks.

"Grandpa was yelling at the radio on our way over here," Laney stage-whispered to Monty, then pulled out a fistful of greasy BBQ chips and shoved them into her wide-open mouth, orange crumbs falling all over her shirt and clinging to her lips.

"I'm not surprised," Monty stage-whispered back, giving her a wink.

"Liam, are you going to come give your old man a hug hello?" Jamison asked his son.

"I'm too old for hugs, Dad." Liam plopped down on the couch next to Nox and propped the soles of his sneakers on the edge of the coffee table. "Can I have a beer?"

"Absolutely. Grandpa will get one for you. Right, Pop?" Jamison asked his father, Mitch.

"Sure! Maybe there's some root beer left in the fridge. Liam, go check. I'm sure your sister wants one."

"Then she can get one herself," he mumbled.

"And you can take your feet off the furniture," Mitch told him.

"Finn has *his* boots on the table."

"That's because he's rude. Don't be rude like this a—" Rez caught himself in time. "*Animal*." He came around the front of the couch and kicked Finn's feet off the table.

Finn shot Rez a silent *I'll-get-you-back-later* promise, planted his feet on the floor and sat up.

"All right. I'm out of here," Mitch announced.

"Bye, Grandpa!" Laney shouted.

"See you kids later." Mitch glanced around the common area and added, "*All* of you children."

Jamison's old man disappeared back the way he came from shaking his head as they all shouted, "Bye, Grandpa!" in unison.

"He needs to dust off his bike and come along on our next run with us. It's been a while. I'm sure he misses it," Crew said to Jamison.

"Mom made him sell it."

"What the fu—*freak*?" Decker shouted.

"Grandma said he's getting too old and brittle and he needs to be careful now and not die. 'Cause if he dies, then he can't help her with the grandkids," Liam announced with his nose buried in his cell phone.

"That's not how she said it," Jamison said with a sigh.

"That's what I heard."

"He's getting older and she doesn't want him getting injured, that's all."

Laney added, "She also said she doesn't want him to cracking open his noggin even though it might knock some sense into him."

"That I believe."

Liam raised his eyes from his phone. "See? I don't lie, Dad."

"That I don't believe," Jamison said dryly.

"Mom said small fibs are okay," Laney said.

"I think you both need your ears cleaned out."

"You sure these two are your kids, Jamison, and not Finn's?" Monty asked with a laugh and tucking a long red strand of Laney's hair behind her ear. Both of the twins had hair close to the same red as Finn's so it was an ongoing joke. Just like Finn always busted Monty on her short hair.

He pitied the teasing the twins probably went through at

school since he'd gone through a shitload about his own red hair and freckles when he was young.

Now he took it in stride. Even when his MC brothers called him Heat Miser.

"Mom didn't have sex with Finn," Laney announced with a serious tone. "I asked her."

"You did what? When?" Jamison asked, his expression a bit shell-shocked.

Laney shrugged. "A million years ago. She said we take after Aunt Ivy."

"And that's true."

Finn grinned at Laney. "I mean, you *could* be mine. But we'll pretend you're not so I don't have to pay the same crazy amount of child support like Crew pays for his kids."

"I don't mind paying for anything my children need. I do mind paying for my ex's lifestyle."

"Yeah, but you pay a ton," Finn said.

"Kids cost a lot," Decker mentioned. He would know since he was raising his four-year-old niece, Valentina.

"They're worth every damn penny. Now the ex on the other hand..." Crew let that drop since there were children in the room.

"Ex's are ex's for a reason," Finn said.

Crew came behind the couch where Finn was sitting and shoved him in the back of the head. "Phew, the sage wisdom coming from that pea-brain of yours."

Nox groaned loudly. "Can we watch the d- *darn* game in peace?"

"Yeah, you all are really annoying," Liam said. "It's hard to concentrate on the game."

Finn dropped his head and covered his mouth with his hand so the kid couldn't see him smirking.

Jamison moved behind his son and plucked his cell phone

from his fingers. "Now you'll have no problem concentrating."

"Dad!" Liam reached up to grab it back but his father moved out of reach.

"I'll hold onto this for a while. You'll get it back when I think you deserve it back."

"Dad!"

Jamison shrugged. "Do you want to go home or do you want to hang out here for the game?"

Liam huffed sharply, crossed his arms over his chest, and slouched down.

Damn, the kid was now looking more like Nox's son.

"I thought so." Axel went and sat with Monty and Laney. "Okay, who wants to make bets to see if the Steelers can turn this damn game around."

"I'm telling Grandpa you said damn in front of us," Liam threatened.

"He's heard me say worse to his face."

"You have?" Laney breathed with her eyes wide. "When?"

"That's a story for when you're older."

Unfortunately, the Steelers did not turn the game around. It was a hard and depressing loss and Finn was currently drowning his sorrows with a cold Yuengling Lager.

Jamison and his kids had left a while ago. Monty a half hour ago. And the only people left at church were his BAMC brothers also on the federal task force.

Crew's salt-and-pepper head popped out from the club's meeting room doorway. "Yo, assholes! Task force meeting. Upstairs. Now."

"Everybody else here?" Decker asked as he and Rez played a game of foosball.

"Yeah, waiting on you turds."

"Where's Nox?" Finn asked.

"Doing something up in his place. I'll grab him on the way." Crew's head disappeared and Finn heard the side door slam a few seconds later.

"Duty calls, boys," Finn announced, downing the rest of the beer and tossing the empty into the recycle bin.

Once they got upstairs, Decker, Finn and Rez settled in empty seats around the long conference table. Like normal, as task force leader, Crew sat at the head of the table. They were joined by Torres, Kruger, Mullins, Powers and Nox. Nine out of the fifteen-member task force team.

It was rare that all of them were able to gather for a meeting, especially if someone was either undercover, like Fletch and Nova, or doing surveillance.

"All right," Crew started, his gaze scanning the occupants of the table. "Since Fletch and Wilder are still undercover, I have them on a conference call along with Butler and Reynolds. I've been meaning to have this meeting to give you the latest updates on the investigation. I met with leaders of the two other groups and this is what we know so far between the wiretaps, the UCs and the surveillance, so pay attention.

"We have three major players involved with this trafficking. That we know of, anyway. A Mexican cartel as the supplier, the Deadly Demons MC as the transporter and La Cosa Nostra as the distributor. More specifically, the Russo crime family out of Pittsburgh. That's the organization funding the trafficking.

"Here's what we've learned so far, some info confirmed, some not. Russos are buying six kilos of 'ice' a month from a cartel. The DEA in Texas is working on discovering which cartel, but if any of you get wind of who that is, get that info to me ASAP. Of course, they're using code and not mentioning the names of the players in any of the wiretaps so far. The Demons are calling the supplier Los Malos MC. We know for a fact Los Malos MC or even a cartel by that name doesn't exist. They're only using it to throw off anyone listening."

"Sounds like they're smarter than we thought," Decker said.

"Maybe," Torres said. The DEA agent and 'plant manager' sat to Crew's left. "But we'll figure it out eventually. With all the wiretaps between the three groups, not one has slipped to actually name the Russos or the cartel, yet."

Crew picked back up there. "Though, whether they're smart *enough* is questionable. They can't figure out when they're being tailed. That's how we discovered where the majority of that meth was ending up. The pipeline breaks down like this... The Demons have a member who's a long-haul trucker and they're using his rig to transport the bricks of meth for the Russos. Side note, even though the rig's in this biker's name, we think the MC paid cash for it. Group one slapped a tracking device on the rig and are setting up more surveillance to notify the DEA in Houston when it's on the move so they can try to identify the cartel. But since they tagged the rig, it hasn't gone anywhere near the border. What we assume is, once a month the Demons are transporting it from the border into West Virginia by mixing it in with legitimate loads of cilantro so it goes undetected.

"Once the load shows up, the MC takes one key as payment. By taking it in that method, they're making more money than being paid outright in cash because of how they're cutting it up and selling it on the streets. Then the Demons are using various methods to deliver the remaining five keys to one of the Russo lieutenants. From what we can tell, the Russos are paying twelve thousand per kilo wholesale. The second it hits Pennsylvania that value doubles."

"That's a hell of an investment," Finn muttered.

"Exactly. But remember, that's only the uncut value. We can safely assume the Russos are then turning around, breaking it down into half and quarter kilos and selling that to street level dealers. Those dealers then break it down even further by cutting it with filler. Our guess is the Russos are making about two-hundred-and forty grand when they sell it to the low level dealers. That's a hell of a return on their original investment of twelve K."

FBI Special Agent Nova Wilder's voice came from the conference phone sitting in the middle of the table. "And why they most likely got involved in this business venture."

"You didn't catch wind of any of this shit while you were undercover with the Russos?" Finn asked her.

"No. There could've been some low-level dealing but my guess is once Frankie, the former underboss, took over, he decided to expand on that. I do know his father wanted to stay out of the drug business. But now with Frank Sr. out of the way, Junior is now boss. This has to be a new venture for them. If they were moving this amount, I can't imagine I wouldn't have gotten a even a slight whiff of it."

"Agreed," Crew said. "This flow of meth only recently hit the DEA's radar, spurring them to establish this task force to squash it. Fletch, you want to add anything from your end, since you're dealing directly with the Demon's Uniontown charter?"

Shane Fletcher, a state trooper currently undercover with the Dirty Angels spoke next. "The Demons are breaking down their kilo by cutting it with cheap baking soda. They're then distributing it to key players within their MC. Those key players have "teams" of fellow MC brothers to sell it on the street, in bars, at bike rallies, wherever. Our contact right now is really limited to Wolf and his crew, but we're working on getting in tighter with him."

Crew picked up from there. "Because of this organized effort the data shows that their club is the fastest growing outlaw MC in the country right now. This all stems back to this hookup with the Russos. Overflowing coffers only makes their MC stronger and is creating a snowball effect by allowing them to expand both sales and territory by adding charters to their club. But that's not all. They're also buying up businesses in PA and Ohio to launder money and expand retail sales. Think back door dealing. They're grabbing locations where their customers tend to hang out, like bars, strip clubs, roach motels, used car lots, pizza shops... shit like that. Places with high traffic. Cash comes in, drugs and washed money goes out."

Torres cut in again. "While all of this might make them financially stronger, it also makes them weaker. The more people involved in these enterprises, the higher the chances of their house of cards falling around them. It just takes one pulled card for it all to tumble."

Crew nodded. "Our three groups are tasked with pulling that card and demolishing that house. But to do it right, we need to take them and the Russos down in a coordinated effort. Especially when it comes time for indictments. It needs to be organized and swift."

"Squash them like the fucking roaches they are." Mullins, a narcotic detective with the Pittsburgh PD, slammed his hand on the table like he was doing just that.

"Anyway," Crew continued, "in the meantime, I have something new we can move on. Rodgers had contact a few days ago with a CI who bought a few ounces out of a strip club right outside of Uniontown. It just so happens The Peach Pit was recently bought by the Demons. Of course that purchase was an immediate red flag. We also heard chatter that they're either using some of the strippers as mules to move product or using them to deal. The info was a bit sketchy on that point. All the CI could tell Rodgers was that he can walk in with cash and walked out with an ounce. We need to confirm that's what's happening. If so, and they're using that location to launder cash, that's another RICO violation, not for the Russos, since they're racking those up, but for the Demons. The more charges we can pin on them and their members, the better to take the whole organization down. And if we take them down, we can choke the flow of meth into PA."

"And that's the reason we're all sitting around this table, right? So, now what?" Rez asked.

"I'd like to set someone up in the strip club. Maybe not long-term but at least long enough to confirm and document that the Demons are using The Peach Pit as part of their drug business. Whether by selling from there, laundering money or using the girls as mules. Or even all of the above."

"You want one of us to go in as a regular?" Decker asked.

"That's one option I'm tossing around. The the other is to have someone work there to get a peek behind the scenes."

"The only female on the team is Wilder. She's already undercover with Fletch and the Dirty Angels." Finn reminded him. "Are you planning on pulling her or bringing someone new on board?"

Crew shook his head. "I'm not pulling her. I want Fletch and Nova to stay put. We can't bring in anyone new because of the budget. I have another idea."

Nova's voice came through the phone. "That's good, because I would say no to stripping."

"Yeah, so would I," came from Fletch.

Nox groaned. "You're not using Monty, right? She won't go for that, either."

"Not Monty," Crew confirmed.

"Then who you got in mind for that fucking job?" Finn asked with a smirk.

Crew's gray eyes landed on him.

Finn knew he was fucked the second the task force leader smirked, too.

Get it here: Beyond the Badge: Finn (Blue Avengers MC, book 2)

If You Enjoyed This Book

Thank you for reading Beyond the Badge: Fletch. If you enjoyed Fletch and Nova's story, please consider leaving a review at your favorite retailer and/or Goodreads to let other readers know. Reviews are always appreciated and just a few words can help an independent author like me tremendously!

Want to read a sample of my work? Download a sampler book here: BookHip.com/MTQQKK

Also by Jeanne St. James

Find my complete reading order here:

https://www.jeannestjames.com/reading-order

* Available in Audiobook

Standalone Books:

Made Maleen: A Modern Twist on a Fairy Tale *

Damaged *

Rip Cord: The Complete Trilogy *

Everything About You (A Second Chance Gay Romance) *

Reigniting Chase (An M/M Standalone) *

Brothers in Blue Series:

Brothers in Blue: Max *

Brothers in Blue: Marc *

Brothers in Blue: Matt *

Teddy: A Brothers in Blue Novelette *

Brothers in Blue: A Bryson Family Christmas *

The Dare Ménage Series:

Double Dare *

Daring Proposal *

Dare to Be Three *

A Daring Desire *

Dare to Surrender *

A Daring Journey *

The Obsessed Novellas:

Forever Him *

Only Him *

Needing Him *

Loving Her *

Tempting Him *

Down & Dirty: Dirty Angels MC Series®:

Down & Dirty: Zak *

Down & Dirty: Jag *

Down & Dirty: Hawk *

Down & Dirty: Diesel *

Down & Dirty: Axel *

Down & Dirty: Slade *

Down & Dirty: Dawg *

Down & Dirty: Dex *

Down & Dirty: Linc *

Down & Dirty: Crow *

Crossing the Line (A DAMC/Blue Avengers MC Crossover) *

Magnum: A Dark Knights MC/Dirty Angels MC Crossover *

Crash: A Dirty Angels MC/Blood Fury MC Crossover *

In the Shadows Security Series:

Guts & Glory: Mercy *

Guts & Glory: Ryder *

Guts & Glory: Hunter *

Guts & Glory: Walker *

Guts & Glory: Steel *

Guts & Glory: Brick *

Blood & Bones: Blood Fury MC®:

Blood & Bones: Trip *

Blood & Bones: Sig *

Blood & Bones: Judge *

Blood & Bones: Deacon *

Blood & Bones: Cage *

Blood & Bones: Shade *

Blood & Bones: Rook *

Blood & Bones: Rev *

Blood & Bones: Ozzy

Blood & Bones: Dodge

Blood & Bones: Whip

Blood & Bones: Easy

Beyond the Badge: Blue Avengers MC™:

Beyond the Badge: Fletch

Beyond the Badge: Finn

Beyond the Badge: Decker

Beyond the Badge: Rez

Beyond the Badge: Crew

Beyond the Badge: Nox

COMING SOON!

Double D Ranch (An MMF Ménage Series)

Dirty Angels MC®: The Next Generation

WRITING AS J.J. MASTERS

The Royal Alpha Series:

(A gay mpreg shifter series)

The Selkie Prince's Fated Mate *

The Selkie Prince & His Omega Guard *

The Selkie Prince's Unexpected Omega *

The Selkie Prince's Forbidden Mate *

The Selkie Prince's Secret Baby *

About the Author

JEANNE ST. JAMES is a USA Today bestselling romance author who loves an alpha male (or two). She was only thirteen when she started writing and her first paid published piece was an erotic story in Playgirl magazine. Her first romance novel, Banged Up, was published in 2009. She is happily owned by farting French bulldogs. She writes M/F, M/M, and M/M/F ménages.

Want to read a sample of her work? Download a sampler book here: BookHip.com/MTQQKK

To keep up with her busy release schedule check her website at www.jeannestjames.com or sign up for her newsletter: http://www.jeannestjames.com/newslettersignup

www.jeannestjames.com
jeanne@jeannestjames.com

Newsletter: http://www.jeannestjames.com/newslettersignup
Jeanne's Down & Dirty Book Crew: https://www.facebook.com/groups/JeannesReviewCrew/
TikTok: https://www.tiktok.com/@jeannestjames

facebook.com/JeanneStJamesAuthor
amazon.com/author/jeannestjames
instagram.com/JeanneStJames
bookbub.com/authors/jeanne-st-james
goodreads.com/JeanneStJames
pinterest.com/JeanneStJames

Get a FREE Sampler Book

This book contains the first chapter of a variety of my books. This will give you a taste of the type of books I write and if you enjoy the first chapter, I hope you'll be interested in reading the rest of the book.

Each book I list in the sampler will include the description of the book, the genre, and the first chapter, along with links to find out more. I hope you find a book you will enjoy curling up with!

Get it here: BookHip.com/MTQQKK

Made in the USA
Coppell, TX
31 May 2023

17513877R00249